A CERTAIN WOLFISH CHARM

LYDIA DARE

sourcebooks
casablanca

Published by Sourcebooks Casablanca, an imprint of
Sourcebooks, Inc.
P.O. Box 4410, Naperville, Illinois 60567-4410
(630) 961-3900
FAX: (630) 961-2168
www.sourcebooks.com

Printed and bound in Canada
WC 10 9 8 7 6 5 4 3 2 1

To Brandt—You are the love of my life. Thank you for believing in me.
To Thomas, JT, and Stephen—Don't interrupt me when I'm ignoring you! Seriously… you are my everything.

One

LILY RUTLEDGE HAD NEVER CONTEMPLATED MURDER before, though she was warming to the idea. The most recent column in the *Mayfair Society Paper* taunted her at the breakfast table. The Duke of Blackmoor seemed to have plenty of time to gamble away his funds in one hell or another, race his phaeton along the old Bath road for sport, and spend every other waking hour enjoying the entertainments of one Mrs. Teresa Hamilton or visiting fashionable bawdy houses throughout Town. Not that Lily was terribly surprised. They were the same sorts of things he'd done for years, though she hadn't cared until now.

"Aunt Lily," called her twelve-year-old nephew, Oliver York, the Earl of Maberley, from a few seats away. "Your face is turning purple again."

Purple indeed. Lily sighed, looking at the boy. What was she to do with him? Especially when she couldn't get Blackmoor to even respond to one of her letters. Of course, he sent funds every time she wrote him, though that was not what she asked for. Infuriating man! Did he even read her letters?

The Maberley estate was not terribly far from London. Visiting Oliver would only interrupt his debauched lifestyle for a day or two at the most. Was that truly too much to ask of her nephew's guardian? After all, he hadn't seen the boy in years.

"Finish your breakfast, Oliver," she directed, glancing again at the maddening society rag. There must be some way to get His Grace's attention. Perhaps if she picked up and went to London—

"I'm through," the young earl responded. "May I be excused?"

Through? Food had been piled high in front of him just moments ago. Lily's eyes flashed to Oliver's plate, only to find it completely empty, as was the sideboard behind him. Not a crumb was left uneaten. Where had he gotten this appetite? It wasn't natural. And how could he possibly have devoured all the food in the room so quickly and quietly? It was another one of the unexplained transformations she'd noticed in her nephew over the last month. "Yes, of course. You would do well to go over your Latin before Mr. Craven arrives."

Oliver scowled as he pushed away from the table. "I'd rather not."

He never wanted to go over his Latin, which was a problem. According to Mr. Craven, his tutor, Oliver was far behind in that particular subject. When he began his first term at Harrow in October, he'd need to do better. That was assuming Lily sent him off to school, and, at the moment, she didn't know if she could do so. It was one of the many things she needed to discuss with that scoundrel Blackmoor.

Lily shook her head. "Mr. Craven says you need to practice, Oliver. Please do so."

The young earl stomped from the room in a manner she was getting unfortunately accustomed to. Just a month ago, Oliver had had the sweetest disposition. Now she barely recognized him. His shoulders were suddenly broad enough to fill a doorway, and he almost had to duck to cross the threshold as he left the breakfast room. Gone was the little boy in short pants. The young earl's valet had replaced Oliver's clothing twice in as many months and had sent more than one pair of trousers to the seamstress to have the seams reinforced.

To make it even worse, Oliver had developed a terrible temper, with the smallest annoyances setting him off. He seemed to rumble more than talk, his singsong voice replaced by a gravely growl. Entry into adulthood was hard, but Lily had never expected it to come on so suddenly and with such force.

Perhaps things would be different if Oliver's parents were still alive. Perhaps things would be different if Blackmoor showed even the slightest interest in the lad. Perhaps if she'd ever raised an adolescent boy before, she'd know if Oliver's *changes* were normal—though she couldn't imagine they were. Lily knew in her heart that something was drastically wrong with her nephew, and she was at a complete loss for what to do.

Blast Blackmoor for ignoring her letters!

An idea occurred to her. If *he* couldn't be troubled

to visit Oliver, she'd simply have to pay *him* a visit instead. His Grace would have an impossible time ignoring her in person. She was hard to miss.

Lily picked up the society rag, rereading it. Everything was there. Everything she needed to know. Where he spent his time and with whom. The Duke of Blackmoor would regret shirking his duties, if making him do so was the last thing she ever did.

The only thing Simon Westfield, the Duke of Blackmoor, regretted was purchasing the services of one whore instead of two. Two would have been a great deal more fun and would have helped ease some of the restlessness that seemed to be his constant companion of late. He could count on the disquiet seeping into the dark recesses of his mind the same way he'd learned to expect the fullness of the moon with each lunar cycle. It just happened. It wasn't something he thought about. He simply began to feel an anxious flutter, a *want*.

To ease the discomfort and restlessness, the duke began his infamous prowl. He'd spent so much time and money perfecting his routine that he'd even been written about in the society pages. He supposed he should feel some shame at being reviewed so harshly. One paper even said that he'd lost more than he had to spend, but that was rubbish. He had a lot more to lose. A lot more to enjoy. He usually won at the gaming tables, even when he had a wench settled upon his knee waiting for him, like now.

He reached around the plump brunette, seated

solidly on his groin, to tap the table, asking for another card. The doxy squirmed in his lap, giggling as he lifted her bottom to put more of her weight on his thigh. "Sit still," he mumbled at her. She squirmed again, becoming more impatient. He sighed and laid his cards on the table, as he lost the hand. "You don't listen very well, do you?" he drawled slowly.

"I follow directions very well, Your Grace," she snickered as she boldly whispered a suggestion in his ear. He dipped his head and kissed the swell of her bosom. She arched toward his mouth, reflexively. If he remembered correctly, this particular woman could arch various parts of her body, because he'd enjoyed her flexibility in the past.

With his cards on the table, he was able to put his hands on her hips and turn her toward him. Her breasts pushed at the top of her bodice, so much skin displayed that she threatened to topple out at any minute.

It wasn't enough. He was past the point where he could take solace in the body of a willing woman. Sadly, the thought of holding those fleshy orbs didn't titillate him. She wasn't going to ease any of the restlessness in him. He knew it. He knew that nothing would satisfy him at this point, nothing that wouldn't scare the wench off. They even scared him, the things he wanted to do when he got to this point.

He forced the beast within him to subside. Reaching into his jacket, he withdrew a guinea and tucked it between her breasts. The tiny jostle caused the creamy flesh to tremble, and the edge of a dark areola peeked over the top of her bodice. The beast reared its ugly head.

What he felt wasn't an attractive desire. It was an overwhelming need to copulate. To force submission. To cover a body with his and *own* it. It was more than he could control. He stood up and placed her solidly on her feet. She put her hands on her hips and stomped a slippered foot.

He laughed and flicked her nose gently with the tip of his finger. "Don't pout, love. I'll be back in a week." It would take a week before he would feel safe enough to be in polite company. Or impolite company, as the case may be.

Simon strolled out of the hell and walked toward the street where his ducal coach waited. His crest, a lone wolf—gold emblazoned against blue—mocked him. He ignored it. His coachman opened the carriage door, and Simon slipped inside, the springs groaning under his weight. He sank heavily into the seat and reached up to loosen his cravat. He hadn't been careful enough. He'd almost gone too far and taken that wench above stairs, even though he knew how close he was to losing control. That could have been disastrous.

This time, he couldn't go to his townhouse. It was time to head for Westfield Hall in Hampshire. He needed a secluded area where he could relax and calm himself. He needed to be locked up for a sennight. But no one was able to do that for him, for his brothers would be suffering the same curse. He would take himself out of harm's way, as he normally did. Of course, the prison was one of his choosing and lacked the cells of Newgate, which is where he would most assuredly be sent should anyone discover his terrible secret. The isolation of the quiet countryside was what he sought. He would go where he could walk the hills at night under the full moon, safe from the intrusion of others. And they would be safe from him.

He slept a fitful sleep the remaining hours of the night, the rocking of the coach his only comfort. He tried to straighten his clothes as he stepped from the coach onto his own cobblestone path, but he knew he still looked disheveled. It was a completely unrespectable way for a duke to present himself to his household. Thank heaven he wasn't a stuffy old member of the peerage. And his staff didn't expect him to be. Of course, they'd also seen him in worse shape.

Not even bothering to tie his cravat or fasten the top buttons of his shirt, he turned toward the front door and drew in a deep breath. It felt good to be home. He was safe again, until nightfall. Thankfully, the desire had dissipated with the darkness. If only the darkness of his soul could be lifted as easily as the sun in the sky.

Simon passed through the doorway with a nod to his butler.

"Welcome home, Your Grace."

Simon immediately knew something was wrong when he saw the normally unshakeable man wipe his sweaty brow. "Is something amiss, Billings?" he asked.

"You have a visitor." The butler gestured toward the closest sitting room.

From his spot in the corridor, Simon had a clear view of the room. The last person he'd ever expected to see here was Lily Rutledge. But there she was, sitting on his settee as though she belonged. With the moonful quickly approaching, that wasn't in her best interest. Simon glared at his butler. Had the man lost his mind? Miss Rutledge could be injured in his presence. "What is she doing here?"

Billings shrugged. "The London staff told her you were here."

Damn! Fight or retreat? He sighed.

Retreat. He couldn't see her. There was no telling what the beast would do.

"Ready the coach to take Miss Rutledge home, Billings." He turned and hastened toward his study.

Simon leaned heavily against the door once he was safely ensconced inside and turned the key. He took deep breaths to try to calm his racing heartbeat. She shouldn't have come. Not when he wasn't fully in control. He couldn't hide from the fullness of the moon. It would take him whether he wanted it or not. Sure, she was reasonably safe during the day, but when the sun sank behind the horizon, the danger would become more and more real.

He knew Lily Rutledge was a strong woman. She was nearly as tall as the average man, standing well above most females. But he wasn't an average man. She only reached his shoulder. He bet that he could tuck her under his chin and still have room to look down at her. He imagined himself doing just that, having her close enough to feel her body against his. He groaned and shifted his trousers.

No matter how strong she was, Simon would still hurt her. He slumped down in the seat behind his desk. As long as Lily remained safely on the other side, all was well.

But then he heard her voice.

"I know he's here, Billings," he heard her cry

from the hallway. Simon flinched when her fist hit the door.

"You *will* see me, Your Grace," she called.

What other woman, he wondered, could make "Your Grace" sound so much like an insult?

Two

LILY COULDN'T REMEMBER EVER BEING SO ENRAGED. How dare the blackguard refuse to see her? How dare he hide out in his study? She pounded louder on the door. "I am not leaving until you see me."

Nothing.

Not a sound came from within. He *was* in there, wasn't he? She knew he was. She'd seen him vanish into the room with her very own eyes. Unless he'd climbed out a window, he could hear every word. Despite last month's mention in the society papers, where he was touted for slipping out Lady T.'s window while the butler helped the inebriated Lord T. to bed, she simply couldn't imagine him folding his big body in two and going out the window just to get away from her.

Lily crossed her arms over her chest. Really, who could imagine the powerful Duke of Blackmoor would be afraid to see *her*?

Over the years, ignoring her had apparently been easy for him, but that was when she was in Essex. Out of sight and all that. It took real effort to ignore her when she was pounding on his door. "I am a most stubborn woman," she warned him. "I'll wait right here as long as it takes, Your Grace."

Still nothing.

Lily jiggled the handle. Locked.

She heaved a sigh and leaned her head against the large oak door. She knew he could hear her, and she was at a loss. Perhaps talking to him would be easier without his penetrating grey eyes focused on her. What did she have to lose?

"I'm worried," she said softly. "Something is not right with Oliver and… Well, I know you don't care for the boy, but his father made you his guardian. So that means I'm stuck with you."

The door was suddenly yanked open, and Lily stumbled forward, right into the muscled arms of the Duke of Blackmoor. She sucked in a surprised breath. Men never held her in their arms. Yet his closed around her as he steadied her. She couldn't really call it *holding her*, since she'd fallen into him like a great oak tree whose roots had suddenly given way.

Lily froze. The heat of his body, coupled with the manly scent of him, was enough to knock her off her feet once more. She steadied herself by placing her hands on his chest. The muscles rippled beneath her fingers. She raised her eyes to his untied cravat and then to the open neck of his shirt, where an improper amount of skin was exposed. She'd never seen such an amazing sight. The light dusting of hair across his chest mesmerized her.

Lily realized that she was standing on her own two

feet, yet his arms were still around her. With her great height, she looked most men in the eye. But she had to tip her head back to look up at Blackmoor. His warm, mint-scented breath blew across her face. Lily closed her eyes and inhaled.

Suddenly, the duke pushed her away from him, a scowl marring his ruggedly handsome face. "Miss Rutledge, shouldn't you be in Essex?"

Shaking off his effect, Lily squared her shoulders. "Do you even read the letters I send you?"

"How much?" he growled.

"How much?" Lily echoed, blinking at him.

"How much money will it take to make you leave?"

Money! Why did it always come to money with this man? Oliver's estates brought in plenty, which Blackmoor would know if he paid the slightest bit of attention to his ward's accounts. She didn't care if she ever saw one farthing of Blackmoor's fortune, for heaven's sake. Lily leveled him with her haughtiest glare. "There is more to being a guardian than proper funds, Your Grace."

"And that's why Lord Maberley has *you*, Miss Rutledge." Then he stepped away from her, stalking down the corridor toward his grey-haired butler. "Is the coach ready, Billings?"

Lily chased after him. He couldn't dismiss her so easily. How dare he try to escape her? "There is only so much I can do, Your Grace. We're entering a realm in his development I know nothing about. Oliver isn't the same boy he was before and…"

The duke turned back to face her. His nostrils flared. His grey eyes darkened to black orbs. A muscle twitched in his jaw. He looked more like a dangerous beast than a refined nobleman.

Lily swallowed her next words, gaping at the imposing duke as a shiver of fear trickled down her spine.

"If you are incapable of caring for his lordship any longer, Miss Rutledge, I will find a replacement. In the meantime, I suggest you return to your nephew."

Replacement? Someone who would care even less about Oliver than Blackmoor did? No one would take Oliver away from her. Not even this great hulking, surly duke. Lily found her voice. "How dare you threaten me? I am concerned about Oliver's well-being, and you won't put me off. *You* are his guardian, for better or worse, and you have duties where he's concerned."

Blackmoor's eyes darkened even more, which Lily hadn't known was possible. She gulped nervously, panicking slightly when she realized his gaze focused on the movement in her throat. The duke had never seemed frightening until now. Of course, she hadn't laid eyes on him in years. Upon reflection, perhaps it was good he hadn't been to Maberley Hall in the last six years.

"No one," his voice rumbled over her, "orders me about, Miss Rutledge, and it would be good for you to remember that." Blackmoor turned his piercing grey eyes on his butler and spoke through clenched teeth. "I assume the coach is prepared, Billings."

The butler simply nodded.

"You can't run away from me, Your Grace," Lily sputtered.

"*I'm* not running away at all." He scooped her up in his arms. "But you, my troublesome Miss Rutledge, are returning to your nephew."

Lily's mouth fell open. "How dare you…"

"You ask that quite a bit. I *do* dare, Miss Rutledge. That is all you need to know."

She squirmed in his arms, though it was no use. They were like steel bands wrapped around her. "Put me down."

"In due time," he growled.

Before Lily could respond, they were on the front stoop and then he was depositing her inside the Maberley coach. "Your Grace!" she managed before he shut the door on her.

She reached for the handle, but the coach started off with a jerk, throwing her back against the squabs.

❧

Simon watched until the coach disappeared down the drive. Lily Rutledge was a formidable woman, and he didn't put it past her to leap from the conveyance. When all seemed safe, he took a calming breath, prayed to keep his temper in check, and then re-entered his home.

Foolish woman! He barely had any control over himself as it was. She shouldn't tempt him with her tantalizing hazel eyes that sparkled with indignation. Her creamy breasts that rose higher with each deep intake of breath. Her slender waist that he could span with his hands, if he was of a mind to do so. The image *that* brought to mind shredded the last of his good intentions. What a blessing she was on her way back to Essex. Just remembering how she had felt in his arms filled him with desire.

Simon tried to tamp down the feelings that suddenly poured through him. It was too close to the full moon to be around women. He'd taken a huge risk when he'd opened the library door. But her plea for help had touched the softness inside him, the softness that even the beast couldn't take out of his soul, not until the night. Not until the night of the full moon.

When he had heard her impassioned plea, he had been in control of those urges. Then he had opened the door, and she'd fallen straight into his arms.

She smelled of all things wonderful—a mix of floral scents, probably a perfume applied behind her ears. Or a touch of flower essence between her breasts. But at this stage of the lunar cycle, his sense of smell was enhanced. When she'd frozen in his arms and swallowed hard, he'd smelled her desire and imagined the flush of wetness that surely must accompany it.

That was when he'd known he had to get her back to the coach and off to Essex as quickly as possible. Otherwise, she would end up flat on her back in the middle of his study with her skirts tossed up around her ears.

The human side of him, now that he was calming down, knew that she deserved better. Despite her advancing age of twenty-three, she was obviously untouched. He could think of nothing worse than a scared virgin being taken by someone like him. He wasn't nearly good enough for such a gentle and *normal* creature.

Simon stomped down the corridor, back to his study. He sank into the chair behind his mahogany desk and began to read the correspondence his solicitor had sent, along with the invitations and notes from the *ton*, inviting him to this party or that.

Would society never realize what he truly was? Would they continue to accept him based on his title alone, despite all the damage he'd done through the years? They seemed inclined to do so.

He'd heard whispers about *the dangerous duke*, and some of his friends had even relayed what was said about him behind his back. That, in particular, pleased him. Part of him wanted them to know what he was, what he was capable of. But no matter how poor his behavior, they still called for him.

Simon sat back in his chair and templed his hands in front of him. He tried to remember what Miss Rutledge had said before she fell into his arms. Something about Oliver needing him. The rest was a blur.

God, he hadn't seen the boy in years. How long since Daniel's death? Had it really been more than half a decade? He winced. Daniel, his cousin and dearest friend, had been one of the few people who understood him. The memories were painful, so he pushed them away.

He called out, "Billings!"

The butler entered the room. "Yes, Your Grace?"

"Do you remember what Miss Rutledge was prattling on about?" He gave a negligent wave of his hand.

"Something about young Lord Maberley changing and her having no one else to turn to. I believe she was soliciting your help, Your Grace."

"Do you think she couldn't deal with a little chest hair? Surely the boy has a valet to teach him to shave." He dismissed the thought. The lad's entry into manhood certainly wasn't something to get so worked up about.

Billings coughed delicately into his hand. "I don't believe she meant *those* kinds of changes, Your Grace. I believe she meant *your* kind."

"My kind?" he asked. His letter opener clattered to the floor. Billings had been with his family since his boyhood. He knew all of Simon's secrets. Yet he still faithfully served. "You don't mean…?" his voice trailed off.

"Yes, Your Grace. That's what I mean. She sees the signs and is frightened."

"She damn well should be," Simon muttered as he stood up and strode toward the corridor. "Ready my horse, Billings," he called.

Three

LILY HAD PLENTY OF TIME IN THE COACH TO PONDER her current predicament. The cad didn't have time for his ward, and he didn't even have time to discuss the situation with her. She would have to figure this out on her own. All she knew was that something was wrong with Oliver, and she planned to find out what. There was a London physician Mr. Craven had mentioned. Lily had rejected his suggestion at the time. Oliver's changes didn't seem medical, but she didn't know what else to do.

She'd love to get her hands around Blackmoor's neck. What had her brother-in-law been thinking to leave Oliver's care to that scoundrel? The blackguard couldn't even be bothered to visit the boy.

After Emma and Daniel died in that tragic carriage accident, Lily was the one who had happily assumed responsibility for the child. She had spent the last six years soothing his worries, healing his injuries, and tucking him in bed when he woke with bad dreams. She wasn't going to let the changes in him continue without addressing them. Not like she had with Emma.

When her sister married the former Earl of Maberley, Lily noticed changes in her as well. Once bubbly and personable, Emma became a bit of a recluse, preferring to stay in the country instead of enjoying the entertainments Town had to offer. She often became withdrawn and refused to see anyone, aside from her husband and child. Most disturbingly, Emma seemed... fearful, which wasn't like her at all.

For years, Lily had berated herself for not doing more, for not demanding answers. If she had, would things have ended differently? Would Emma have left Daniel? Would she not have been with him that fateful day?

Lily was determined not to make the same mistakes with Oliver. The situation wasn't the same at all, but she had learned her lesson from sitting back and doing nothing with Emma. She wouldn't ever do that again. She was going to get to the bottom of this by finding out what was wrong with Oliver and coming up with a plan to help him.

She needed answers before he went off to Harrow. The clock was ticking.

෧෩

Simon handed his riding crop to Billings and shrugged into his greatcoat. Lily Rutledge had an hour's lead on him, but, atop his hunter, he could intercept her. Though what he'd do with her when he found her was a mystery he hadn't quite worked out yet.

He started for the door but reared back when it opened of its own accord. Standing before him, like a sudden gust of unexpected wind, his brother William raked his gaze across Simon's form. "You can't be leaving. I just got here."

"Why *are* you here?" Simon asked suspiciously. Will had a habit of showing up at the most inopportune times.

"You have quite the way of making a fellow feel welcome, Simon."

"I am losing my patience, William."

His brother smirked and then strode past him, tossing his hat to Billings, who caught it in mid-air. "You make it sound as if you had some to lose." Will continued toward the study, no doubt looking for Simon's best whisky. "Besides," he called over his shoulder, "if you ever bothered to read your correspondence, you'd know I intended to spend the week with you."

Will stopped in his tracks and sniffed the air. Then he turned around, a rakish grin plastered across his face. "*You* brought a female companion? No wonder you're not happy to see me. What happened to, 'It's too dangerous to have women about during a full moon'?"

"It *is* too dangerous," Simon growled. Not that he had a choice at the moment. What would he do when he caught up to Lily Rutledge? How could he keep her safe? It was perilous enough for her to be around *him*, but now with his brother here, too…

As usual, his temper did nothing to faze Will, whose smile only grew. "So you say. Who is she then?"

"Miss Rutledge, and she arrived uninvited."

"Miss *Lily* Rutledge?" Will asked with an appreciative grunt. "How fortuitous."

In the blink of an eye, Simon had Will's back against the wall, his feet dangling six inches off the floor. "You won't touch one hair on her head. Understood?"

With the strength of ten regular men, Will pushed Simon off him, slid back to the floor, and loosened his cravat. "A simple, 'She's mine,' will do, Simon. There's no need to mark your territory."

She's mine? Ha. After he'd watched Emma Maberley cower in fear when she learned what Daniel was? No woman would ever be his, not in that way. Lily Rutledge or anyone else. It was too dangerous.

He was wasting time with Will. Simon started again for the door, then stopped in his tracks. "Benjamin isn't headed here, too, is he?" If there were going to be three of them, preparations would need to be made. He'd need to make a concerted effort to pay more attention to his post in the future or hire a bloody secretary who could keep track of everything for him.

Will shook his head. "Still in Scotland. But I'll be sure to let him know Lily Rutledge is off limits when I see him next."

"You do that," Simon growled. Lily Rutledge had enough problems of her own. She didn't need the brothers Westfield chasing her skirts. He stalked out the door and down to his stables.

Abbadon was saddled and waiting for him, the sun glinting off his sleek, black mane. Simon mounted his hunter and raced for the edge of Westfield Hall, hoping the solution to his problems would occur to him before he intercepted Lily Rutledge.

❧

Lily was starving. She'd barely touched her breakfast that morning, worried that she wouldn't be able to find Blackmoor or that his butler in London had sent her on a wild-goose chase all the way to Hampshire. Now she rather wished he had. She wasn't certain at all what to make of her encounter with the duke.

She'd been terrified, excited, and furious all at the same time. It didn't even seem possible, yet it was; and the further she traveled from Westfield Hall, the more her encounter felt like a strange dream. She hadn't slept particularly well the night before, and she wondered if that was related.

The carriage slowed, and Lily looked out the window. A small coaching inn was within sight. Thank heavens. It would do her good to stretch her legs and enjoy some dinner while she tried to get her thoughts in order.

When the carriage stopped, the coachman, Jenkins, opened the door and helped her to the ground. "I need to rest the horses, Miss. I do wish you'd stay with the coach. I don't like the looks of this place."

Lily glanced around the coaching yard. A couple of burly men, unshaven and unkempt, lounged about. However, as she had recent dealings with the Duke of Blackmoor, none of these men seemed particularly dangerous. Besides, she was hungry and had no intention of sitting in a stationary coach; sitting in a moving one was tiresome enough. Who knew when they would rest the horses again? As it was, this stop needed to be quick, because the skies were darkening and the threat of rain imminent.

She shook her head. "No need to worry about me, Jenkins. I'll order some light fare and be back shortly so we can be under way."

Lily started toward the inn, ignoring the coachman's grumblings about independent-minded women.

Of course she was independent-minded. If she didn't take care of herself, who would? It wasn't as though she had a line of suitors clamoring for her attention in Essex. She was firmly on the shelf at almost twenty-four. Emma had once told her she was *willowy*, but that really meant she was skinny and too tall for most.

Those traits could easily be ignored if a woman had ample funds to turn a suitor's head. Lily had none. Perhaps that's why she became so enraged when Blackmoor sent a bank draft instead of answers. He made her feel like a poor relation he was trying to appease, rather than an aunt with legitimate concerns for her nephew. Did he think he could buy her silence, since she had nothing? That money would titillate her so greatly she would drop her suit?

But she didn't have *nothing*. She had Oliver.

Perhaps she was going about this all wrong. Blackmoor was his guardian, but he wasn't Oliver's only cousin. Maybe Lord William or Lord Benjamin would be easier to deal with. They couldn't be any worse at correspondence than their older brother, in any event. So what did she have to lose?

Lily stepped inside the inn and shuddered slightly when the door shut behind her. It was nearly dark as night in the taproom, and the place reeked of unwashed bodies and ale. As her eyes adjusted to the darkness, she found that her stomach and her nose were in complete agreement, that anything prepared in this place would not be palatable.

She turned to leave but found the exit blocked by a man. Her gaze flickered over him as she clutched her cloak tighter around her body. She raised the edge of her wool cloak to cover her nose, trying to block the smell that drifted off him in waves. She took two steps back.

Lily jumped when her backward footsteps bumped her into a solid object, and she spun around. Another man, equally as horrid as the first, leered at her. She shivered and stepped to the side so she could keep them both in her line of sight.

"Good afternoon, my good men," she began, amazed that only a small tremor was present in her voice. She glanced around the room, searching for the innkeeper, but she found no such source of assistance.

"Did you hear that? She called us good men," one man taunted her.

"Do you come this way often?" Lily thought to distract them with small talk while she backed away from them. But they followed. They stalked.

The wind from outside blew the hair into her eyes when the door swung open. Lily, afraid to take her eyes off the predators, didn't even look to see who came inside.

"Miss Rutledge," a familiar voice said quietly, the sound no more than a low growl. "How nice to see you here."

The duke! Lily had never been so happy to see anyone in her twenty-three years.

"Y-your Grace." Lily nodded at him, unable to keep the tremor from erupting.

Blackmoor held one hand out to her. "Come," was all he said.

"Here now," one of the men started. "We were just havin' a little fun," he protested as Lily stepped toward the duke.

Blackmoor's warm, strong hand closed around Lily's own, and she finally let her gaze drop to the floor as she took a deep breath. She was safe!

The duke tugged her gently toward him and brushed that wayward lock of hair from her eyes. "Are you all right?" he asked.

"I'm fine," Lily whispered, wanting nothing more than to lay her head on his chest and weep with joy. But she maintained her composure.

He opened the door and pushed her gently outside. "Go to the coach," he said quietly. "Get inside and stay there."

Lily didn't even think about not obeying his order. She walked out the door and toward the coach, just as he said. Tears welled up in her eyes as she walked across the inn yard. She shivered as she thought of what might have happened had Blackmoor not arrived when he did. Her chest constricted, and it became harder to breathe. Between her quivering knees and the lack of breath, Lily didn't think she could take one more step.

But then she felt warm, comforting, strong arms surround her. "There, now, dear," the man started. "You're just fine." Lily thought it was odd that Jenkins would draw her to his chest and allow her to cry a river all over his coat. Maybe he had daughters of his own. She sobbed and clutched his shirt as the sobs wracked her body. He held her. Stroked her back. Let her cry it out.

But even that comforting moment was cut short when the duke barreled out of the inn. She looked up in time to see that his grey eyes were now black as night and he looked fiercer than any wild animal she had ever seen pictured in books. She moved to step behind Jenkins. But then she realized the coachman stood to her right, and that he was much smaller than the man who'd held her.

The dark-haired gentleman reached out and took her hand in his, raising it to his lips. He lingered only briefly, until Blackmoor roared, "If you want to keep that hand, I suggest that you remove it from Miss Rutledge's person."

Four

SIMON DIDN'T KNOW WHAT INFURIATED HIM MORE—
seeing Lily Rutledge as she was about to be eaten
for lunch by two men inside the inn or seeing her
wrapped up in the arms of his brother William. Simon
thought he *might* allow Will to live if he would step
away from the woman, but when Will's lips touched
Lily's gloved hand, Simon nearly lost control.

"Miss Rutledge and I were getting reacquainted,"
William gloated, as only a younger and irritating brother
could. "What on earth did you do to cause such a storm
of tears?" He turned toward Lily again. "He has a bit of
a temper, dear," he said with a slow grin.

Lily looked confused as she brushed her auburn hair
from her eyes. Simon wished he could do that for her,
to soothe her, but he couldn't with William between
them. He growled low in his throat.

"Try not to bare your teeth, dear brother," William
said. "You'll frighten the lady."

Simon stepped closer to Lily and took her elbow,
propelling her toward the coach. "What were you
thinking, going into a place like that?" he asked

her. Then he turned toward Jenkins, who looked positively green. "And you," he said to the worthless driver, "why didn't you protect her? I *should* sack you on the spot."

Jenkins sniffed. "I work for the Earl of Maberley."

"Which is the same as working for me," Simon snarled. "I don't appreciate insolence in my staff. It would be best for you to remember that."

The coachman blanched and then turned toward his box, muttering something about stubborn women. Had the dolt seen Simon two minutes earlier, he would not have dared to sniff nor mutter.

"You have blood on your sleeve," Lily said as her gaze slid across his body. "Are you all right?" she asked, her voice pitched a little higher than before.

"It's nothing," he growled as he pushed her toward the carriage door, hoping to get away from this place quickly.

"No, I think you're hurt," she insisted, her eyebrows drawing together, pinching her pert little nose at the top. Why hadn't he ever noticed she had freckles?

"The blood is not mine," he muttered, hoping she would let it go at that.

She blinked twice. "Those men inside?"

He simply nodded, feeling better as he got the beast back under control.

"What did you do, Simon?" William asked, his body now at full alert, nostrils flaring.

"I don't remember," he said to Will, his voice no more than a whisper.

Will simply nodded and walked into the inn.

"I should have listened to you this morning," Simon said gruffly. "You'll come back to Westfield Hall, and I'll send someone for the boy."

Tension seemed to vanish from her pretty face, but she shook her head. "Oliver's never traveled without me before."

Simon frowned. "I'm certain he'll manage, Miss Rutledge." He wasn't going to let her out of his sight. Who knew what other trouble she could get herself into? The idea struck fear in his heart.

At that moment, Will exited the inn and cheerfully announced, "Well, you owe me two hundred quid for the tables and chairs I had to pay for. But it was quite worth the expense to see the state of those men, I have to admit." Once he reached Simon, Will added quietly, so only his brother could hear, "They're alive, but they'll bear the scars of that encounter for a lifetime."

Simon could do no more than nod. He'd known that he shouldn't leave Westfield Hall this close to a full moon. But when he'd realized why Lily was so frightened, he knew he'd have to take desperate measures to retrieve Oliver before he could do harm. Now *he* seemed to be the one they should be worried about.

A drop of rain fell onto Simon's hair. He looked up at the dark clouds as a crack of thunder split the day. He could either ride Abbadon and get soaked to the skin, which would not improve his disposition in the slightest, or he could stay warm and dry in the coach. With her. He was safer on horseback. So was she. But as he turned to mount his hunter, he saw William slide into the coach along with Lily. Bloody hell. Now he had no choice.

"You," he called to the driver, "attach these two horses to the back of the coach." He pointed to Abbadon and his brother's chestnut mount. Of course William had paid no mind to his own horse. As soon as the rogue spotted Lily, Simon was certain, every other thought had left his brother's mind.

He hauled the coach door open, glowering at William, whose innocent expression didn't fool him in the least. Simon settled himself beside Lily, across from his brother.

When the coach began moving forward, Simon leaned his head against the leather squabs and closed his eyes, willing the journey to be shorter than it was. If he didn't look at her, maybe he could control his lustful thoughts or maybe he could sleep.

It didn't work. She smelled delightful, like sweet magnolias, and he imagined himself tasting every inch of her. Simon groaned. He nearly jumped through the wall of the coach when her hand touched his cheek.

What the devil was wrong with her?

His eyes flew open to find Lily gaping at him with a horrified expression. Well, she should be horrified. She shouldn't go around touching creatures like him, not when she smelled the way she did. "What?" he growled.

"You made a sound." Her voice was very small. "Are you sure you're not hurt?"

He was about to *hurt* William, whose brow rose with mirth. "I already told you," Simon began, looking once again at Lily, trying not to notice that she'd unbuttoned her traveling cloak while his eyes were closed, trying not to notice how the swells of her breasts rose with each breath she took. "I'm *not* injured."

"I'm sorry—I mean, I'm glad—oh, never mind." She sat back in a huff, folding her arms across her chest and staring out at the darkening sky.

Simon winced. Didn't she know that made her breasts rise even further? Was she *trying* to get herself mauled?

He glanced across the coach at his brother, who'd noticed the same sight. If William touched her, Simon silently swore, he would break every bone in his younger sibling's body. The sneer he sent William was rewarded with an unrepentant wink. To hell with breaking Will's bones, he was simply going to kill him, quick and easy.

Simon turned his attention back to Lily, who seemed oblivious to everything else going on in the coach. He cleared his throat. "Miss Rutledge, my apologies. I'm not quite feeling myself at the moment. I didn't mean to bite your head off."

Fortunately, she uncrossed her arms, and then she turned to face him. "Thank you… for everything."

The image of her terrified expression in the taproom flashed in his mind. "What *were* you doing back there, Miss Rutledge? What are you doing traipsing across the countryside without a chaperone, for that matter?"

"A chaperone?" Her hazel eyes sparkled, and the most delightful laugh escaped her throat. "Honestly, Your Grace, I am quite on the shelf, raising a troubling twelve-year-old boy all by myself. Traveling alone is the least of my worries."

Thunder cracked overhead.

"Is Oliver twelve already?" Will asked, leaning forward in his seat, close enough to touch Lily's leg if he was of the mind to. He had better not, Simon thought. "He seemed a little scrap of a lad when I last saw him."

"He's hardly little anymore," she muttered to herself, though Simon clearly heard her, his senses more keen than most. Lily frowned at Will. "You last saw him, both of you, right after his parents died. I'm certain he's not the child you remember at all."

There was a rebuke in her voice. Simon chose to ignore it. He didn't know the first thing about raising a child, and Lily Rutledge had offered her services at the time. If she was unhappy with the arrangement, she should have said so earlier. "You say there've been changes in the boy?" he asked, hoping Billings was wrong in his assessment. "His development is worrisome?"

His brother's icy blue eyes flashed to Simon as understanding stretched across his brow. "His *development*?" Will echoed.

Lily nodded. "It's come on so suddenly. He's nearly doubled in size in no time at all. Just a month ago, he was quiet and sweet natured, but now he's angry and loud most of the time. I hardly recognize him."

Rain began to pound against the top and sides of the coach. Simon closed his eyes, remembering when the change had first come upon him. It had been like a nightmare he'd been unable to wake from. At least he'd had his father to help guide him through his new life.

He'd been foolish not to check on Oliver before now. Twelve years old, for God's sake! Time had somehow gotten away from him. It didn't seem like six years had passed. She was right to be annoyed with his guardianship. Daniel would have expected more.

The coach wheels slid on the muddy road, and Lily gasped beside him. Before Simon could pull her safely to his side, the carriage tilted on two wheels, tossing him onto her. One moment they were all upright, and the next they were on their side.

Simon stared at Lily, trapped beneath him, and scrambled off her. Terror overtook him when he saw blood trickle from her hairline.

≈

Lily tried to grasp Blackmoor's forearm as the coach tilted, but she could only flail her arms wildly. Her elbow sunk into the flesh of the duke's nose, but he didn't even grunt. Her shoulder slammed into the side of the carriage, her head into the window frame.

Darkness danced along the edges of her vision.

"Lily?" She heard a voice call from a great distance. A warm hand brushed across her forehead, testing the wound, pressing gently but insistently.

"Lily?" It persisted. Why couldn't he just let her sleep? "Lily, you need to wake up, dear."

Someone else's chuckle broke through the urgency in Blackmoor's voice and reached her. "You've become awfully familiar with Miss Rutledge there, Simon," Lord William taunted. "Using her given name *and* a term of endearment. Tsk, tsk. One would wonder when you plan to offer for her." The chuckle became a laugh. Then a loud yelp.

"Must you talk?" the duke growled at his brother.

"Not if talking will elicit such a forceful blow to the side of my face. Have a care, won't you? I have an image to uphold."

"You'll heal within moments," Blackmoor murmured.

"Doesn't make it any less painful," Lord William complained.

"Miss Rutledge?" the duke persisted.

The darkness lifted, and she could finally look up at him, his body limned by the light from the window. He was a study in masculine proportions. Broad shoulders. Dark hair that fell in a tumble across his forehead. A simple silver streak over his left temple that was highlighted by the light when he turned his head. He was beautiful, and not because he'd saved her life earlier.

"Now that sounds more like the brother I know. Never let a woman get too close to you, not when the moon is nearly full to fading. Isn't that what you always say?"

Blackmoor growled low in his throat.

The driver of the coach opened the door, which was now above them. Jenkins poked his head inside, drenching them with a pool of water. "Everyone well?" he asked.

"We most certainly are not well," Blackmoor retorted, his voice harsh. "Who taught you to drive a coach?"

Jenkins quickly retreated from the doorway. "I'll just go gather the horses," he said as he vanished from view. Lily thought she heard him say something about poor-mannered noblemen.

She reached up to touch the wound at her hairline and winced.

"Be still," Blackmoor commanded her.

"Can you go five minutes without giving me orders?" she asked as she sat up. "I'm fine. Just a bump on the head." The walls of the carriage spun as she stood up.

The duke growled.

"I do like her," Lord William said as he pulled himself up through the open doorway to kneel on the top of the coach. "Not even drizzling anymore." He held out his arms. "Here, pass her up to me."

Blackmoor hesitated. Lily slipped past him, her body brushing against his, and raised her hands up toward Lord William, feeling rather like a baby waiting to be picked up by her parent.

Lily gasped when Blackmoor's warm hands spanned her waist. Having his hands on her person felt almost scandalous. Yet wildly comforting at the same time.

He lifted her effortlessly toward his brother's outstretched arms, which pulled her safely and quickly out of the coach. "Welcome back, Miss Rutledge," Lord William laughed.

She had to admit she enjoyed his easy-going nature, which was so unlike his rigid brother's. He had a boyish grin and a rakish twinkle in his eye, the contrasting traits mixing nicely in the man.

Before she could speak, the duke pulled himself from the coach and sat beside her on top of it for a moment. She could see Jenkins slogging down the muddy road in the distance as he led the horses back to the coach. If there wasn't too much damage, maybe they could soon be on their way.

In one graceful leap, Blackmoor was on the ground

and holding his arms out to her. He beckoned with the tips of his fingers. "Come on, now."

Lily sat down on the side of the coach and slid into his arms. Instead of catching her at the waist, as she expected, he wrapped his arms around her and let her slide down the front of his body.

She couldn't fight back the gasp that rose in her throat. Her hands clutched at his shoulders and then slipped down to his chest as she made her descent. Her heart thudded. Could he hear it? Certainly he could, because her heartbeats sounded as loud as the pounding of hooves to her own ears.

"I hear there will be a beautiful full moon in a few days," Lord William said as he jumped down from the coach himself.

Blackmoor thrust her forcefully away from himself and went to join his brother and Jenkins as they prepared to flip the coach. Surely the three men didn't think they could lift the heavy conveyance on their own?

Yet, within moments, the coach creaked and groaned as its mighty hull shifted and landed forcefully back on its wheels. The coach must have been much lighter than she thought. No wonder it had tilted over.

Lily was anxious to sit down inside the coach again. Her head spun like a child's top after the string had been pulled. Blackmoor reached out to take her arm.

"We need to have someone take a look at your head," he said, concern etched in his features.

"Not in this coach, you won't," Jenkins said. "Broken axle." He pointed toward the front of the carriage, where Lily couldn't see.

Blackmoor cursed under his breath.

"Looks like Miss Rutledge will just have to ride to town with me. She can ride your mount, Simon." Lord William smiled as he untied his large chestnut gelding from a nearby tree where Jenkins had secured the horse.

Lily's vision grew darker. She shook her head, trying to shake off the queasiness like a hound shakes off water. That only made things worse.

"It's fairly obvious that Miss Rutledge can't sit a horse." Blackmoor looked down at her and scowled.

"Oh, delightful luck, there. She can ride double with me," Lord William said as he reached down toward Lily, a sparkle in his icy blue eyes.

"I don't think so," the duke replied, mounting his own hunter before pulling Lily onto his lap. She leaned into him for support, and his arms came around her as he took the reins. She settled in closer to him and sighed. His chest was solid and strong.

"Perhaps someone *should* look at my head," she said quietly, the smallest noise making the thump in her brain renew itself.

She felt a breeze stir around her calves and reached to adjust her skirts.

Blackmoor brushed her hands away and accomplished the task himself. Heaven forbid that she should show a bit of leg around these men. Though she had to admit she rather enjoyed having the duke arrange her clothing.

Five

SIMON HAD TO ADMIT HE RATHER LIKED ARRANGING Lily's skirts, though he would much rather remove them all together. He was content to see the turn of her ankle and a slim calf, but he wasn't particularly happy that Will was able to enjoy the same sight. Simon bared his teeth at his brother before the insolent pup smiled and dutifully turned his head.

"We need to reach the next village before dark," Simon said.

"Haslemere is just a few miles up the road," the coachman informed them. "It's fairly good-sized, so there's got to be someone in a coaching yard who can fix this up with plenty of time to spare."

Plenty of time to Jenkins and plenty of time to Simon meant two very different things. Even if they found a fellow to repair the axle as soon as they reached the village, when they returned, it would be too late for them to continue on this day. Lily couldn't ride in a carriage with him or Will after dark.

During the daylight hours, he could honestly say he was more aware of her injury than her body. He had the beast firmly under control—for the time being, though he wasn't so sure how long he could maintain his composure after the sun went down.

"I think that's a good idea," Will agreed good-naturedly. "We'll send someone back for you, Jenkins."

His brother nudged his gelding forward, and Abbadon dutifully followed. Simon noticed Lily wince from being jostled on the horse, though she didn't utter a complaint. He sighed.

"Will!" he called. When his brother pulled up on his reins, Simon gestured toward the road in front of them. "Your speed isn't conducive to Miss Rutledge's injury. Go on ahead, and find someone to fix the axle. We'll follow at a more leisurely pace."

"Whatever you say, Simon." Will had the audacity to wink at him.

Simon glowered at his brother. "And we're going to need rooms at the inn. See if you can't get the innkeeper to track down the local doctor before we arrive."

"Anything else, Your Grace?" Will raised one eyebrow at him.

Simon wasn't sorry at all for his tone. Being alone with Lily while her body was pressed against his would be some of the hardest work he'd ever done. No reason why Will shouldn't have a few chores of his own.

Lily stirred in his arms and looked up at him. "Shouldn't we see if the coach can be fixed first, Your Grace? It's not that much farther to Westfield Hall, is it?"

It might as well be on the other side of the Atlantic, for all the good it did them. They'd never make it in time. He shook his head. "It's too dangerous to travel these roads at night, Miss Rutledge. We'll stay in Haslemere."

Will chuckled. "My brother thinks *everything* is too dangerous."

"Be off, you dog," Simon ordered.

Will smiled at Lily. "His bite is much worse than his bark, my dear. Keep that in mind."

"William!" he roared.

Will tipped his hat, then pressed his heels to the side of his gelding, and raced down the road.

Simon was surprised when Lily laughed against his chest, her warm hazel eyes twinkling in the fading light. Having her close, smiling at him, made him wish for things that could never be. A pang of regret pierced his heart, and he urged Abbadon on. "What could you possibly find amusing, Miss Rutledge?"

"The two of you. Emma and I used to bicker like that... Well, not exactly like that, but close enough."

"He's infuriating," Simon huffed.

"You're very close," she said. "It's easy to see you adore each other."

"We're connected," he amended.

Lily rested her head against his heart and closed her eyes, an endearing smile lighting her face. For a moment, Simon thought he could stare at her for hours, for days, and never tire of the sight. Then he snorted and shook his head. When had he become a fool?

Lily's brow furrowed as she opened her eyes and lifted her head. "Are you feeling all right, Your Grace?"

Simon nodded. "I've never felt better," he lied.

Lily's frown deepened. "Are you certain? Your heart is racing, and you're nearly burning up through your shirt."

He and his brothers were warmer than most other men. By the time most women realized it, they were too caught up in the passion of the moment to mention it. No one had commented about the beating of his heart, however. Perhaps it was because *she* was sitting across his lap. Or perhaps it was simply something no one had ever noticed before.

Lily gently cupped his jaw and then pulled her hand back as if she had been burned. "You *are* feverish, Your Grace."

"It's nothing to concern yourself with, Miss Rutledge."

"I can't even believe you can stand up, let alone ride."

Simon heaved a sigh. She was persistent. "You have a terrible habit of not listening to me. I'm neither injured nor ill. Now let it be."

She pursed her lips, and Simon wished he didn't imagine kissing them. Ignoring Lily Rutledge would be easier if her every gesture wasn't innocently seductive. She had no idea the precarious position she'd put herself into with him.

Why hadn't she married some country squire or local vicar or... someone respectable? Her mere existence tempted him to do things he knew he shouldn't. He couldn't be the only man to find her so... intoxicating. Firmly on the shelf, she'd said. It was ridiculous.

Lily Rutledge should be somewhere in Essex raising a brood of children and tending to some decent man's needs. Not draped across *him* in the middle of nowhere, making him want things he couldn't have.

"You are very grumpy," she said quietly. "Are you certain you're not ill?"

Simon ignored her. He didn't need someone worrying about him and trying to coddle him. Besides, answering her hadn't done him any good up to this point. She kept asking the same questions, unsatisfied with his responses, and he could never tell her the truth. But he had to admit he did enjoy her attention, no matter how poorly advised it was.

Lily sighed a breath of relief when she spotted Haslemere in the distance. Blackmoor had stopped talking some way back, and her head throbbed. Every time she adjusted her seat, trying to get comfortable, the duke either flinched or grunted. He would tense, and then it took moments for him to relax again.

Her thoughts went back to Oliver. She hadn't planned to be away from Maberley Hall for so long. Hopefully, he was all right. What would he think when Blackmoor's servant arrived to transport him to Hampshire? And why was the duke so adamant about bringing Oliver to his estate?

Lily looked up at Blackmoor to ask him. The question died on her lips, however, when she noticed the intensity of his stare, which was focused on her. She nearly lost her breath.

"We're here," he said, his voice low and gravely.

Lily shook her head, bringing herself back to the present, but the motion caused the throbbing pain to reoccur. Sure enough, they were in front of a quaint inn, two stories tall with a good-sized stable.

Lord William strode toward them, his dark hair windblown and a charming grin on his face. "Ah, there you are. I was starting to think my brother had absconded with you."

Lily smiled. What a ridiculous thing to say. "He's been ignoring me for years, Lord William. I hardly think he wants anything to do with me at all."

"I would beg to differ on that point, Miss Rutledge," Lord William said as he walked closer to the duke's mount.

Blackmoor growled.

His brother clasped his hand to his chest, feigning insult. "Lord William? My dear Miss Rutledge, we are practically family. Call me Will."

Behind her, Blackmoor grumbled something unintelligible.

His brother roared with laughter. "So charming, Simon." He lifted Lily from the horse and placed her on the ground, offering his arm. "Come on, my dear. Dr. Albright will be along shortly. I do hope you'll let me call you Lily."

She didn't have much of a choice, not that she was fussy about that sort of thing. She nodded. "Of course."

"Brilliant," Will gushed, escorting her into the taproom, which was much brighter than the frightening establishment they'd been to earlier.

A bosomy barmaid rushed to Lily. "Oh, you poor dear, his lordship said you'd been injured."

"Indeed," Will said with a frown. "Do you have Her Grace's room prepared, Molly?"

Her Grace!

Lily took a surprised step back. A strong hand

squeezed her shoulder, and Lily turned her head to see Blackmoor behind her, a deadly frown on his face. "I would like for my wife to lie down until your doctor arrives."

Lily's head began to pound, and she thought she might faint. Apparently Blackmoor did, too. Before she knew it, the duke had scooped her up in his arms. What was it with these men who felt the need to lift and carry her from place to place?

"Right this way, Your Grace," the bosomy girl said in a panic.

Blackmoor carried Lily up a flight of stairs at the back of the taproom, depositing her in the middle of a small bed. He waited until the tavern wench shut the door before sitting on the edge of the bed beside her.

Lily gaped at him. "What was that about?"

The duke shook his head. "I do wish Will had warned us, but he is right. It wouldn't do for someone to know that an unmarried lady traveled with the two of us. This is for your own good."

"My reputation?" Lily closed her eyes, wishing the pounding in her head would subside. There were so many more important things to worry about. Like the fact that he was sitting on the end of her bed, with the door closed.

"Yes, your reputation."

Either she was slightly addled from the knock on the head or he thought she was an idiot. She wasn't sure which.

"Surely you can do more than just repeat what I say," she said as he fluffed a pillow and placed it under her head, urging her to lie down. She batted his hands away.

Blackmoor scowled at her. "If it was found that you traveled unescorted with us by coach, tongues would wag and you would have to marry one of us."

"Twenty-three years and no one has ever offered for me, so it might be quite a novel experience. One I would have to turn down, of course."

She had to admit he looked quite dashing with his hair tumbled over his forehead. But the vee between his eyebrows was slightly unattractive.

"Your Grace, you're looking at me as though I've sprung a second head."

She didn't expect it when he reached out to move a lock of hair from her eyes. His fingertips lingered at her temple before he turned his hand and brushed her cheek with the back of it, his knuckles trailing all the way down to her chin. "If no one has offered for you in twenty-three years, the loss is certainly theirs, Miss Rutledge. Not yours."

She snorted. "The loss *would* be theirs, Your Grace. The lack of a dowry makes me a poor prospect for marriage." She shrugged. "But I am quite happy with Oliver, taking care of him."

"Speaking of that," the duke began. "We'll need to discuss his present living situation. I have decided that Oliver will come to live with me at Westfield Hall, at least for a short while."

Lily sat up quickly. "Why on earth would you want to do that?" she exclaimed. She grabbed her head when the pounding started again.

"Stop that," the duke rebuked her. "Lie down

before you keel over." He grasped her forearms, one in each hand, and pushed her back onto the bed.

He had to be the strongest man ever, because Lily found herself unable to fight him, no matter how much she wanted to do the opposite of what he instructed.

"Let. Me. Up." She must have spent too much time in the duke's company, because she heard the growl in her own voice. Perhaps surliness was contagious.

He leaned over her, his body mere inches from hers. "I will let you up when you promise to lie still, Miss Rutledge."

"I will promise you nothing," she said loudly.

"Then I'll just have to hold you like this forever," the duke replied.

Six

SIMON WASN'T SURE WHICH WAS WORSE, THAT MISS Rutledge was injured and needed to be restrained or that he was the cause of her agitation.

On second thought, Simon realized that he should have used a bit more tact when he apprised Miss Rutledge of his plans to foster Oliver, at least while the boy needed his guidance. Oliver was obviously important to her, so important that she still fought against his hold.

Or perhaps that was the woman's temper coming to the surface. Despite her willowy frame, tall but thin, she was quite strong. Of course, not strong enough to move a man like him from atop her person.

Atop her person. Simon looked down at her. He was on top of Miss Rutledge, in a bedroom, with the door closed, his body hovering only inches above hers. When she struggled, he felt her body brush against his.

"Be still," he tried a softer tone. He wanted to see her eyes open so he could enjoy the amber flakes close up. "Please?" he added. Miss Rutledge opened her eyes and looked at him, the anger merely simmering below the surface.

Simon was lost. His gaze traveled from her eyes, down her pert little nose to her amazingly full, pink lips. Lips. Simon watched her lips. He wanted nothing more than to touch them to his own. But she had them pursed tightly together, her anger still evident.

The hands that clasped her forearms gentled, his thumbs in total disagreement with his head as they began to trace loose circles on her tender skin.

She stilled beneath him. The struggle eased out of her in one slow breath. Simon inhaled deeply, enjoying the floral smell of her, the *Lily* smell of her. His nose took a path down the side of her neck and back up to her hair.

"Your Grace?" she asked.

"Yes, love," he said, distracted by her to the point where all reality ceased to exist.

"You can let me go now," she said quietly.

"In just a moment."

Simon released her right arm so that he could bring his hand up to her face. "So beautiful," he said, unable to keep from smiling at her. She surprised him when she smiled back and used that free hand to clutch his forearm.

With that simple acquiescence, Simon allowed himself to touch his lips to her forehead. Then her temple. The corner of her eye. Her cheek.

Simon pressed his lips to the corner of her mouth, lingering, his kiss much softer than he'd ever thought possible.

Lily inhaled quickly beneath him. Her heartbeat sped up; he could hear it thumping in her chest. The soft scent of her breath tickled his nose. But more than just her scent titillated him. He smelled her *desire*. And that was when he lost control.

Simon pressed his lips against hers, immediately lost to the sensation. She tentatively pressed back. If she'd been kissed before, it wasn't by anyone who'd taught her how to do it. Just the thought of another man kissing her raised his hackles. He wanted to own her.

"You have never been kissed?" He lifted his mouth long enough to whisper the words.

"Of course I have," she said saucily.

"Liar," he growled before his lips met hers again.

He deepened the kiss, finding her lips soft, warm, and willing beneath his. His tongue flicked out to touch her lips. She gasped, and he seized the opportunity to enter her mouth. Just that one act, his tongue entering her warm depths, and he knew he had to be closer to her.

Simon raised himself off her quickly, the cold brush of air when her body separated from his momentarily jarring. He stretched out above her, spreading her legs with one of his. The tangle of her skirts prevented more, but he was content for the moment with what he had.

She surprised him when she raised her head to meet his next kiss. Her lips touched his of their own free will. He rejoiced. Her mouth opened of its own accord. He reveled in the sensation. Tilting his head, he aimed to consume her. His tongue slid into her mouth, his hands coming up to hold her face. Both of her hands were now free, and she used them to grasp his forearms, then his chest. She held tightly to the lapels of his jacket and pulled him closer.

Closer. Yes. He wanted to be closer. And closer. And closer still. He moved the leg that was situated so nicely between hers, anxious to seat more of himself in that spot. His knee brushed her thigh, and she opened to him, all the while their tongues tangling in a sensuous circle.

Simon pressed himself against her, letting her feel the length of him against her hip. Immediately, her hand traveled down his chest, her nails raking his skin through the fine lawn of his shirt. He nearly swore because it was so delightful. Pleasure. Pain. Lily.

A knock at the door broke Simon from his trance. Will barreled through the door. "Simon, the doctor—" he began. "Well!" He cleared his throat. Turning on his heel, Will faced away from the pair. "Simon, whenever you're finished mauling Lily, the doctor would like to take a look at her."

Simon heard the door click shut. His gaze moved to the open window, where he saw that the sun was about to set in the sky. "Bloody hell," he bit out before he extricated his knee from between Lily's legs and eased himself off her body. He stood up, righted his clothes, shifted the most painful erection of his life, and tried not to look at her as he quit the room.

He was a goddamned fool.

❦

Lily bit back an oath of her own when Blackmoor stormed from the room without even glancing in her direction. She touched her lips, where his had just claimed hers so pleasantly, and shivered.

She couldn't quite understand what had come over her. She'd never done anything so wanton in her life, but she couldn't help herself. She'd been completely powerless to do anything except submit to him.

Her face heated, and she cringed. What must he think of her?

There was a knock at the door, and then it opened. A portly old man bustled inside, smiling brightly. "I'm Dr. Albright, Your Grace. I understand you've been injured."

Your Grace, indeed! How would anyone ever get used to such a thing? Not that she needed to, since the title was only temporary.

The doctor frowned, waiting for her to reply. So Lily nodded. "It's just a bump. Truly, too much has been made of it." It was certainly the least of her concerns at the moment.

Had she really just lain in bed with the Duke of Blackmoor? Run her hands along his body, while he pressed her into the mattress? No matter everyone in this establishment thought she was his wife; she wasn't, and it was a foolish thing to have done.

"Ah, well," the man began, pulling a chair up to the side of the bed, unaware of her inner turmoil. "Let me be the judge of that, shall we?"

He gently prodded the bump above her hairline.

"Your Grace, you should remove your pins, so I can have a better look."

"Oh?" Lily hadn't thought her mussed chignon would be a hindrance. She sat up slowly and pulled a handful of pins from her hair, allowing her tresses to tumble to her shoulders.

"That's better," the doctor said. Then he ran his fingers over the bump, making little sounds to himself. "There's just a bit of blood." He walked across the room and poured some water into a small bowl.

He returned to the chair, dipped a cloth into the water, and pressed it against her injury. "Have you been experiencing headaches, ringing in your ears, or dizziness?"

Lily frowned. "A little dizziness. Mainly it just feels like it's throbbing."

Dr. Albright removed the cloth and applied a bit of ointment to her wound. "I'd say that's fairly common for someone who overturned in a coach, Your Grace. You're quite fortunate. I've seen much worse injuries."

So had Lily. "My sister died in a coaching accident." If something had happened to her, Oliver would be alone again. The sudden thought made her heart lurch.

He wouldn't be completely alone. He'd have Blackmoor. Though Lily wasn't certain that was good at all.

Just then, the door quietly opened and William Westfield poked his head inside. "May I come in, Lily?"

She wished he wouldn't. She wished she never had to lay eyes on him again after what he'd witnessed earlier between herself and the duke, not that she could voice that opinion. Lily nodded. "Of course, Will."

He stepped inside, looking much more serious than he had the entire day. "So, Doc, what's the verdict? Will my sister live?"

Dr. Albright nodded and then rose from his seat. "Yes, she'll be just fine. But I am going to give her a sleeping draught to get her through the night."

"Splendid," Will said. "I'm sure my brother will be relieved. See me before you leave, Doctor, for your payment." Then he looked at Lily, a frown marring his handsome face. "Sleep well, all right, dear?"

❧

Will wasn't at all surprised to find Simon sitting alone at a far table in the taproom. That was understandable. That was Simon.

Finding him earlier, stretched out across Lily Rutledge, looking like he was going to take her… Well, that had been a surprise. Not that Simon was a saint. He was far from it, as were he and Benjamin; but as a rule, none of them dallied with innocent misses. The strictest rule-follower of the pack was Simon.

For a moment, Will felt a twinge of guilt for so mercilessly hounding his brother all day. But only for a moment. He'd enjoyed himself immensely and, had the tables been turned, he was certain Simon would have done the same. Benjamin would have been even worse. He shrugged off the feeling.

However, watching his brother nurse a glass of whisky, looking more miserable than he had in the past six years, Will felt his enjoyment of the situation fade.

He crossed the room in just a few strides and fell into the seat across from Simon. "Bit early to be so deep in your cups, don't you think?"

"Bugger off," his brother snarled.

Will smiled. He deserved that after all he'd put Simon through today. "Brilliant suggestion. Though I think I'll wait for Molly."

Simon glanced up from his glass, frowning. "Who?"

Will gestured at the buxom barmaid across the room. "Molly. Pretty little thing, isn't she?" He winked at her, and she waved back.

"For God's sake, Will, it's too close—"

"—to the full moon," Will finished. "Yes, I know. That didn't seem to stop you earlier with Lily Rutledge."

Simon groaned and took another sip of his drink. "I don't know what's come over me."

It had looked, to Will, as though Simon had come over Lily Rutledge, but he chose to keep that thought to himself. He didn't particularly care to have a whisky bottle smashed over his head. "Well, it's obvious you have some feelings for the girl."

"I'm a goddamn fool." Simon downed what was left of his glass.

"So Ben's been telling me for years." Will grinned. "But, honestly, Simon, do you think getting properly foxed is going to change all that…" He pointed to the staircase that led to the sleeping rooms.

"I'm hoping it will help me forget."

"That is a good plan." Will nodded understandingly. "And in your position, I'd probably do the same thing."

Simon grunted in agreement.

"The only problem with it," Will continued, "is I don't think *Miss Rutledge* is likely to forget."

A truly tortured look marred Simon's brow. "Oh, God, Lily. I'll have to talk to her."

He started to rise, but Will grabbed his arm, pushing him back in his seat. "Yes, but not tonight." He'd never seen Simon so troubled. It was probably best for his brother to get a good night's sleep. "The doctor gave her a sleeping draught. She won't wake 'til morning."

Will waited until Simon seemed more in control before adding, "She's not some tavern wench or merry widow, Simon."

"Don't you think I know that?" his brother grumbled.

Will sighed. "I think you need to think about what that means. Go for a walk. Clear your head, for God's sake. You're going to need it in the morning."

Simon shook his head. "She deserves someone better than me."

Will couldn't help but smile. "True, but she'd probably settle for you anyway."

Seven

SIMON SNEAKED INTO LILY'S ROOM AFTER DAYBREAK, when the moon had fallen in the sky and the sun was rising to take its place. He watched her sleep somewhat fitfully under the effects of the sleeping draught, but beautifully, nonetheless.

She had removed the pins from her hair the night before, and her auburn locks spread like a fan across her pillow. She lay on her back, still in her serviceable traveling gown, with a thin counterpane spread over her. He wanted nothing more than to peel back the covering and lay beside her. He wouldn't even have to touch her. He just wanted to feel her close to him.

She stirred in her sleep, her hand jumping on the pillow beside her face as she clenched her fist. Probably thinking about wringing his neck for the way he'd mauled her the day before. He deserved no less. He'd treated her terribly, like she was a common whore with whom he could toy and then never see again.

But, oh, he definitely wanted to see Lily again. He wanted it more than the next breath he would take.

He settled into a chair, which was not nearly big enough for his size, and stretched out his body. He wished he had an injury so he'd have an excuse to take some of Lily's sleeping draught and escape from it all. But men like him didn't suffer injury. Sure, they aged, but they healed quickly, even if they did happen to find an adversary large enough to wound them.

Finally, after he relaxed to the cadence of her breaths, he slept.

⤜✦⤛

Lily blinked. Bright morning light poured in through the windows. She was groggy, the sleeping draught apparently still in her system. She strained to sit up. That's when she noticed him. Simon Westfield slept slumped in a wooden chair, much too small for him, with his legs kicked up on the edge of her bed.

Why had he slept in *this* room? Certainly there was some place else he could have stayed. Even under the ruse of playing her husband, she hadn't expected him to share her room.

Her movement must have woken him because his head shot up and his eyes flew open. "How are you feeling?" he asked, scratching the dark whiskers along his jaw.

Tired, sore, and... foolish. "Um, fine. You?"

He drew his legs from the edge of her bed and rose from his seat. The frown she'd grown so accustomed to over the last day was once again in place. "Miss Rutledge, er—Lily." He cleared his throat and began to pace around the small room. "I spent half the night thinking about your predicament."

It was about time. Lily smiled at him, relieved he wasn't the beast she'd thought for so long. "I do hope, once you see Oliver, you'll have some idea what to do. I didn't know who else to turn to, and—"

Blackmoor shook his head. "No, no. I'm certain the boy will do fine at Westfield Hall. What I meant to say, Lily, is that I greatly appreciate all you've done for Oliver. Daniel wasn't just my cousin. He was my closest friend. I should have been more involved with his son before now."

An uneasy feeling washed over Lily, and she leaned forward, not wanting to misconstrue what he was saying.

"In any event, I feel I owe you for your time and dedication to the boy. You say you haven't got a dowry, and… Well, I'd be happy to supply you with one. You've certainly earned it—"

Lily leapt off the bed, and he stopped in his tracks. "How dare you?" she fumed, stalking toward him. He was large and intimidating, but she wasn't about to let that stop her. "Emma was my sister, and I've raised that boy. He's like a son to me. You can't take him from me. I won't let you."

Blackmoor stepped backward, surprise in his grey eyes. "If you'll just listen to reason—"

"Do you think I'm looking for compensation? Do you think I've been caring for him in hopes that you'd offer me a dowry? Do you honestly think I can be bought, Your Grace? I love that child, and I wouldn't take one farthing from you."

His face contorted to a dark scowl, his eyes narrowed dangerously. "There are things you don't understand, Miss Rutledge. Things you don't *want* to understand. Now allow me to help you, and—"

Before she even knew what she was doing, Lily raised her hand, pulled it back, and slapped him across his stubbly cheek. The sound reverberated around the room.

Oh, the man had a hard head. But he accepted the blow with dignity, as a man of his station would be expected to do. He barely turned his face. But his nostrils moved in and out as he breathed heavily through his nose.

Then he stepped toward her.

She took one step back.

He stepped closer, his eyes dark and brooding.

Lily found herself out of room to maneuver when her legs hit the side of the bed. But she refused to be cowed. Not by this man or any other. She lifted one pointed finger and poked it into his chest. Then poked it again. He didn't take his eyes from her face.

"You will not take him from me. You simply can't," she said as a lone tear escaped and ran down her cheek, her voice cracking despite her intention to show bravery.

"Would that I could leave him with you, Miss Rutledge," he murmured softly, wiping the tear from her face with the pad of his thumb. "I have not set out to hurt you, despite the fact that it's the unfortunate outcome. I wish that I could take it all away."

"By taking Oliver from me?" she asked. "You're taking away my *life*." She grabbed the lapels of his jacket and tried to shake the nearly unmovable man.

All she succeeded in doing was tugging his clothing, like a silly child.

The duke took her hands in his, lifted them to his mouth, kissed her bare knuckles, and stepped away from her. He opened the door and stepped out into the hallway. Lily could do no more than drop to the bed, lower her face to her hands, and sob.

Simon sank into a seat in the back of the taproom. Thunder rumbled in the distance, matching his mood. When he'd offered Lily a dowry, he'd truly meant to help her. She'd said she was on the shelf because of her lack of a dowry. Though he couldn't imagine any man not wanting her, even if she was penniless. So, he'd offered to do away with that obstacle, making it easier for her to find a husband to love. Someone decent.

He'd never expected her to become so angry. Or to cry. It had nearly wrenched his heart out when that tear had fallen onto her fair skin.

He was taking Oliver for her own good, so she wouldn't be in danger from a pup who hadn't learned to control his basic instincts. No matter how much Oliver might love her, he needed someone to guide him through these changes. And that someone was him.

He had to push Lily Rutledge far, far away from him. From both of them. If that mean marrying her off, so be it. Though the image of her smiling at someone else, kissing someone else, holding someone else made his stomach tighten.

"You look like a storm cloud," Will said and then plopped himself down in a seat across from Simon.

"I'm in no mood to converse with you, Will." He was in no mood to converse with anyone.

Will leaned back in his chair, studying his older brother. "No, apparently you're simply in the mood to bark at young ladies. Congratulations on that, by the way. Splendid performance. You were perfectly ruthless."

"I was no such thing," he mumbled.

"My room is next to Lily's. It's not as if the walls are thicker than parchment in this place."

Simon closed his eyes, hoping his brother would get tired of pestering him and leave him in peace.

"You can't honestly want to marry her off," Will said quietly.

Simon took a deep breath, rose from his seat, and glowered at his interfering brother. "Go pester someone else."

"You're making a mistake, Simon."

"It's mine to make then, isn't it?" But he wasn't making a mistake. He was doing the right thing, hard as it was. What did Will want from him? "Now go find someone who actually enjoys your company."

Eight

SIMON DIDN'T KNOW WHAT WAS WORSE, HIS INTENSE attraction to Lily Rutledge and his inability to act on it, or having her hate him so much. Her feelings about him emanated from her body in great waves as they rode back to Westfield Hall. The blasted rain continued to pour, so he was unable to ride outside the coach. Not that he would if he could, not when Will was so solidly ensconced in the seat beside her.

As they'd left the inn, Lily had grabbed hold of Will's arm, talking animatedly with him. She smiled at Will. She laughed with Will. Yet she continued to ignore Simon. It was as though he no longer existed.

Simon's mood darkened more and more as they rode toward Westfield Hall. Not only did Lily talk to Will, she touched him. She reached out to his brother, pressing her fingers to his arm when she wanted to make a point. The tinkling sound of her laughter was painful to his ears.

To make it even worse, Will ignored him as well. All of his attention was centered on Lily. *Go find someone who actually enjoys your company*. He could kick himself for saying those words to his brother. Not once did Will look at him and grin. Or tease him unmercifully. Or take his eyes off Lily's delectable form.

When Simon finally got Will alone, he would box his ears. He might not even wait to get him alone. He might have to attack him and rip him limb from limb in the coach. He wondered if he would get blood on Lily if he chose to kill his brother in such close quarters. She probably wouldn't enjoy the sight.

Simon was relieved to find that being around her during the day was getting easier and easier, despite the coming of the full moon. That first day, he'd been ready to take her, even in the broad light of day. But yesterday, when he'd kissed her, he'd been in control of the beast.

Simon could not have been more relieved when the coach finally stopped. Jenkins opened the door, and Simon stepped out, turning to raise a hand to Miss Rutledge. She ignored it and took the driver's offered hand instead. He fought back a groan of displeasure.

"Welcome home, Your Grace," Billings said as he stepped through the threshold. Simon didn't even respond as he turned toward his study, anxious to get as far as he could from Lily Rutledge as quickly as possible.

❧

"Well played there, Lily," Will said quietly to her, as the duke stalked away from them. Lily worried her bottom lip as she watched Blackmoor throw his hat and coat at Billings, who barely caught them before the force of the items nearly knocked him from his feet.

"I'm sure I don't know what you mean," Lily said sweetly, smiling at Will.

He used one crooked finger to tip her chin, forcing her to meet his eyes. His blue eyes, so unlike the duke's, sparkled with mirth. "You know exactly what I mean," he chuckled. "You would do him a better service if you had him strung between two horses and pulled limb from limb. Poor fellow."

Lily sighed. That suggestion had merit. It would certainly make her feel better, easing some of the ache around her heart.

"Careful how you play him, Lily," Will warned quietly, his gaze penetrating hers. "It may not be a game you enjoy."

"What am I going to do, Will?" she asked. "I can't just let him take my life from me without even asking my opinion or giving me a choice in the matter. He wants to *marry me off*, for heaven's sake!" She nearly shrieked the last but quieted her voice when Will glanced toward the duke's study.

"Lily, there are some things you don't understand," Will sighed.

"Then explain them to me! Please! *You* don't understand. I…" She stopped when he took her shoulders in his hands.

"The next card is Simon's to play, dear. You laid down the first card. Now it's time to see if he picks it up." He flicked her nose before passing his hat to the butler.

"Billings, can you be sure Miss Rutledge is comfortable, while we wait for the Earl of Maberley to arrive?"

"Yes, my lord." Billings simply nodded.

"I'll leave you to it, then. There's some whisky in Simon's study that needs to be tested. For quality, you know," he added. Then he winked at her and walked away.

∾

Simon was already absorbed in the ledgers Billings had left for him to check. He needed something to focus on besides the pain in his chest, to keep him from foolishly searching out Lily and begging for forgiveness.

He dropped his head into his hands, wondering how in the world he was going to handle his present situation.

"You won't find redemption for your latest sins in that book, Simon." Will broke him from his reverie.

Without speaking or even looking up, Simon tossed the open ledger at Will's head. His aim was deadly, but the man was agile and fast enough to duck before it could strike him.

Undaunted, Will poured himself a glass of Simon's best whisky from a sideboard and took the chair across from him. He dangled one leg over the arm of the chair in a supremely relaxed male pose.

"So, what are you planning?" Will asked congenially. "And how long will you torture yourself before you give in and take Lily to bed? The full moon is nearly upon us, yet you have her secured here at Westfield Hall, right in the path of danger."

"I *know*!" Simon roared, standing up so fast that his chair toppled over behind him. He pressed the heels of his hands against his eyes, hoping to push back some of the confusion that wracked his brain.

Will took a deep breath. "You know, Simon," he said calmly. "Our parents had a wonderful relationship." He let that thought trail off.

Simon raised his head and glared at his brother. Will simply shrugged. "You know it's true. Father was one of us. He faced the same beast we face every day, and Mother loved him."

"Lily *can't know*!" Simon groaned. "She simply can't."

"Why not?" Will asked, as though he'd asked what was for dinner. But, to Simon, he might as well have been pondering the makings of the universe.

"You saw the way her sister was with Daniel. She married him, and then she became a fearful little waif. She was scared of her own shadow."

"Daniel never had anyone to teach him to be a man," Will said quietly. "You are a very different person than he was."

"I am the same *type* of person he was, Will. You seem to have forgotten. All it took was one full moon. He shared himself with her on one full moon, and she would never let him come near her again, not in that way. I wouldn't be able to stand it, to see Lily hurt the way Emma was." And he couldn't. It would kill him for Lily to fear him or, worse, to pity him.

"Tell her, Simon. And let her make the choice," Will said before he extricated himself from his slouch in the chair and started for the door.

Simon flung his inkwell at Will, and it crashed against the now closed door, splattering black liquid all over. He had to fight the urge to give chase and throttle the man when he heard Will's laughter from the hallway.

Lily sighed, running her fingers along the book spines in the Westfield library. With the weather simply horrid, she hadn't left the manor house, though she desperately wanted to do so. She felt trapped and dismissed all at once.

How could she possibly get Blackmoor to change his mind about Oliver? She didn't think begging would work. She wished she had something to barter or wager. The duke did a fair amount of gambling, after all. But she had nothing even to tempt him with. Even if she had something of value, she didn't know the first thing about gambling.

"Ah, there you are," Will's voice came from the doorway. "Looking for a good book?"

Lily turned around and graced him with a smile. "I'd much rather be out of doors, but in this weather…"

He strode further into the room. "How are you holding up?" he asked quietly.

Lily wished Lord William had been made Oliver's guardian. He'd be so much easier to work with. Blast Daniel for leaving the boy to that obstinate ox instead! She shook her head. "What is the easiest card game to cheat at?"

His blue eyes widened, and his mouth fell open. "Cheat?" he echoed.

Lily shrugged. "I need to find some way to keep Oliver. I thought a game of chance…"

"Where you held all the cards, so to speak?" he chuckled. "Simon will definitely have his hands full with you."

"Have you a better idea?"

A feminine giggle from somewhere close caught Will's attention, and he winced, his usual smile faded away. His reaction immediately piqued Lily's interest. "What's wrong?"

"Not what. Who," he grumbled.

With a world-weary sigh, he turned back toward the door and looked down the hallway, like a child checking for an escape route. Lily couldn't help but laugh. "Who then?"

"A neighbor." A second later, he groaned. "It's too late. We could hide, but she'd still find us."

Lily couldn't imagine Lord William Westfield hiding from anyone. She brushed past him and peeked around the corner of the door. The most beautiful woman Lily had ever seen was just a few feet away. Ebony hair, knotted at the base of her neck, draped over one shoulder. Violet eyes twinkled beneath a pair of slender brows. An expensive day dress peeked out from beneath a long coat.

The striking woman smiled. "You must be Miss Rutledge. Please tell me William is cowering behind a bookcase."

Lily choked on a laugh. Her guess was fairly close to accurate.

Will stepped into the hallway, glowering. "My dear Prisca, you do suffer such delusions of grandeur."

The beautiful woman's eyes narrowed to little violet slits. Then she stepped forward, focusing on Lily. "Uncivilized beast. Since his lordship is either incapable or unwilling to introduce us, allow me, Miss Rutledge. Prisca Hawthorne of Langley Downs."

She unbuttoned her coat and then thrust it in Will's hands.

"Oh, do let me take your coat," he said mordantly.

Lily smiled. "A pleasure, Miss Hawthorne."

"Ah, Prisca, please. I insist."

"Prisca, then." She gestured to the library behind them, "Would you care for tea?"

Prisca arched one perfect brow and pierced Will with a haughty stare. "Pretty *and* polite. I can't imagine why she would waste her time with you, William."

Will looked past Prisca, down the hallway. "Where *is* Emory? Tell me he didn't turn you loose on Westfield property. I'll have to end our friendship."

"Oh, please do," Prisca countered. "My brother would do well to end his association with you." Then she linked her arm with Lily's. "Tea does sound delightful, thank you very much, Miss Rutledge."

"Lily," she offered quietly, slightly surprised by the whole interaction.

As they stepped into the library, Will followed. "Tell me, Miss Hawthorne, do you sharpen your tongue at night, on the off chance you'll get to use it on me?"

Prisca laughed, a sweet melodic sound that filled the room. "And *I* am the one who suffers delusions of grandeur? On the contrary, William, I hardly ever think of you. I heard a rumor in the village that one of Blackmoor's prodigal brothers had returned. I'd so hoped it was Benjamin."

Will stopped dead in his tracks, a frown marring his handsome face.

Prisca smiled beatifically at him, and Lily was certain she'd never met a more stunning woman. "Emory is visiting His Grace, if you're of a mind to find him."

Will glared at her and then bowed to Lily. "We'll finish our discussion later."

After he left, a genuine smile lit up Prisca's face. "Please tell me you haven't lacked for female companionship for too long. If I'd known Blackmoor had guests, I'd have come much earlier. I can't imagine they have much to entertain you with, if you've had to resort to speaking with William."

Lily shook her head. "Actually, Lord William has been quite gracious. Do you truly dislike him?" It was hard to imagine anyone could do so. She would have been completely lost without him.

Prisca furrowed her brow. "I much prefer Blackmoor, if truth be told. At least one knows where one stands with the duke."

A stab of jealousy pierced Lily's heart. No matter that she was furious with Simon Westfield, that she'd envisioned strangling him more than once that very day—she could never forget how it felt to have him touch her, kiss her, make her lose all thought and reason. Lily was certain she would appear terribly drab next to such an exquisite creature as Prisca Hawthorne.

"Are you all right?" Prisca asked, alarm in her voice.

"Yes, of course," Lily lied. Something was wrong with her nephew. She'd kissed his guardian, who threatened to take Oliver from her. Her life had been completely turned upside down on every level. "I am surprised you prefer His Grace. He seems quite unapproachable."

Prisca smiled. "You just have to know how to deal with men. God punished me with five brothers, but having them has trained me well. Do you have brothers, Lily?"

"I lost my only sister six years ago."

Prisca's smile faded. "Lady Maberley. I met her once. You've been caring for the young earl, I understand."

Lily nodded, willing herself not to cry.

"How long will you be visiting?"

Until Blackmoor threw her out of the house or forced her into a marriage she didn't want. With those thoughts, Lily lost the battle with her tears, and they spilled down her cheeks.

"There, there." Prisca said, offering her handkerchief. "It can't be all that bad."

"It's awful," Lily sobbed. Prisca hugged her tightly. "I don't even know you, and look at me… I'm crying all over you. I'm terribly sorry." She dabbed at her eyes.

"Nonsense! Whatever it is, you should get it all out."

Lily sniffed back her tears. "You're very kind."

"Don't let William hear you say that. I've got a reputation to protect."

Lily laughed.

"What I was going to ask, Lily, was whether you'd be here at the end of the week. Friday, there's a ball at the assembly room. Nothing large. Not by Town standards, for sure. But it is delightfully fun. And if you've been cooped up here with the brothers Westfield, I'm certain you'll need an escape."

A ball? Lily couldn't remember the last time she went to a ball. Years, at the very least. She shook her head. "Oh, I think not. I wouldn't have a thing to wear."

Prisca's eyes lit up. "Is that all?"

Lily sighed. "Truly, I wasn't planning on staying long at all. I certainly didn't bring anything appropriate for a ball, small or otherwise."

Prisca clapped her hands together. "Perfect. I've been looking for a project. And I love to sew. I've got a magnificent green silk. I think it would perfectly bring out your eyes. Please say you'll stay and let me make you a magnificent dress."

"Oh, I don't know." She had so many worries. A ball seemed so frivolous compared to them all.

Prisca's violet eyes twinkled. "No, Lily, you must come. If you agree, then that scoundrel William Westfield will have to escort you, and there's nothing *he* hates more than a small country ball."

"Oh, I could never," Lily began. She didn't want to make Will angry. He was her one hope at getting Blackmoor to change his mind about Oliver.

"Go ahead and agree, Lily," Will said from the doorway. "She'll never let up until you do." Then he focused his eyes on Prisca. "Do save me a waltz, Prissy."

Nine

SIMON GAPED AT HIS BROTHER. WHAT HAD THE FOOL been thinking? "Absolutely not! No balls."

"Sorry, Simon. I already agreed." Will examined his fingernails as he leaned against the wall. "That pest Prisca Hawthorne goaded me into it."

"But Friday!" Simon paced around his study. "That's—"

"The night after the full moon. I know. By then, the worst of the affliction will have passed."

"But the wildness will still remain," Simon reminded his brother. He couldn't fathom why in the world William would want to put himself in the position of being on guard for an entire torturous evening, fighting the basest of instincts. Every scent of a woman, every brush of a body on the dance floor, every clasp of a hand, even in innocence, would be impossible to ignore.

"The wildness is there *every* day, Simon," Will replied as he clasped his hand to his brother's shoulder.

The tinkling sound of Lily's laughter drew Simon from his study. This was, of course, the first time he'd heard it since their arrival at Westfield Hall.

But that sound would draw him from the depths of hell.

Simon turned the corner into his gold parlor, Will in his wake, to find Lily laughing with his old friend Emory Hawthorne and his sister. Simon had thought their neighbors had already left. He couldn't imagine why the pair was still there until he saw the look of infatuation in Emory's eyes as he gazed at Lily.

The beast rose in him once again. Must every man stare at her in such a way? "Miss Rutledge, I'll have a word with you," he clipped out. Lily and the Hawthornes turned toward him, surprised expressions on their faces, yet he did not regret his tone. She would be well served to heed his mood and remove her fingertips from Emory's hand. Immediately.

Lily raised her nose at him. "I'll be along in a moment, Your Grace." Then Emory regained her full attention.

Simon felt his hackles rise and was one step from baring his teeth at one of his oldest friends when Will stepped forward. "I imagine we'll see you at this ball your sister seems obsessed with, Emory." Will touched the man's shoulder and turned him toward the door, shooting a warning glare at Simon. Will's warning should have been saved for Emory because *he* was the one in imminent danger, Simon thought.

Emory was oblivious to the fact that his life was in jeopardy. "Miss Rutledge, I would be honored if you'd allow me to escort you to the assembly room on Friday night."

Simon growled.

"Well, I—"

Simon snarled, "If Miss Rutledge insists on attending a party, she will be escorted by me, Hawthorne."

"I will?" Lily asked, one hand fluttering to land on her chest.

If only his lips were upon that chest, Simon thought. He tore his gaze away from Lily's cleavage when Will said, "Why don't we all go together, Emory? We can meet you both at Langley Downs beforehand."

"Oh, William," Prisca began, feigning sweetness. "If you wanted to escort me to the ball, you had only to ask. No need for an elaborate ruse to get me into your coach." She winked at Lily.

Will muttered under his breath, "If it saves your brother's life, I would agree to take you to the altar." Simon's keen hearing picked up the words, though he was beyond caring.

Simon stalked slowly toward Emory Hawthorne, who still stood too close to Lily for comfort. Emory paid no heed to the warning look he sent him, so Simon bumped his shoulder against the man.

Emory stumbled to the side.

"Pardon me, Hawthorne," Simon said as he took Lily's elbow in his hand and prodded her away from the group.

"Honestly, Blackmoor," Lily complained. "I told you I'll be along in a moment." She yanked her arm from his grasp. He allowed it, but only for a moment.

"*Now*, Lily!" he said, grasping her elbow more firmly. He was prepared to drag her, if need be, though it would be better for the neighbors if she came willingly.

"It's all right, Lily," Prisca said, her eyebrows drawn

together in concern. "You'd best do as he says. He looks ready to devour you right here and now."

Only Prisca would make such an incendiary statement in such a public place. Though Simon supposed his behavior warranted her waspishness.

"I'll send a coach for you tomorrow, Lily, so we can prepare for the ball," Prisca continued as Simon pushed Lily around the corner.

"Thank you," Lily called back as he led her into his study and slammed the door. Then she glared at him, her pretty, hazel eyes darkening. "Honestly, Your Grace!"

"Simon," he said absently, running a hand through his hair in desperation, trying to rein the beast back under control, trying to figure out why it drove him to distraction to see other men fawning all over her.

"Simon what?" she asked, confusion on her face.

"I'm tired of you 'Your Grace-ing' me. You call Will by his name."

"Is that what this is about? Why you manhandled me in front of your neighbors?"

"I did not manhandle you."

"You most certainly did. That had to be one of the rudest displays of temper I have ever seen." Lily rubbed her elbow.

Had he harmed her? Simon looked over her person. Her chest was pink and rosy, a symbol of her anger. Her cheeks were bright red, and her breasts rose with every agitated breath.

Her breasts. Her breasts rose with every breath. His gaze danced across her *décolletage*, willing the flesh to rise a little more so his eyes could greedily devour her skin. She noticed his stare and covered her chest with her hand.

"Perhaps, *Simon*, you should just undress me and get it over with, instead of simply undressing me in your mind."

Simon instantly hardened at the thought. He took two steps closer to her. "Perhaps I shall."

❧

Lily immediately forgot the pain in her elbow as he walked closer. What was he doing? She hadn't really laid down a challenge. She held up one feeble hand, as though that would hold him off.

It didn't.

Lily danced sideways, putting a chair between them. Simon pushed it over. As it thumped against the rug, she fled to stand behind his desk.

"Simon, what has come over you?" she shrieked. Her voice sounded painful to her own ears. Though it did not affect his, not if his present conduct was any indication.

"I want to see if I hurt your elbow, Lily," he said quietly, his voice no more than a low hum.

"Then why are you stalking me?" she asked, happy that the desk was still solidly between them.

He laughed mirthlessly. "What an odd thing to say, Lily. I am not stalking you."

However as he advanced toward her, all Lily could think was that she was about to become his dinner. What a silly notion. Though at times, Simon did remind her of a wild animal. Now was no exception.

He reached one hand across the desk and said

quietly, "Let me see if I hurt you." Did a bit of guilt cross his face?

Lily extended her elbow, pointing it at him as she rolled her eyes. "You really should have worried about this *before* you grabbed me in front of everyone. In fact, you shouldn't have grabbed me at all," she rebuked him.

Simon took her elbow in his hand and regarded it quietly, noting the redness of her skin where his brutish hold had clasped her so roughly. He lowered his lips to the spot and touched it gently.

His dark eyes rose to meet hers, and she saw remorse in their depths. But she also saw... *hunger*? She batted at his hand. "That's enough, Simon. I'm fine."

His gaze never left hers as he said, "Never pull away from me, Lily. I can't bear the torture."

"What has come over you?" One moment he was standoffish, offering to pay her dowry to the first available man who would take her off his hands. Then he was trying to devour her. And what of his comment about undressing her? It was best left forgotten.

Lily jumped as Simon suddenly leapt over the desk, the contents of the desktop scattering to thud onto the rug. Within seconds, he was mere inches from her. How had he moved so quickly? And so quietly?

"Allow me to apologize properly," he said as he lifted her elbow again and graced the inside of her forearm with his lips. Was that a question? He certainly wasn't waiting for permission.

Lily was still peeved. "And if I choose not to accept your apology?" she asked, trying to tug her arm from his hand.

"Then I shall have to convince you of my sincerity.

Let me kiss it and make it better," he said. With the last, his eyes met hers, a bit of boyishness dancing in the depths.

"I think you have kissed me quite enough, Your Grace," she sighed.

His hands dropped her elbow, moving to cup her face. Gentle thumbs played around her jawline as his fingers splayed toward the back of her head. His glance dropped to her mouth just before his lips touched hers. "Never enough, Lily," he growled.

Ten

SIMON KNEW THE MOMENT LILY ACCEPTED HIS
advances. She reached up to place her hands flat
against his chest, nearly igniting him. Initially, he
thought she intended to push him away. But she
simply curved into him and returned his kiss as
fervently as he offered it.

Forgotten was the elbow that had begun this
encounter. In fact, what had started this tryst were
Emory Hawthorne and his desire to accompany
Lily to the local assembly hall. Simon would wipe
all thoughts of Emory from her mind. He would be
sure she had very little mind left, except for thoughts
of him and what he could do for her, what he could
make her feel.

Simon's arms snaked around her waist, drawing her
closer to him, as though he could pull her right into his
body. Her arms inched up around his neck, pulling his
head down as she pressed even more firmly against him.

Simon was amazed he still had his wits about him,
but he realized how much he liked her height as she
returned his kisses. Most women were diminutive in

comparison to him, but not Lily. She fit against him as though she was made to be there. Her breasts pressed against his chest, hard nipples grazing the fine lawn of his shirt, the pinpoints in stark contrast to the bounty of her chest.

Simon used one hand to play around her bodice, teasing the sensitive skin. She arched into him. She gasped against his mouth, a quick intake of air, as he moved his hands down to cup her bottom and then picked her up and turned to sit her on the edge of his desk. But she didn't pull away.

Simon pressed her knees apart so he could settle his body there. She gave no resistance, opening willingly to him as he pulled her to the edge of the desk so that he could seat himself as closely as possible to her heat.

Smelling her desire, Simon grew harder than he'd ever thought imaginable. His lips trailed down the side of her throat, weaving a gentle path across her tender flesh. *Gentle. Be gentle, Simon.*

"Gentle?" she whispered. Had he spoken aloud? "I don't want gentle. I want you," she breathed.

But she had no idea what she was asking. She wasn't aware of what firm control it took for him to stay sane. She didn't have any idea how close he was to devouring her like a sweetmeat before dinner. It took every bit of his humanity to remain in the moment.

No matter, he wasn't ready to stop. He would push his control a little farther. And test hers at the same time. As his lips moved across her flesh, he pressed her back until her arms were forced to leave him to hold her weight up. Her new position brought her breasts forward, pressed against the fabric of her gown, calling to him.

Simon cupped one breast in his hand, testing the weight of it. She inhaled sharply, her head falling back so that her throat was exposed, her eyes closed in sublime pleasure.

His thumb grazed her nipple as his other hand rose to cup her other breast. Lily's eyes closed tightly as she absorbed the sensation and reveled in it.

She broke his trance when she suddenly sat forward, taking his hands in hers and removing them from her body. Her chest heaved, her breath coming in great gulps.

"No," he ground out.

"Do you hear that?" she asked, looking toward the door.

Her heartbeat? Yes, he heard it. It was nothing to be ashamed of. "Quite normal," he said softly.

"Simon, would you *listen*?" she said more loudly.

That was when he heard the angry stomp of footsteps in the hallway. Then he heard Billings tell whomever it was, gently but forcefully, that the duke was unavailable.

But Lily was already pushing him away. She dared to straighten her clothing? When he wanted nothing more than to tear it off?

A voice called from the hallway, "Aunt Lily, are you here?"

The Earl of Maberley had finally arrived.

Lily flew from Simon's study, nearly barreling right into an overgrown adolescent boy. Simon managed to keep his mouth from falling open. Looking at Oliver York was like staring into the past. The young earl was definitely his father's son. He had Daniel's chestnut hair and dark chocolate eyes and the build of a man instead of a boy.

Oliver barely spared him a glance, holding tightly to his aunt. "Why did you leave like that? I thought you were only going to be gone a day."

Lily kissed his cheek and backed away from the lad. "My plans changed a bit, Oliver."

"Well, why did you bring me *here* in such a rush?" he asked, irritation evident in his voice. "The driver barely stopped to change horses. I'm sore and—"

Simon stepped forward. "*I* brought you here, not your aunt." This was the child Lily would fight him for, tooth and nail? This young man lacked the innocent boyishness of youth. Simon couldn't imagine Lily rocking him to sleep or singing him lullabies. So, why was she so willing to give up her chances for a good match to spend time caring for this recalcitrant youth?

He knew it must be difficult for the boy to keep his temper, especially with the changes that were taking place in his body, but Simon wasn't about to let him use a disrespectful tone of voice with Lily.

Oliver's brown eyes flashed to him, and his brow furrowed angrily. "So *you're* him?"

Lily stepped forward. "Oliver, please," she said softly. "This is your cousin, His Grace, the Duke of Blackmoor. Do be on your best behavior."

The boy's scowl darkened. Simon mirrored his look, not understanding why the boy behaved with such impertinence. Full moon approaching or not, the whelp had no excuse for his conduct. He'd need to have a conversation with Oliver sooner rather than later, but he couldn't do so with Lily hovering. For a moment he wished Prisca Hawthorne hadn't left. At the very least, she could have distracted Lily.

"Lily love, will you give me a moment with the earl?"

"Why?" She blinked innocently at him, and he felt his desire for her mount.

"I would like to have a word with my ward. We'll find you. Go make certain Will isn't still smarting from his encounter with Prisca, will you?"

She nodded reluctantly and then started down the corridor. Simon pulled his eyes away from her disappearing form and gestured to his study. "After you, Maberley."

The boy stepped inside but stopped, looking around the room and frowning. "What happened in here?"

Simon winced. If he hadn't been so distracted by Lily's delectable form, he would never have brought Oliver into his study. Chairs were toppled over. His desk was wiped clean. Ledgers and several pieces of foolscap littered the floor. "I, uh, have a bit of a temper at times. It would be best for you not to bring it out in me." He shot the youth a subtle warning before he righted one of the chairs and pointed to it. "Sit."

As Oliver took his seat, Simon walked around his mahogany desk and dropped into his own chair. "Your aunt is worried about you."

"Why did you call her 'love'?" The child had the nerve to growl at him.

The pup didn't know who he was dealing with. "I didn't bring you to Hampshire for you to ask me questions, but the other way around, my boy."

Oliver shook his head. "I'm *not* your boy. Aunt Lily

begged you for years to visit me. A little late for you to be interested now."

Simon had never had a twelve-year-old chastise him before. Obviously, the lad was in serious need of a strong male in his life. He leaned forward in his seat, leveling the young earl with a serious look. "You're still a boy, Oliver. It's not too late for anything. In fact, it's the perfect time. Now tell me what's been going on with you."

"Nothing. Certainly nothing that would warrant a summons from you," he grumbled.

Simon tried a different approach. There had to be some way to get a pleasant response from the young earl. "Did you know your father lived here for a while as a boy?"

Oliver shrugged. "Is that supposed to mean something to me?"

Simon rubbed his jaw, amazed Lily wanted to keep the brat. He hoped the boy's transformation was to blame and that he didn't act like an unruly scamp for Lily on a regular basis. For the time being, Simon was giving Oliver the benefit of the doubt, but his patience was quickly fading away. "Let me explain something to you, Oliver. I understand you are experiencing some *changes*. You don't feel the same. You don't feel like you're in control of yourself, not your thoughts nor your body. You feel different on many levels, and that has to be frightening."

For the first time in their conversation, Oliver looked vulnerable, like a child.

Simon breathed a sigh of relief. "What you're experiencing is *normal*. Well, normal for us. Me, my brothers, your father, you, and handful of others out there."

Oliver frowned but didn't say a word.

"There are ways you can control these feelings, these urges you don't understand. I brought you here to help you, to train you."

"Train me?"

Simon nodded. "You can live a normal life, for the most part. A few days out of the month will be completely out of your control, but I can help you learn how to live with the rest of them."

"You make me sound like a monster."

How many times had Simon thought the very thing? "Not a monster, just different."

"But you said it was normal, and now you say it's different."

"Normal for *us*, Oliver. Other people aren't like us, and they can't understand the changes and turmoil. I'm sorry I wasn't there for you sooner. I should have been."

Oliver's expressions danced between relief and anxiety. "Aunt Lily said—"

"Your aunt doesn't know. It needs to stay that way." It was easier to focus on what should be done with Lily when she wasn't in the room, he realized. "In a few days, I'll send her back to Essex, but you'll stay here."

"No!" Oliver shot out of his seat. "If she goes, I do, too."

"You're not the one making decisions, my boy," Simon said calmly, hoping that when the time came, he could let Lily go. It was best for her, regardless of what he wanted for himself. "Your father left me as your guardian because he trusted my judgment. You'll have to do the same."

"I don't want to stay without Aunt Lily."

Neither did Simon.

Eleven

LILY FOUND HERSELF SEATED BETWEEN OLIVER AND Simon at dinner. Her nephew was unusually quiet, and Lily was anxious to talk with him privately. Simon was also quiet, and Lily couldn't keep herself from wanting to see him privately as well. They needed to sort out what was going on between them.

Simon seemed to be clutching her to himself at the same time he was pushing her away. He was a dichotomy. Though she also was having a difficult time coming to terms with her own feelings.

Lily wasn't sure what had come over her in the last few days. Until now, she'd never considered the possibility that she'd find a man she could care for. There hadn't been a point in wishing for something that wasn't likely to happen. However, circumstances had brought her to Simon's door, and Lily had never felt so confused. Her heart seemed to beat only for him, but she wanted much more than he seemed willing to give.

She sent a sideways glance toward Simon, only to find him staring back at her with an intensity that stole her breath. He felt it, too, whatever this was, and she couldn't understand why he wanted to send her away.

Across the table, Will stabbed a carrot on his plate with a frown. "Irritating chit," he grumbled.

Lily furrowed her brow. "I do hope you're not speaking about me, Will."

He looked up from his plate. "Oh, I didn't realize that was aloud. Apologies, Lily."

"What has you so upset?"

"I'm not upset," he snapped.

Simon touched her hand, sending a jolt of awareness through her. "My brother and Miss Hawthorne love to annoy one another. They've been doing so for years. Quite successfully, I might add."

Lily had noticed that. "Why?" she asked innocently.

"Indeed?" Simon quirked a grin at his brother. "William, do tell."

"I'd rather not." Then his icy blue eyes flashed to Lily. "But watch yourself over there tomorrow. She's crafty and—"

Lily giggled. "I hardly think she wants anything from me."

"Where are you going?" Oliver demanded beside her, making Lily jump.

Simon squeezed her hand. "Don't bark at your aunt, boy."

"What do you care? You're the one sending her away."

Lily sucked in a surprised breath. Oliver was getting more belligerent as the days went by. Her sweet nephew would never have said such a thing a few months ago. She slid her hand from Simon's and turned in her chair to focus on Oliver. "I'm only visiting a neighbor's home tomorrow. I'm not leaving."

"But *he* said—" Oliver began, glaring over her shoulder at Simon.

"Nothing's been determined," she assured him. "My place has always been with you, Oliver. I have no intention of leaving you."

"Lily," Simon growled, though he was drowned out by Will's laughter.

"Good for you, Lily. Stand your ground."

Anger rolled off Simon, and Lily turned her head to see him glaring daggers at his brother. "Mind your own affairs."

❧

Lily looked at the trunk of clothes lying in the middle of her chamber. Thank heavens, Oliver brought nearly her entire wardrobe with him. She'd been wearing the same two gowns for days and was anxious for a change.

She washed, slid into her yellow cotton nightrail, and closed her eyes. It felt so nice to have the soft material against her skin.

There was a light knock at the door, and Lily slid her arms through the sleeves of her matching robe. She tied the sash around her waist and called brightly, "Come."

Oliver poked his head inside the room, frowning when he saw how she was dressed. "I didn't know you were ready for bed, Aunt Lily. I'll talk to you tomorrow."

She shook her head, walking toward him. "Don't go. I want to know how your conversation with His Grace went."

Oliver opened the door wider and stepped inside. "I don't want to stay here. I want to go back to Maberley Hall with you."

Lily crossed the floor to him and took his hand in hers. "I won't leave without you, Oliver."

"Why does he want you to go? If I have to stay, why can't you stay, too?"

Good questions, ones she would find answers to. Lily led him to a pair of chintz chairs near her window. "Don't worry yourself, dear. I'm certain I can make His Grace see reason." Simon couldn't *really* want her to leave, not with the way he looked at her, the way he touched her.

"I won't stay if he makes you leave," Oliver vowed.

A loud knock sounded on the door, which made Lily nearly jump out of her skin. She patted Oliver's hand and then quickly crossed the room to the door. She pulled it open to find Simon standing on the other side, his grey eyes dark as he took in her state of dishabille.

"You shouldn't have Oliver in here with you."

Lily blinked at him. "I beg your pardon."

"It's too dangerous," he said quietly, before pushing the door wider. "Maberley, it's time for you to retire to your own room."

Oliver frowned. "I'm just talking to my aunt."

"And you can continue your conversation on the morrow. It's late." He inclined his head toward the door, a subtle hint of authority.

But, of course, Oliver balked. Oliver balked if *she* asked him to do something. Of course he would balk if someone else spoke to him with a tone of authority, especially someone with whom he was unfamiliar.

"I'm no longer in leading strings, Blackmoor. I'll decide when I'm ready to go to bed. Right now, I'm speaking with my aunt."

Lily was unable to choke back her gasp. What a disrespectful tone to take with the duke! She covered her mouth and watched Oliver return to his seat in the chintz chair.

Lily raised her finger, planning to scold him, but Simon pushed her hand back down to her side. That made her want to scold Simon as well.

"Oliver, I think you need to apologize to His Grace," she said. Despite the glower her comment received from Simon, she continued, "You may not know him well, but the man is your guardian."

"That doesn't give him the right to order me about," Oliver sniffed.

Simon interrupted his show of obstinacy. "In fact, it gives me the right to do anything I want with you."

Tension nearly crackled in the air as Simon stepped toward Oliver, who merely lifted his nose a few inches and turned his face away from the duke in a supreme show of feigned indifference. Lily knew the boy was anything but indifferent. But it would take much more to win Oliver's confidence.

Unfortunately, Simon didn't appear interested in gaining her nephew's confidence, not in the slightest. The situation reminded Lily of when she was a child and had offered to help the cook by going to the henhouse to collect eggs. Invariably, two of the roosters would begin to fight, each battling for supremacy.

That's what the duke and her nephew looked like as

Simon crossed the room. But Lily knew Oliver would be the one to get hurt. She stepped between them.

"Move, Lily," Simon said.

"Not if you're going to hurt him, Simon." Lily held up one finger, much the way she would if she were scolding Oliver. Realizing how ineffectual the gesture was when he smirked at her stance, she lowered her hand to her side.

"I won't hurt him, Lily. Not if he listens and does as I tell him." He looked around her at Oliver and bellowed, "Now!"

When Oliver didn't move, Simon took another step toward him.

William called from the doorway, "Are you all involved in a game of charades? I can hear your bellow all the way from downstairs." He glanced around the room. "Why is everyone in Lily's room when she's in her nightrail?" Will glanced down at her bare feet and smiled wickedly. "What beautiful toes you have, Lily." He attempted a casual tone, Lily could tell, as he tried to break the tension in the room. It had little effect on Simon, and Oliver took even less notice.

Despite his casual manner of speaking, William was suddenly on guard as well. He circled around Simon, coming to stand close to her. She watched as he met eyes with Simon, almost as if a silent communication passed between them. Within seconds, his arms were around her, and he took her to the side, cradled in his hold. At the same time, Simon advanced toward Oliver, and the rest was a blur.

It seemed like only moments later that the room

was empty, except for William who reluctantly loosened his hold on her.

"I'll let you go, Lily, but only if you promise to let them be. Simon needs to teach him something, and this is the time to do it."

Twelve

SIMON HAD KNOWN THAT THE TIME WOULD COME FOR
him to assert himself as the leader of the pack. But he
knew quite well how disastrous the situation could be
if anyone else was caught in the middle of the altercation when it happened.

He was incredibly relieved when Will walked through
the door. He knew Will would remove Lily from the
line of danger while he took the pup to hand.

The boy was stronger than he looked, and it took
every bit of effort Simon had to drag Oliver from the
room and into the hallway. As he stepped through the
threshold, Simon closed Lily's door. The crash of the
door slamming seemed loud, even to his ears.

He held the young earl's face against the wall,
one hand bending his arm behind his back. The boy
kicked and squirmed, refusing to give in, even in his
current position.

Simon tightened his hold on Oliver's arm, pressing
more forcefully but taking care not to hurt him. It
took every bit of concentration he possessed not to
simply knock the obnoxious little pup to the ground

and stomp on him. But he imagined Lily would take exception to that.

He moved his face close to Oliver's and growled, "If you can control yourself, I will let you go." Oliver stopped squirming. While Simon had the boy pinned against the wall, it was time to tell him the rules. "You have more power in your fingertip than your Aunt Lily has in her entire body. If you fly into a rage when she's in the vicinity, there's a very good chance that you will hurt her, even if you don't mean to." He loosened his hold on Oliver's arm but didn't let him go.

"Do you understand what I'm saying?" Simon needed to know before he would fully release him.

Oliver nodded, a bit of contrition apparent in the way he held his body when Simon finally let him go.

"I know you don't understand what's happening to you and your body," Simon said as he led the way to Oliver's room. The boy followed slowly. "What you're experiencing is more than just the approach of manhood. It's the approach of manhood for *us*, for our kind. And it can be dangerous."

"I wouldn't hurt Aunt Lily," Oliver sniffed.

"You wouldn't *intend* to hurt your aunt, but you may do so without even realizing what you're doing." He opened the door to the boy's quarters and motioned for him to precede him into the room. "Do you *want* to know what's happening to you?"

The boy nodded.

"If you truly want to learn, William and I will take you out with us tomorrow night, when the moon is full in the sky. We will educate you about what's happening to you, and I'll be there to help you learn to control it. And embrace it. Because only by fully embracing it can you make it a part of you, rather than an enemy." Simon grew pensive as he regarded the boy. "Your father never learned to fully embrace it because he didn't have anyone to teach him how to be a man."

"But you'll teach me that?" Oliver surprised him when he asked.

The boy reminded him so much of Daniel. How things might have been different if someone had been able to guide his cousin. Simon swallowed the lump in his throat and nodded. "As long as you promise to keep an open mind and behave yourself." He shot a pointed look at him. "No more shows of obstinacy." Then as an afterthought, "And you must promise not to tell your Aunt Lily."

Oliver seemed instantly accepting of the camaraderie that came with working together to keep something from his aunt, as Simon had expected him to be. He laughed and clasped the boy's shoulder. Despite the look on the youth's face, Simon could still sense a bit of rage boiling below the surface. He would leave him to it. After all, that beast lived in him as well. He understood it.

Simon looked Oliver in the eye and said, "Go to bed. And stay there."

Oliver nodded. Simon turned and left the room, closing the door behind him. As soon as he stepped into the hallway, he heard the sound of breaking glass. Probably the crystal vase that sat upon the armoire. Then another smash. That one was probably his mother's antique clock. Simon couldn't contain the chuckle that crept from his belly. He'd broken more than one frivolous item of décor in his younger days. And was still prone to it now. He would let the boy have his fit of pique and then discuss it on the morrow.

As for Lily, he wanted nothing more than to go to her, to explain, but as the moon was now high in the sky and nearly full, that would be the worst idea he'd ever had. He retreated to his study with a bottle of whisky instead.

It wasn't until he was very well into his cups that he heard movement above stairs.

❧

Lily sat in her room and stewed, her bare feet fretfully tapping the carpet. She took out her knitting but wasn't able to concentrate. She crossed to the window and looked into the distance. The estate was a mass of dark shadows, the light of the nearly full moon illuminating everything in its path. Lily watched as a rabbit darted across the lawn, heading for its hidden burrow. But the animals of the night only held her attention for a moment.

What she wanted to do was to go and see Oliver, to be sure he was all right. William had stayed with her for no more than a few minutes before he encouraged her to get a good night's sleep and kissed her forehead, as if she were nothing but a child.

If one more man told her what to do, she would scream. *She* would be the one to throw the fit. And they would all be very sorry.

Who was she kidding? No one would care if she yelled loud enough to bring the house done. They would say *"It's for your own good, Lily. You wouldn't understand."*

She understood much more than they credited her for. She understood that the men in this house, all three of them, were some of the most poorly behaved men she'd ever seen.

If they could be poorly behaved, so could she. She would check on her nephew whether they liked it or not. She needed to assure herself that Simon hadn't hurt Oliver when he'd dragged him from the room.

Lily cracked her door open and peered outside, her gaze darting left and right. She stepped out into the hallway once she'd assured herself that everyone else was abed.

Lily padded softly down the hall, her bare feet sinking into the luxurious carpet that lined the corridor, and found Oliver's room. The door slowly opened and creaked only slightly as she stepped inside. She would take a moment to watch him sleep, as she'd done almost every night since he'd come into her care.

Oliver's dark hair lay tousled against the pillow. He was at once a child replete with all the physical characteristics of a man. The full brow drew down in a frown even in sleep. Lily reached out and touched his hair, instantly relaxing him. He sighed softly and settled more deeply into the bed.

These were the moments she loved, the moments when her little boy was still a child. They were few and far between, and Lily was starved to crawl into bed with him and pretend he still needed her.

She glanced around the room, taking in his clothes that were flung about the floor. He'd always been a bit of a messy child. However, he was an earl and always had servants to keep his rooms clean and his clothes tidy. But then she noticed the broken shards of glass on the floor. He must have been in quite a temper when Simon had brought him to his room. She got up and went to pick up the larger pieces. She would have to apologize to Simon in the morning on Oliver's behalf.

"Why are you in here, Lily?" a voice asked quietly from the doorway. Simon leaned against the door frame, glowering at her.

"I just came to check on Oliver," she whispered as she stood up and placed the largest shards of glass on the side table. "He's sleeping soundly, so I'll go back to bed now." She took a step to brush past him but winced as her bare foot picked up one of the remaining pieces of glass. She lifted her foot and winced.

"What's wrong?"

"Just a piece of glass in my foot, Simon," she sighed.

His expression immediately softened. "A great excuse to hold you," he said softly as he scooped her up in his arms.

"Simon, put me down," she scolded him. "Why is it that you think I can't walk on my own two feet?"

"Because one of your two feet is injured, Lily love." She heard the laughter in his voice and couldn't help but smile at him. The scent of whisky caressed the side of her face.

"Simon, I think you're foxed," she smiled. "Put me down before you drop me."

"I'm not so foxed that I can't carry you to bed." He met her eyes with that suggestive comment. She felt the heat creep up her face.

"Perhaps you should drop me at my door," she murmured.

"Perhaps you should be quiet and let me decide what I'll do with you," he goaded her as they entered her room and he tossed her onto the bed. Before she could scramble to her feet, he had her injured foot in his hand. Even foxed, he moved faster than any man she'd ever met.

When he'd tossed her onto the bed, her nightrail had risen, exposing her calves. She tugged at the hem, trying to find some modicum of decency.

Alas, Simon was no help at all.

"I have seen your ankles before, Lily. Now be a good girl and sit still," he ordered as he closed one eye and tried to focus on her injury.

"How much have you had to drink, Simon?"

"Way more than I should have," he murmured. He stilled her foot and pulled the shard from her tender skin. Smiling, he held the small sliver up for her perusal. "Got it."

It was rare to see Simon actually smile. A scowl was much more like him. He got up, crossed to the water pitcher, and wet the handkerchief from his pocket. She held her hand out to him when he returned with it. But he took her foot in his hand again and said, "Let the doctor work, will you?"

He gently washed the bottom of her foot until he'd cleaned it enough to satisfy his own need to assist. Then he took her foot in his hand and peered at it closely. "I have never understood what makes you women think you need to keep your ankles hidden." His hand slipped up to cup her slim calf.

"Simon, that's not at all proper," she reminded him, tugging at the bottom of her nightrail again.

"A view of your foot doesn't particularly make me lose all control, Lily."

"Well, that's good to know, Simon." She rolled her eyes and tugged her foot, trying to pull it from his grasp.

But he held strong. "It's not like it's your calf, love," he said as his hand trailed up the back of her leg, his arm pushing her nightrail with every caress of his fingers.

"Now, when I see this, I can't help but think naughty thoughts." He smiled lewdly at her.

"Simon," she said more forcefully.

"*Simon*," he mocked her, making a face that caused her to giggle. But then he sobered. "Do you know why I think naughty thoughts when I see your calf?"

Lily's heart thumped in her breast. "W–why?" she stuttered.

"Because I know that above this knee," he said as he slid his hand up the back of her knee to the sensitive skin of her thigh, "lies what I want above all things, Lily," he murmured as he bent to kiss her.

Before he could touch his lips to hers, she breathed against his mouth, "You want *that* above all things?"

"Mmm. More than anything." He nodded, his lips barely brushing hers.

And that was all it took. He may as well have doused her with a big glass of water.

He'd dismissed her. He'd tried to send her away, to marry her off. He'd kissed her. He'd touched her inappropriately. And, above all things, he'd made her want him to do it all over again. But she needed to keep her wits about her.

"Simon," she whispered. "You need to leave."

He frowned at her. "Don't ask me that, Lily. I need you."

"For now," she added quietly. "Tell me, when morning comes, will you need me then? Or will you still be intent on sending me away?"

She saw a number of emotions flash across his face. Then he shook his head and stumbled backward. "I shouldn't be here. I'll see you in the morning."

Lily brushed away a tear as she watched him leave her room, wondering if she'd just made the biggest mistake of her life.

Thirteen

SIMON AWOKE WITH A SPLITTING HEADACHE, BLINKING painfully when the morning light flooded his vision. What had he done the night before? Ah, yes, finished off a bottle of whisky. He'd started it before his encounter with Lily and finished it after. He was playing with fire where she was concerned. She was fortunate he'd been so deep in his cups last night, dulling the intense call of the moon, or he wasn't sure what would have happened.

What a lie.

He knew exactly what would have happened. He'd have taken her beneath him and ruined whatever chances she had at a normal life. He wasn't at all certain that her protests would have even hit his ears until it was too late. Thank God he'd been foxed.

Simon pulled himself from bed, noting the room spun if he moved too quickly. "Parker!" he bellowed, covering his ears when they rang.

A moment later, his valet threw open his dressing-room door. "Yes, Your Grace?" The young man's eyes were wide, taking in Simon's form.

He must look even worse than he felt.

"Prepare my bath, and…" his voice trailed off, certain Parker would know what he needed.

Soon he sank down into the warm water of the bath and closed his eyes. How would he face Lily after the things he'd done last night? More importantly, how could he keep her safe from himself tonight, when he transformed into something that would terrify her? His drink had saved her last night, but it wouldn't help her this evening. He could imbibe all the whisky in Scotland beforehand, but it wouldn't make a bit of difference. The full moon would have him in its grips regardless.

After his morning ablutions, Simon made his way to the breakfast room where he found Will slicing his sausages on his plate. He barely looked up when Simon fell into a spot across from him.

"If you're looking for Lily," his brother began with a glower, "you're too late. She's already gone."

Simon's heart lurched. Gone? "Where?" he couldn't help but ask, though he had no right. It was the best decision for her. Still, a cold emptiness settled over him. He couldn't imagine going through the day if he didn't get to see her. She'd left? Just like that? No warning? No good-bye? Just… gone? He must have terrified her.

Will looked at him as if he were the village idiot. "To the Hawthornes'."

Simon released a breath he didn't know he held. "Oh, yes, of course." Thank God.

Will shook his head. "You're just making it worse on yourself, you know. You should have taken care of the situation last night when you had the chance."

Will's hearing was as keen as his own. No doubt he had overheard the entire exchange with Lily, even if he tried not to. Simon scowled at his brother, hating that his privacy had been compromised. "She asked me to leave, as I'm sure you know."

Will scoffed. "Like you've been asking her to do? Neither of you mean it. You're obviously made for each other."

"Why are you in such a sour mood?" Simon finally asked, after a footman had placed a plate of baked eggs and sausages in front of him.

Will's blue eyes shot up, piercing him. "Prisca Hawthorne not only sent her father's carriage for Lily, she also came along for the ride. Insufferable chit takes special delight in making my life hell."

Simon raised one brow, the memory of his carriage ride with Lily fresh in his mind. Turnabout was fair play, after all. "I don't know why you don't just bed the girl and put the rest of us out of our misery." He took a bite of eggs, relishing the glower Will sent his direction.

"Ha! I'd wake up with a knife in my back."

Simon nearly choked. "I do believe, William, that if our dear Prisca put a knife in your back, you wouldn't wake up, but it might well be worth it."

"Go to hell."

He'd already been, when he thought Lily was gone for good. He was going to have to rethink this whole sending-her-away plan of his.

What if he set her up in a little house nearby? He could visit whenever he wanted, staying away when it was too dangerous for her. It was the perfect solution.

She didn't want to leave Oliver, and she would be close enough to see the lad as often as she liked... mostly.

He couldn't wait for her to return from the Hawthornes' so he could tell her.

❧

Lily gaped at the emerald green dress Prisca held up for her perusal. The beautiful silk shimmered in the afternoon light and made her catch her breath. She'd never worn anything so exquisite, and she couldn't believe Prisca had accomplished so much in so little time. She hadn't even taken any measurements before she left yesterday. "How did you manage this?"

Prisca beamed. "I told you. I love to sew, and I have a good eye, even if I do say so myself. Do try it on."

Before Lily could respond, Prisca's lady's maid began to unbutton the back of her serviceable, blue-sprigged muslin, which paled considerably in comparison to the work of art her new friend had created.

In no time, Lily stood before a floor-length mirror admiring herself. The green silk flowed gently down her length, while, at the same time, it forced her bosom higher. Prisca was on her knees with a pincushion, hemming the bottom of the gown.

"Hum. I thought a white ribbon would finish this nicely, but now I'm thinking gold would be better. With your coloring, it will go perfectly." Prisca stood up to examine her handiwork. "You look stunning. Almost like a duchess."

Lily's face grew hot. Simon didn't even want her to stay at Westfield Hall. He certainly didn't want to marry her. "Oh, Prisca, His Grace isn't... I mean I'm only at Westfield Hall so the duke can become more acquainted with my nephew."

Prisca retrieved a wide golden ribbon from her bedside table. When she returned, she wore an all-knowing smile. "It might have begun that way, Lily, but I'm certain things have changed."

Lily shook her head. "He wants to send me back to Essex as soon as possible."

"But you're still here. He's had ample time do to so. Raise your arms." Prisca ran the gold ribbon under Lily's bosom. "Listen, the brothers Westfield and Hawthorne were inseparable. I've known Blackmoor my entire life. He's always seemed the most serious of the lot to me, but I've never seen him look the way he did yesterday."

Lily frowned. "What do you mean?"

Prisca returned to her table, retrieving a pair of sewing shears. "I thought he might tear Emory limb from limb."

She hadn't noticed any difference in Simon. He was just as surly as he'd been since she met him. "Why?"

Prisca giggled. "Because of his attention to you. Honestly, Lily, you had to notice. Blackmoor practically dragged you away from my brother. Had you not allowed him to shove you down the hallway, he would have picked you up and carried you."

Lily fought back the blush she knew must be creeping up her neck as the memories of what he did to her after he had her alone flooded her mind. "He seems the same overbearing brute he always was to me."

"He *has* kissed you." Prisca's violet eyes twinkled. "I can see it on your face."

So much for fighting back the blush. For a moment, she considered denying it, but perhaps Prisca could help. She seemed much more sophisticated than Lily, and she did seem to know how to manage men. Lily nodded. "Then he offered me a dowry to go search out a husband."

Prisca's smile faded. "He did not," she said, her voice dropped dangerously low.

Lily shrugged. "So I don't think being a duchess is in my future."

"The lout!" Prisca almost growled herself. Then she grumbled something unintelligible, though Lily did recognize Will's name somewhere in her hushed rant.

"I don't need to be his duchess, Prisca. But I don't want to leave my nephew."

"Go search out a husband," Prisca repeated, a frown marring her beautiful face. "Stupid Westfield scoundrels." She started to pace the room, and then she stopped suddenly. "If that's how he wants to play it, Lily, I say you pick up the gauntlet."

"I beg your pardon?"

Prisca shook her head. "You are beautiful. I was quite jealous of you when I first laid eyes on you. But then you were so sweet, it would be hard to hate you."

Prisca Hawthorne thought *she* was beautiful? Lily couldn't believe it, and she gaped at her friend.

"I can make certain every eligible bachelor within three villages is at the assembly hall tomorrow. We'll see how Simon Westfield enjoys a little competition, especially when he's the one supplying your dowry."

Lily's mouth fell open. "B-b-but…"

"And you won't go back to Westfield Hall tonight."

"I won't? But Oliver—"

"Survived several days in Essex without you. He can manage one night with those Westfield barbarians watching after him. They're not completely inept, just with women."

Lily bit her bottom lip. The chances of angering Simon were enormous, but it was worth the risk of catching him. She nodded her acceptance.

Fourteen

"BILLINGS!" SIMON BELLOWED AS HE STRODE THROUGH the corridors of Westfield Hall, growing more and more anxious with every step. He'd searched her room, the music room, and half a dozen parlors, and had even walked through the gardens, but he couldn't find Lily anywhere. The sun was about to set, and he needed to talk to her before he no longer could.

He was impatient to tell her of the plan he'd concocted, because he knew how pleased she would be that he'd come up with a solution that solved all their problems. She would be nearby. She could see young Maberley as often as she liked. And they could be together, as often as the moon allowed.

Billings appeared as if from nowhere, answering Simon's bellow. "Yes, Your Grace?" he asked.

"Have you seen Miss Rutledge?" Simon asked as he sat down at his desk and began to open his correspondence, all of it well over a week old.

"She is still at the Hawthornes'. She sent a note, Your Grace," the butler informed him.

Simon shuffled restlessly through his mail. "Then where is it, Billings?" He raised one sarcastic eyebrow.

The butler coughed delicately. "It wasn't for you, Your Grace. It was for the young earl."

"And what did it say?" Simon snapped. Why hadn't she sent word to him? Had he well and thoroughly terrified her last night?

"I'm not sure. I didn't open it." Billings grew fidgety. Obviously he knew more than he let on, which only made Simon more anxious.

"I expect better from you, Billings," Simon growled as he walked by the butler on his way out of the study. He *would* find out what was in that note if it was the last thing he did.

He found Oliver in the library with William, where the two were discussing the earl's dislike of Latin. He watched them as they leaned over the boy's Latin text. Despite Will's lack of decorum and teasing nature, he was quite a scholar in his own right.

"Have your studies included any text on Lycanthropic lore?" William asked as he held up one finger, silently urging Simon to be quiet. Didn't his brother know how important it was that he find out what was in that note from Lily? Why wasn't she home?

He interrupted anyway. "Oliver, did your Aunt Lily send a note to you today?"

"Yes, Your Grace," Oliver replied, narrowing his eyes at Simon.

"And what did it say?" He tried to force the impatience from his voice. Belatedly, he remembered that the boy had senses similar to his own and could probably smell his agitation.

"It said that Sir Herbert Hawthorne had invited her to stay for dinner and she'll be staying the night."

"She said *what*? Let me see the letter." He held out his hand, waiting for Maberley to show him exactly what she'd sent.

The boy shrugged. "I don't know where I left it."

"Your aunt should be here," Simon said under his breath, but they all heard him. Damn those overly sensitive ears.

Simon wondered which of the Hawthorne brothers had taken a liking to Lily. Probably Emory, if the besotted look on his face when he was with her was any indication.

"Billings," he bellowed. The man appeared. "Get my horse."

"Stop, Billings," William said to the butler. The man waited patiently in the doorway. "Where are you going, Simon?"

"To retrieve Lily," Simon said matter-of-factly. As though he needed to explain? Wasn't it obvious that she should be at home? His home. With him. Under him.

"Tonight is the full moon, Simon," Will reminded him, nodding imperceptibly at the boy.

"And?" Simon asked, still completely focused on retrieving Lily, on seeing her again, smelling her again, holding her again.

"And she's safer where she is."

"Why isn't Aunt Lily safe here?" Oliver asked, his eyes darting from brother to brother.

Simon scratched his chin and gave it some thought. She probably *was* safer at the neighbors'. He tried to calm his beating heart.

Then he motioned to Oliver and said, "Have a seat. We need to have a talk."

The young man asked rather intelligent questions, Simon was surprised to hear. The most poignant question of the bunch being, "Was my father *really* one, too?"

Just before the moon reached its highest peak, the point where it would beckon uncontrollably to those of his kind, Simon clapped Oliver on the back and asked, "Ready?"

The boy simply nodded, worry knitting his brow. As they stepped into the garden, Simon already felt the pull of the moon, the rush of power that surged through him. He looked at Oliver and knew that he felt it, too, even though the boy probably was unable to distinguish between the wildness of the event and the act of moving from humanity to... *not*.

Simon wound through the woods on a trail notice-able only to those of his kind. He followed his nose, noting that an elk had recently followed a similar path. Will sniffed the air and said, "No humans."

Simon nodded. For this one event, they would all stay together. Changing was usually a solitary moment, but they feared Oliver would need guidance and the attendance of at least one of them.

Simon and Will began to remove their shirts, boots and stockings after they reached a clearing, a place devoid of shadows so there would be no trees to obscure the light of the moon. For modesty's sake, they left on their trousers, even knowing the garments would be destroyed when they changed. On most occasions, they removed all of their clothing and left it where they could find it before the moon sank and was replaced by the sun. They became wild before the wildness could even take them. But not tonight. Tonight, they wanted to do all they could to keep Oliver calm, so they didn't strip but instead brought extra clothes to don later.

As usual, Simon would be the first to change. As the leader of the pack, he always felt the call of the moon a little more strongly than the others.

Simon closed his eyes and lifted his face to the moon. It was then that humanity fell away and the beast was freed. His body began to change, painful as he knew it would be. Yet he did not cry out because he craved the freedom that came with changing. He wanted the clenching of muscles. He desired the lengthening of his spine. He needed the change of his face to something that was not human.

When his change was complete, he stood still and watched Maberley's face. Fear filled his eyes. In a singular act of goodwill, he walked closer and nudged the boy's arm with his nose. Oliver took two steps back. Simon nudged him again. It was best to let him know that the Lycans still recognized friendships, families, and loyalty. The boy would not be alone.

Oliver watched as Will went through a similar transition, changing into something more than feral, something more than wild. Simon knew the two of them, so similar in human appearance, looked similar even in Lycan form, the only distinguishing characteristic being Simon's streak of silver hair, which followed him even into the beastly world.

Oliver cried out as he began to change, perhaps surprised by the pain, yet oddly comforted by it, if he felt at all the same way Simon did when he, himself, changed. The boy would be fine. He would be there for him. He would nurture and tutor him. He would chew up the world and spit it back out if that's what it took for Oliver to take part in it.

When the three transformations were complete, Oliver followed Will into the darkness. Simon crested the hill, climbing higher and higher until he stood at the top overlooking Langley Downs. There Lily slept, her beautiful head on a pillow. He could imagine her scent, her feel, and the way her skin might taste behind her ear. He licked his lips, salivating a little at the thought. Even now, he was aroused at the very thought of her.

But this side of him she could never know. She could never encounter this part of him, or she would turn from him in disgust. He raised his head toward the moon and called out to her, knowing that she would not hear, that she would not understand. Yet he did. He understood it all too well.

❧

Lily sat bolt upright in bed. What was that? She was almost certain she'd heard Simon call her name. She was obviously a candidate for Bedlam, as he was surely sound asleep at Westfield Hall.

There it was again, a feeling as if he called out to her. Lily blinked in the darkness. Then she heard a faint howl off in the distance. She rose from bed and peered out the window. High in the night sky, the full moon illuminated the countryside.

She shook her head. It was probably her imagination.

Fifteen

PRISCA HAWTHORNE DID KNOW HOW TO COMMAND a room. Lily watched in awe as her friend deftly managed the overcrowded parlor, filled with hulking Hawthorne men.

Only Sir Herbert and his oldest son, Emory, had been at dinner the night before, but now there were three others, all of them similar in build and looks. Tall, though none as tall as Simon or Will. Dark haired, ranging from a chestnut brown to nearly black. There was Mr. Garrick Hawthorne, a quiet man who, Prisca told her, had recently taken the post of vicar in a neighboring village to be closer to his family; Lieutenant Darius Hawthorne, who had returned from Waterloo the previous summer and now spent most of his time in London; and Mr. Pierce Hawthorne, a *tradesman*. Prisca had whispered that bit as if it were a sin. He'd made a small fortune in shipping in South Hampton.

Lily was surprised that all of their eyes seemed to follow her, as she'd never commanded this much attention in Essex. Of course, at home she wasn't a novelty.

Despite all the activity at Langley Downs, Lily missed Simon more than she could have ever imagined. After she'd woken the night before, she'd had a difficult time getting back to sleep. She wanted nothing more than to be back at Westfield Hall so she could tiptoe into Oliver's room, touch his cheek, and slip back out. She wanted to argue with Simon and banter with Will. But she'd lain awake, listening to the wind buffet her window, alone.

Oliver. Simon. Will. Westfield Hall. None of those things were hers. She would do well to remember that and cease her pining for a life that wasn't, and probably never would be, hers.

What if Prisca's elaborate plans for tonight did nothing, and Simon still wanted her to leave Hampshire? What if all his kisses had just been something to pass the time? He *was* known all over England for his female conquests. Would she be just another successful tryst he could add to his list?

She made her way to the large window and stared off into the distance, toward Westfield Hall.

"Why do you look so sad, Miss Rutledge?" the vicar asked, coming to stand beside her.

Lily plastered a false smile on her face. "Just woolgathering, Mr. Hawthorne."

⤲⤳

While she should have been listening to Emory and Darius banter back and forth, Prisca watched Lily talk with Garrick and tapped her chin mindlessly. There was so much to do, and not a lot of time. She'd have to find recruits.

"...Prissy?" Darius said.

Prisca's attention snapped to her middle brother. "I *know* you did not just call me Prissy." No one did that. Not anymore.

Darius chuckled. "Indeed, it was the only way to get your attention. You must have been a thousand miles away."

"Obviously incorrect, as I am right here, Dari."

He shook his head. "What are you up to with Miss Rutledge?"

Prisca cocked her head toward her brother. "What am I up to? I don't think I like your insinuation."

Darius draped his arm around her shoulders. "You're my sister and I love you, but there's not one generous bone in your body. So you must be up to something."

Beside them, Emory laughed at her expense. Prisca leveled both of them with her haughtiest look. "Something you want to add, Emory?"

"No, no," her eldest brother said, raising his hands as he backed up a step. "I think Darius has it well under control."

Well, fine, they all thought she was looking after her own interests. That shouldn't bother her. This *was* a selfless act on her part, however, whether her irritating brothers believed it or not.

Maybe she could use their unflattering view of her to Lily's advantage. How fortuitous. "Very well, I wasn't going to tell either of you this, but since you seem to think I only think of myself, I'll have to prove you wrong."

"By all means." Darius grinned at her.

"Lily is looking for a husband, and I don't see why it can't be one of you."

"She seemed so focused on rearing her nephew." Emory's eyes flashed across the room, landing on Lily. Prisca had to bite back a smile. This would be too easy.

"True," she said, sliding out of Darius' hold. "That was before Blackmoor decided to take his guardianship seriously. Besides, the boy's bound for Harrow for the Michaelmas term. To show his gratitude for all her years of service, Simon Westfield has bestowed upon Lily a grotesquely large dowry."

Now Darius' eyes flashed to Lily and Garrick across the room. "You make us sound like piranha, Priss. What do we care about Blackmoor's funds? She's a pretty girl to be sure, but you can't mean to leg shackle one of *us* to her? We barely know her."

Prisca rolled her eyes. Not very ladylike, but the two fellows were her brothers. "Well, why not you? Lily will marry someone. She's pretty and kind, and I might enjoy being the relation of a duke, even distantly."

"Indeed?" Darius grinned. "Is that why you and Will…" But his voice trailed off when her glower darkened dangerously.

"I don't have any idea what you're talking about," she bit out.

He looked at once like a remorseful little boy. "Sorry, Priss, I didn't mean…"

She shook her head. "William Westfield means nothing to me. In fact, as Lily is hunting for her husband, I think I shall hunt for mine." She pretended to ignore the twin looks of surprise her brothers exchanged. Then she feigned an innocent frown, reeling them completely in. "I do hope there will be several eligible bachelors there this evening."

Emory proudly thrust his chest out. "If you are serious, Prisca, I can personally guarantee a full house."

She graced him with a most charming smile. "Well, I *should* have choices, and so should Lily—especially if none of you are interested in scooping her up."

As predicted, both of her brothers' eyes flashed back to her friend, now alone, as she stared out the window. They really were too easy to manipulate.

Simon was more anxious than he could ever remember being before. It had been *two* days since he'd seen Lily. Two days without her melodic laugh. Two days without her smile, her scent, her twinkling hazel eyes focused on him.

This blasted ball at the assembly room couldn't happen soon enough to satisfy him. He rushed Parker through the chore of readying him for the event and was pacing the floor of his parlor two hours earlier than necessary.

Will peeked inside the room, grinning ear to ear. "Ready, are you?"

His blasted brother wasn't even dressed to go. "Why aren't you?"

"It's hardly time," Will responded, dropping onto a light blue settee. "Relax."

"Get dressed," Simon ordered.

Will simply chuckled. "For God's sake, Simon, you're wound more tightly than a child's top. Have a drink or something to calm your nerves."

Simon glowered at him. "You *could* just meet me there."

"Or I could stay away completely," his brother suggested with a grin.

"That's a fabulous idea," Simon replied, starting for the door. Then he threw over his shoulder, "I wish you'd declined the invitation to begin with. I'd much rather have Lily here tonight."

"You are a man besotted."

"Just anxious. I want to discuss a proposition with her."

"A proposition?" Will echoed. "Down on one knee and the whole bit?"

Simon stopped short. Marriage. He wished it could be that. It wasn't even safe to keep her in Hampshire, but to live with him day in and day out, to be his wife… He couldn't put her in that sort of danger. If anything ever happened to her, he'd never forgive himself. "I didn't say 'proposal.'"

Will's blue eyes seemed to stare right into him. "You're making a mistake."

"You keep saying that, and I have yet to ask for your advice." Simon quit the room and headed out of the house.

He stepped lightly down the steps, anxious to be inside the coach, on his way to Lily.

"Your Grace." His coachman bowed, then opened the door of his carriage.

"Langley Downs," Simon instructed him.

He had a good twenty minutes before he reached the Hawthornes' estate, and he leaned his head back against the squabs, closing his eyes. Lily hadn't made any comments about wanting to marry him, just that she didn't want him to send her away. Everything would be fine, if he could just see her again.

When he arrived at Langley Downs, Simon nearly bowled the old butler over on his way inside. "Y-your Grace," the man stuttered, righting himself.

"I'd like to see Miss Rutledge," Simon announced.

The butler shook his head. "Miss Rutledge and Miss Hawthorne are preparing for the ball. Would you like to wait for them in the parlor?"

He'd like to stomp right up the Hawthornes' stairs, knock down Prisca's door, and throw Lily over his shoulder... Though he didn't really have a choice. "The parlor?"

The Hawthornes' butler nodded. "We have a full house today, Your Grace."

"Indeed?" Simon soon found himself at the threshold of Langley Downs' yellow parlor. One, two, three, four... Every Hawthorne brother was in attendance, save one. "Where's Blaine?" he asked in way of greeting.

Emory looked up from his perusal of *The Times*. "Still at Cambridge. How are you, Simon?" He stood, crossed the room, and offered his hand, which Simon clasped.

Every other Hawthorne brother offered his welcome and then went back to his previous activity. Garrick and Pierce returned to their game of chess, and Darius focused his attention on a piece of foolscap.

"Brandy?" Emory asked him, as he headed for a decanter.

Simon nodded. What were they all doing here? Emory was generally the only one in residence. "What brought everyone home?"

Emory handed him a tumbler and shrugged. "Prisca, it seems, is intent on finding a husband for your Miss Rutledge, and she thought to start with us."

Simon nearly broke the glass in his hands. He had to rein in his control to keep from doing so. "She what?"

Emory smiled. "Did you really bestow a grotesquely large dowry on the chit? That doesn't seem like you."

They'd never discussed amounts. Although Lily said she wouldn't accept even a farthing from him. Simon's vision got bleary. Lily wouldn't do this. How many times had she told him she wanted to stay?

"You all right, Blackmoor?" Emory asked, concern in his voice.

Simon nodded. "I'm, uh, just surprised she told anyone, is all." Why would she have told Prisca Hawthorne, of all people? He would strangle any Hawthorne brother who thought he could take Lily from him.

"So it is true?"

"I said it, yes." Could he take it back? March up the stairs and demand she forget any man except him? That idea had promise. "I would like to see Miss Rutledge."

Emory smirked. "Good luck with that. Prisca said they'll be down when they're ready and not a moment before."

Sixteen

Simon's breath whooshed from his lungs. Dear God! Was *that* Lily?

Lily wore an exquisite green gown that accentuated curves she generally kept hidden. Her pretty auburn locks were loosely piled on her head, adorned with tiny gold roses. Though she was gorgeous, Simon wanted nothing better than to strip her bare and remove every blasted rose.

When she saw him, her face lit up, and Simon couldn't help but grin like a fool.

"Simon," she whispered.

He was before her in less than a heartbeat. Two days without her was too long. "Lily."

She blushed, and he felt his heart expand. Was there a way to forgo this stupid ball?

"I wish there was a way I could speak with you privately, Lily," Simon said quietly as he looked at her. He wanted to offer his plan to her before the ball, so he could get this unbearable burden lifted from his chest. Simon glanced around. There wasn't a quiet corner available, anywhere. "Might we take a walk in the garden?" Simon held out his arm to her. Her smile warmed his heart.

"I'm not sure that would be quite proper," Lily hedged, throwing a glance at Prisca and raising a questioning eyebrow.

"Of course you can take a walk in the garden together. The man is giving you a dowry so you can find a husband. I feel certain he has no designs upon your person," Prisca responded. Her violet eyes twinkled.

Simon tugged Lily's hand until they were out of the manor and alone on the garden path. The scent of roses hung in the air. But nothing smelled as delectable as she did. "I've missed you," he said as he pulled her gently beneath the arbor and wrapped his arms around her.

"Really?" she asked quietly.

Simon gently and tenderly touched his lips to hers. Despite the waning of the moon, he was fully and completely in control of the beast. Where he could not have been gentle with her yesterday, he could be today.

She immediately softened in his arms and pressed her length against his. He fought back a groan as he set her away from him. He needed to tell her of his plan.

"I think I have come up with a solution to our problems, Lily."

"You plan to send Oliver back home with me after all?" Her face lit with hope.

Simon winced. "No. That's not something I can offer you. I need for him to be with me. It's complicated, and it's something I can't explain."

"Yet you expect me to accept it with grace?" she asked, her eyebrows drawing together in a frown.

"I think the solution I want to propose to you will make you very happy." He took both her hands in his and held them close to his heart.

"You want to be close to Oliver," he started. She nodded.

"I want to be close to you," he continued.

She smiled.

"I cannot offer you marriage because of my… lifestyle."

She frowned. Oh, this was going poorly.

"Your lifestyle, Simon?"

"Yes. I need to maintain the lifestyle to which I'm accustomed." He held tighter to her fingers when she tried to jerk them from his grasp.

He took one large breath of air and said, all at once, "I want to set you up in a small house nearby so that I can see you when I'm available and you can see Oliver as often as you like because you would be nearby."

"What?" she asked.

Oh, he really didn't want to repeat it. It was hard enough to say the first time. "What part did you miss?"

She finally succeeded in tugging her hands from his grasp and backed away from him warily. Then she began to pace.

"Let me be sure I understand you, Simon. You want to make me your mistress?" Her eyes flashed. Her face reddened.

This was not going well at all.

"No." He took a step toward her. "Not a mistress. Not really," he added.

"Simon, you want to put me in a house." She began to tick items off with her fingers. "Pay my bills, I assume?" She arched her eyebrows in question.

He nodded. "Of course."

She ticked a third finger. "Let me see Oliver when I wish."

"Within certain boundaries, yes."

"And you and I would have relations of a sort." She added another finger.

He groaned, lust immediately encompassing his brain, and took a step toward her. "Of course."

She stepped back.

"That, Simon, is a mistress. And do you know what I'll do? I believe I will take you up on your offer."

He smiled and reached for her.

"Your offer to provide me with a dowry, that is. So that I can find a husband." Her voice grew louder and louder. "You *will* honor the offer you made to me of a dowry." She shook her finger at him. "You *will* honor that offer, and I *will* accept. Because I will *not* be any man's mistress, not even yours."

She stomped past him, her green dress lifting in her wake. He chased after her, but she slammed the door in his face. By the time he caught her, she was ten steps from the parlor. She stepped around Will, who had finally arrived, without sparing Simon more than a glance.

He watched as she approached the Hawthorne men and said, "Gentlemen, I believe we have a ball to attend." Her smile was radiant. She was completely composed. Then she added, "Because I need to find a husband." She laughed, a beautiful sound that was the most painful noise he'd ever heard.

Will bumped his shoulder with his own. "Told you it was a really bad idea."

Simon wanted to roar. He wanted to shout.

Will continued softly, "One of these days, you will learn that younger brothers do know a thing or two about some subjects."

"I still have yet to ask your advice," Simon rumbled as he watched Lily take Emory's arm and head for a Hawthorne coach.

"Perfect," Will added, as two of their childhood friends ambled their way. "We get Darius and Pierce. It's been an age."

"So nice of you to escort *us*," Darius teased as he reached the ducal coach.

"Flattered," Pierce agreed.

༄

Lily tried her best to keep from crying. Prisca's tight grip on her hand and stoic expression did help. She hoped that neither Sir Herbert nor his sons asked anything of her, as she paid no attention at all to the conversation in the Hawthorne coach.

By the time they arrived at the local assembly room, the sun had begun to set, as did Lily's hope for the future. *Mistress*. How could he think she would agree to such a thing? Her cheeks warmed. She had acted like a wanton with him, though that was no excuse.

The coach rambled to a stop. If she never laid eyes on Simon Westfield again—

The coach door opened, and Simon stuck his head inside. "Lily."

She gritted her teeth. There was no way to graciously refuse his hand.

Prisca put her hand in Simon's. "Oh, Your Grace,

thank you. That was such a trying ride. I do need a breath of fresh air."

Simon glared at Prisca but helped her from the coach, leaving Lily to accept Will's outstretched arm. She'd never been so grateful to see someone... Well, there were other times she'd been more grateful, but she pushed those from her mind.

Will led her inside a large Georgian building nearly overflowing with men of all shapes and sizes. "Don't be too hard on him," Will said softly.

Lily's eyes flashed to his. "You have no idea what he asked of me."

"I have a fairly good guess. I know how his mind works."

Lily ignored that last bit and looked around her. The assembly room wasn't terribly large, and there was very little room to move about. "I never attend balls," she admitted. "But I'd always heard there were very few gentlemen to go around." That was certainly not the case here. At least two men for every female in attendance.

Will heaved a sigh. "I'd imagine your new dearest friend had a hand in it."

Lily glanced in front of them to see Prisca admiring the turnout with a glow in her eyes. How had she managed this? Lily was in awe. "Well, she did say she intended to hunt for her own husband here."

Will stopped in his tracks, an instant grimace appeared on his face. "She said what?"

Lily looked up at Will. Something did seem to be going on between the two of them. "What is the history between the two of you?" she asked.

He simply shrugged. "She wants more than I could

ever give her." He looked away nervously, as though she might uncover some deep, dark secret if he actually met her eyes.

"That seems to be a theme amongst the Westfield men."

"You don't understand—" Will started.

But she cut him off with a cutting glance. "It seems as though I've heard that once tonight already, doesn't it? Pardon me, but I didn't believe it then, and I don't believe it now."

Seventeen

Prisca took it upon herself to act as Lily's matchmaker for the night, arranging introductions, filling her dance card, and keeping Blackmoor at bay. She made certain Lily never missed a dance, even if she had to prod her brothers to fill the space. Prisca was delighted to see Lily embrace all the attention lavished upon her and accept all the invitations. By all appearances, Lily was having a grand time, though Prisca knew that the poor dear's heart was breaking.

Having dealt with a Westfield man of her very own, she had a good idea of what Lily was going through. She had to admit she felt a certain sense of satisfaction as she watched Simon pouting among the fronds of the plants that hugged the outer edges of the ballroom.

His eyes never left Lily, and every time the dance changed, Simon made to approach her. But someone else always got there first, sweeping her back onto the dance floor. He became more and more surly as the night went on, barking at anyone who dared to speak to him.

Prisca watched as Mrs. Bostic, the local vicar's wife, made her way across the ballroom. She was approaching

Simon of all people? Then inspiration struck. Prisca knew how to solve this problem for Lily.

She edged around the ballroom until she stood near Simon. But he disregarded her presence, as though she was inconsequential. She would show him inconsequential.

"Mrs. Bostic," Prisca called to the woman. She turned and walked toward Prisca, her hands outstretched. "How wonderful it is to see you."

The woman returned the greeting. "Quite a lovely event, isn't it? Such a turnout," she remarked absently as she turned to stand between Prisca and Simon.

"Oh, it's indeed lovely," Prisca smiled. "It looks as though my new friend Miss Rutledge is having a grand time." She pointed to the dance floor. She smiled as she noticed the slight tilt of Simon's head as he heard Lily's name.

"Who is the gel, Miss Hawthorne? I don't believe we have met." She tapped her fan against her hand, searching her memory.

"Miss Rutledge has been staying at Westfield Hall. Her nephew, the Earl of Maberley, is the duke's ward. She brought him for a visit." Simon stepped closer, almost imperceptibly, but not quite.

"She has certainly captured everyone's attention, hasn't she?"

Prisca nodded. "Indeed, I know His Grace is awfully fond of her."

This made the older woman frown, and Prisca had to bite back a smile. After all, the Duke of Blackmoor was rarely fond of *respectable* girls. "Is her chaperone here?" Mrs. Bostic asked. "I should like to introduce myself."

Prisca forced herself to laugh delicately. "She doesn't have a chaperone, Mrs. Bostic. She came here this evening with my brothers and me."

Ms. Bostic's eyes narrowed. "But I thought you said she has been *residing* with the duke for a short time?"

"Yes, she has," Prisca replied, finding it difficult to keep a straight face as Will stepped up to her side. Oh, how delicious. The vicar's wife was fully enthralled in the tale of Lily's whereabouts.

Mrs. Bostic pursed her lips together in such a tight line that a ring of white showed around them. "That is not at all proper."

Prisca lowered her voice and said, "I wasn't certain it was, either. But Lily is firmly on the shelf. So, who am I to judge?"

Mrs. Bostic fidgeted nervously. "I must go and find Mr. Bostic, dear. It was delightful to see you." The woman stomped off, scowling at Simon. He didn't even notice, poor man, as he was too engrossed in watching Darius spin Lily around the dance floor.

"What are you doing?" Will hissed in her ear as Mrs. Bostic vanished into the crowd. "That termagant will show up on Simon's doorstep tomorrow demanding one of us marry Lily."

Prisca shrugged, not daring to make eye contact. "Come now, William, you and I both know *you're* not the marrying sort."

"That's hardly the point," he growled. "What gives you the right to meddle in Lily's life?"

"Knowing you," she answered. Slowly she focused her eyes on him. She did wish that her heart didn't still flutter whenever he was near. "I've been in Lily's position, and I wish someone had been looking out for me."

"You think setting *Mrs. Bostic* on Lily is looking out for her?"

Prisca nodded her head. "Yes. I'm forcing Blackmoor's hand. *He* won't be able to simply turn his back on her and pretend she never existed."

Will closed his eyes, and she could tell he was reining in his temper. "Prissy, I didn't—"

"Don't call me that," she cut him off. Then she squared her shoulders and tossed her head back, as if she didn't care at all what he thought. "Do excuse me. This dance, I believe, is Mr. Fielding's."

Lily had expected the ball to be a sedate affair. But it was far from that. As soon as she entered the assembly hall, she found herself besieged by men. They came in all shapes and sizes, from tall to short, from thin to rotund, from young to old. But as she danced with them one by one, she realized sadly that they were after one thing, her dowry. Not a single one of them was interested in her as a person.

It was a painful realization to make. Here she was at a ball full of eligible men, and the only thing they were interested in was a gift Simon had given to her. It seemed quite ironic that she was trying to lure a husband to the altar with a gift from the man she loved.

Oh, goodness! Love? As she twirled about the floor, she realized slowly that she did love him. She loved him despite his temper. She loved him despite his reputation. She loved him despite the fact that he obviously didn't love her back.

He'd spent the entire night glowering at her. As she'd been swept from one dance to another, his scowl had grown larger and larger. She only hoped he wasn't trying to decide which man would be right for her. That would add insult to injury if he thought, by providing her dowry, he could also have some decision-making power in her choice of a husband.

Of course he wouldn't think that. She was a grown woman after all, responsible only to herself. She had no family to speak of, aside from Oliver, and she was quite capable of making her own decision about a husband.

She'd learned quite a bit about the men who were present as they danced. Many of them appeared to be fortune hunters. One even went so far as to mention his gambling debts. Only a few showed any interest in her as a person. Yet, even with those few, she still found herself very happy when the dances ended so that she could take a moment to rest. But that didn't seem very likely.

Lily wanted nothing more than to retreat to the retiring room so she could wipe her moist brow in peace. She wanted to sit down, take her slippers off, and stretch her toes. She wanted to take the smile off her face for just a moment, because maintaining the tilt at the corners was becoming quite painful.

Just when she thought she might have an opportunity to slip away, Emory Hawthorne approached her. "May I steal you away from your many admirers, Miss Rutledge? So that we can take a turn about the floor?"

Lily sighed. "Of course you may, Mr. Hawthorne." Perhaps he saw the pain in her face because his eyebrows scrunched together in a frown.

"Are you quite all right, Miss Rutledge?"

"To tell the truth, I am a bit exhausted," she groaned, flexing her toes inside her slipper.

"Then I have just the thing, Miss Rutledge," he said, offering his arm. She took it tentatively.

"Don't worry. I won't make you walk far." His dark eyes danced at her.

"Promise?"

"On my honor," he said as he covered his heart with his hand.

"I pray that I will find a man who has some," Lily mumbled.

Mr. Hawthorne laughed out loud, a rich sound that warmed her heart.

He placed a hand at her back to gently prod her through a set of double doors. He led down a winding path into a vast garden lined with hedgerows. The wind picked up the tendrils of hair at her neckline and instantly cooled her.

"Nice, isn't it?" he asked as she lifted her face to the breeze.

She sighed with pleasure. "Very."

He pointed out a bench and encouraged her to sit, then joined her. Lily relaxed, completely at ease with this man who'd saved her from hordes of money-hungry men.

"Thank you so much," she said. "This is just what I needed, Mr. Hawthorne."

"Emory. Please." He smiled at her. She simply nodded.

"I kept waiting for Blackmoor to sweep in and steal you away from those who kept seeking your attention."

Lily shook her head. "He doesn't think of me in that way." She met his eyes, hoping the pain she felt at the mere mention of Simon's name wasn't displayed on her face.

"Oh, Lily." He chuckled. "That is where you are wrong." He raised one finger to trail it across her cheekbone. "He would have to be an imbecile *not* to feel that way for you."

The finger that touched her cheek didn't alarm her, but it didn't ignite her, either. Not like Simon's touch. Why must she compare every man to Simon?

Emory continued, "I have known Blackmoor for a very long time. And have never seen him act the way he does with you."

"But he doesn't want to *marry* me," she said. Heat suffused her face as she realized what she'd almost revealed.

"He would be a fool not to feel *that* way about you as well," Emory said quietly, his hand reaching to clasp her own.

"Do you think I could bother you to get me some punch, Emory?" she asked hesitantly. She needed a moment to herself. Just a moment was all it would take to right her thoughts.

"Certainly," he said as he rose. "I'll be back momentarily."

She watched him until he was through the double doors. Then she rose and wandered further down the garden path. She slowly trailed her fingertips in the fountain. A breeze blew across her skin, lifting goose-flesh along her arms.

"You let him touch you."

Lily spun quickly to find Simon standing in the shadows. His normally grey eyes had changed to black. His hair hung over his brow in disarray, as though he'd been running his hands through it.

"What did you say?" Certainly she hadn't heard him correctly. "What are you doing here? Did you follow me?"

He approached her, anguish in his eyes as he cupped her face. He repeated, "You let *him* touch you."

"He was just being friendly, Simon." She shook her head to throw off the hand that held her cheek, but he refused to let her go.

"He *wasn't* being friendly, Lily. He wanted you, just like every other man here." He looked down at her *décolletage* and then brushed his fingertips along her shoulder. She shivered. This wasn't fair. *He* was what she wanted more than anything.

"I think you've had too much punch, Simon," she snapped. Then she could say no more because the air whooshed from her lungs when he pulled her to himself, hard and fast.

"I have had a bit," he said quietly against her lips. "But now I plan to have a bit more."

That was when she realized he wasn't talking about punch.

❧

Simon had watched her the whole night. He'd watched her laugh and dance with other men, their hands at her waist, her hand in theirs. And he'd grown more frustrated and apprehensive. It should have been him. He should be the only one she danced with. The only one she'd touched.

When he'd seen Emory approach her, it had been all he could do not to bellow across the dance floor. It took all of his strength to stop himself from crossing the room and tearing Emory limb from limb. He could imagine himself flinging small pieces of the man into the fronds of the plants. He hoped a piece wouldn't land in the punch bowl. That would be quite improper.

But then Emory had led Lily outside. Into the dark. Into the night. Into his domain.

The moon still hung high and full in the sky. It wasn't as powerful as before, but it still led him. It did not control him, but it did lead.

He watched as Emory trailed his finger across her cheek. She didn't shove him away. Perhaps she'd enjoyed it. Then Emory took her hand in his. He'd wanted to jump through the bushes that separated them and carry her away. But he held himself back, watching her reaction.

Now she had the nerve to look at him as though he'd done something wrong. He would show her. He would show her what *he* could do for her. He would show her what she'd be missing if she chose anyone else over him.

He bent at the waist and hoisted her over his shoulder.

"What are you doing, Simon?" she gasped.

"Do be quiet, Lily love. Or you'll draw a crowd. I'm sure you don't want that, since I'm about to have my way with you."

"You will do no such thing," she gasped.

"Watch and see, Lily." He chuckled to himself as he slipped his hand beneath her skirt and clutched the back of her thigh. She hit at his back with her fists. The blows were more annoying than painful, like a bug that flies in your face but never stings you. He strode further down the darkened garden path.

As soon as they were far away from the light of the assembly hall and any wayward strollers who might also want to take advantage of the cover of darkness, he stopped and put her down. Her face was red, the silky skin of her neck and shoulders blotchy.

She moved to walk around him. "I am going back, Simon. I don't know what you think you're doing."

He stopped her by grabbing her wrist and spinning her around. He ran his knuckles across her cheek. His hand shook with the effort it took to go slowly. "Did his touch feel like mine?" he asked.

"You're being ridiculous, Simon." She stomped, but she also leaned her face into his hand. He knew she didn't intend to, but she stretched into him like a cat who wanted to be stroked. And stroke her, he would.

He cupped her face as her hand came up to hold his. His lips hovered over hers, barely brushing them as he said, "Tell me my touch is better."

She tried to fight it. He knew she did. He saw the battle as it played across her face. She failed miserably.

"Tell me," he breathed as he brought his free hand up to cup her breast. His thumb brushed her nipple. Her eyes closed, and a breath rushed from her.

"Yes," she said quietly, looking into his eyes as his lips touched hers softly. But she still hadn't said it. She hadn't done what he wanted.

"Yes, what?" he teased as he brushed her nipple again.

"Your touch is better," she acquiesced before pulling his lips firmly against hers.

Simon took the time to tease her, to play with her mouth. He touched his tongue to her lips. They opened, and she tentatively met him. He tilted his head so he could delve deeper. She pressed back.

Simon groaned against her mouth and pulled her hard against himself. He cupped her bottom, pulling her belly against his arousal so she could feel every inch of him.

Simon removed his coat and spread it in the shadows beneath a tree. Her body was supple and pliant as he picked her up and laid her gently upon the coat, anxious to cover her body with his own and sink into her.

Slow, Simon, he chided himself.

Gently, he pulled her gown off her shoulder and replaced it with his lips. Her skin felt like silk and smelled better than the sweetest ambrosia. He fought the beast to maintain control, to make it good for her.

He tugged her sleeve down further and, in doing so, bared the swell of her breast. He dropped slow kisses against the fevered flesh. Her breaths rushed in and out, causing the plump flesh to tremble. One more tug, and her breast popped free.

Simon groaned and waited a moment simply to feast upon the sight of her. Her pert breast, round and full, was topped by a perfectly peaked nipple. He looked into her face as he touched it with his tongue. Her eyes closed briefly.

"Open your eyes, Lily, and see what a happy man I am," he said quietly. She did and touched her hand to his hair to hold his head in place as she arched her back.

"Again?" she asked quietly.

He laughed as he took the peak fully into his mouth. She squirmed against him. He used his free hand to uncover her other breast, where he began to wreak similar havoc with no more than his fingertips.

Lily began to purr like a kitten beneath him. Her hips rose to press against him. "I'll take care of that for you, Lily. I promise," he whispered as he bunched her skirts in his hand. They rose higher and higher until he felt the silken smoothness of her stockings. Then he walked his fingers slowly up to touch her bare skin.

She stilled as he ran his thumb along the crease between her thigh and stomach, following it to rest his hand against her drawers. They were already wet with the dew of her passion.

Without even looking beneath her skirts, he let his instincts guide him as he found the ribbons that held her drawers. He quickly untied them and slid his hand inside. All the while, his lips continued to play relentlessly with her breasts.

Her legs spread of their own accord when he touched her. He trailed one finger through her slit, feeling how wet she was. He groaned, "So sweet, Lily."

She laid her head back against the ground as he slid one finger inside her. He would allow her to close her eyes this time, wanting her to give in to the sensations, to realize how wonderful it could be between them.

She arched her hips toward him when he pressed deeper. She closed around him like a silken glove.

"Simon," she cried softly. "Please."

She probably had no idea what she was even asking for, but even an innocent knew there had to be some release from the sweet torment he was trying to inflict upon her.

His thumb rubbed once across her nub, and she arched toward him, pressing his finger deeper. He wanted to be inside her but not until he'd given her pleasure. Then he would do it again.

He stroked across her center again and took up a rhythm of small circles. He reveled in the fact that she responded to him so beautifully. She rocked against his hand, her cries soft and mewling.

And he knew when it was about to happen, when she was about to topple over. She closed her eyes tightly and threw her head back and forth, the pins falling from her hair across the ground. Then she pressed against his hand one more time and exploded. Her body pulsed, milking his finger as he swiped across her heat time and again, wringing the last bit of pleasure from her center. She cried out, clutching his arm. And she said his name. He felt immense satisfaction when she cried, "Simon!"

She stilled beneath him, slowly coming back to reality. Her eyes opened apprehensively, as though she was afraid of what she'd see when she opened them.

"How was that, love?" He couldn't help but smile at her.

Her breaths returned to normal. Her pulse began to quiet. But that was all right. He could bring her back up. But then she began to tug at her bodice, covering her breasts before she rolled away from him.

She quickly stood up, smoothing down her skirts. Her hair tumbled wildly about her shoulders, the pins long since forgotten. Then she looked down at him, confusion clouding her pretty face.

"That's not all there is, love," he said, tugging her hand to bring her back down.

"Are you happy, Simon?" she asked quietly. Before he could even answer, she said, "You certainly should be. Because, despite my desire *not* to be your mistress, you made me your whore instead."

Eighteen

WHAT HAD SHE DONE?

Lily clutched her skirts in her hand and ran back down the darkened path toward the assembly hall. Simon called after her, but she paid him no attention. Tears began to stream down her face. He'd never marry her now.

She found Emory Hawthorne on the bench where he had left her, a cup of punch in his hand. When he noticed her tears, he dropped the cup and raced toward her. "My God, Lily, are you all right?"

She doubted she'd ever be right again. Lily managed to shake her head.

Emory pulled her into his arms, and she cried even harder. Why couldn't she feel something for this man or one of the others? Why was Simon Westfield the only man who had ever made her pulse race?

"I'd like to go home," she whispered.

Emory nodded. "Of course, Lily."

"Hawthorne!" Simon's voice boomed from the darkened path. "You won't take Miss Rutledge anywhere."

Emory stared into the darkness. "Blackmoor?"

Simon emerged from the shadows, looking darker and more menacing than Lily could remember, even more so than when he saved her from the awful men at the coaching inn. She shivered.

"Lily is staying at Westfield Hall, and I'll take her home. Your services aren't required."

"Now see here, Simon," Emory began, puffing up like a peacock. "Lily can stay wherever she wants. I'm sure Prisca would enjoy her company again."

Simon chuckled darkly. "Good luck with that, Hawthorne. She'll never leave her beloved nephew. Not for you or anyone else."

Oliver. Somehow she'd lost sight of him. Simon was right. She'd never leave Oliver, not if she had a say in it. Lily brushed her cheeks and stepped away from Emory. "Excuse me."

"Lily." Simon started toward her.

She shook her head. She didn't have a choice. She'd go back to Westfield Hall, but not without Will. Simon wouldn't do or say anything untoward with his brother nearby.

Lily dropped onto her own bed at Westfield Hall, after turning the lock in her door. She was of no temper to entertain guests in the middle of the night.

Simon had fumed the entire way back from the assembly room, and Will hadn't been in the mood to use his charm to make the ride more palatable for anyone. Lily was more lost than ever.

She had never felt so connected with another soul as she had in the garden with Simon. Then the interlude had ended and reality came crashing back around her. No matter how deeply she had fallen for him, Simon didn't love her and he wouldn't offer what she truly needed.

It was time to leave.

She'd say good-bye to Oliver in the morning and start back to Maberley Hall. In a few months, he'd head off to Harrow and wouldn't need her as much as he had up until this point. No matter that Simon couldn't be what she needed, she didn't believe he'd let any harm come to Oliver.

Her decision made, she snuggled under the counterpane and cried herself to sleep.

❧

"You should know," Will began, as he slumped in an overstuffed leather chair in Simon's private suite of rooms. "True to form, Prisca has stirred up a bit of trouble for you."

Simon shrugged out of his coat and threw it across the room to land on a slight Chippendale chair. "What's she done?" He couldn't possibly have more trouble than he'd made for himself. Lily wouldn't even look at him, and his heart had ached when he heard her turn the key in her lock and start to cry. Perhaps she would see reason in the light of day.

"Got Mrs. Bostic all worked up that Lily's been living here without a chaperone." Will threw back a whisky and closed his eyes.

The vicar's wife? Simon grunted. He couldn't care less what the old bat thought. He couldn't even remember the last time he'd stepped foot in a church.

He was many things, but hypocritical wasn't one of them. He picked up the decanter of whisky and started to pour.

"I know you don't play by the rules," Will continued. "Well, not their rules, anyway; but this is bad for Lily. She's ruined, Simon. Living with two bachelors, neither of whom have pristine reputations, and with no one watching out for her virtue. No chaperone. Her name will be dragged through the mud tomorrow morning."

Simon crushed the whisky bottle in his hands. Shards of glass penetrated his skin, while blood and drink pooled on the floor at his feet. Will didn't even look surprised or pull himself out of his seat. "Damned Hawthornes." Simon dropped what was left of the bottle to the floor and pulled a piece of glass from his palm. "That woman is a menace. Why would she hurt Lily like that?"

Will scoffed. "Prisca is calling your bluff. She doesn't think you'll let Lily be called a whore, that you'll marry her instead."

God! Simon winced. She'd called herself a whore, which wasn't even close to the truth. He'd spent many a night with women who were, but Lily Rutledge couldn't be counted in their number. He'd kill anyone with his bare hands who would speak out against her. "I'd like to get my hands around her neck."

Will growled. "You stay away from Prisca. She's only trying to help Lily, as unorthodox as it seems."

Simon pulled the last piece of glass from his hand and wrapped his once snowy white cravat around his wound. He shouldn't bother ruining the cloth; he'd heal in no time, but he was at a loss for what to do, what to say.

"What are you going to do?" Will finally asked.

Simon didn't have a clue. "I can't marry her, Will. She doesn't want to know about all of this." He moved his injured hand about, gesturing to both of them. "I can't ask that of her."

Will shook his head. "You'd rather she be branded a whore?"

"Don't you ever say that again," Simon snarled.

"I won't need to. Everyone else will."

There had to be a way around the situation. He could send her back to Maberley Hall. He could send her to his family's old estate in Scotland. "She wants to go back to Essex."

"Did she say that?" Will asked.

"Not to me, but I can feel it."

Will shook his head. "It's no matter, Simon, this will follow her anywhere. You're you, and what you do—and who you spend time with—has a way of making it in the papers. Mrs. Bostic isn't known for keeping her tongue."

"I could rip it out of her head," Simon suggested, offhandedly.

"Charming."

Simon glared at his brother.

"Look, Lily doesn't have to know. You were going to set her up in a house nearby anyway. So you set her up here instead. Marry Lily. Protect her. But when the moon calls, you'll tell her you're going hunting with me or Ben. Make plans. Be somewhere else. Stay with her the rest of the time but keep her in the dark a few days. It's the best solution there is."

"It's not fair to her," Simon said as he buried his head in his hands.

"Let her decide, won't you?"

Nineteen

LILY WOKE AND DRESSED BEFORE THE SUN CAME UP, needing the time to bolster her confidence. She paced the length of her room, practicing what she would say to Simon, Oliver, and Will—and even what she would say to Prisca and Emory Hawthorne.

She could just imagine how Emory viewed her at this point, having seen her run from Simon into his arms. She'd seen herself in the mirror when she'd arrived home. Her hair hung tangled and wild about her shoulders; gone was the elegant upsweep that made her look so sophisticated. In its place was the whore that she'd become.

Could she still salvage her reputation? She would have to leave Oliver and return to Essex. Of course, she would refuse Simon's offer of a dowry. No one would want her now, not once word got out about her wanton behavior.

Oliver would be safe with Simon. Despite his lack of interest in providing supervision in the past, he would care for the boy. He would be firm yet loving. And Oliver would have Will as well, someone who was already having a positive effect on him. William had even managed to coerce Oliver into practicing his Latin, which was a miracle in itself.

Lily descended the stairs slowly, listening for sounds of footsteps in the foyer. She was slightly relieved to find no one moving about. But as she turned the corner, she heard voices from the breakfast room.

Simon and Will.

Her task seemed more difficult now that she was here, and her heart pounded ruthlessly. But it had to be done. She took a deep breath and steeled herself to face them. To face Simon.

Lily pressed forward and stepped over the threshold. At once, Simon leapt to his feet. Anguish marred his brow.

"Lily," he said as the air rushed out of him.

Will slowly rose and smiled at her. "I'll leave you two alone."

Lily shook her head. "That's not necessary, Will."

"Oh, I think it is." He winked at her and quickly quit the room.

Lily watched him go and then turned her head back to Simon, only to find him right next to her. How could he possibly have moved so quickly? She took a step away from him, not able to look him directly in the eyes. "Your Grace, I—"

"We're a little past 'Your Grace,' Lily."

Heat infused her cheeks, and she nervously smoothed her skirts. "Your Grace, I have no excuse for my behavior, and I think it best if I leave for Maberley Hall today."

Simon's knuckles brushed against her cheek, sending tendrils of desire straight to her core. The sooner she left, the better. She couldn't trust herself alone with him at all. Who knew what she'd do next?

"I can't let you leave, Lily," his deep voice rumbled over her.

Lily closed her eyes, wishing herself away from him. Wishing this could be easier. "I won't be your mistress, Simon. I can't. It's time for me to leave."

"No," he said, his voice strained. "Not my mistress, Lily. You're going to marry me."

She must have misheard him. Simon Westfield couldn't possibly want to marry her. She would interfere with his lifestyle. Wasn't that what he'd said?

Slowly, Lily opened her eyes. His penetrating grey gaze bored into her. His brow was furrowed. A muscle twitched in his jaw. Whatever was going on, Simon was the furthest thing from happy. "Marry you?" she asked.

He nodded. Once.

A feeling of dread settled in her belly, and Lily shook her head. "Why would you ask me such a thing?"

"It's necessary."

"Necessary?"

Again, he nodded.

"Why?"

He quietly watched her, and, for the longest time, Lily thought he wouldn't speak at all. Did he really not want to lose her? Her heart expanded at the thought.

"We don't have a choice." Simon's voice interrupted her thoughts, dashing her hopes.

Unsure what to say to that, Lily blinked at him.

Simon shook his head. "If you don't marry me, Lily, you're as good as ruined."

"I *am* ruined," she reminded him with a whisper.

Simon closed the distance between them and tipped her chin back, forcing her to look at him. "Lily love, you are far from ruined. Last night I gave you pleasure; I didn't take your innocence."

She wasn't quite sure what the difference was. She felt the furthest thing from innocent.

"Will has a connection to the Archbishop. He'll leave for Lambeth Palace this morning to acquire a special license, and we'll be married in three days time."

Lily shook out of his hold. "Why don't we have a choice?"

Simon raked a hand through his black hair. "Damn it, Lily! I thought this would make you happy. You were prepared to settle for Emory Hawthorne or one of the other dolts from last night."

Not really. Not that she could tell him how much he'd hurt her with his offer. "That was different."

He glared at her. Lily had never expected to receive an offer of marriage from anyone. She didn't have lands, connections, or money to offer a prospective husband. If she had ever let the stray thought enter her mind, Simon's proposal was far from what dreams were made of. There were no declarations of love, no looks of adoration, nor promises for a happy future.

She was already a poor relation. The last thing she wanted was to be stuck in a loveless marriage. She'd seen that with Daniel and Emma, and had no desire to live in one herself. Not that there wasn't love on her side; there was. But Simon obviously didn't return the sentiment, and she didn't think she could face a lifetime with him, knowing he never really wanted her. That she was an obligation.

If her heart wasn't already broken, this would certainly have done the job.

"Look," Simon began gruffly, "I wish it could be different, Lily. Really, I do. You're better off without me, but there isn't a better solution."

She didn't believe that. "Why?" she asked skeptically.

"Because word has gotten out that you've been living here with me."

"But I only came to speak to you about Oliver, as you couldn't be bothered to return a letter."

"It's no matter. You're a young, unmarried woman staying under my roof without a proper chaperone."

"Young?" She snorted. "Heavens, Simon, I'm almost twenty-four. I'm Oliver's spinster aunt. I don't need a chaperone."

One black eyebrow arched. "You are hardly a spinster. Not one man last night thought so."

They hadn't wanted her either. They were after her funds, or Simon's funds, as the case may be. She didn't realize she was crying until Simon brushed a tear away with the pad of his thumb.

"Why would you consider marriage to that pack of fools, but not to me?" he asked softly.

Lily's eyes flashed up to him. He was the only man she'd ever wanted in any way, shape, or form. "Because you don't want me."

His arms snaked around her waist, and he pulled her length against his. She could feel his arousal through her skirts, and heat crept up her face.

"Certainly you can feel how much I want you."

"For a tumble, for an arrangement. You don't want to *marry* me, Simon."

"I never wanted to marry anyone, Lily. If things were different, if *I* was different, it would be another situation all together, but I am who I am. Somehow we'll find a way to make it work."

"What about your lifestyle?"

He blanched. "We'll find a way to make it work," he repeated.

"Simon—" she began, but he placed his finger on her lips, silencing her.

The intensity of his grey eyes pierced her, and Lily lost her breath. She did want him. He was offering respectability and his name, if not his heart. Perhaps that would come. She prayed it would.

Lily nodded her consent.

Simon thought his heart was going to leap out of his chest, right up to the moment she nodded her head. When she finally nodded her acquiescence, he was sure he looked like a besotted fool. Surely she would turn her head and laugh at him any moment. But he couldn't be romantic, could he? He had to let her believe his offer of marriage was simply to protect her reputation. But it was far from that.

Well, it was partly that. He could already imagine the society pages when the scavengers reported that someone had finally shackled the Duke of Blackmoor. He was notorious for his escapades; he'd spent years cultivating his image, after all. He could only imagine how Lily would feel when the gossipmongers began to speculate about an eight-month baby. They might even make wagers in the London clubs about how long it would be before a blessed event would occur. Even though he and Lily hadn't been intimately involved, she would be slaughtered by their poisonous pens.

Simon turned away from Lily and scrubbed a hand across his face. How best to protect her?

"Is something wrong, Simon?"

"No, no, Lily," he said, suddenly distracted by his wayward thoughts. "Nothing is wrong."

"Simon," she said as she laid her delicate little hand on his chest. "You don't *have to* marry me." His heart sped up beneath her touch.

"Oh, I do," he murmured, already feeling aroused from her innocent touch.

"I can survive a bit of scandal…" she started.

"There is no need, Lily."

"I can't imagine forcing you into something you don't want to do." She turned away from him. Then she spun back quickly. "Will you hate me?"

"I can't imagine anyone hating you," he said, tipping her chin up with his finger. "And you will make a perfectly beautiful duchess."

"Oh, my, Simon." She smiled. "I almost forgot about that part."

"You will be perfect," he said, looking into the amber depths of her eyes.

"Who will make a beautiful duchess?" Oliver asked as he breezed into the room. He stopped and looked at the pair of them, his stance one of supreme bullhead-edness. He stomped like a horse as he walked toward them and plopped into a chair.

"Really, Oliver," Lily said. "Mind your manners."

Oliver had the nerve to smirk at her. "Why?" He looked at her with the utmost disrespect, reminding Simon of a young pup who's just learned he has teeth but hasn't yet learned how to use them to his advantage.

"Because an earl is expected to behave properly." Lily's eyebrows scrunched together.

"Aunt Lily," Oliver said. "My manners are certainly not the only thing that's improper about me. If you only knew…"

"Enough!" Simon barked, worried the boy would reveal too much.

Oliver snapped his mouth shut and sat up straight. That was much better, Simon thought. He really didn't want to take the pup to heel. Not again. Not today.

"So, who is going to be a duchess?" Oliver asked again.

"It appears as though I am," Lily sighed. Simon's eyes sought hers. She sounded as if she had just said *"I'll be going to the gallows tomorrow"* or *"I have three days left to live."*

"Well, that was fast," Oliver said. "You met a duke last night? And he has already offered for you? It's that dowry, isn't it? I had a feeling…" he trailed off when Simon shot a look at him.

"No, Oliver," Simon began, adjusting his stance to lean casually against the door frame. If he wanted the boy to be less of a peacock, he might try by setting an example, so he attempted an air of relaxation. "Your Aunt Lily has agreed to marry me." Before he could even attempt a smile at the lad, the boy was up and stomping across the room.

But what tipped his hand was when he grabbed Lily's upper arms and shook her slightly. "Are you daft, Aunt Lily? You simply cannot agree to marry a man like *him*."

Simon fought the beast to maintain control when he pulled the boy away from Lily. It was difficult but not impossible. He picked the lad up by the scruff of the neck, grasping his shirt tightly, and set him away from Lily.

She already had red marks appearing on her upper arms, and she reached to rub them, a scowl on her face. "What is *wrong* with you, Oliver?" she demanded.

Simon wanted an answer to that, too. So, he stood between them, waiting for Oliver to speak.

"You don't know what he is," Oliver snarled.

Lily rolled her eyes, a movement Simon found to be quite endearing simply because it was so improper. "I know all about him, Oliver." Simon's heart expanded as she slipped her tiny hand into his. "I have read every scandal sheet, every rumor posted in *The Times*." She met Simon's eyes. "And there were a lot of them." His heart hurt with that last statement. "But people change."

"Oh, he does *change*, Aunt Lily. You don't know the half of it," Oliver said, reaching for her again.

"Out, Lily!" Simon ordered before the boy could hurt her. She looked as though she was going to hesitate. "Now," he barked.

Billings appeared in the doorway, as if he'd been summoned. "This way, Miss," Simon thought he heard him say. Though he honestly couldn't hear anything over the roaring in his own ears.

Twenty

LILY REFUSED TO TAKE ONE MORE STEP AWAY FROM the morning room where Simon was behind closed doors with Oliver. She heard a crash and reached for the doorknob, only to have Billings brush her hand away. The old man was surprisingly fast. Sometimes he seemed to appear from nowhere. She assumed that was a trait of a good butler. Unless it kept her from her goals. Then it was a nuisance.

"Miss Rutledge, His Grace will not be happy…" Billings' voice trailed off as he saw the look on her face.

"I am not terribly concerned with anyone's happiness at the moment," Lily snapped. "I am simply concerned about my nephew's safety." Another bump sounded from the room.

Billings cleared his throat, and Lily leveled her iciest glare at him. "You are excused, Billings."

After the butler grudgingly departed from the corridor, Lily frowned at the door. If she went back in, her presence might make matters worse. She'd have to talk to Simon alone once he finished with her nephew. She paced a circle in front of the door until the noise slowed and then stopped. She could just imagine the disarray caused by the altercation. She remembered how easily Simon had flipped the furniture in his study when he was simply playing with her. And wondered what in the world was happening in the breakfast room.

She heard words every now and then like *change* and *unnatural*. Then she heard part of a sentence in which Oliver said something about something not being fair to her.

What *were* they talking about? Lily placed her ear next to the door, straining to hear better.

"Tsk, tsk," Will's voice came from behind her. She nearly jumped out of her slippers at being caught eavesdropping. "Listening at doors, Lily?" he asked.

She stepped away from the door, her cheeks on fire. "I'm worried about Oliver. For some reason, he thinks Simon is unnatural."

Will draped his arm over Lily's shoulders, steering her toward the blue parlor. "Our brother, Benjamin, has the same complaint."

She blinked up at him.

Grinning, Will chucked her chin. "I'm teasing you. Of course, Oliver thinks Simon's unnatural. He's his guardian. I always thought my father was unnatural, too. It's the way of men, Lily dear. Think nothing of it."

Reaching the parlor, Will directed her inside. "Oliver wasn't always this…" She searched for the right word. "…insolent, Will. It's very disconcerting."

They sat together on the settee, and Will squeezed

her hands. "Every boy goes through an adjustment when he starts becoming a man, Lily."

She scrunched up her face. Oliver's changes seemed so… different.

"So, tell me," Will began charmingly. "Are congratulations in order?"

Her betrothal. Lily bit her bottom lip. "You knew. That's why you left."

He winked at her. "Seemed the thing to do. Are you happy?"

Was she happy? Yes and no. "He doesn't want this, Will. I feel terrible this has been forced on him."

"Perhaps it's all for the best. He's been known to be a bit stubborn in the past. He might not ever have made the decision on his own."

"I wish he had," she said softly.

Someone cleared his throat in the doorway, and Lily's eyes flashed to find Billings, looking stoic as usual, standing sentry. "Miss Hawthorne has arrived to see you, Miss Rutledge."

Will tensed beside her, grumbling something unintelligible.

"Oh, do show her in, Billings." As soon as the butler departed, she frowned at Will. "Be nice to her."

"It's not me you need to worry about," Will replied.

"Ah, Lily!" Prisca's cheerful voice came from the doorway, causing Will to stand and bow slightly.

"Prisca."

She barely spared him a glance, focusing her attention on Lily. "You left so suddenly last night. I wanted to make certain you were all right." She crossed the floor and sat in a chintz chair near them.

"Should you really be visiting the home of a bachelor alone, Miss Hawthorne?" Will asked, irritation in his voice. "Highly dangerous."

Lily's face flushed. Why would he say something like that in light of her predicament? "Will!"

Prisca simply beamed at him. "Don't mind him, Lily. I don't intend to." Then she pierced Lily with her beautiful violet eyes. "Do tell me you're all right. I worried all night."

Will snorted.

Lily folded her arms across her chest. "As Prisca came to see me, perhaps you should go busy yourself somewhere else."

He smiled tightly. "I'm certain my horse is ready anyway." Will stood up.

"Going somewhere, William?" Prisca asked, examining her fingernails.

"London."

Her eyes darted back to him. "London? But you've hardly been here."

"If I didn't know better, I'd think you'd miss me. As it is," he continued, "I wouldn't try Simon's temper, were I you, Prisca. Don't stay too long."

She sat back in her chair with a huff. "Missing your light skirts already, are you?"

"Happy husband hunting." Will strode purposefully from the room, never looking back.

Lily stared after him, and then she turned to Prisca, who was brushing her knuckles across her cheek. "Are you all right?" Lily asked, rising from her seat.

Prisca smiled, pretending she wasn't crying. "Perfect. Tell me you're doing well."

Lily pursed her lips. "His Grace asked me to marry him."

Prisca leapt from her seat and threw her arms around Lily. "Oh, that is wonderful. I'm certain you'll be happy."

Lily wished she could be just as certain.

Simon had been tested more times than he could count on two hands and two feet. He'd been pulled naked from the bed of a married woman by the angry spouse. He'd been in more than one drunken brawl. He'd been pummeled by his brothers. And even by a friend or two. But he'd never had his patience tried like he did with Oliver.

For Lily's sake, he tried not to kill the boy. That wasn't easy to do. Oliver had an amazing strength, which often came with the youth of their kind. Fortunately, he didn't know how to use it yet. Once he'd toppled a few chairs and uprighted the table, he simply stood before Simon, his chest heaving as he tried to catch his breath.

Having two younger brothers, both with similar tempers, Simon had learned the hard way that it was easier to let them get the rage out of their systems rather than stifling it. As with a plugged-up teapot, the steam would find a way to escape one way or the other. As long as no one around Oliver could be hurt, Simon would let him blow off some steam.

"If you ever put your hands on your Aunt Lily again," Simon seethed. "I will personally lock you in your room for so long that you will *wish* you were in Newgate."

"You can't truly expect me to be happy about Aunt

Lily marrying someone like *you*," Oliver shot back, sneering the last word.

"You mean someone like *us*, don't you?"

"Like us," the boy whispered as he turned toward the window. "I wouldn't want any woman to be shackled to someone like us."

"I am pretty happy with the situation," Simon began. "And your aunt seems to be quite content with the idea." He tried not to smile, but he felt the corners of his mouth tilt, regardless.

"That's because she doesn't know," Oliver reminded him. Simon bit back a wince.

"She doesn't have to know."

"You would marry her and not tell her?"

"Yes, and you won't tell her, either. No one knows about us, except us. And it will stay that way. Unless I decide she's ready to hear it at some point in the future." Simon sighed.

"And what will you do when the moon calls?"

"I'll go away for a few days every month, Oliver. I'll probably take you with me." It would be safer that way, because Oliver might not be able to control himself.

"And what happens when you have a child? Another one like me?"

Simon hadn't given any thought to having children, but he had to admit his heart warmed at the idea of it. A piece of him, combined with Lily, growing inside her. And it would be even more fun creating a child. He coughed to hide the smile that nearly erupted.

"You *have* to tell her," Oliver said, crossing his arms in a move so reminiscent of Lily's stubbornness that he had to chuckle.

"I'll tell her when I simply cannot avoid it," Simon acquiesced.

"You need to tell her before you bed her," Oliver said quietly, his face coloring slightly.

"What do you know about bedding a woman?"

Oliver's face colored even more. "Will told me about it. About how we must claim our mates. He gave me books about Lycanthropic lore. There's a lot of truth between the pages, he said." His eyes scrunched together, his comment more of a question for Simon, obviously.

"If they're the same books our father gave him, and I suspect they are, there is a lot of truth between the pages. The majority of what you've read is true."

"Is it true about the claiming of your spouse?" The boy was more tenacious than a dog with a bone.

"I don't think you're old enough to be told about…" Simon began.

"I am old enough to change but not old enough to know about the things I truly need to know?" His gaze met Simon's own. "If Aunt Lily knew, she might not *choose* to marry a Lycan."

"I know." Simon pinched the bridge of his nose between his thumb and forefinger. He had a definite headache coming on.

"You will deceive her. And that's not right," the boy sniffed.

"It's not really deception, Oliver. Just a little omission."

"And the claiming?"

"I'll never be able to claim Lily. Not when the moon is full. Not in the way you're describing." It was quite disconcerting to talk about such matters with an adolescent. But he imagined there would be many more such talks to come.

"You'll not hurt her?" Oliver asked, suddenly looking like a child.

"Never on purpose. I promise."

A knock broke their silence. "A moment," Simon called. "Are we all right, now?" he asked Oliver.

A nod was his only answer.

Simon turned to the door, "Enter," he called.

Billings stepped into the room. "Your Grace, you have visitors in the yellow parlor."

This was certainly not the time to deal with anyone. Simon rubbed his brow. "Who is it, Billings?"

"The vicar Mr. Bostic and his wife, Your Grace."

Perfect, Simon thought mordantly and hung his head in defeat. "What else could possibly go wrong?" he moaned quietly.

"Well, Your Grace. They did bring their son with them. The fellow was seen practicing in the front yard."

Simon's head snapped up. "Practicing what?"

"Dropping to one knee, Your Grace. Over and over."

"God, will this day never end?" Simon grumbled as he strode through the door, heading toward his yellow parlor with his heels clicking across the floor in his haste.

Twenty-One

LILY SAT ACROSS FROM THE VICAR AND HIS WIFE, WHILE their sheepish son huddled in the corner, muttering to himself. Entertaining the trio was a chore, and Lily tried to keep her composure. However, it was getting more difficult by the moment. She listened to the woman prattle on about the weather and how bumpy the carriage ride was. She fought to keep from rolling her eyes.

"How long do you think it will be before His Grace joins us?" the woman finally asked before pursing her lips.

"I'm not at all certain. He is with the Earl of Maberley at the moment. Would you care for some tea while we wait?"

"Thank you," the meek vicar replied.

Lily smiled at the man and then started toward the sideboard, where Billings had left a fresh pot of tea.

"Do tell me how you came to be here in His Grace's house, Miss Rutledge," the woman had the nerve to ask.

"I arrived with the earl, Mrs. Bostic." She tried to keep the annoyed tone from her voice but feared that she failed miserably. "My nephew needed to spend some time with his guardian." She began to pour the tea, happy to have something to keep her hands busy.

The woman consumed a plate of lemon cakes within minutes and then looked around as though she thought someone had stolen them from right under her nose.

"And did you think it proper to stay with His Grace without a chaperone?" The woman looked at Lily as though she'd grown two heads.

Lily didn't answer, but sat back against her chair and lifted a teacup to her mouth.

The woman had the nerve to continue. "Is it true that His Grace has offered a healthy dowry to any man who marries you, despite your recent behavior?"

Lily nearly choked on her tea. The vicar sighed nervously.

"I beg your pardon?" Lily asked, as she put down her cup and stood up quickly. How dare the woman speak to her that way!

"I imagine that means yes," Mrs. Bostic said, smiling broadly at her husband. Then she snapped her fingers at their son. "Timothy."

The vicar's son gulped and stepped forward, cringing as he looked at his mother. He was a mousy little fellow, his skin so pale it was nearly translucent. His eyes were rimmed in red, as though he'd been sneezing. Or crying. She would have cried, too, if Mrs. Bostic were her mother.

Lily looked down at him; he was at least five inches shorter than she was, and she could see a bald spot appearing on the top of his head. If she remembered correctly, they were close to the same age. At the rate he was losing hair, he would be bald by the age of thirty.

"You may do it now," Mrs. Bostic directed.

The poor fellow dropped to his knee in front of Lily. "M-Miss Rutledge—"

His speech was cut short when Simon strode into the room. "Bostic, off your knees if you want to keep them."

Timothy Bostic scrambled back to his feet. "Y-your Grace?"

Simon turned his irritated grey gaze to the vicar's wife. "Did my dear Miss Rutledge tell you our good news?"

The woman sucked in a breath, her face starting to turn an unflattering red. "N-news?"

Lily bit back a smile. Did Simon make everyone stutter?

"Indeed," Simon replied, crossing the room and sliding his arm around Lily's waist. "I was going to have to pay you a visit later today, Mr. Bostic. But as you're here, you've saved me the trip. This amazing woman has agreed to marry me." He smiled down at her. "Once Lord William returns from Lambeth Palace, I'd like for you to do the honors."

The vicar's eyes grew round. "A special license, Your Grace?"

Simon nodded. "I find she has quite captured my heart, and I'd rather not wait for the banns."

The man stumbled to his feet. "I-I-I... Of course, Your Grace. Whatever you require of me."

Mrs. Bostic squeaked, and Simon flashed his eyes on her. "Did you say something, ma'am?"

"But you were offering her a dowry—"

"True. Miss Rutledge will still have it. I'll put the funds in trust for her."

"I see." The woman frowned.

"Well," the vicar said, rising from his seat. "I believe we will be on our way then. When you have the license, Your Grace, do let me know."

Simon inclined his head.

Once the Bostics left, Lily sighed deeply and rested her head on his chest. She wished the words he'd said to the vicar and his family had been true, that he'd really lost his heart to her. "I had no idea money turned people into such terrible creatures."

Simon chuckled and then dropped a kiss on her brow. "Mrs. Bostic has always been a terrible creature, Lily. I am sorry you had to endure her."

Lily tipped her head back, gazing at his ruggedly handsome face. He did seem happy. More so than he had this morning. "Is Oliver all right?"

He nodded. "The little monster is fine for now. You should have come to me years earlier. I don't know how you ever managed him alone."

For years, Oliver had the sweetest disposition. Something Simon would have known, if he'd ever showed the slightest bit of interest in the boy. How long would his interest last in Oliver, or in her? How long before his lifestyle called to him? What did that even mean? Did he intend to return to the hoards of women he'd left in London? She wasn't certain her heart could take it.

"Lily," he said softly, interrupting her thoughts. "You look so sad."

She forced a smile to her lips. "Just woolgathering."

"About what?" he pressed.

Lily sighed. Should she tell him of her concerns? Would it matter? "I suppose I don't know what to expect from our marriage," she hedged. "What it will entail."

A slow smile lit his face. "Ah, well, let me show you."

Lily batted his hands away from her person as he reached for her. "You know that's not what I meant."

Simon took another step toward her and she backed up, but she couldn't hide the smile that erupted, no matter how hard she tried.

"Oh, but it's what *I* meant," he said, his grey eyes twinkling. She'd never actually seen the man laugh before. He was handsome even when he was sour, but when he laughed, he completely captured her heart. "You wanted to know what to expect from our marriage, and I want to show you."

He stepped toward her again. She put a chair between them.

"Will every room in my house be left a shambles because of you and Maberley? Before you arrived, I had quite a lovely home," he said as he slid the chair over. Lily ducked behind a second chair.

"You are the one who keeps making messes of the furniture, Simon. Not me," she said, shaking her finger at him. Then she laughed and ran as he casually flipped another chair. They seemed to be nothing more than playthings to him.

"When we're married, you will no longer be able to rearrange the furniture. I won't have it." She tried to look stern and unforgiving. She failed miserably.

He simply smirked at her and pushed the final chair out of the way.

Lily squealed as she turned to run, but his hands snaked around her middle. He pulled her to himself, her back to his front, and leaned forward to say quietly in her ear, "Got you."

Lily couldn't hide from the sudden warmth she felt as his body pressed along the length of hers. One of his hands splayed on her belly, pulling her into the cradle of his hips. The other brushed the hair away from the nape of her neck.

When his lips touched the sensitive skin where her neck met her shoulder, she thought her knees would buckle. Thank goodness for that hand on her belly that held her tightly to him.

"Simon," she sighed. "This is quite improper."

"It's not nearly as improper as what I did to you last night," he reminded her. She felt the heat creep up her face as she remembered his hand in her drawers, his mouth on her breasts, and that sweet, sweet release.

He must have sensed her hesitation because he simply said, "When we're married, I'll be able to kiss you here." He pressed his lips to the skin beneath her ear. "And here." He kissed her shoulder and spun her around.

"And here," he said as his lips hovered over hers. *Oh, please kiss me, Simon*, she wanted to shout. But he didn't. He simply stayed close to her. She finally gave in and reached for him, her fingers threading through his hair as she pulled him close enough to touch her lips to his.

When she finally allowed him to lift his head, he simply smiled and said, "Forceful little thing, aren't you?"

"I am not little, Simon," she gasped as his hands ran

up her side slowly, moving closer and closer to her breasts. Her heart beat like she'd just run up the stairs.

"Compared to me, you are quite small."

"You're the exception."

"I had damn well better be the exception. There will be no comparisons to other men."

"I have nothing to compare you to."

"And it will stay that way."

Lily nodded, quite unsure of what to say next. She bit her bottom lip.

"What's bothering you?" he asked as he lifted his head and looked into her eyes.

"Well, you have mentioned your lifestyle more than once. If you don't plan to share me, then I don't plan to share you, either." She winced and closed her eyes, waiting for callous words to flood her ears.

"Done," he said.

"What about this lifestyle you keep referring to? The one you want to maintain."

"It doesn't involve wenches, woman," he growled softly.

Lily's heart leapt. That was the one hesitation she had about marrying Simon. But he'd acquiesced so easily. Almost too easily.

She would worry about it later, because Simon was taking all her attention. His hands stroked her as if she were a cat just waiting to be petted. She looked into his eyes.

Oh, now she was in big trouble, because his dark eyes reminded her of a predator. And that meant she was the prey.

❦

Simon could hear her heart thumping in her chest, beating a rhythm as old as time. "Can we get back to what we were doing before you started the marriage negotiations?"

"It wasn't a negotiation," she said. He really should do a better job of seducing her so he could take her mind off all that.

"And when we're married," he said, reminding her where they'd left off. "I will kiss you here," he whispered as he pressed her back against the wall. His lips touched the skin above her bodice before he lowered his head and found her nipple, aching and waiting for his touch. He very gently nipped it between his teeth, through the fabric of her dress.

Simon smelled the evidence of her desire. It was the scent of sweet Lily and her flowers. But now it contained something else, something wild and free. As her body warmed to his touch, more of her fragrance reached his nose.

"You go too far, Simon," she said, her voice a throaty whisper.

"Yet you want me to go farther," he countered. He certainly hoped she did. He had never gone so long without a woman. It had been days since she'd arrived. It felt like a lifetime.

She didn't deny his statement. Her fingernails dug into his biceps as she clutched his arms. He reveled in the sensation. She had sharp claws, and he would enjoy every minute he spent teaching her to use them on *him*.

Simon tugged the shoulder of her gown, but this one didn't give as freely as the one the previous night. He wanted to press his lips there, to cup her breast in his hand and lift it to his mouth. He could always just rip the dress off her. But he imagined that might scare her. It wasn't the only thing about him that would scare her. Compared to his other secrets, his desire to rip her clothes off was a minor issue.

Simon spun her away from him and began to work the laces of her gown.

"What are you doing?" she asked, looking over her shoulder at him.

"Taking this thing off you so I can show you how it will be once we're married." His fingers couldn't work fast enough. He needed her to be out of that gown.

But a voice broke his concentration on his task. Lily gasped and stood up straight and tall. They both saw the interloper at the same time.

"Simon, get rid of the light skirt. We need to talk."

Simon sighed deeply and pulled Lily to him in a tight embrace. "I'm so sorry," he said to her. He wished he could apologize profusely and was, in fact, already planning what sorts of flowers to buy for her as his penance for what was about to happen. "Hello, Mother."

Twenty-Two

MORTIFIED, LILY CLUTCHED HER SAGGING GOWN tightly to her chest. Perfect! Her future mother-in-law thought she was a light skirt. Not that she could blame her. She must look like one. Lily didn't think she would ever be able to carry on a conversation with the woman, not after this.

Lily closed her eyes to avoid gazing at Alice Westfield, the Duchess of Blackmoor. If she didn't know better, it would be hard to believe the frail, old woman was Simon's mother. All that they shared were their grey eyes, eyes that seemed to burn a hole in Lily's skin.

Simon kissed her forehead. "Be brave, love." Then he stepped in front of her, shielding her from the duchess' view. "Mother, why don't we wait in my study? Miss Rutledge will join us shortly."

Lily cringed. Was it possible to delay the interview all together? She didn't need to postpone the meeting for long. Only forty or fifty years or so. She watched as Simon steered his mother from the room, preventing her from looking back at Lily and her embarrassing state of dishabille.

He closed the door behind them, and Lily sank into the last upright chintz chair. She released a sigh and the tight grip on the top of her bodice.

Heavens! Lily looked around at the disheveled parlor. No wonder the duchess thought she was a light skirt.

The door creaked open, and a little chambermaid bustled inside. Dark curls escaped her cap. "Billings said you needed assistance, miss."

Assistance. That was the very least of what she needed. A place to hide would be better. However, Simon had asked her to visit with his mother. It wasn't something she could really refuse.

"Indeed," Lily replied, resigned to her fate. She stood up and beckoned the young maid forward. Hopefully the girl could right her clothing, and she could get this over with.

~

"What do you mean 'marry her'?" his mother asked, her brow furrowed.

Simon sat back in his chair grinning widely at his mother. Over the years, he and his brothers had tried their best to surprise and shock her. They were rarely triumphant. He had to admit, however, that he'd finally found success today with this endeavor.

"I don't know how to be more clear, Mother. I do wish, however, that you'd refrain from referring to Lily as a light skirt. I'm certain she didn't appreciate it. I *know* I didn't." He said that last bit in an attempt to embarrass her. Even if Lily had been a strumpet, his mother shouldn't have said so in her presence.

"Then perhaps you shouldn't treat her like one, Simon," his mother rebuked him.

He frowned at that. How he and Lily spent their time was really none of his mother's concern. "Why don't you tell me why you arrived at Westfield Hall completely unannounced?"

She snorted. "What would be the point in writing to you with my intentions? You never pay any attention to your correspondence. It's a waste of time, ink, and foolscap."

Apparently, he did need to employ a secretary. Or perhaps Lily wouldn't mind taking over those duties as well as the more intimate ones he would be expecting from her very soon. The image *those* thoughts brought to mind made him smile.

"…Simon!" his mother's irritated voice interrupted his daydream.

"Yes, Mother?"

"I'm worried about Benjamin," she admitted, her frown darkening. "I haven't heard a word from him for far too long."

That was what had led to this visit from his mother? "I never send you letters. Does that mean you're worried about me all the time?" he asked, trying to charm her.

"Who needs to hear from you? You're in all the society rags, all the time. Besides you can't compare yourself to Benjamin. In fact, the three of you are all very different from each other."

He raised his brow at that. The three of them were all too similar in the most important of ways.

She continued with a frown. "If I ever received a

letter from you, I'd be worried. But Benjamin writes me several times a week. This isn't like him."

Several times a week? Simon bit back a smile. He had no idea his youngest brother was such a mama's boy. He couldn't wait to tell Will. Ben would never live it down. "For God's sake! He's a grown man, Mother."

A light knock interrupted their conversation. "Come!" Simon called.

The study door pushed open, and Lily tentatively peeked around the corner. Simon's smile grew. His lovely bride-to-be always stood toe to toe with him, never backing down. But she was intimidated by his *mother*? A strong wind would blow the duchess away. His mother couldn't be all that scary. She was tiny and old, the only member of the Westfield family no one of sound mind should fear.

"Ah, Lily love." He gestured to the seat beside his mother. "Sit, please."

She gracefully slid into the wingback chair he'd indicated, worrying her bottom lip. The movement made Simon long to dismiss his mother, wipe his desk clean, and finally claim his bride-to-be.

His mother coughed delicately. "Simon?"

He shook his head, hoping to clear his lustful thoughts and bring his attention to the matter at hand. "Um, Mother, you remember Miss Rutledge. She's been keeping a watchful eye on Daniel's son for me."

"Indeed?" his mother asked, raking her grey eyes across Lily's form. Hmm, perhaps Lily did have a reason to be frightened, after all. "Do you really intend to marry my son?"

Lily gulped but nodded slightly.

"I do hope you're not always so meek, Miss Rutledge. My son can be quite the bully, and he needs a wife who will bring him to heel."

Simon's mouth fell open. "Mother!" Lily didn't need any help standing up to him.

She spared him only a glance. "Don't interrupt your mother." Then she refocused on Lily. "Stand up to him *now*, or it will never get any better for you."

Lily's eyes widened. "I don't let him bully me, Your Grace."

His mother's eyes began to twinkle. "Glad to hear it. Now what date have we planned on?"

Simon shrugged. "Whenever Will returns with the special license."

The duchess' mouth fell open. "Special license! You should wait for the banns. Don't you know what people will say?"

They were already saying it, not that he could tell his mother that bit of information. It was better she not know, at least not yet. He'd like to get his paws on Prisca Hawthorne for thrusting them into this situation. "They'll say I'm impatient to marry my bride. That won't come as a surprise to anyone who knows me."

His mother pursed her lips and turned in her seat to focus on Lily. "Do you know what you're getting yourself into with my son?"

Lily shook her head. "No, but we'll make it work," she replied, echoing his earlier sentiment.

The duchess exchanged a meaningful glance with Simon. Lily hadn't really answered the question his mother was asking. She silently berated him for keeping Lily in the dark. However, he'd never let his mother intimidate him, and he wasn't about to let her start.

Distraction had often worked when he was a lad.

"So, Mother, Will tells me that Benjamin's in Scotland. There's no need to worry about him. You should probably return to Hampton Meadows and wait for his mountain of letters to arrive."

His mother narrowed her grey eyes at him. Distraction hadn't worked at all. "I'll leave Westfield Hall when I'm ready, Simon. Thank you for making me feel so comfortable." She touched Lily's hand. "Do tell me Oliver's here. I'd so like to see him again."

Lily nodded. "Indeed, Your Grace. I'm certain he'd love to see you, too."

Simon held in a snort. Oliver couldn't care less about meeting ancient duchesses. He'd have to make certain his mother didn't become too attached to Lily or let anything slip that shouldn't.

"Oh, and, dear, please call me Alice. We're both to be duchesses very soon. There's no point in being so formal."

Simon nearly groaned.

Twenty-Three

LILY MUTTERED TO HERSELF AS SHE WALKED THROUGH the garden. All she'd wanted was to coerce the duke into spending more time with Oliver. Yet here she was—ruined, engaged to the scoundrel, and still just as confused about Oliver as she had been *before* she made the trip.

Lily kicked a stone in her path, sending it skittering into the grass. She wished it was Simon's head.

She'd just spent a perfectly horrid afternoon and evening with the duchess. For all intents and purposes, the duchess was probably a splendid woman. But Lily felt grossly inadequate around her. It wasn't even that she felt inferior to the woman. It was because she obviously knew something Lily didn't.

Throughout dinner, every time the duchess began to talk about the marriage, Simon had efficiently changed the subject. It was almost as if there was something he didn't want her to know.

She stopped and kicked a bench beside the path. Once again, Simon was her target, but this time she imagined the chair leg to be his shin. "What am I missing?" she muttered to herself.

Lily paced back and forth along the pebbled path, wracking her brain, trying to find the missing piece of the puzzle that was Simon. She kicked the bench again.

"Do I need to step in and save that piece of furniture from your wrath, Lily?" Simon said as he stepped from the shadows.

"Don't be silly, Simon." She fought the urge to roll her eyes.

"I do believe my furniture will be much worse for wear once you're a permanent resident. The pieces indoors seem to have a hard time staying upright, and now I find you beating the poor bench into submission. Poor thing," he crooned to it. "And she seemed like such a wonderfully docile woman just a few days ago."

This time, Lily wasn't able to stop the rolling of her eyes, nor could she avoid the frustrated sigh that escaped her lips.

Simon's eyes narrowed. He caressed the back of the bench. "Don't worry. I won't let her hurt you," he said to the furniture.

"I have no plans to attack your furniture, Simon," she snapped, one hand fluttering in the air as she dismissed his complaint. "You, on the other hand, may not be so lucky."

"Lily love, I'm not at all sure I know what you mean." The look of innocence he tried to feign was far from genuine. He took her fingertips in his hand and tugged her over to the bench. "Come and let the poor bench do its job." She flopped down much more heavily than she knew was ladylike. "It will think you don't appreciate its talents, since you were determined to do it harm."

Lily found it difficult to concentrate on her conundrum with his thumb drawing little circles on the sensitive skin between her forefinger and thumb. His thigh touched hers, and she felt the heat of him all the way to her toes. And everywhere in between.

"Are you trying to distract me, Simon?" she asked.

"From your pursuit of the poor bench, which you seem bound and determined to torture? Of course, I am. What did it ever do to you?" His grey eyes twinkled, and the corners of his mouth twitched up.

Lily groaned. Insufferable man!

"Simon, stop teasing me."

"But I do enjoy it so much."

"Yes, I can tell." She could tell how much he liked annoying her. As though it were a sport. Perhaps that was the reason for the subterfuge she could sense in the background. Did he simply think she was something to play with? To entertain him?

He sobered. "What's bothering you, Lily?"

"Nothing." She stared into the garden.

He leaned close to her, his breath blowing across the sensitive ridge of her ear, and said softly, "Liar."

Lily sniffed and pulled her hand from his. He immediately reached to capture it again. And didn't let go.

"One thing we need to be very clear about is that you are never to pull away from me. I might annoy you to the end of time, but you mustn't take yourself away from me. Not any part of you. From your hands to your feet. In fact, I believe we should solidify this rule right now."

Lily's heart jumped in her chest. "Rule?" she was able to choke out.

"Yes. You may beat my furniture. You may even strike *me* when you're so frustrated with me you just can't tolerate any more, but you will never take away what's most important to me. And that's you."

Where was all this coming from?

"You say this to all the women, don't you?" she countered. "That's how you earned your reputation. By wooing unsuspecting females."

"I have never set out to *woo* a woman until now. Before I met you, I just wanted to bed them." Lily felt her heart expand.

"You don't want to just bed me?" She felt like a ninny. But she was finally getting closer to having answers to her questions, so she wanted to take advantage of the moment.

"Oh, no," he chuckled, his gaze sliding over her like a caress. She shivered. "I most certainly do want to bed you."

"You know that's not what I meant. How will I be different from any of the thousands of women you've been exposed with in the society rags?"

"Thousands is exaggerating just a bit, Lily."

"Not by much." She was finally able to yank her hand from his and stand. She stood in front of him and put her hands on her hips. "*Why* are you marrying me, Simon?"

Simon leaned forward and grasped her hips, pulling her to stand between his spread knees. She tried to take a step back. "No pulling away," he said, looking into her eyes.

"*Why*, Simon?" she insisted.

"Because I want to protect unsuspecting yard

furniture around the world from your wrath. You can simply abuse mine, and the rest of the world will be safe." He pulled her closer, his hands snaking around her thighs to clasp just below her bottom.

"Oh, you…" she groaned. She'd never wanted to hit anyone so much in her life.

"All right," he sighed. His hot breath stole right through her dress, he was that close. It touched her belly like a gentle rub. "One: you're ruined. And it's my fault. So, there's a bit of obligation there."

Lily felt tears choke her and tried to push them back.

He must have noticed because he said, "Wait," and held up one finger. "That's not all."

Lily sniffed and swallowed hard.

"Two: you're Oliver's caretaker, almost a mother to him, and he's going to live with me. So, having you live with me, too, will serve a dual purpose."

Lily had never heard such a poor excuse for marriage. She clasped his wrists in hers and tried to pry his hands from the back of her thighs. He didn't budge. The man had really strong arms, which infuriated her.

"Three: there's the fact I *really* want to bed you," he said quietly as he looked up at her again. He trailed slow kisses across her belly, his hands sliding up to grip her bottom through her dress.

Lily gasped and immediately felt a flip in her belly. *Don't let him distract you, Lily.* She swallowed the lump in her throat. "Well, of course you want to sleep with me. You want to sleep with everyone."

"Not any more. I haven't even thought about another woman since you walked through my door."

❧

Simon knew how dangerous it was to bare his soul to the woman, but he could sense she needed a bit of reassurance. Despite the fact that he truly did want to marry her, he also wanted her to be happy and feel secure in the situation. As safe as she could be with someone of his ilk.

"You haven't thought about anyone else?" she croaked. He almost had to grin at her discomfiture.

"How could I when you're right here, taunting me with your charms all day?" He gathered her skirts and put his hands below them, grasping the back of her thighs, pulling her closer to where he still sat on the bench.

"I don't taunt you."

"Oh, yes, you do." The woman had no idea how sensual she was. He would just have to show her. "And you don't even intend to do it, which makes me want you even more."

"Simon, I'm almost twenty-four years old. No one has ever wanted me."

"I want you," he said, removing one hand from her skirts to clasp her own and bring it to press the front of his trousers. Her fingertips skittered across the fabric, testing the feel of him. He bit back a groan.

"That's...?" she asked, a question in her voice.

"That is how much I want you." And much, much more, he thought. "I want to be with you." He punctuated the sentence with a kiss to her belly. "I want to be on top of you." His hand slid beneath the legs of her drawers to knead her bottom. "And I want to be inside you."

The scent of her arousal caught his nose, and Simon felt like he could devour her in that moment.

She broke him from his concentration when she shook his shoulder. "Simon," she nudged. "Simon," she whispered vehemently. "Someone is coming."

"No. That comes later, love."

"Simon," she nearly shrieked, pushing his arms from beneath her dress. Or trying to. She wasn't very successful. Thank God, she was such a little thing, he thought, or she could win by sheer strength of will.

"Simon," his mother's voice rang out from the edge of the garden. "I think I told you to stop treating Miss Rutledge like a harlot."

Simon finally raised his head and looked up at Lily. "Oh, God," he groaned, knocking his forehead gently against her belly in frustration. She smiled down at him and laid one hand on the top of his head.

"Simon," his mother called again.

"What do you want, Mother?" he barked.

"Why, to protect Miss Rutledge's virtue, of course. It's amazing she has any left with you chasing her skirts all day." The duchess motioned to Lily. "Come along, dear. We'll leave the big, bad wolf to sort out his own misery."

Lily extricated herself from his arms and followed his mother down the garden path. What else could possibly go wrong?

❧

Alice Westfield linked her arm with her future daughter-in-law's and towed her back toward the manor house. Simon would need some time to recover from his current state, which meant she could get a few uninterrupted minutes alone with Lily Rutledge. Minutes that were sorely needed.

Never, in all her years, had anyone ever considered Alice a fool, and it was in poor form that Simon did so now. He'd obviously compromised the poor girl, which was why he'd sent William on his quest for a special license. It was the honorable thing to do, after all. But did he really think he could keep her from realizing this? Alice wasn't a fool, but Simon, apparently, was.

Lily seemed to care for Simon, which was a relief, especially considering his differences. Considering the sort of women he generally associated with, Alice had been frightened the man wouldn't ever settle down. He had a duty to his title after all, and Alice rather thought Lily would fill the role as his duchess quite nicely.

If Simon was to have a successful marriage, he couldn't keep one of the most important parts of himself a secret from his wife. Doing so was the fastest way to doom their relationship. She wished for the millionth time that Jonathan was still alive. He'd given their sons such excellent direction, and Simon obviously was in need of it now.

She sighed as they neared the back terrace. Men were stubborn enough creatures, but Lycans were very nearly impossible.

"Alice," Lily's voice interrupted her thoughts. "Are you all right?"

Alice smiled at the girl. She was a sweet thing. She was certainly capable of learning the truth about Simon without running into the woods screaming like a bedlamite. At least Alice thought so. It would be best to make sure. "Indeed. I was simply thinking about you, dear."

"Me?"

"Of course, you. Very soon, you'll be my daughter-in-law, and if anyone understands the difficulty of dealing with a Westfield man, it's me. I was married to one and raised three."

Lily smiled as they climbed the steps to the terrace. "Is it more difficult than raising a York man, I wonder?"

"I believe it is much the same, dear." Alice couldn't help from smiling back. Oliver York was his father's son in every way. Not only did he look like Daniel, but he'd inherited his father's other abilities as well. She had known that instantly when she laid eyes on him the day before. With his impressive size and irritability, Oliver reminded her at once of Simon, Will, and Ben when they were his age.

It was amazing Lily had done so well with the lad all by herself. That was another reason Alice thought Lily could handle the truth about Simon. No matter how difficult Oliver had become the night before, Lily's love for the child had never wavered.

She led Lily to a set of table and chairs in the far corner of the terrace. From that position, she could see the grounds and know when Simon was near. Not that she could keep him from overhearing them. She'd learned early in her marriage that Jonathan could hear any word spoken even three or four rooms away. At the moment, she didn't mind. Simon should hear what was on her mind.

"It is obvious how much you love Oliver."

Lily's face lit up. "I adore him. I do wish you'd

seen him before now. He was the sweetest child you'd ever meet."

"He's different now, though," Alice said. The change must have been difficult for her to face, not knowing what was happening. Poor girl.

"Simon and Will say it's natural. I've never raised a boy before, Alice," Lily admitted. "But it doesn't seem natural to me. It feels as if I'm missing something."

Alice patted her hand understandingly. "Lily, what if you're right? What if there is something else going on with Oliver? Something you can't understand. What if he could never be the sweet child you raised ever again?"

Lily shuddered at the thought, and Alice clutched her hand tighter.

"I don't know how to answer that."

"Well," Alice prompted, "would you stop loving him? Would you turn away from him? Abandon him?"

Lily snatched her hand away, looking appalled at the suggestion. "Never. I love him more than life. I might not have given birth to him, Alice, but I feel as if he's my child in every other way."

Alice smiled. She was hoping Lily would say something along those lines. "No matter what?" she asked, knowing Simon hovered at the bottom of the terrace listening to every word.

Lily nodded her head, clutching her hand to her heart.

"So you are capable of unconditional love. That is good, dear. As a wife, you will need that ability. There may come a time when it is tested, and I do so hope you choose wisely."

Lily blinked at her. Obviously the girl didn't have any idea what she was talking about, though Alice was certain she'd find out soon enough. Simon couldn't keep his secret forever, and he shouldn't have to.

Twenty-Four

EARLY MORNING LIGHT POURED INTO LILY'S ROOM, and she blinked her eyes open. Why hadn't she closed the drapes the night before? She lay quietly, staring up at the pale green canopy above her.

Strange. In almost no time at all, Westfield Hall was beginning to feel like home. She supposed that was a good thing, since it was to be her home shortly.

She sighed and then swung her legs over the edge of the bed. Almost instantly, she heard a light knock at her door. It was a little early for visitors.

Lily tightened her wrapper about herself and crossed the room to the door. She opened it and was surprised to find Simon standing on the other side. Instantly, she was worried something had happened. "Is it Oliver?"

A grin broke out on his face. "No, love. It's Will. He returned in the dead of night."

Will? Her eyes widened in surprise, and Simon pushed the door wide. "I've sent word to Mr. Bostic and expect him this morning. I thought you might want help picking out your wedding dress."

As if she would trust his taste in that regard! Lily heaved a sigh. She was still getting accustomed to the idea that Will had returned. She would marry Simon today. Her life would never be the same.

Lily moved to shoo him from the room. He stood his ground. "I need to get dressed, Simon." She motioned toward the door with her hand again.

"I had thought to help you with that," he murmured, bending to kiss her cheek softly.

Lily patted her hair, smoothing the stray locks that had escaped her braid during the night. "I must look a fright."

"The only thing I find frightening is how much I want you," he said candidly, his eyes suddenly dark as night.

Lily shivered and drew her wrapper closer about her body.

"Simon," a voice called from the hallway.

"Lily, if Ben ever goes missing again, I'm going to kill him. Because if she wasn't worried about him, she never would have descended upon *me*."

Lily couldn't hold back the snicker that erupted.

"Simon!" his mother's voice called more urgently. The sound of doors opening up and down the hallway made Lily smile even more. She was obviously opening every door, looking for her son.

"Do you want to climb in the wardrobe?" she whispered.

"If I thought you might fit in there with me, I probably would." His gaze raked from her bare feet to the top of her head. The man was dangerous.

"Simon!" his mother called as her head poked

through Lily's open door. "Out!" She stepped behind him and pushed.

"You had better go," Lily warned him. His mother appeared to be perfectly serious in her intent.

"I just wanted to give Lily a gift, Mother," Simon said, planting his feet and refusing to move.

"And I can just imagine what sort of gift you want to give her, Simon," Alice said sarcastically.

Lily couldn't control her blush. She'd never met a family that discussed such things. But she had to admit they were adorable. They honestly loved one another.

"What kind of man do you think I am, Mother?" he said as he picked an invisible piece of string from his jacket.

"Oh, I know exactly what kind of man you are, Simon. Out!" She held up one finger and pointed toward the door.

Simon took a box from his pocket and gave it to his mother. "I did have good intentions. Even if I do get distracted easily around her." He winked at Lily. "I'll see you in just a bit?"

As though she would change her mind. Not a chance. He stepped across the threshold, and Alice came to stand before her. "Are you ready?"

Lily could only nod. She thought she was ready. She assumed time would tell.

"Then let's get started." Alice clapped her hands together, and servants immediately arrived carrying buckets of steaming water. They filled the tub and then left. Maids bustled through Lily's wardrobe, removing clothes, undergarments, and slippers and lining them up for the duchess' inspection.

"Into the tub, dear," Alice directed as she began to peruse the assembled dresses.

Lily stepped into the tub, and the hot water lapped against her calves. Then she sank deeper until she was almost completely covered. While one of the maids washed her hair, another scrubbed her arms and legs. Lily felt like a child. She couldn't remember the last time someone had bathed her.

Too soon, she was plucked from the water and wrapped in a robe, while a maid went to work drying her hair with one plush towel after another.

Finally dry, Lily opened her eyes to find Alice regarding her quietly. The duchess's gaze was nearly as dark as Simon's. "I have a feeling you are quite unprepared to marry my son. But I will do my best to rectify that." She held out the box Simon had passed to her. "Let's start with this, shall we?"

Lily opened the small satin box, and the air rushed out of her lungs. A translucent grey stone, oval in shape, lay inside. It was unusual in its color. Lily ran her fingers over the smooth surface, and then she lifted the stone to look at it closer.

"It's beautiful. What is it?" she whispered. She laced its delicate gold chain through her fingers. As it caught the light, the stone shimmered.

"It's moonstone," Alice answered, touching her shoulder. "It belonged to his grandmother."

Lily's heart began to pound. What a sweet gesture. Not one she would have expected from Simon.

"Now," Alice's voice broke into her thoughts, "about your dress…"

Lily turned her attention to the line of her serviceable

gowns laid out on her bed. Only one dress looked even close to what a duchess would wear. Alice ran her fingers over Lily's new green silk. "This one is very lovely."

"Thank you. Prisca Hawthorne designed it for me."

Alice smiled at that. "Such a sweet girl, and very talented." She picked the gown from the bed and handed it to Lily. "This is the one, dear."

Lily agreed. There wasn't another viable choice.

"Nervous?" Will asked, handing Simon a whisky.

"Why would I be nervous?" Simon sank down in the chair behind his mahogany desk, hoping his brother didn't notice the amber liquid tremble in his hands. He placed the tumbler on his desk. He didn't need to imbibe this early.

"I don't know," Will replied, slipping into an empty chair. "I've often heard that some men get nervous right before their freedom is sucked away."

"I'm fine," Simon barked.

Will chuckled. "Yes, fine indeed." He downed the whisky in his own glass and placed it on the edge of Simon's desk. "In all honesty, it was probably time for you to settle down anyway."

The last person who should tell him to settle down was Will. His brother had cut a larger swath through London than Simon had. "Well, then I suppose you'll be next, William."

His brother scoffed at the same time there was a scratch at the door.

"Come," Will called, apparently not wanting to discuss his turn to find a bride.

Billings peeked inside. "Your Grace, the vicar Mr. Bostic has arrived. I put him in the blue parlor."

"Excellent." Simon rose from his seat. "Is he alone, Billings?"

The butler cracked a smile. "The vicar left his wife at home, Your Grace. If that is what you are asking."

"Thank God!" Simon started for the door with Will quick on his tail. "Please inform Miss Rutledge and the duchess that we are all waiting for them, Billings."

"Yes, of course."

Simon and Will started down the corridor toward the blue parlor. When they stepped over the threshold, Simon was surprised to see that Mr. Bostic was not alone. Prisca Hawthorne also sat on the settee, talking to the vicar.

Will sucked in a breath beside him. "I thought Billings said he was alone," he grumbled, only loud enough for Simon to hear.

"No. He said the man didn't bring his wife," Simon whispered back. Then he stepped toward the vicar. "Ah, Mr. Bostic, thank you so much for coming."

"Miss Hawthorne, what a surprise," Will said, bowing over Prisca's hand.

"Indeed. I felt certain you had turned tail and left forever, William."

"Wishful thinking," Will answered.

At that moment, Lily and the duchess entered the parlor. Simon could sense Lily even though his back was to the door. He inhaled deeply, her sweet scent tantalizing his nose. If he thought about it, he would be able to taste her on his lips. He finally turned to look at her. Simon gaped at his bride. She was resplendent in her green gown, the gold sash lifting the tempting swells of her breasts for Simon's eye to feast upon. The necklace he had given her rested right above her cleavage. His mouth went dry.

Will cleared his throat and clapped a hand to Simon's back. "Time enough for that later, *mon frère*."

Simon crossed the room, took Lily's hand in his, and pressed a kiss to her gloved knuckles. Very soon, he'd strip the gloves from her hands and have her bare skin touch his. Very soon, he'd strip her of everything except for the necklace and finally sink into her. "You look beautiful, Lily."

A pretty blush stained her cheeks, and Simon couldn't keep the smile from his lips. He hooked her hand on his arm and led her to the other side of the parlor, where Mr. Bostic was waiting for them.

The vicar had them repeat their vows, though it was all a blur to Simon until he heard the words, "Your Grace, you may now kiss your bride."

Twenty-Five

LILY STILL HAD DOUBTS, RIGHT UP TO THE MOMENT he kissed her. Standing in front of the vicar, Oliver, her new mother-in-law, and Will and Prisca, Simon pulled her hard against him and pressed his lips to hers. What could have been a simple seal of their marriage wasn't simple at all. It was much more.

It was very nearly carnal in its intensity. His arms wound around her waist, his fingers splayed wide to pull her to him as his lips descended to touch hers. He wasn't gentle. He wasn't soft. He wasn't proper. He was Simon. And she reveled in his desire for her.

Lily pushed up onto her tiptoes as her arms rose to clasp his neck, her fingers touching the hair at the nape of his neck. She gasped against his lips when his hands snaked down toward her bottom.

"Your Grace…" the vicar tried to interrupt and then coughed behind his hand. A very distant part of Lily's mind heard him but paid him no heed.

And Simon obviously didn't hear him at all. The vicar didn't steal Simon's attention from her for even a moment. He continued to plunder, to assault, to worship her mouth. And she kissed him back. She forgot all the other people in the room. She forgot where she was. The only thing that was important was that she was in Simon's arms.

But then Oliver finally got her attention. "Aunt Lily?" He was the one who broke through. She pushed Simon's chest until he finally stepped back. Simon reached for her again, but she evaded his grasp.

Simon's eyes sought hers, dark and brooding. His breath heaved from him in small gasps. She laid one hand over his heart and smiled.

"Patience," she whispered, unable to keep from smiling at his bewildered expression.

She left her hand on Simon's chest even after she turned toward Oliver. Simon covered her hand with his own and pressed it to his heart.

"Congratulations, Aunt Lily," Oliver said quietly. He tilted his head and smiled slowly at her. Despite his growth over the past few months and his surliness, he *still* was the little boy she'd raised.

Lily hugged him close with her free arm, as Simon refused to relinquish the other. She was about to let Oliver go but stopped when he whispered, "Be careful, Aunt Lily."

Lily looked over at Simon, who'd obviously heard the comment, if the scowl on his face was any indication.

"Oliver," he warned, his eyebrows scrunching together in frustration.

Oliver turned and walked away.

Lily cast a questioning glance at Simon. "What was that about?"

Simon slid closer and wrapped his arm around her waist. The boy was a menace. He would have to talk to him. Again. He was obviously scared Simon would devour Lily whole when he took her to bed. He had to admit he'd planned to do a little of that, but not the way Oliver was afraid of.

"Just boy stuff," Simon said as he looked down at her. "I'll talk to him. Tomorrow."

"All right." Lily snuggled deeper into his side. He loved the way she fit him, her curves matching up with his body. Her height was a blessing. Her slender form his curse. All he wanted to do was strip her right there. But he imagined that he would offend his guests if he ripped her clothes from her body, pushed her against the wall, and surged into her. He grew hard at the thought.

Simon pulled Lily to stand in front of him, his arms sliding around her waist. "How long until we can retire?" he whispered to her.

She shrugged and smiled at him over her shoulder. "I think I heard your mother say she had a day full of events planned for everyone." Her eyes twinkled with mirth.

"Even my mother isn't tenacious enough to keep me from you now that you're mine." He brushed a loose curl from her shoulder and kissed it quickly. He couldn't wait to get her to his room so he could remove the pins from her hair and run his fingers through it.

"Yours?" she asked quietly.

"All mine," he said, his voice rough with emotion.

"Not yet, Simon," his mother broke in. "You will endure a celebratory breakfast before you cart her away."

Simon simply sighed when Lily followed his mother into the breakfast room. All he could do was follow like a faithful puppy chasing her skirts.

The sway of her hips had his total attention until Will clapped him on the shoulder. "Congratulations, Simon. I hope the two of you will be very happy together."

"If I can ever get her alone, I'm sure we will be," Simon growled. Will simply laughed. Simon was caught in a lustful hell, and Will could only tease him. Oliver glared at him from across the room.

"What's wrong with Maberley? Do you know?" Simon asked.

"He's still worried about Lily," Will said, coloring slightly.

There was no reason for him to worry. Simon would never harm her. He'd sever his own arm first. "Damn you for giving him those books!"

Will shrugged. "There's a lot of information in them that he should know."

"But not about the claiming, you fool." Simon hit his forehead with the heel of his hand. "That's what's wrong with him. He thinks I'll devour her on sight."

Just the thought of claiming Lily made his blood run hot. He watched her as she talked with his mother. She lifted a spoon to her mouth, and her full, pink lips slid off the end of it. He wished it was him. That her lips were on him at that moment.

"I'll talk to Oliver again," Will sighed.

"I'll never be able to claim Lily, so you can assure the boy she's safe."

Will's eyes narrowed. "*Never* claim her?"

"Oh, I'll have her. But never when the moon is full. Never when I might be out of control. Never when there's a chance I could hurt her." Simon fought a bit of melancholy at the thought of it. But then the spoon slid from between her lips again. She smiled at him.

Simon had to adjust his trousers. One more look from her, and he would cross the room, pick her up, and carry her upstairs. Then she pressed her fingertips against her lips, kissed them, and blew a soft kiss to him. He was immediately lost.

Twenty-Six

LILY HAD NO IDEA WHAT MADE HER DO THAT, WHAT made her blow a kiss to him from across the table. But he looked so serious as he sat there with Will. His forehead was marred by lines of worry, and his body was tense, his movements terse and choppy.

She simply wanted to soothe him. But what she didn't expect was for him to slide his chair back with a scrape against the hardwood floors, the noise of which was loud enough to make every head turn. He strode quickly across the room and stopped at her side.

"Lily," he said softly, as though something pained him. He took her hand in his and pulled her to her feet. And before she knew it, he'd scooped her up and was striding out of the breakfast room.

"Simon, put me down," she squealed as he started up the steps, taking them two at a time. "This is highly improper."

"Then I get to be your improper husband, and you'll just have to be my improper wife, won't you?" He smiled wolfishly at her, his eyebrows wagging at his own joke.

He strode through the door of his bedchamber, and she expected him to place her on her feet. But he didn't. He unceremoniously tossed her into the middle of the bed, where she hit so hard that she bounced.

"Simon!" she shrieked a she reached out to steady herself. But he was lost in his chores. He closed the curtains, nearly drenching the room in total darkness. Then he turned and lit a candle, which cast soft shadows about the room.

The bed dipped under his weight as he sat down and began to remove his boots.

"What are you doing, Simon?" she asked.

He finally turned toward her. "I have every intention of making love to my wife," he said slowly, his eyes dancing from the top of her head to the soles of her slippers. "Unless you have an objection?"

"None," she squeaked, cringing when she heard the sound of her own voice. "None," she repeated with more conviction. "But you'll have to show me what to do. Because I fear I may be really bad at it." She swallowed hard.

"Not possible," he breathed, before his lips claimed hers.

His touch didn't start out rough, but it certainly wasn't soft. His lips slid across hers, pressing hard enough to steal the air from her lungs. His hands stole into her hair, pulling the pins out one by one until her auburn locks fell freely about her shoulders.

His fingers threaded into the hair around her temples as he consumed her. She tried to pull back, but he growled against her lips and held her tighter. She whimpered when his teeth nipped her lip a bit too hard.

The sound of her whimper brought Simon back to his senses. For a moment, he'd allowed his basic instincts to take control. But Lily was an innocent. He pressed his forehead into hers and drew in great gulps of air.

"I'm sorry," he breathed.

Her only answer was her hand sliding across his jaw to cup his face and bring his lips back to hers. Tentatively, she kissed him, testing his control. Her eyes were wide open, staring into his own.

He pressed softly back against her, his tongue sliding between her lips to caress hers. This time she moaned. He must be doing better.

Simon sat back and said, "I think you have entirely too many clothes on, Your Grace." He picked up her foot and slid her slipper off, the tips of his fingers dancing across the sensitive skin of the bottom of her foot. She giggled.

He couldn't help but smile. Laughter wasn't the sound he'd hoped for when he thought about bringing her to bed, but it beat the fear that had escaped her moments before. He repeated the motion with her other foot. She tried to tug her leg from his grasp. He held firm.

"No pulling away," he reminded her.

She simply nodded, a smile hovering around her lips.

Simon walked up the bed on his hands and knees until he was behind her. His hands moved to unlace her dress. As he exposed her shoulder, he replaced the fabric with his mouth. Her freckles were illuminated by the candlelight, and he planned to kiss each and every one before the day and night were over.

He smiled against her skin, his fingers still working at her laces.

"What's funny?" she asked quietly, reaching back to touch his hair.

"Nothing," he murmured. "I'm just happy."

"Really?"

"You doubt it?" he asked as he moved in front of her. She clutched her sagging gown to her chest.

"I know you didn't *want* to marry me, but I'll try to make you happy."

"You already do," he said as he pushed her back to lie on the bed. She gasped as he pulled her hands from her bodice and tugged to expose her breasts. "So beautiful," he murmured, his gaze traveling over her flesh. To have her breasts exposed tested his control. But he reined the beast back, determined not to scare her, no matter how aroused he was.

His erection strained against his trousers, aching to be free. But not yet. Not until she was ready.

Simon tugged her gown down over her hips. Lily lifted to help him pull it from her body. The ribbon that tied her undergarments hissed as he tugged the knot free, allowing him to pull them from her in one swoop.

Lily moved to cover her breasts, her face coloring under his gaze. But he captured her hands, laced his fingers with hers, and pressed them to the bed beside her head as he leaned over her, sliding one knee between her thighs. She instinctually adjusted to make room for him.

"Mine," he growled as he took a hard peak into his mouth. Lily gasped beneath him, arching to meet his mouth. Her hands moved under his, her fingers opening and closing, as he toyed with her, his tongue flicking out to tease the turgid flesh of her nipple.

Her heart beat heavily beneath him, thumping faster and louder as he moved from breast to breast.

Her fingers opened and closed again. "Let me touch you, Simon," she said softly, her voice catching as his mouth lifted from her nipple with a pop.

His hands released hers, and she immediately brought them to his shirtfront to loosen his cravat and then to unbutton the tiny buttons at his throat. Her delicate little hands tugged frantically at his shirt, yanking it from his trousers. She wasn't happy until they were flesh to flesh, man to woman, beast to beauty. Only then did she sigh with contentment.

This was how he wanted her always. Her face flushed with heat. Her body warm and pliant beneath him. Simon adjusted his body so he could remove his pants and then settled himself, entirely naked, in the cradle of her thighs.

"Please," she whispered.

৩৯

Lily could feel the length of him between her thighs, touching her center but not entering her, not even pressing against her. He was content to lie there, to torment her. His breath brushed heavily against the side of her face as he asked, "Please what?"

He smiled when she arched against him. She didn't know what. She just knew she needed. She needed him.

His hand moved between her thighs, one finger swiping across her heat. She couldn't keep from crying out. Her center throbbed, like a fire waiting to be stoked. Like a pot that simmered, just before the steam.

"So wet," he breathed against her ear. She closed her eyes tightly, and he stopped the movement of his hand.

"What's wrong?" she nearly begged. Surely he wouldn't stop now. Surely he would ease this torment.

"Open your eyes," he said. She did, only to find his eyes, dark as night, staring into her own. "Know that it is me who takes you."

Lily's hand trailed down his chest, her nails raking his belly as she reached lower. And lower still. She took the heat of him in her hand and pressed him to her center. She rocked against him, but he didn't move. He didn't answer her thrusts. He simply looked at her. He watched her torment.

Lily wrapped her legs around him, her heels at his buttocks, pressing them insistently to pull him into her. And finally he did. He entered her slowly, inch by inch.

His arms shook on each side of her as he held himself above her, slowly sliding farther and farther inside. There was a moment of discomfort as he pressed forward. He slowed and kissed her eyelids, pulsing inside her. She bumped his buttocks with her heels again, and he pressed forward, seating himself fully inside her.

"I am inside you," he said softly.

"I know," she gasped out as he began to slowly withdraw. "No!" she cried. But he quickly surged back into her. He set a rhythm as old as time, moving in and out of her in quick strokes. Grasping her hips, he tilted her and went farther. He consumed every inch of space inside her and still asked for more. She graciously gave it.

He stoked the fire within her, taking her up and over the place where he'd taken her in the garden, making this oh-so-much-better simply because he shared it with her.

When she finally erupted, she called his name. He pressed his face into her neck, his arms sliding under her, holding her closer than she'd have ever thought possible, and then he joined her.

Twenty-Seven

LILY STIRRED IN HIS ARMS, AND SIMON PULLED HER closer to him. With her eyes closed, she gently kissed his chest and then tried, once more, to pull away from him. "Stay where you are," he ordered softly, intertwining one of his legs with hers.

"Simon," she giggled against his chest. "Shouldn't we return to the others?"

He rolled her onto her back and pressed his lips to hers. "We could just stay here forever."

"We could," she agreed, grinning at him. Lily's gaze drifted across his naked torso and stopped. Her eyebrows drew together. She lifted one finger to touch a mark below his shoulder.

"What's that?" she asked.

"Birthmark," he said quietly as he nuzzled her neck.

"Oliver has one that's similar."

"As do Will and Ben, and even Daniel had one. Family trait." He lifted his head to look into her eyes. "Does it bother you?"

"Why would it bother me?" She looked puzzled. Then she did the unthinkable and lifted her face to press her lips to the moon-shaped mark. "I think it's quite handsome."

The warmth of her lips pressed against the very thing that marked him as a beast made him pause. Simon closed his eyes tightly and savored the moment. Never before had he felt so accepted.

"I believe Oliver's is on his thigh."

"Then he will be a very lucky man the day he finds a woman to kiss it, won't he?" Simon laughed.

"Oh, Simon," she punched his shoulder. "We should get up," she sighed, a contented smile hovering about her lips.

"You'd like to see about Oliver?"

Her smile vanished. "He seemed worried, didn't he?"

"Just overprotective," Simon growled. *Irritating little pup.*

Lily cupped his face. "No reason for that."

None that she knew about anyway. "Don't be so sure, love. I can be quite dangerous."

She giggled again. "You're not frightening in the least. I think that persona you wear like a cloak is all for show."

Simon nuzzled her neck. "Naïve wench." She was so soft and pliant beneath him, and he could easily take her again. He longed to do so, but it was too soon.

Lily caressed his back, and Simon groaned, not yet wanting this to end. But the time had come. He lifted his head and dropped a very chaste kiss on her cheek. "Get dressed, Lily, and go see about Oliver."

He slid from the bed and ran his fingers over her naked form. She was a vision, her hair tousled, her hazel eyes darkened with passion, her lips swollen from his kisses. God willing, he'd see this same vision every day of his life… with, of course, a few exceptions.

He picked up her rumpled green dress and inhaled her sweet floral scent. "I should take you to London with me."

"London?" she asked with a frown, sitting up and clasping the counterpane to her breasts.

"Yes, London," he replied. Why wouldn't she want to go to Town? "Do you not like it there?"

Lily shrugged. "I've not been that many times, Simon. But after…" her voice trailed off, and she looked away from him.

Concerned, Simon sat on the edge of the bed and brushed his hand down her bare back. "What is it, love?"

She worried her bottom lip and then tentatively turned to face him. "All the columns about your exploits… Well, I just thought we might stay in Hampshire for a while."

Simon bit back a smile. She was worried he'd return to his debauched haunts and forget her. That wasn't even a possibility. The only woman he wanted was her. The only entertainment he sought was her. He had no need of anyone else. Though he didn't know how to convince her of the fact. "Lily, I only thought I'd take you to Town so we could enjoy it together."

Her innocent frown lightened only incrementally.

He dipped his head and touched his lips to hers. "Let me show you off, Lily. Let me shower you with gifts. Let me order you an entirely new wardrobe. Let me drape you in jewels…"

Lily's hand moved to the delicate chain around her neck. "Thank you for the necklace, Simon. It is beautiful."

"Will you let me give you more?"

Again, she innocently bit her lip. "I don't need anything."

Simon's smile widened, and he pushed her back to the mattress, hovering over her. "Of course you don't *need* anything. That's why it's fun."

"Do you really want to show me off?"

Simon nodded his head and tugged the counterpane from her hands, once again baring her breasts. "But this is all for me," he murmured before closing his mouth around one peaked nipple.

∽∾

Will closed the door to Simon's study and sat down across from Oliver. The boy had frowned the entire day thus far. In fact, when Simon kissed Lily after the ceremony, Will had been forced to keep his arm on the lad, as Oliver nearly charged Simon at that point. Perhaps, Will thought belatedly, he should have waited a while before giving the boy his books on Lycan lore. Of course, at the time, he hadn't thought Simon would marry Lily. At the time, he hadn't thought Simon would ever marry anyone.

"Maberley," he began in his most stern voice. "You are out of your league. If you'd like to keep your tail, you'll take a step away from Simon. He isn't going to put up with your insolence for much longer."

The boy's nostrils flared. "But Aunt Lily—"

"Is his wife. And there's not a thing you can do about it." Certainly not now. The marriage had been well and thoroughly consummated, Will had no doubt.

Oliver slumped back in his seat, folding his arms across his chest. Anger rolled off him in waves. "I can protect her from him."

Lily was a saint to have raised this child. She must have the patience of Job, which she could probably use in her role as Simon's duchess. Will sighed, rubbing his brow. "She is his territory, Maberley, and you *will* respect that."

The young earl snorted.

Will narrowed his eyes. "I'm trying to help you, but if you keep up this unwarranted animosity toward Simon, no one will be able to help you."

Oliver glowered back at him. "May I be excused now?"

Will nodded. "Remember what I said."

"How could I forget?" Oliver grumbled as he stormed out of the study.

Will let his head fall backward, and he looked up at the ceiling, vowing to himself never to father a child. He hadn't realized what a trial they could be. Of course, he never spent any time with boys Oliver's age either.

"Your mother is worried about Benjamin," Prisca's melodic voice said from the doorway.

Will instantly rose from his seat at her presence. For some reason, God had cursed him. Every time he saw Prisca, she was more beautiful than the time before. He schooled his features to reveal nothing of his inner torment. "The dolt has apparently been sending

Mother multiple letters every week. Then when he holes himself up," *probably with some buxom widow*, "and doesn't send word, he gets her all upset."

"It is strange," Prisca said, stepping further into the study. "Benjamin is such a regular correspondent. Her Grace says he was going to take a sojourn to Scotland, but none of the letters he sent me mentioned the trip."

Will's blood began to boil. He must have misheard her. "Are you saying *Ben* has been writing you?" He hoped he'd managed to keep the jealousy out of his voice.

"Why shouldn't he?" Prisca clasped her hands behind her back, raising her tempting breasts for Will's perusal. Did she do that intentionally? He believed in his heart that she did such things simply to torture him. "*Ben* has never forgotten me."

"For the love of God, Prissy, I did not forget you."

Her violet eyes pierced him, and he felt it in the depths of his soul. "Then that's worse." She took a steadying breath, never looking away from him. "I won't have this argument again, William. There's no point to it. That's not why I wanted to talk to you anyway."

"What then?" he whispered.

Prisca took a step away from him and began to pace a path in the study. "I find myself worried about Benjamin. I'd talk to Blackmoor, but I believe he'll be occupied with Lily, at least for the next little while. But you…"

"But I what?" he asked, knowing full well what she wanted of him. She wanted him to travel to Scotland, to yank Ben out of whosever bed he was in, and

march him back to Hampshire, so she could see he was
safe. And, fool that he was, Will was considering it just
to see Prissy smile in his direction again.

She stopped mid-pace. "He *is* your brother, William.
Aren't you the least concerned?"

He had been a bit concerned, but only a bit, right
up until he realized his younger brother had been
carrying on a correspondence with Prisca for God
knows how long. Now he'd like to get his hands
around Ben's neck. Disloyal mutt! "Ben is a grown
man. He can take care of himself."

"But what if something's happened to him? It's not
like him not to write at all."

Will's vision turned nearly black. Ben had better
stay hidden for a very long time, if he knew what was
good for him. What was he doing writing to Prissy?

She walked toward him, and, with each step she
took, Will's heart pounded faster. Prisca laid her hand
on his chest, tilting her head back to look at him.
Will's fingers twitched, aching to touch her again.

"Please," she whispered.

Will tightly closed his eyes before opening them
again. He was still a bloody fool where she was
concerned. He stepped away from her, not able to look
upon her any longer. Then he strode out of the library
and down the corridor toward the terrace doors.

Billings stopped him before he could make his
escape. "Lord William, are you all right? You don't
quite look yourself."

Will didn't quite feel like himself either. "Tell His
Grace that I've gone to Scotland."

The butler quickly masked his surprise. "Scotland?"

Will nodded tightly. Then he strode out the doors and down the path to the stables before he had the chance to come to his senses. When he found his younger brother, there was a very good possibility that he'd strangle him.

Twenty-Eight

"Billings!" Lily called loudly from Oliver's room.

Simon was already in pursuit of her when he heard her call. He stepped into the room and immediately knew something was amiss. She paced from one side of the room to the other, chewing on her fingernails. Simon crossed the room and plucked her hand from her mouth, then kissed the back of her knuckles.

"What's wrong, love?" he asked, his hand trailing up and down her arm in an attempt to comfort her. What he really wanted to do was drag her back to bed.

"Simon, Oliver's g-gone," she said. A tear pooled over her lashes and fell onto her cheek.

"I'm sure he's here somewhere," Simon said as he wiped the tear away with the pad of his thumb. "Don't fret."

Lily thrust a piece of foolscap into his hand. "No, Simon," she nearly wailed. "He's *gone*."

He took the paper from her hand and read it.

Dear Aunt Lily,

   Please do not be mad at me. I hate that you married the duke, but there is nothing I can do about that. Though I do not have to stay at Westfield Hall and watch your unholy union. Please be careful. If you ever got hurt, it would kill me. I love you so much.

                     Oliver

It was all Simon could do to keep from baring his teeth. The little bugger had turned tail and run. And had the nerve to try one of the oldest tricks in the book. Guilt.

Lily took the paper back from him and asked, "What does he mean by all that, Simon? What does he think is going to happen? Why on earth would he be so distrustful of you? He barely knows you."

Lily resumed her pacing. Simon scratched his jaw and wondered what the best way to answer would be. *Because he's afraid I'll forget how to treat you in a fit of lust and claim you as a Lycan mate*, he almost said. No. He couldn't say that.

The boy did know how to ruin a perfect day. He'd had Lily under him and planned to do it again before the day was over, but now she was worried about her nephew. She wouldn't stop pacing long enough to look at him, much less let him have his way with her.

Lily wore torment on her face like an uncomfortable mask. "You'll wear a hole in the floor if you keep that up," he said, attempting to lighten the situation.

"Do be quiet, Simon," she snapped, never ceasing her back-and-forth movements across the room. He had to admit he liked the fact she wasn't afraid to stand up to him. She had a strength he would never have expected.

Simon held up his hands in mock surrender.

"Where do you suspect he's gone?" Lily asked, her voice only showing a tiny bit of whininess.

The boy had only lived one place in his whole life. "My guess would be Maberley Hall," Simon answered.

"But that's so far away, and he's all alone!" Lily cried, her voice finally cracking under the strain.

"Don't worry, love. We'll find him," he assured her. And then he was going to kill the troublesome little wolf.

Luckily, Lily let him wrap his arms around her for comfort. Simon held her close, silently vowing to find the young pup and give him a tongue-lashing he would never forget for upsetting his aunt. "We'll go talk to Dorn and see what he knows."

Lily sniffed and then nodded her head in agreement.

Simon led his bride to the stables, where he grilled the head groom about Oliver's whereabouts.

The color seeping from his face, Dorn looked shocked to learn the young earl had run off. "Honestly, Your Graces, if I'd known 'e was gonna do somethin' like that, I'd've never saddled Erebus for him. I thought he was just goin' for a ride around the property."

Erebus! Simon winced. The gelding was one of the wildest in his stables. He'd like to berate the groom on the spot for giving the unruly beast to the boy, but he didn't want to alert Lily to the danger. She was worried enough as it was.

"How long ago did he leave, Dorn?"

The groom shuffled his feet, looking at the ground. "A couple o' hours. I was just startin' to get worried about the lad."

Simon made a note to have a long conversation with Dorn once he returned to Westfield Hall. In the meantime, he gestured toward the main road. "Prepare Abbadon," he commanded.

The groom nodded at the same time Lily called after him, "And a mount for me as well."

Simon's eyes shot toward his wife, and he shook his head. "Lily love, I'll find the lad and bring him home."

She furrowed her pretty brow. "I have to be there, Simon. I have to know why he would do this."

"And those questions will be answered when I return with Maberley." He had a few things to say to the young pup first, things Lily didn't need to hear.

With a stubborn tilt of her head, Lily glared at him, her hazel eyes boring angry little holes into his skin. "Simon Westfield, I am going. And don't you even think about keeping me from it."

Simon heaved a sigh. At least he could use a coach ride to his advantage. Having Lily beneath him instead of Abbadon did have its merit. "All right, love. Dorn, ready the carriage instead."

Lily's frown deepened. "We can go faster on horseback."

Simon returned her scowl. He wasn't accustomed to someone challenging his every edict, and he didn't enjoy that one bit. "Lily, I am allowing you to go with me, but you'll follow my direction. I believe this very day you vowed to do that exact thing."

A blush pinkened her cheeks at his words, and, for a moment, Simon felt like a cad. But only for a moment.

Once they were under way, Simon put his arm around Lily's shoulders and pulled her to him. She sat stiffly against him, unyielding in her anger. Even the gentle rocking of the coach didn't relax her into his side.

He brushed a lock of hair from the side of her face. "You're beautiful even when you pout, you know?" he taunted her. She rose to the bait, as he'd expected. If there was one thing he was learning about Lily, it was that she didn't back down from a fight.

"I am *not* pouting," she said, following the comment with a harrumph noise. She crossed her arms beneath her breasts. That only served to push them up where he could better see them. Simon found that he rather liked the display.

"Oh, yes, you are pouting," he said quietly, his lips touching her cheek briefly. He would tease her out of this mood if it was the last thing he ever did. "But I think it's quite attractive."

"I can't *believe* he let Oliver take off for God-only-knows where. He's *twelve*, Simon. Twelve!" She scooted out from under his arm and across the seat to stare out the coach window.

"Believe me, love, when we return to Westfield Hall, Dorn and I will have a long chat. In the man's defense, he had no reason to think Oliver would bolt."

She sniffed and turned her attention to stare out the window.

"With luck, we'll find him before he even reaches

Essex," Simon reminded her. Then she would have Oliver back clinging to her skirts, which was exactly where *he* wanted to be, except he preferred to be under them.

"I just don't understand why he thinks so poorly of you. Is there something I don't understand? Did you hurt him in the breakfast room the other day? Or in one of your heated exchanges?"

Not in the slightest. Oliver was just as tough as any other Lycan. The boy wasn't even afraid of him.

Simon frowned. He didn't need Lily to distrust him. "If anyone should be angry, Lily, it's me," he said, changing tactics.

She gasped and swung her gaze to him. "And what reason, please tell me, could *you* possibly have for being angry?"

"Don't you think the fact that my wife is sitting as far from me as she possibly can is enough? I hadn't planned to spend my wedding night in exile. I had planned to spend it wrapped up... in... you."

She flushed at his comment, just as he'd hoped. Having her once wasn't nearly enough.

Yet she still put her nose in the air and turned back to the window. If that pup ruined his chances of staying in Lily's good graces, he would make him sleep with the hounds.

❧

Lily watched the Hampshire countryside pass by her window. With the way Simon was looking at her, it was really quite difficult to stay angry with him. He settled deeper into his seat and looked at her, his eyes half-closed. Lily's heart jumped when he licked his lips.

"Come here," he said quietly.

Oh, dear.

"No," she answered, fully aware that her voice cracked. She hated her traitorous reflexes for responding to him.

"I didn't *ask* you." He crooked a finger at her. "Come here."

With a conscious effort, she turned to look out the window again. But then she felt the brush of his hand against the side of her breast. She closed her eyes and sighed, unable to deny how pleasurable the sensation was.

"Your body wants me," he taunted her.

"Well, of course it does," she sighed.

"Yet you want to deny it."

"Yes, I do." She very nearly caught a smile erupting. But pushed it back.

"I think I'll let you sit there and simmer," he said as he placed his hands in his lap.

She immediately felt the loss. She narrowed her eyes at him. "Why would you do that?"

"Because I'm going to wait. Until you ask me for it." He smiled a greedy little smile. "Or until we reach the next coaching inn. Whichever comes first."

Twenty-Nine

LILY COULD BARELY WAIT FOR THE NEXT COACHING inn. She felt like a violin that had been strung too tightly. She had been worried that Oliver was in danger nearly the entire day. But now she was worried that she would simply erupt if Simon didn't touch her some time soon. When he'd said "come here," she'd nearly climbed into his lap and begged him to take her.

But she wasn't willing to concede quite so quickly. She wanted to know what he was hiding from her. Something was going on between him and Oliver. She knew it.

When they finally stopped, Simon jumped from the coach and held out his hand to her. He showed an abnormal level of detachment when he simply took her hand in his, rather than taking her hand and caressing it or teasing her unmercifully as she'd become accustomed.

"Something bothering you?" she asked him as they stepped toward the inn. Perhaps he was feeling guilty for keeping her in the dark.

He simply smiled politely. "Not a thing. You?" He didn't allow his gaze to stroll up and down her body. Nor did he stroke her with the timbre of his voice, the way he normally did. He put a hand at her back to guide her through the door. But that was where his familiarity ended.

As soon as they turned the corner into the taproom, Lily heard the squeal. It was an unexpected noise, the noise of a child opening presents on her birthday. Yet it came from a woman who was obviously more than a child. Flaxen curls framed her lovely face. Cherubic cheeks rested under the bluest eyes Lily had even seen. The woman was curvy and wore a sinful smile.

Simon stepped away from Lily and toward the woman, who raised her hand to place it in his. He smoothly lifted it to his lips. Lily could not believe he actually kissed that woman's skin.

She fought the red haze that clouded her vision. She stepped closer to Simon and touched his arm. "Introduce me to your friend, dear," she said, smiling sweetly, though anger rolled through her in waves.

The woman looked at Simon as though he was her own personal savior.

"Lily, this is Mrs. Hamilton." The woman looked up and down Lily's frame and obviously found it lacking, as she scrunched up her nose in distaste.

Of course, Mrs. Hamilton was petite with large breasts and a pixy nose. She was every man's dream, everything Lily was not.

Mrs. Hamilton, Mrs. Hamilton. Lily wracked her memory trying to recall where she'd heard the woman's name. Then it hit her, and she nearly fell to the floor as she realized Mrs. Hamilton was the not-so-discreet widow Simon had been linked to in the *Mayfair Society Paper*. Her husband hadn't even been gone a month before she started catching the attention of every gossip in London with her scandalous affair with the even more scandalous Duke of Blackmoor.

Mrs. Hamilton had the nerve to touch Simon before she asked, "And who is this, Your Grace? Your sister?"

❧

Teresa Hamilton knew perfectly well that he had no sister. The randy widow knew much more about him than that, including the fact that he had a mole on his inner right thigh and a scar on the inside of his left arm. But Simon could see his former paramour's desire to hurt Lily brewing behind her infinite charm. He'd never thought of Teresa as catty before.

"Mrs. Hamilton, this is my wife—Her Grace, the Duchess of Blackmoor," he said, feeling an overwhelming need to protect his darling Lily.

The color drained from Teresa's face. Perhaps, Simon thought, he should have lessened the blow somehow. Teresa had angled for the position herself, after all. He smiled, trying to lighten the mood. "What brings you to Hampshire, Teresa?"

The buxom blond pulled her eyes away from Lily to stare daggers at him instead. "I was headed to Westfield Hall at *your* invitation, Simon."

Oh. He'd forgotten that he'd asked Teresa to visit him. After Lily stormed into his life, everything that happened before her seemed to vanish from his mind.

Simon wondered what else he'd failed to remember in the last fortnight.

Lily's nails dug into the skin on his forearm, where she still held onto him, bringing his attention back to her. She was definitely going to leave a mark. Thank goodness he healed quickly.

Simon pried Lily's fingers from his arm. "Love, give me a minute, will you?"

Her hazel eyes glared at him, and he had a sinking suspicion that his wedding night was going from bad to worse. Still, it wouldn't do to have Lily overhear his conversation with Teresa. It couldn't get any worse than that. "Lily?" he patiently asked again.

His irritated wife took a staggering breath, then quietly turned on her heel and stormed back out to the coaching yard. That did not bode well for him. He'd never known Lily not to say anything.

Simon shook his head. He'd have to buy her something nice to make up for it. In the meantime, dealing with Teresa was a necessity. He gestured to a small wooden table on the other side of the taproom. "Ale?" he asked her. Teresa was always more accommodating after she had a few drinks.

Teresa shook her head.

Well, it had been worth a try. Simon started toward the table himself and waited for her to follow him. It only took a second for her to fall in a half-step behind.

"Since when do you have a wife?" she hissed.

Simon held out a chair for her and waited until she sat. Then he walked to the other side of the table and sank into a seat across from her, so he could keep an eye on the door. "Since today," he informed her. "I should have sent word, Teresa. I am sorry."

Her pretty mouth fell open. "Sorry! Simon, I'm just a few hours away from reaching your doorstep. How would that have looked?"

Rather bad, he thought with a sigh. "I forgot you were coming, Teresa."

Apparently that was the wrong thing to say, as her spine straightened and she pinned him with a furious glare. "How very charming."

"I just mean that life has been rather complicated since Lily and…"

"Oh?" Her voice raised an octave. "Do tell, Your Grace," she sneered. "As you were in my bed the night before you left London, I am dying to hear about Lily. Why did you never mention her? You led me to believe that I—"

Simon held up his hand to stop her onslaught. "I never did."

"You said you wouldn't ever marry," she spat the words at him.

He had said that. Many times over. Though it never stopped her from trying to wriggle a proposal out of him in the most intimate of moments. "And you never believed me."

She slid her seat back from the table, scraping it along the floor. "And all this time you had that… that… Lily," she fumed.

Simon winced. This really could be going better. "Teresa, it wasn't like that. What we had together was quite enjoyable and—"

"What we *had* together." Teresa leaned forward, giving him quite the view of her charms. Reflexively, his gaze lowered to her cleavage, though he was surprised to find it didn't have the effect it used to. "I hope you don't mean it's over. Is that what you're trying to say, Simon?"

Yes, but apparently he was doing a very poor job of it. "Teresa, I'm married now."

"And *I* was married when you seduced me. So I don't see what that has to do with anything."

Teresa had a point. She had been well and truly married to her husband when he'd invited her to visit with him. But she'd readily accepted. He hadn't even had to work to sway her decision. That conquest was easily won.

At that moment, Lily re-entered the taproom, and Simon leapt back to his feet. "It has everything to do with everything, Teresa. We need to keep our distance."

"Distance?" she whispered vehemently. Her eyes narrowed on him. She smiled a vindictive little smile, which should have been his first clue that she was up to no good. She held out her hand to him. As he clasped her fingers in his, he felt the hard, cold metal of her room key pressed into his palm. He nearly hung his head in defeat.

On the other side of the room, Lily folded her arms across her chest. There was no easy way to return the key to Teresa without Lily noticing.

"I had planned to stay the night and come to you tomorrow," Teresa said quietly. "But you're a smart man. You can find a way to come to me," she breathed, before she turned on her heel and walked away.

Simon swallowed hard and pocketed the key, unsure how he was going to explain any of this to his wife, and still he had to find that irritant Oliver. He started toward the innkeeper. Before he and Lily returned to his coach, they needed sustenance.

෴

The door to their private dining room closed, and Lily stared across the room at her husband. For the first time ever, he looked a bit nervous.

Simon shrugged out of his coat and draped it over a nearby chair. Lily allowed him to pull her seat out before she dropped daintily into it, and he sat across from her.

"Lily, I can explain," he started, as he closed his eyes and rubbed his forehead, his elbows resting on the table between them.

"Explain what, Simon?" She lifted her wine glass to her mouth and took a sip. She fought for control. And lost.

Simon began to speak, but she cut him off. "Explain how you married me when you already had a woman traveling from London to come and spend time with you. Alone. It's fairly obvious what kind of relationship you had."

"That was before," he started.

Lily fought the urge to bury her head in her hands and cry. Instead, she allowed the anger that roiled just below the surface to overflow. She stood up to face him. He rose from his seat quickly as she approached. Even with her height, he still towered above her.

"I never *asked* to be married," she said quietly, tilting her head back to look into his eyes. She poked her finger into his chest. "I never *asked* to be ruined," she continued, jabbing once again with her finger, her voice rising in anger.

He reached to take her hand, but she jerked it from his grasp.

"I never *asked* for you to make love to me," her voice cracked on those last few words, and she turned away from him to wipe the tear that fell down her cheek.

"Lily," he said.

She spun quickly to face him. "Don't 'Lily' me, Simon. The only thing I asked was for you to help me with Oliver. And that's the only thing I didn't get." She began to tick items off on her fingers. "I was ruined. I was forced to marry. I was made love to." That one was certainly a lie. "But, in all of that, I never did get the one thing I wanted. And *that* was help for *Oliver*," she said again.

Lily turned her back on him. He pressed a hand to her shoulder. She shrugged him off. "Perhaps you should ask for the carriage to be prepared. I am ready to leave."

Without a word, he turned and stepped out of the dining room. The door closed quietly behind him.

Then, and only then, did she allow herself to collapse. She sank into his chair and dropped her head in her hands. She was much too proud to sob, but she did brush a tear or two from her face.

Lily berated herself for falling so completely and totally under his spell. He had never really guaranteed faithfulness. So, wishing he would be loyal was her first mistake. The second mistake was falling in love with him, when it was so obvious he didn't return the sentiment. Lily reached into Simon's pocket and tugged the handkerchief she knew he'd have there. She flipped it open to wipe her nose and try to compose herself before he returned.

But when she opened the piece of fabric, a metallic clank sounded against the wooden floor. Lily looked down to find a metal key. She picked it up and turned it over in her hand. They hadn't planned to stay the night. Why would he have a key? Then it hit her. Teresa Hamilton? Simon wouldn't dare. Would he?

Thirty

SIMON TOOK THE STAIRS TWO AT A TIME. HE'D ALREADY informed his coachman that they needed to depart sooner than planned. But he needed to take care of one more task before they could leave. He had to tell Teresa that he was well and truly married, and quite happy at that. Lily was all he wanted, and he couldn't imagine that changing any time soon.

When Lily had nearly cried in front of him, all he'd wanted to do was sweep her into his arms and hold her close to him while he soothed away all of her worries. But he needed to dispense with Teresa before he could do that.

Simon knocked softly on Teresa's door. He turned the knob and stepped inside when she called, "Come in." Unfortunately, he didn't realize until he'd already stepped through the door that she was in a state of undress. She stood beside the bed wearing nothing more than a silk nightrail. He'd seen it before. He'd even bought it for her.

It was bright red with black lace, and it hugged every curve of her body. Her breasts threatened to tumble from the top. The slit up the thigh showed a good portion of her leg. Simon turned his head away quickly.

"Teresa, we need to talk," he started, still looking away from her body.

"I knew you wouldn't be able to stay away for long," she said. Simon couldn't fathom how her voice had once delighted him. Now it reminded him of a screeching crow.

"Actually, that's not why I'm here," he tried to begin again.

"Did you put your mousy little wife to bed?" she asked, tossing her hair over her shoulder.

"Lily's not mousy," he shot back, instantly feeling the need to defend her. He'd never had that urge before. "Actually, she's quite fabulous." He couldn't contain the small smile that erupted.

Teresa sat down on the edge of the bed. She raised one knee to the side, in a pose that he'd seen more than once. While it appeared to be one of mere comfort, he knew she had practiced it with more men than just him. She raised her arms above her head to fluff her hair, outlining her breasts. He instantly felt pity for her, because she couldn't compare to his Lily. She didn't stir him in the least.

"I am quite devoted, and plan to stay devoted, to my wife," he began. She stood up and walked slowly across the room toward him. She wore a devious smile that immediately angered him. Funny that she'd never elicited any other emotion in him, aside from lust.

Teresa reached up to cup his face in her hand. He

captured her wrist but, before he could pull her hand away, the doorknob turned.

❦

Lily wanted to turn and run screaming from the building. But her feet refused to move. She should have known better than to go looking for a confrontation. She should have just picked up her belongings, gotten in the coach, and continued on to Essex, to Oliver.

There Simon stood, just inside the room, with Mrs. Hamilton's hand cupping his face. She was in barely anything, looking perfectly sinful with her hair hanging about her shoulders. And there was Simon—right where she'd hoped he wouldn't be.

Lily glanced from his face to hers. Teresa Hamilton wore a look of supreme satisfaction. She'd won.

Lily quietly and purposefully laid the key on the bureau and left the room. Her legs moved like there were leaden weights attached, heavy and cumbersome. She forced her feet to lift, one after the other, until she reached the lower level. With all the dignity she could muster, she crossed the room, moving toward the door.

But then she heard his voice call to her. "Lily," was all he said. She ignored him. So, he said it louder. He reached her in three strides.

"Keep your voice down, Simon. Everyone will hear you," she hissed.

"Darling." He smiled that sinister smile at her. "I am the Duke of Blackmoor. No one expects me to behave well."

He said it loudly enough that a snicker erupted from a nearby table. Would her mortification never end?

To make matters worse, he grabbed her forcefully and pulled her body close to his. She felt his hardness pressed against her hip. How dare he get aroused by that woman and then come to her?

"Let. Me. Go," she cried, pushing against his chest. Scene be damned. She would not allow him to misuse her.

He grabbed her chin and turned her head toward him. "Never," he said, just before he scooped her up in his arms.

"Simon," she cried, struggling in his grip. But it was useless. He was much stronger than she. The innkeeper rushed to open the door so he could carry her through it. She fought him all the way to the coach, until he tossed her inside and turned to take a basket of food and his coat from the innkeeper. He climbed inside and slammed the door.

But before she could even adjust herself in the seat, he picked her up and placed her in his lap, wrapping both arms around her.

She still struggled against him. "Keep moving against me like that, and I'll toss your skirts up and take you right here," he said quietly.

She instantly stilled. And her traitorous body responded to his tone. To his arms around her. To his hardness pressed against her bottom.

"That's what I thought."

She wanted to hit him.

"I can't believe you did that," she bit out, trying to

stand and move to her own seat. He refused to allow her to retreat, tightening his arms.

"Did what?" he smiled, his white teeth flashing in the darkness.

"I can't believe you made a scene like that," she replied, crossing her arms under her breasts. The coach moved off, heading toward Essex, she assumed.

"I already told you, I am the Duke—"

She didn't allow him to finish. "Of Blackmoor," she mocked his tone. "And I don't care what anyone thinks or how disgraceful my behavior is," she finished.

"Stop it, Lily."

"Let me up, Simon," she said, once more trying to rise from his lap.

"Not on your life," he sneered. "In fact, I told you that if you didn't stop squirming, I would do more than just hold you on my lap." He arched an eyebrow at her.

Drat. She stopped moving. "Don't even *think* you will do a thing with me after being with that woman," she said.

"I didn't do anything with that woman," he said as his hand stroked up and down her arm. Her traitorous nipples peaked in response. "I went to tell her that my wife is the only one I want."

"You're a poor liar," she said without looking at him.

"No. I am a wonderful liar. I have had years of practice. But I am telling the truth." He caught her chin in his hand and forced her to look at him. "I never had a reason to tell the truth before. But I am telling you now that you need to trust me. You have to give me a chance."

Lily sniffed. "Then why was she touching you?" She knew she sounded like a petulant child, but she couldn't help it.

"Because she wanted me," he stated blandly. "And, more than that, I imagine she didn't want you to have me."

"Your conceit knows no bounds."

"That scene was played badly, I admit. But I needed to tell her that things between us are over. And I did." His lips touched hers briefly.

"Really?" she sniffed.

He had the nerve to chuckle. "Really."

She moved in his lap again, turning toward him.

"That's it," he groaned. "Don't say I didn't warn you."

&

Simon's last thought was that if she wiggled in his arms one more time, he would have to take her. He would have to push her skirts up and pull her down on him. He would teach his little innocent about making love in a carriage.

Then she moved. And he had his opportunity. He lifted her from his lap only briefly, ignoring her gasp as he gathered her skirts in a ball around her hips and drew her down to straddle him. He let her skirts fall.

"This is highly improper," she sniffed, pulling away from him again. He tightened his hold on her bottom, pulling her forward to rock against his length.

"*That* is improper," he whispered just before his

lips touched her neck. She leaned into his kiss, so he immediately knew he had her interest. Yet she still had a point to prove, he assumed.

"Let me up, Simon," she whispered. Her hot breath blew across his ear.

"I'll let you up," he whispered as he reached beneath her to unfasten his trousers and pull himself free. He grasped her bottom and pulled her forward to ride the ridge of him. The dampness of her soaked him through her drawers.

He reached beneath her and tore them, moving the offending fabric out of the way so he could surge against her moist heat.

"Simon!" she shrieked when she heard the fabric tear.

"I'll buy new ones for you," he chuckled. "Or you can just go without so they'll never be in my way again."

Simon tugged her bodice until he could see the rigid peaks of her nipples.

"You do want me," he said as he took a peak into his mouth and began to tease the other with his fingertips.

"I don't want to," she cried, arching her back and threading her hands in his hair to keep him at her breasts.

"You don't want me to be inside you?" he asked, searching her face for the answer.

"No, I don't want to want you," she whispered, just before she inched forward on him.

"But you do." It was a fact. She was soaking wet and purring on top of him, even if she still wanted to deny it.

"I do," she breathed and then touched her lips to

his. Her tongue entered his mouth at the same time he entered her body. She moved to accommodate him, sliding down his length.

"Easy," he whispered. If she moved too fast, he would explode long before she finished.

"Nothing with you is easy," she whispered, her breath catching as he took her hips in his hands and raised and lowered her on top of him.

This was how he wanted to see her always. Completely uninhibited. Her eyes half-closed with passion. Trusting him.

Simon reached between them, his hand stealing into her curls to rub her heat. As she rode him, tight as a glove and much silkier, he toyed with her. She gasped and clenched around him when he found the source of her pleasure. Within moments, she was crying out against his shoulder as her body erupted around him. He quickly followed.

Simon pulled her against his chest to stroke her naked back. She drew deep breaths against him, her breath tickling his chin.

"I can't believe you would use me like that," he said, brushing her hair back over her shoulder. He couldn't help but laugh when she balled up her fist and hit his chest.

"Quiet," she whispered. "Let me enjoy this before more of your secrets intrude."

Thirty-One

LILY AWOKE TO A BRIGHT STREAM OF MORNING LIGHT that poured in through a crack between the drawn shade and the carriage window. She blinked her eyes open, realizing she'd slept in Simon's arms all night. His dark head rested against the wall of the coach, a slight rumbling snore escaping him. Even rumpled and unshaven, he was the most handsome man she'd ever seen. And he was her husband.

Her husband.

That thought brought a smile to her lips as Lily leaned back against his massive chest. Never in all her days did she think a man could make her feel such passion. Never in all her days did she think she'd ever fall in love. She certainly never thought she'd marry, not a man like Simon anyway. Yet she had inexplicably done so.

She sighed, wondering if it was possible he felt the same for her. Then the unwanted image of Teresa Hamilton flashed in her mind and Lily's smile vanished. She doubted the sight of the stunning widow wrapping herself around Simon would ever leave her mind.

"A world of emotion crosses your face, love. Did

you know that?" Simon's baritone voice startled her, and Lily nearly leapt from his lap. However, his arm tightened around her, securing her safely against him. "Good morning, Your Grace."

Lily offered him a shy smile. "How did you ever get accustomed to being called that?"

He kissed her brow and then grinned at her. "I never thought about it. My father was the duke before me, and I always knew I would assume his role. Does the title make you uncomfortable?"

"A little," she admitted. "My father *wasn't* a duke."

Simon chuckled. "Don't worry, love. Soon you won't even cringe when someone calls you that. It'll just take a little time."

"Are you certain?"

He laughed again. "Every woman I know wants to be a duchess, Lily. There must be something to having the role."

"Hmm," she agreed. "Having you." Apparently she was daring this morning. It must have come from spending the night on his lap. Lily looked up at him and pressed a kiss to his stubbly chin.

Simon's arms tightened around her. "Watch yourself, love, or I'll ravish you again."

A giggle erupted from her throat at the thought. There was something very primitive about Simon, and Lily discovered she enjoyed that aspect of him quite a bit. "You beast."

His arms slackened, and he frowned at her.

Lily immediately missed his tight embrace and couldn't imagine what would change his mood so quickly. "Simon, what is it?"

His grey eyes bored into her as his frown deepened. "You think I'm a beast?"

That's what he was upset about? Lily ran her fingers along his jaw. "Yes," she said honestly, "but I like that about you."

Simon sat back against the squabs, his eyes widening in surprise. "You do?"

Lily nodded. "I *love* that about you."

The tiniest smile lifted his lips before he pulled her back against his chest. Just as he was about to capture her mouth, the coach came to an abrupt halt.

Lily's forehead met with Simon's chin, and he reared backward.

"Ouch!" she said, clutching her head.

"What the devil?" Simon growled. He pulled back the shade and sucked in a breath. "Maberley Hall," he informed her with a frown.

Lily glanced out the window, looking at her home of the last six years. The light-stoned Tudor manor house towered above them, and Lily closed her eyes. *Please, let Oliver be here!* She didn't know where to begin if he wasn't.

Simon touched her cheek. "He'll be all right, love."

She blinked her eyes open. How did he know what she was thinking? Before she could ask, he opened the door of the carriage and stepped out into the morning light. Simon offered her his hand, and she allowed him to help her from the coach.

Together they walked from the drive up the stone steps to the grand, arched doorway. "Miss Rutledge!" the wide-eyed butler greeted her, as they stepped over the threshold. "We weren't expecting you."

"Findley," she replied. "Please tell me Maberley is here."

The butler shook his head as he shut the door. "Miss Rutledge, the Duke of Blackmoor sent a carriage for his lordship more than a week ago. Did he not arrive at Westfield Hall?"

❧

Simon frowned at the elderly butler. Oliver was here somewhere; he could sense the pup. He could almost smell him. What was the man's game? "If you'd like to keep your post, you'll lead me to the whelp this instant."

"Simon!" Lily whispered at the same time the butler's eyes grew to the size of billiard balls.

"Sir?" the old man managed.

"Findley," Lily began, with just a hint of mortification in her voice, "this is His Grace of Blackmoor. Maberley did arrive at Westfield Hall, but he's vanished. We had hoped he'd returned here."

Findley turned his attention from Simon to Lily. "Miss—"

"Her Grace," Simon corrected.

For a moment, he thought the old man's eyes were about to pop out of his head. "H-her Grace?"

Lily nudged Simon in the ribs. "Simon, please." She refocused on the butler. "He's not returned then?"

The old man shook his head. Simon narrowed his eyes on the fellow. There wasn't a question in his mind that Oliver was here.

It had been years since he'd been to Maberley Hall, but he'd spent some time here as a lad. It shouldn't be too difficult to tear the place apart, find the pup's hiding place, and toss him back in the Blackmoor coach. Then he'd deal with the insolent butler. "Maberley!" he bellowed.

"Your Grace!" Findley cried. "I tell you the earl is not here. I would never keep him from Miss… er… your duchess."

"Simon, Findley is honorable. If Oliver was here, he would say so."

The old man vigorously nodded his head. "Of course, Your Grace."

Simon sniffed the air. He couldn't catch the boy's scent, not recent scent anyway. Still, he knew they were close. "Very well, Lily. You stay here and wait for him." He started back for the door.

"Wait!" she called after him. "Simon, where are you going?"

"I'll search along the lanes." With that, he strode out the front door.

The sky above looked ominous, reflecting Simon's darkening mood. He paid no heed to the gardeners who gaped at him as he made his way down the stone path that led to the Maberley stables. Simon cursed the rain, which made it nearly impossible to use his keen sense of smell.

He spotted a boy, younger than Oliver, with a bucket in hand, just about to enter the stables. "You!" he beckoned.

The stable boy turned around, dropping his bucket of oats. "Yessir?"

"I'm looking for Maberley."

The child stared blankly at him.

"The earl," Simon clarified. "Have you seen him?"

The boy shook his head. "Not for days, sir."

Erebus! Oliver would have to stable him. Simon stalked forward. "And what of horses? Have you any Anglo-Arabians here?"

Again the stable boy shook his head. "No, sir."

"Well, I'll just take a look." Simon brushed past the child into the stable, his nostrils flaring at the odors that assailed his senses. He wouldn't be able to catch Oliver's scent here, but if he could locate Erebus, it would be a good first step.

He walked the length of the stables, peering into every stall. Neither Oliver nor Erebus was there, which didn't make any sense at all. Simon would swear the boy was there. He couldn't see him and he couldn't smell him, but he could sense his angry presence.

He turned back to the stable boy, who was now speaking with a groom at the entrance and pointing at Simon.

"You," he called. "Have your fastest stallion saddled for me."

"I beg your pardon?" the groom said, stepping forward, a frown marring his face. "Who are you?"

It was a trial not to be at his own estate where his every dictate was immediately leapt upon. How much time had he wasted today dealing with Maberley's inept servants? "The Duke of Blackmoor. Now do as I say."

He stalked out of the stables as a streak of lightning raced across the sky. Damn Oliver York! Where was the little beast? Simon looked across the estate as dark clouds rolled overhead. He sniffed at the air to the south. Nothing. He turned to the east and sniffed again.

There it was.

The scent was faint, so faint that he'd nearly missed it. He inhaled deeply to be sure. Oliver was out there. Somewhere to the east, Simon was certain.

Within minutes, he mounted a chestnut stallion and tore off toward the east as thunder cracked above him. It had been years since he'd ridden this land, but at one time he and Daniel had explored every part of the Maberley estate. The area was not completely unfamiliar to him.

He raced past one copse of trees and then another, looking in all directions for some sign of his insolent ward. A large drop of rain splashed onto Simon's cheek. When a flash of lightning lit up the dark sky, Simon heard a faint whinny in the distance.

He urged his borrowed mount on as a deluge fell from the sky. Simon squinted, trying to see through the blinding rain, and he hoped his horse knew the terrain better than he.

He kicked his mount's belly, pushing him toward the darkness that now appeared to be shelter of some sort. His horse pressed forward, stopping only when Simon pulled up on his reins.

A crofter's cottage.

A momentary haven. There was a lean-to on the side of the cottage. He could tie his horse, wait for the worst of the storm to pass, and then continue his search for Oliver.

Simon hopped from his saddle and led his horse to the make-do shelter. He stopped in his tracks, drenched from head to toe but incredibly relieved to have found a dry place to wait for the storm to pass.

The scene that greeted him made his heart soar. Because, panicked and unhappy, Erebus already occupied the lean-to.

Thirty-Two

THERE WASN'T A LOT OF EXTRA ROOM IN THE SMALL shelter, but Simon managed to secure his horse to a rail beside Erebus. He patted his gelding's nose. The Anglo-Arabian was of the twitchy sort and hated thunderstorms. If he panicked badly, he could tear down the cottage. "There, there, boy. I'll see you home. A little patience."

Erebus calmed a bit at his touch, and Simon stroked his neck. The poor thing was traumatized. It was yet another sin to add to his long list of grievances against Oliver.

Simon left the horses with another round of soothing words and stepped back out into the rain. He bolted for the front door of the cottage and threw it open, as rain poured off him in rivulets.

At his entrance, Oliver leapt up from a small bed in the far corner of the room. The boy's face was ashen white, as well it should be, because Simon's blood boiled at the scene inside the cottage.

While Simon had been caught out in the pouring rain looking for the pup, Oliver had been snug and warm in the cottage. Rain poured from Simon like water from a waterfall, yet Maberley was dry and comfortable.

Simon shrugged out of his coat and shook his head like a dog. Water flew from his hair, and Oliver was forced to raise his hands in front of his face to avoid being drenched. It was no more than he deserved. The boy needed to learn what it meant to play with the big dogs. If not for him, Simon would be back at Westfield Hall with Lily.

"How did you find me?" the boy had the nerve to ask.

Simon scratched his bristly jaw. Then he tapped his temple with his forefinger. "Superior intellect. Wins every time." Simon flopped down in a chair heavily, all bounds of propriety suddenly absent, along with the desire to find them again. He crossed one foot over his knee. "You remind me so much of your father," he said, shaking his head in wonder. The boy looked just like Daniel, from the stubborn jut of his chin to the feral glint in his eye.

Oliver sat forward but didn't say a word. Simon could tell he had the boy's attention at the mere mention of Daniel. "I found you because your father and I explored every inch of the grounds of Maberley Hall when we were young." He couldn't push back the smile that came with his memories. "There are not many secrets about these grounds that I don't already know." Simon took a deep breath. "We're also blessed with expanded senses." The puzzled look on the boy's face encouraged him to continue. "I smelled you. You haven't noticed that we have a greater sense of smell? That you can suddenly catch scents that you never would have caught before?"

"I noticed," Oliver mumbled.

"I thought you might. What else have you noticed?"

Oliver turned his head to look toward the wall. The rain continued to pound outside the tiny cottage. Simon decided patience would be a great virtue. He would be truly grateful if he was ever granted some. He was trying desperately to find just a bit.

"I'm sure you've noticed that you're growing. You're much bigger and stronger than other lads your age. And, despite your bulk, you're faster than they are."

Oliver nodded but still refused to meet his eyes. Simon pressed on.

"Does it bother you to be one of us?"

Oliver shook his head. "It doesn't bother me," he mumbled.

"Yet you still don't think I'm good enough to be married to your Aunt Lily."

Oliver's gaze finally swung to meet his. "That's not it."

"Then why don't you tell me what it is so we can get this over with." Lily would be proud he hadn't picked the pup up by the scruff of his neck and shaken his secrets from him. He still wasn't completely opposed to that idea.

Oliver just regarded him solemnly.

"I remember when your father found out about our heritage, when he went through the change. He was two years younger than me, so I'd already been through it. But a Lycan is sworn to secrecy. It's never to be mentioned that you're different, except with members of your own kind." Simon wondered if Will had shared that with him. "You haven't told anyone yet, have you?" he asked, suddenly worried that the boy had been screaming it from the rooftops.

"Like anyone would believe me," Oliver mumbled.

Simon chuckled. "That's true. It does seem a little odd, doesn't it?"

"Odd doesn't begin to describe it," Oliver said.

"You'll learn to live with it in time, Oliver—" he started.

"You never should have married her," the boy suddenly said.

Finally, they were getting somewhere.

Simon narrowed his eyes at him. "I know you don't think I'm good enough for her. But I care about her, and I promise to be kind to her."

"But you'll claim her with the next moon. And hurt her," Oliver whispered, horrified.

Simon sighed. He really hadn't thought he would be forced to discuss his sexual relationship with a twelve-year-old. But apparently there wasn't another way to make Oliver understand. "That's where you're wrong," he admitted.

"What do you mean?"

"Every Lycan has the choice of whether or not to take a mate. I know you've read about it and you know what occurs." He raised one eyebrow to prompt a response from the boy. Oliver nodded.

"But what the books don't say is that a Lycan is not forced to claim his Lycan mate, even if he takes her as a wife."

"I don't understand."

Neither did Simon. "I took Lily to be my wife. She's mine. In every way." He prompted the boy to nod again and only continued once he did. "But I'll never take her as a Lycan mate."

"Why not?"

"Because she doesn't know what I am. And I prefer to keep it that way. I want her to have a normal marriage. And I want to share my life with her."

"What about when the moon calls?"

"When the moon calls, I'll do what I do now. I'll travel to Westfield Hall where I can seek the solitude of the forest. Alone. Then, when the moon begins to wane, I'll come back to her."

"You won't bite her neck? And hurt her? Like the book said. Like my father did to my mother?"

"How do you know about that?" Simon asked.

"I remember she was afraid of him and tried to keep me from him. I was too young to wonder about why. She just did. And she always made sure her neck was covered, but I saw it once." Oliver frowned, looking at his own hands. "I didn't know he had done that to her until I read about the claiming in the book."

Damn Will to hell. Daniel, too, for that matter. No wonder the boy was so fearful. Simon's heart ached for the pain he saw reflected in Oliver's eyes. "Your father and I are very different." When the lad started to speak, Simon held up a hand. "Wait, Oliver, because you need to listen first."

Oliver nodded, his jaw twitching as he ground his teeth.

"Your father didn't have anyone to teach him to be a man. Or a Lycan. His own father died when he was a boy, and though my father tried to help him, it wasn't enough."

"And that's why he hurt Mama?" the boy's voice broke on the last few words.

"Yes, he did," Simon said, refusing to show any emotion, though it rolled through him in waves. The boy needed strength, and he could show him that. "But your father loved her."

"Then he shouldn't have hurt her!" he growled at Simon.

He was quite glad the pup still had his milk teeth, because he would be a formidable foe when he was fully grown.

"You're correct. But he didn't know any better. Daniel loved Emma so much. He wanted to share every part of himself with her. He did tell her about himself. And she chose to be with him, in his Lycan form, when the moon was full. She accepted that risk and trusted Daniel, but he couldn't control the beast."

Simon stood and began to pace across the room. "Not until it was too late. He realized what he'd done after it was nearly over. But by then, he'd hurt her, shattered her trust, and she withdrew. It nearly killed him. And her. Because she'd wanted so badly to be *that person* for him. It wasn't his failure. And it wasn't hers."

Simon knelt in front of Oliver where he still sat on the edge of the bed. "Are you afraid that will happen to you? And to someone you love? And to Lily?"

Oliver simply nodded.

"It won't. Because I won't let it," Simon snarled,

suddenly even more sure that his decision to keep his Lycan ways a secret from Lily was a good one.

"You will promise?" Oliver asked.

"I will promise to guide you and teach you what you need to know, just as a Lycan father should. I'll never try to replace Daniel, but I'll try to teach you as he would. As someone should have taught him."

Oliver stood alongside him and was nearly able to look him in the eye. He almost knocked Simon to the ground when he threw his arms around him and hugged him fiercely. All Simon could do was plant his feet, tighten his arms around Oliver, and accept the only bit of affection the boy had ever offered him.

Lily paced back and forth across the foyer, biting her fingernails and mumbling to herself. It had been hours since Simon left. As soon as he'd turned the corner of the house, the skies had opened and rain had fallen from the heavens.

While she waited, she and Findley had searched the entire residence. Not even the smallest wardrobe was left unsearched. Oliver was nowhere to be found.

Now she didn't know what to do to keep busy. Where else would he have gone? Was he hurt somewhere? Had something happened to him? She'd never forgive herself if he came to harm.

And then there was Simon. Shouldn't *he* have returned by now? Not that she was worried about his safety. Simon was indestructible, or at least he seemed that way to her. Hard. Solid. Strong. She so wished he was there. His presence would calm her. She wouldn't feel quite so alone.

Lily returned to her old chambers. It felt odd being here again, like a glance into the recent past. So much had changed since she'd left Maberley Hall. Her journey certainly had turned into something she had never envisioned.

She ran her hand over her old comfortable counterpane, while looking out the window at the drenched grounds beneath her. Thank heavens, it had stopped raining. Hopefully, that meant Simon would return soon, and together they could decide where to go from here. She would go mad if she had to figure this out alone.

Movement caught her eye off in the distance, and Lily pressed her fingers against the cool pane of glass. She strained her eyes. It looked like two riders, but from where she stood, she couldn't be certain. Glued to her spot, she watched as the figures came nearer. As soon as she noticed Simon's distinctive build, she raced from the room, through the corridor, and down the grand staircase.

Overjoyed, she didn't stop. Lily tore from the house, leaving a gaping Findley in her wake. She ran down the stone path toward the stables, reaching it right as Simon and Oliver rode up.

Tears spilled down her cheeks, and relief engulfed her at the sight of her nephew. Lily closed her eyes and silently thanked God for keeping him safe. "Oliver," she cried as he dismounted.

He hung his head and shuffled his feet. "Sorry, Aunt Lily. I didn't mean to worry you."

She threw her arms around his neck. The last of

her composure fell away. Holding him, her heart overflowed. It wasn't her imagination. He was before her and safe and... Lily owed Simon everything for finding him.

Her eyes flashed to her husband's. Drenched and scruffy, Simon was a complete mess, but she'd never seen a more handsome man. He barely inclined his head in greeting before he dismounted his chestnut stallion.

She pulled back from Oliver, shaking her head at him. "Don't you ever do something that foolish again. It nearly killed me."

He nodded, his brown eyes drooping like those of a scolded puppy. "I know, Aunt Lily. I'm sorry."

She hugged him again. "I'm so glad you're safe." She felt a large, familiar hand on her shoulder.

"I'm sure Maberley has learned his lesson, love."

Lily drew back from Oliver and threw her arms around Simon's neck. He was sodden from head to foot, and the wetness seeped into her clothes and against her skin. Lily didn't care. "Oh, thank you, Simon, for finding him."

He chuckled against her neck. "Lily, you'll catch the ague if you don't let go of me."

She leapt away from him as if he was on fire. "Oh! You'll be sick. Let's get you out of those clothes."

"That's the best idea I've heard today." His husky voice rumbled over her, causing her cheeks to burn.

Honestly, did the man only ever think about one thing?

Thirty-Three

SIMON DECIDED HE ENJOYED MARRIED LIFE QUITE A BIT. He'd always been so solitary; he hadn't thought he'd like a woman fussing over him.

But he did.

Lily clasped his hand and towed him up the stony path. "You look like you fell in a lake, Simon. I wonder if I shouldn't send for Doctor Sanders."

He held his smile in check. "There's no need for a doctor, Lily. I'm fine."

"But you were gone so long, and there was so much rain. Now I feel guilty. I was thinking while you were away that there was no reason to worry about you as you seem so indestructible, but now…"

"Now?" he prompted, trying to keep the merriment from his voice.

"Seeing you in such a state, I… Well, I don't know what I'd do if something happened to you."

Simon stopped on the path, pulling Lily back to him. "Nothing is going to happen to me."

She was so adorable when she worried about him.

Her nose scrunched up a bit, and her brow creased with concern, with love. It warmed his heart.

"Simon," she began softly, blinking her pretty hazel eyes at him. "Aside from Oliver, I've lost everyone I have ever cared about. I don't intend to lose you, too. Now get inside the house, and take off these clothes." She tugged on his greatcoat for emphasis.

Once they entered the manor house, she asked Findley to ready Maberley's largest chamber for him and ordered a hot bath to be sent up as well.

"Yes, Your Grace," the butler replied evenly. "I took the liberty of preparing the late earl's chamber for the duke and the countess' chamber for you."

Lily shook her head at that. "Findley, that isn't necessary. I can stay in my old room for a night."

It was necessary, however, in Simon's mind. The earl and countess' chambers connected, and he had no intention of being separated from his bride. He cleared his throat. "Love, Findley had the right of it."

"Are we only staying one night?" Oliver asked from behind them.

Simon nodded. "Indeed. Take the opportunity to get whatever you'd like to have with you at Westfield Hall, anything you might have left behind."

"Of course, Your Grace," the boy said with more respect than he'd shown thus far. Then he bounded up the staircase.

The tone caught Lily's notice, and she glanced up at Simon. "What was that about?"

He feigned ignorance and shrugged. After all, he couldn't give her any details.

Lily's eyes narrowed on him.

"Aren't you going to show me to my chambers, love?" he asked, offering her his arm.

She took it but frowned slightly. "Simon Westfield, what exactly are you trying to hide from me?" Lily asked as she led him up the stairs. "And why are you drenched and Oliver dry as a bone? Where was he? What happened with the two of you? And why—"

Simon couldn't help but laugh. "Lily, have you ever heard the term 'Don't look a gift horse in the mouth'?"

She stopped at the top of the stairs. "Of course I have, but I don't see how that is fitting in this situation."

He prodded her along. "You wanted Oliver found. I did so. You wanted me to take an interest in the boy, and I've done so. You wanted Oliver to accept our marriage, and now he has. Simply smile and say, 'Thank you, Simon.'"

Lily directed him toward the master's chambers. "I am happy, Simon. Thank you, but—"

"It's this door, isn't it?" Simon asked, hoping to distract her.

She nodded, "Simon—"

He silenced her by pulling her against him and wrapping his cold, wet arms around her. "I don't have my valet, Lily. Can I beg you to help me out of these clothes?"

She blushed, smiling up at him. Finally, he had her attention where he wanted it.

"Simon, I'm certain you can manage that all on your own."

"Yes, but it would be much more enjoyable with your assistance," he whispered, as he opened the door to the suite of rooms.

Then someone coughed delicately behind them. Simon looked over his shoulder to find Findley's eyes on Lily. "Your Grace," the butler said to her. "We weren't expecting you, and Cook needs to begin preparing dinner. Could you please come see her about the menu?"

Lily slid from Simon's arms. "Yes, of course, Findley." She threw a glance back at Simon as she followed the butler down the corridor.

Don't look a gift horse in the mouth! Lily frowned. Something was wrong. Something had happened, and Simon was trying to keep it from her. What was it?

Lily went through the tedious task of choosing cucumber soup, roast beef, Yorkshire pudding, fresh vegetables, and lemon tarts for dessert. She then assured Findley that there wouldn't be any changes to the household after her and Oliver's departure.

That thought brought her back to her conundrum. What had happened between Oliver and Simon that had rendered such an obvious truce? Before the storm, she'd had the feeling Oliver wouldn't have poured a bucket of water on Simon even if he'd been on fire. Now she felt like their feelings had changed.

Oliver had needed the influence of a father for quite some time. She'd often thought about marrying, simply so he could have a male presence in his life. But the situation never presented itself, and she never went in search of a husband. She was much more content to lead a rather solitary existence.

Lily twisted the wedding band on her finger. Until now, that is. Now all she could think about was how to get back upstairs to Simon. She flushed as she imagined him shrugging out of his sodden clothes. Then he would sink his lean body into a warm bath.

Lily called for Findley. The man appeared as if by magic. How *did* they do that? She shook her head. No matter.

"Findley, would you have Cook send lunch up to His Grace's room, please?" The man simply inclined his head. Lily turned to run up the stairs. Findley's voice stopped her.

"For two, Your Grace?"

Lily couldn't avoid the blush that she knew must stain her cheeks. "That would be lovely," she replied with quiet dignity.

She raced up the steps in very unladylike fashion. Thank goodness, no one was watching. Or they would think she was in a hurry to get to her husband. Then they would assume to know why.

And they would be completely right. She wanted him to enfold her in his strong arms and hold her tightly. But even more than that, she wanted answers about Oliver.

Lily didn't even knock before stepping into Simon's room. He was her husband, after all. She couldn't suppress a shiver. The door clicked closed behind her, and she walked farther into the room.

"Simon?"

"Yes, love?" She would never get over the thrill that came with that term of endearment.

"May I talk to you?" she called.

"Not very effectively if you stay that far away," he called back.

"Are you decent?"

He chuckled. "I have never been called decent in my whole life. Why should I begin now?"

"Simon," she scolded him.

"I think you enjoy the fact that I'm not quite decent most of the time. Don't you?"

Thirty-Four

Simon couldn't help but tense up to prepare himself for her answer. She'd alluded to the fact that she liked his beastly behavior in the coach. It would be beyond his wildest dreams to know that she accepted him just as he was.

Of course, he would never be able to fully reveal himself to her, but it would be nice to know that he didn't have to pretend every minute of every day.

When she didn't answer, he called, "Lily?"

"Yes, Simon." She stepped from behind the bathing screen and immediately turned her head to look the other way, her face coloring prettily. "I'm so sorry," she started.

"Lily love." Simon allowed his gaze to travel down her body. "I have been *inside* you. I don't think it will hurt for you to see me in the bath."

Her hands fluttered nervously. If he wasn't in the bath, he would have gone to her in an attempt to calm her. Unlike any woman he'd ever been with, she was a novice to all of this. He usually chose women who were as jaded as he.

"You shouldn't say things like that out loud, Simon," she gasped.

"Say what?" He couldn't keep himself from teasing her.

"That you have been… there."

"I'm planning to go *there* again when I get out of the bath."

"Oh, my," she said, as her hand fluttered to land on her chest. "You're incorrigible." The corners of her mouth finally tilted into a grin.

"There's that smile I love." He did love to see her happy.

"You like to embarrass me."

He did. He liked to see her out of sorts. He liked to surprise her. He liked that all this was fresh and new for her. But would she feel the same way about him if she knew the truth? Would she still laugh at him? Or would she be disgusted? Would she turn and run from him? He wasn't willing to take that chance.

Lily watched the play of emotions on his face. "What is it, Simon?" She took a step closer to the tub. "What are you not telling me?"

"I don't know what you mean," he said, avoiding her gaze.

"I think there's something you're keeping from me." Lily closed her eyes and took a deep breath. "I know you didn't want to marry. Or to be a father."

"Who implied that?" he suddenly barked.

"You *do* want to be a father?" she asked.

"I think I have made that perfectly clear," he said

as he stood up and took a towel from a nearby chair. Water sluiced down his naked body and puddled on the floor when he stepped from the tub. "I came all the way here on our wedding night to search for Oliver. Then I went out in the pouring rain to find him. Then I actually made peace with the little pup. If that's not acting the role of father, I'm not sure what is."

Lily turned to face away from him. He crossed the floor in three quick strides. Lily gasped as he took her shoulder and turned her around, then pulled her close to his naked, wet body.

"Don't ever assume that I'm not a normal man. With the same wants and desires as any other."

"Wants and desires?" she managed to croak out.

"Those, too," he said, shaking his head. "But listen to me, Lily."

She nodded, the water from his body soaking the front of her gown. But she paid it no heed. The intensity in his eyes had her total attention.

"I want you to be my wife. I want to raise Oliver like he's a son. I want you to be the mother of my children. I *want* to share my life with you in every way." His lips pressed against hers quickly. "I just wish…"

"You wish what, Simon?" Oh, please talk to me. Tell me what's in your heart.

"I just wish I were a different man for you," he finally admitted before he turned away to pat himself dry with the towel. "Could you ring for Oliver's valet?"

"I could help you," she offered. She really wasn't ready to be dismissed.

"The boy's valet will do." He walked away from

her, apparently forgetting his earlier promise of inti-
macy. Lily was left with a soaked gown, wounded
pride, and just as many questions as she'd had before
their conversation began.

She went to the bell pull and tugged harder than
was necessary. "Simon," she began, "I asked Findley
to have lunch delivered to you here. I'm certain
you're famished."

"How thoughtful," he replied, looking out the
window with his back to her.

"I thought we might enjoy the meal together. I
thought we could talk."

She saw the muscles in his back tense at those words,
which only made her more suspicious. "Simon?"

"Lily, it's been a long day," he said quietly.

She frowned at him, not understanding him in the
least. "What secrets are you keeping from me, Simon?"

He laughed and glanced over his shoulder at her.
"Secrets? Lily, you yourself said you knew them all
after keeping up with my scandalous exploits through
the gossip columns all these years. What else could I
possibly have to hide?"

That was a very good question, but Lily was certain
he was hiding something. "I am your wife. You do
know I'm trustworthy, don't you?"

Simon sighed. "I'm certain you are. If I had any
secrets, Lily, I would lay them at your feet."

At that moment someone scratched at the door.
"Come," Lily called.

When Oliver's valet opened the door, Lily knew she
had run out of time. At least with Simon. Oliver, however,
might very well shed some light on the situation.

She strode purposefully down the hall and around the corner to her nephew's room. She knocked lightly and then pushed the door open. "Oliver," she began.

"Aunt Lily!" When Oliver leapt off the bed, a book thudded to the floor at his feet.

"What's that?" she asked, stepping forward.

Looking more guilty than she'd ever seen him, Oliver shrugged. "Just one of my father's books. I found it in the library."

Lily shook her head. Oliver wouldn't feel guilty over a book. He was far from studious. She must have misinterpreted the expression. If he wanted to study some of Daniel's old books, she'd gladly welcome the activity. "I suppose it's too much to hope that it's Latin."

Oliver nodded his head vigorously. "There is some Latin text, Aunt Lily."

Now she didn't believe him at all. But old tomes belonging to the late Earl of Maberley were not her highest concern at the moment. "Oliver, may I ask you a question?"

"Of course," he answered, dropping back to his spot on the bed and kicking the book under the counterpane.

Lily took a spot beside him. "Why did you run off?"

⚞⚟

Oliver hated to lie to his aunt, but the duke had made the rules very clear. Blackmoor had told Oliver what to say, and he hoped he'd be able to carry it off.

"I was jealous," he repeated his contrived response.

"Jealous?" Aunt Lily echoed, a crease marring her brow.

He nodded while guilt consumed him. "Well, when I arrived at Westfield Hall, Blackmoor seemed to demand all of your attention. And you seemed taken by him."

"Oliver York," she said quietly, "you have always been my life."

He shrugged. "Not anymore. I'll be going off to school, and you have the duke, and…"

Aunt Lily kissed his cheek, just like she always did when she was trying to soothe him. Oliver swallowed his guilt about deceiving her. He did want her to be happy. She deserved all the happiness in the world. Knowing what he was, what the duke was, wouldn't bring that to her. So he squeezed her hand and continued his ruse.

"I am sorry, Aunt Lily. I shouldn't have run off. I suppose I thought you'd be so consumed in your new life, you wouldn't miss me."

"Oh, Oliver!" she said, brushing tears from her cheek. "I was so worried about you. How could you think that? When you go off to Harrow, I will miss you more than you will ever know."

He hugged her then. Fiercely. "I love you, Aunt Lily."

Thirty-Five

LILY WAS A TAD BIT DISGRUNTLED THE NEXT MORNING when Simon shook her awake. "Time to get up, love," he said briskly. "I thought we could travel to Harrow today and give Oliver a tour of the school. I'd like to show the boy my old stomping grounds."

"When did you come to bed?" she asked as she rubbed the sleep from her eyes.

"It was late." He simply shrugged. "I don't remember the time. I did like finding you in my bed, though," he said and winked at her.

After dinner, Simon had mentioned that he wanted to look through the steward's reports to be sure Maberley Hall was being cared for properly. Of course, he received quarterly statements, but he wanted to tour the grounds himself and see if any issues might need his assistance. When he'd taken Oliver with him, Lily certainly hadn't been able to complain, since he was finally spending time with the boy.

He'd kissed her quickly before he walked out the door with Oliver and said, "Back soon."

She'd watched as the sky grew darker and darker. Then she finally put on her nightrail and went to Simon's room to wait for him.

"What kept you out so late?"

"I wanted to show Oliver some of the places Daniel and I used to go. That's all." He turned away from her.

Lily was quickly learning that Simon tended to turn away from her when he wanted to avoid directly answering her questions. She slowly sat up and regarded his profile as he looked down at the lawns below.

She had two options. She could travel to Harrow with the two of them and try to figure out what was going on. Or she could let them go on without her, and she could return to Westfield Hall alone. Feeling slightly uncharitable, Lily was leaning toward the second option.

If Simon couldn't be honest with her, if he couldn't tell her what was in his heart, if he couldn't even be bothered to wake her when he returned in the middle of the night, she wasn't certain she wanted to spend a day with him.

"Well," she began carefully, "I think the two of you will enjoy your time together tremendously. I can't wait to hear all about it."

He spun on his heels to face her. "Why do you make it sound as if we're going without you?"

Lily swung her legs off the bed and slowly started toward the door that connected her chamber to his. "I don't really see why I'm needed for the excursion, Simon. The two of you will get along fine without me."

His grey eyes darkened, and a chill raced down her spine. However, she wouldn't let him know that, and she continued toward the connecting door.

"I want you with me," he growled.

Lily shrugged, hoping he couldn't tell how he affected her. "One certainly wouldn't know it."

"What is that supposed to mean?" Simon asked, stalking toward her.

She took a calming breath and raised herself to her full height, refusing to be cowed. "Exactly what I said. Ever since we arrived in Essex, you have found one excuse or another to abandon me. It will be much easier for you two to carry on without me being in your way."

"Lily." He frowned, planting himself in front of the connecting door.

"You can tell me all about Harrow when you return to Westfield Hall."

He folded his strong arms across his chest. "I don't find pouting to be an attractive trait."

Lily plastered a fraudulent smile across her face. "Indeed? *I* find boorish behavior to be particularly distasteful, myself. You are in my way, Simon."

"Have I behaved boorishly?"

"In more ways than I can count. Now, please remove yourself from my path."

"Lily."

"You and Oliver really should get a start on the day. Do excuse me." She tried to brush behind him and escape into her own chamber, but she found him more immobile than an elephant with a mule's disposition.

He grasped her waist and pulled her flush against him. The intensity of his stare left her nearly breathless, which was infuriating. After putting up with his ill treatment the previous day, she didn't want her pulse to race when he held her. She didn't want to notice how lovely and strong his lips were. She didn't want to feel his muscles and sinew through the thin material of her nightrail.

"You are my wife, Lily." His dark voice warmed her and settled in her belly. "And you won't escape me."

"Ha!" she shot back, hoping to regain her composure. "You're the one who has been escaping me, Simon Westfield. Now unhand me."

"I've not been escaping you."

She narrowed her eyes at him. "As soon as we arrived, you took off. Then yesterday you made it seem as if you wanted my attention while you bathed, but then you pushed me away. You kept yourself apart from me the remainder of the day, except for dinner, as I'm certain you couldn't find a plausible reason to avoid me, and then…" She poked his chest with her finger. "Then you stayed away all night and didn't even wake me when you returned."

Simon frowned. "I'm not accustomed to having to answer to anyone, Lily."

"I'm not just anyone, Simon. I am your wife, which I suspect you are now regretting."

"I told you my lifestyle wasn't conducive to marriage. You're going to have to be patient with me."

Lily didn't feel like being patient. She wanted answers—and sooner rather than later. "What are you hiding from me, Simon?"

He shook his head. "Nothing, Lily. Whether you believe me or not. I don't know how to convince you."

"Why did you push me away?"

"I'm not accustomed to having anyone else in my life. As I said, it will take me time to adjust. Dear God, Lily, this is all new to me."

Was that all it was? She started to second-guess herself. Was she being silly and insecure? She stared into his grey eyes and felt warmth spread across her body. "You're not trying to avoid me?"

He shook his head.

"Why didn't you wake me last night?"

His lips formed a lopsided smile. "Because you looked so tired. After the exhausting day we had, I couldn't bring myself to rouse you, though I wanted nothing more than to do so. Believe me, if I'd known you'd react this way, I would have done so."

"Truly?" she asked, her voice very small.

"If I promise to ravish you every night, will you promise to avoid histrionics every morning?"

Her cheeks warmed, and she felt like a fool. She'd never been prone to dramatics before.

"Is that a yes?" he asked, dipping his head down to hers. "I promise to keep my part of the bargain, Lily."

"To ravish me every night?"

A wolfish grin spread across his face. "And some-times in the morning."

When Simon's lips captured hers, all other thoughts left Lily's mind. His strong hands splayed across her lower back and pressed her against his arousal.

Lily couldn't think when he held her this close, when his eyes darkened to flint and his nostrils flared. She could only feel. And feel she did. Every inch of him pressed against her belly, hot and hard.

"Can we start with this morning?" Lily felt the heat

creep up her cheeks when he raised one eyebrow. Perhaps she was being too bold. But then he picked her up and took her back to bed, and all thoughts of being too pushy fled quickly from her mind.

Simon draped his arm around Lily as the coach rocked her back to sleep. On the other side of the carriage, Oliver watched with a sad smile on his face. The boy had been quiet most of the journey, and Simon wondered what was on Oliver's mind. "Something wrong?" he asked quietly.

Oliver shook his head. "Just thinking about Aunt Lily."

She stirred in Simon's arm at the sound of her name but quickly stilled. "What about her?"

Oliver shrugged. "I just don't want her to get angry with me when she finds out."

"She's not going to find out."

Oliver glanced out the window at the passing countryside. "Aunt Lily always finds out everything. I hope she forgives me for not telling her."

Guilt niggled at Simon's conscience. "Oliver, she's happier not knowing. Enough about this. We should be talking about your upcoming visit to Harrow."

Oliver straightened in his seat. "You said there are safe places for me to go when..." his voice trailed off.

Simon nodded. "My father, yours, Will, Benjamin, and I were always safe at school. You will be, too. The difficult part is controlling yourself as the moon waxes. Its pull gets stronger as the days pass. Yet you have to maintain your personality so those around you won't notice the changes occurring within you."

"How do I do that?"

"When you begin the term, keep to yourself as much as possible. Count the days on the calendar. Everyone is different, but most of us feel the pull of the moon four to five days before it's completely full. When you see the dates approaching on the calendar, you should take special care to be cognizant of your emotions and reactions. When you feel like you are not in control, go somewhere safe.

"As time goes by, your control will strengthen. You will learn to manage your wildness, instead of it managing you."

Oliver nodded, his gaze wandering to the passing scenery out his window.

"You look as though you don't trust me."

"No. It's me I don't trust," Oliver sighed.

"It'll come with time. Have faith in yourself. As I have faith in you." It was obvious the boy needed a confidence primer. Wasn't that something fathers did? He rather liked the thought of being the one to do that for Oliver. Would he be the same with his own children?

Simon looked down at Lily, who was beginning to stir again. Children. With her. He couldn't help but smile and draw her more closely to him.

☙

It was nearly impossible for Lily to lie completely still when she wanted to hear what they were saying so badly. She'd nearly been asleep when Simon had spoken. To hear him ask Oliver what was troubling him initially warmed her heart, but as she listened further, she simply became more and more puzzled.

Lily tried to maintain a relaxed pose, but it was difficult. Her heart really wanted to thump right out of her chest.

Why in the world would Oliver ever think she'd be disappointed in him? She'd always told him what a good boy he was. And, despite the fact that he didn't study his Latin text, he was truly a joy to be around. Sure, over the last few months, he'd become a bit surly. And he'd gotten aggressive with her a few times. But maybe that was just normal adolescent behavior. What did she know? She'd never raised a child.

…She's not going to find out… Find out what? Was there some manly secret that women weren't aware of? Women pretended that their monthly courses didn't exist and they were never spoken of, but it really wasn't a secret. Surely, men didn't have any ailments that couldn't be discussed.

Lily wanted to sit up and force them to tell her the truth. But she had a feeling Simon would quickly and effectively change the subject. She would get more answers if she pretended to sleep.

…There are safe places to go… Why would Oliver need a safe place to go at school? To escape bullies? For personal time? To meet girls? There were no girls at Harrow, aside from the staff.

…Calendar… Control… Lily grew more and more agitated. She stirred in Simon's arms, fully prepared to sit up and have a go at them both. She would stop the carriage and refuse to go one more inch until someone

told her what these secrets were about. But Simon pulled her closer to his chest and locked his strong arms around her. She couldn't have moved if she'd wanted to.

Will knew the secrets. Oliver obviously knew them. Even Simon's mother had alluded to facts that weren't yet apparent.

Was there madness in the family? They all seemed quite sane most of the time. But she could think of no other explanation for wanting to keep her in the dark.

This mystery would gnaw at her like a dog with a bone until she unraveled the details. She would find out what was going on. And she would do it soon.

Thirty-Six

ST. MARY'S CHURCH IN HARROW-ON-THE-HILL WAS A remarkable medieval structure. Lily had never seen it before and was surprised that she could look down on London from her position in the churchyard. She had heard Lord Byron loved this church and spent many hours whiling away his years at school in this very courtyard. The beauty of the place made it easy to see why he'd done so.

Still, as lovely as she found the village and its quaint surroundings, Lily anxiously awaited Simon and Oliver's return from the school grounds. She wished they'd let her go with them on their tour, but Simon had adamantly shaken his head, informing her that a woman would be a distraction on campus.

The thought made Lily frown. A distraction. *That* she highly doubted. More likely, he and Oliver couldn't discuss their plans with her awake. Whatever this was about, Simon guarded his secret fiercely. He wasn't likely to tell her what was going on even if she asked nicely or if she demanded, stomping her foot and acting the role of a fishwife.

She'd have to get her answers from someone else. She could probably force it out of Oliver. She had lots of experience in that realm, but she hated to use her nephew in such a way. If Will was at Westfield Hall, she was certain he would tell her; at least, she thought he would.

Her mother-in-law. Alice was the only woman who seemed to know the secret. If she couldn't finagle an answer out of her, she would set her sights on Oliver. One way or the other, she'd get to the bottom of this mystery.

Simon took great pride in showing Oliver around the Harrow grounds. For most of the tour, the headmaster accompanied them, leading them down one corridor or another and even allowing them a peek into one of the boys' chambers.

The visit brought back many memories for Simon. The years he and Daniel had spent there together, the scrapes and adventures they'd shared. He wished again that his closest friend had survived that awful carriage accident. There was no doubt in his mind that Daniel would have been proud to see Oliver grow into a man before his eyes.

The headmaster gave his permission for Simon and Oliver to explore the grounds alone. The countryside wasn't different from Simon's memories, so he was able to direct Oliver down a secluded path that very few people knew about. It had been used by one Lycan schoolboy after another through the years. Even after all this time, Simon easily found his way through the thick foliage until they reached a small circular clearing.

"This is where you'll come," he told Oliver. "When the moon is full, this place will be your haven." He pointed to the sky above them. "The light will hit you in the middle here." He gestured to a circle of white rocks just a few feet from where Oliver stood. "After the transformation, you'll be free to roam the grounds, like we did at Westfield Hall. Then you'll return to this spot when the time has come to resume your human form."

Oliver quietly looked around the clearing. "Will there be others like me?" he finally asked.

Simon didn't have a clue. He supposed he could take a look at the rolls. "It's possible there are others. When I attended Harrow, it was just Daniel, Will, and me. I'll see if I can find out for you."

Oliver circled the pile of white rocks. "What is this?"

"I never thought to ask. It has always been here, even in my father's time."

Oliver nodded, sniffing at the air. "It does smell as if someone has been here."

Simon did the same. A faint scent lingered, yet the breeze rarely found this place. "Do you hope there are others? Are you afraid to be alone?"

The lad's back straightened instantly. "I'm not afraid of anything," he boasted proudly. "Just curious."

Simon bit back a smile as he remembered saying something similar to his father years ago. "My apologies."

After he sniffed back his indignation, Oliver glanced around the clearing once more and nodded. "All right, Blackmoor. I think I've got the lay of the land."

"You sure?"

The boy let go a sigh. "If I know Aunt Lily, she's wearing a path through that churchyard. She doesn't like to be kept in the dark."

Somehow, Simon knew that. He clapped a hand to Oliver's back and directed him back down the secret path. "We'll have to distract her then. Does your aunt like the theatre?"

Oliver pushed his way through the dense flora. "She likes to read Shakespeare. I don't know that she's ever seen a play."

That brought a grin to Simon's face. "Well, I'll have to remedy that. We'll stay in London a few days. Get you fitted for new school clothes." *Order something sheer for Lily, or several somethings. A new wardrobe befitting a duchess. Jewels. Ribbons. Hair combs.* "You won't mind us going out at night and leaving you alone, will you?"

"No," Oliver answered and then jumped back when a tree limb smacked him in the arm. "I'd like to read more about Lycans. I found a couple of books at Maberley Hall. They're different from the ones Will gave me."

Same information, however. Simon kept that bit of fact to himself. As long as Oliver wanted to study up on their heritage and lore, he would support him. Keeping the boy occupied would also leave Simon and Lily to their own devices. He looked forward to offering London on a platter to her. Starting tonight with his box at Drury Lane.

❧

When the ducal coach rambled to a stop in front of St. Mary's Church, Lily finished her walk through the churchyard. The sunlight reflected off the Blackmoor crest, and the sight made her shiver. The door opened, and Oliver scrambled out, a boyish grin on his face. Lily's heart warmed. It had been so long since he'd looked carefree.

"Aunt Lily!" he cried, running toward her.

She laughed as she embraced him. "Well, you obviously enjoyed yourself."

Oliver pulled back from her and nodded. "I do wish you could have seen it."

So did Lily, but seeing Oliver so happy, she felt her annoyance melting away. "Do tell me about it," she said as they walked toward the coach.

Simon stepped from the conveyance at that moment, his eyes light with merriment. "Isn't St. Mary's lovely?" he asked.

Lily nodded as he took her hand. "I can see why Byron enjoyed his time here."

Simon chuckled, helping her into the coach. "You'll have to ask Will about him some day."

"Oh?" Lily asked as she settled herself against the squabs. "Did he know him?" She couldn't keep the scandalized tone from her voice. As lovely as Lord Byron's poetry was, he'd very recently been exiled; the offenses were too shocking to speak of in polite society.

Simon took the spot next to her, just as he had the entire journey, and draped his arm around her shoulders, pulling her against him. He smelled of sandalwood and the outdoors. "They were in the same year."

Oliver climbed inside the coach, sat across from them, and rolled his eyes. "Must you go about touching her *all* the time?"

With a warm laugh, Simon squeezed her arm. "As she's my wife, I don't see where you have anything to say about it, Maberley."

Oliver groaned, closed his eyes, and rested his head against the wall of the coach. "It's enough to turn a fellow's stomach."

"Well, we'll give you a reprieve tonight then, my boy."

"Oh?" Oliver asked, sitting forward in his seat.

"I believe I will take Her Grace to the theatre tonight. I can trust you to stay out of trouble for one evening, can't I?"

Lily looked up at Simon. "The theatre?"

"We have a box at Drury Lane. I believe *Richard III* is on stage. At least it was when I left Town a few weeks ago."

Shakespeare? Drury Lane? Giddiness spread through Lily.

❧

Simon loved seeing Lily's expression of awe when they entered his home on Curzon Street. Having grown up with all the grandeur of one ducal home or another, Simon enjoyed seeing his world through her eyes.

The Rutledge family was landed gentry, but foolish investments had left them penniless. He'd been surprised when Daniel had insisted all those years ago on marrying Emma. They were both so young at the time. She hadn't had fortune or connections to lend him, only herself. She was a quiet girl with simple tastes. But she spoke to a part of Daniel that Simon was just now beginning to understand.

He wanted to give Lily everything. Jewels, gowns, new experiences, anything to make her smile and see her pretty eyes grow wide with surprise. To that end, he went to the safe in his study, certain he had more of his grandmother's moonstone jewelry there.

Pulling back a portrait of his grandfather, he worked the combination until a cough from the doorway halted him. Simon stepped away from the hinged portrait to find his butler, Anderson, standing just inside the study.

"Yes, Anderson?"

The middle-aged man appeared uncomfortable and shifted in his spot, which was not like him at all. Simon had never known the butler to hedge.

"Well, Your Grace, it is Friday."

Simon raked his gaze across the man. What was this about? "Is that supposed to mean something to me?"

The man barely met his gaze. "The, um, well, the society pages came out today."

Something Simon never cared about. "And?"

The butler gestured to his desk, where a small stack of papers sat, awaiting his perusal. "Well, Your Grace, I'd rather not have to speak the words aloud. Perhaps you could read them for yourself."

"Why don't you just tell me what's going on?" Simon barked. He really didn't want to waste his time like this.

The butler shook his head. "Speaking frankly, I've seen you in a bit of a temper in the past, and I'd prefer not to be the messenger. Though," he pointed again at the stack of papers, "I thought you should be aware of the word about Town."

Thoroughly annoyed, Simon dismissed the man and sat at his desk. He first opened the *Mayfair Society Page*. He clenched his mouth shut after reading the first paragraph. *Bloody hell!*

Thirty-Seven

SIMON STEPPED FROM THE COACH AND HELD HIS HAND out to Lily. He smiled a smile she was sure he intended to be encouraging. However, it did little to ease her nerves. She'd never attended the theatre before, and, though she was excited, the prospect was a bit intimidating. She fingered the moonstone that rested right above her cleavage. She'd been shocked when Simon had presented her with matching earbobs before they left Curzon Street.

For years, the talents of Edmund Kean had been gushed over in one review after another, ever since he'd portrayed Shylock in *The Merchant of Venice* on the stage in Drury Lane. Lily never imagined she'd see Shakespeare performed in a London theatre, and she certainly never thought she'd actually see Kean himself on the very stage where he'd made his name.

When Simon had informed her that they would watch the famed thespian in the role of Richard III, Lily could barely contain her excitement. Apparently, being a duchess had its advantages.

Bridges Street was clogged with carriages as drivers maneuvered their horses toward Drury Lane. Men and women moved en masse toward the entrance, all dressed in their finest clothes for their night at the theatre.

Lily glanced down at her own dress. "I suppose I should be eternally grateful to Prisca for making this gown for me." She felt a little chagrin at wearing the green silk dress again, but it was the nicest one she owned.

Simon pulled her hand into the crook of his arm and smiled down at her. "Tomorrow, we'll commission London's most expensive modiste. You deserve a grand new wardrobe."

"My reward for putting up with you, Your Grace?" she laughed.

"*My* reward is you putting up with me." His gaze traveled up and down her body. "Among other things."

"Simon," she scolded him. "Do behave yourself." But she couldn't hold back the smile that threatened to erupt. "You're positively incorrigible."

His eyes narrowed at her. "And I thought beastly was the only description you had for me." He made the comment and looked away without meeting her eyes.

"I have a lot more, Your Grace." She stopped walking and tugged his arm. She raised one hand to cup the side of his face. "Beastly is my favorite, though."

He leaned into her hand. "Would that it could be true," he said quietly.

"You doubt me?"

He looked away and changed the subject, just as she'd known he would. "I can't wait to show off my lovely wife at the theatre." His eyes caught hers. "But I must warn you…"

Before he could even finish his sentence, a booming voice said, "Well, there's the Duke of Blackmoor. Finally out of seclusion, I see."

The man approached slowly and extended a hand to Simon. His height was nearly equal to the duke's, and the family resemblance was unmistakable. He shared the same black-as-night hair and grey eyes. Lily wracked her memory to come up with a name, but it eluded her.

"Lily, this is Mr. Alstott, a distant relation on my father's side. Charles, meet my duchess." Lily's heart did a little flip when he said her new title with such pride.

"Lovely to meet you," Lily replied.

"Your Grace, I knew it would be a lady such as you who'd finally get Simon to the altar," Mr. Alstott said, pressing his lips to her gloved fingers.

"I'm not sure if I should take that as a compliment or not," Lily said quietly.

Simon simply laughed and whispered dramatically, "It's a compliment, love. You may take it as one."

"Most definitely," the man boomed. "It would take a woman of great strength to finally collar this pup."

Simon narrowed his eyes and shook his head slightly, almost unnoticeably, at his distant cousin. At first, Lily thought she'd imagined it, but she knew she had not when Mr. Alstott tilted his head to one side in confusion. Then Simon made his signature move and changed the subject.

"Where is your lovely wife?" Simon asked.

"She's gossiping with friends, as usual," Mr. Alstott answered, as he searched the lobby with his eyes. Then he caught his wife's attention across the room and gestured her toward them. "Mary," he began when

she reached them. "Meet the Duchess of Blackmoor."
After the introduction, he draped his arm around his
wife's slender shoulders.

"Lily, please. I'm not quite used to the title yet."

"Charles and Mary will be sharing our box
tonight," Simon informed her and directed her
toward the staircase.

"Oh, how nice," Lily replied.

Beside them, Mary Alstott leaned toward Lily, her
brown eyes wide. "I think it's quite brave of you to
come out in society like this after the…"

Charles coughed loudly, interrupting his wife's
statement. Mary stopped talking to place her hand on
her husband's chest. "Are you all right?"

Lily frowned as she watched them. All the male
members of the Westfield family seemed to share
the same predisposition toward untimely changes of
subject matter.

"Yes, yes, of course," he said. "I am a bit parched,
however. Come, Mary. We'll find some wine."

"Perhaps we should take our seats," Simon suggested.
He ushered Lily through the crowd and up the stairs
to his box.

The number of theatre-goers was slightly overwhelming. Lily had never imagined such a crush. One
lady after another looked at her out of the corner of
their eyes, and Lily was certain she wasn't dressed
nearly nice enough for this. "Perhaps we shouldn't
have come," she muttered to herself.

Simon stopped walking and frowned at her. "Why?"

"I beg your pardon?" Lily blinked at him.

"Why shouldn't we have come?"

Lily shook her head. How was it possible he'd heard her? "I... um... Well, I feel a little underdressed."

A roguish smile lit his face as he directed her down the corridor past one box after another. "You're beautiful, Lily. And you're the Duchess of Blackmoor. You could walk in here wearing rags if you wanted."

"Rags?" She couldn't hold in a giggle.

"Personally, I prefer you wearing nothing at all."

"Simon!"

He ignored her rebuke, pressing her lower back toward one of the boxes. "Ah, here we are. Sit right near the front, love, so you have a good view of the stage."

Moments later, the Alstotts joined them and the theatre grew dim, signaling the remaining patrons to find their seats. Lily sat forward against the rail, excitement coursing through her veins as the stage captured her attention.

Simon's hand clasped hers when the play began. With a sidelong glance, she saw his bright smile in the darkness and it warmed her heart.

⤛⤜

Simon couldn't concentrate on the play even the slightest. He held Lily's hand clasped comfortably in his for fear that, if he let go, he would lose her. It was a foolish thought. She was safely seated beside him, entranced by Kean's performance.

Still, the worry persisted. Both Charles and Mary had very nearly told Lily the word about Town. The society rags were full with the news of his nuptials and rife with unflattering speculation. Not one column mentioned how wonderful Lily was.

Instead unsubstantiated gossip filled the pages. One author after another suggested Lily was already expecting Simon's child before their nuptials, hence the swift wedding.

One enterprising columnist had discovered Lily's dowry. They wrote that when no one would take Blackmoor's bribe to take Lily and the child off his hands, he had no choice but to marry her himself.

To add insult to injury, not only was her virtue maligned, but there were many uncomplimentary comments about her appearance, from her hair color to her height.

Simon's gaze traveled over her body in the darkness. She was perfect. She was tall and lithesome. Every part of her fit every part of him.

At first, he'd wanted to cancel their excursion and return to Westfield Hall, but that would only give credence to the reports. It would be better for them to hold their heads high and ignore the lies all together.

When the curtain fell for intermission, Lily stood up to stretch, exuberance sparkling in her hazel eyes. "This is amazing," she gushed.

Simon caressed her knuckles. He loved seeing her so happy. "Would you like some refreshment, love?"

"No, but thank you. I'll return in just a moment, Simon," she said as she pulled her hand from his grasp.

"Where are you going?" he asked, rising from his seat, ready to trail her like a faithful puppy.

"Women have to have some secrets," Mary broke in. "Come along, Lily. I'll accompany you to the retiring room."

Lily hooked her arm with Mary's, promised to return soon, and stepped out of the box. Simon watched her go, and a feeling of dread seeped over him.

Charles brought his attention back to the present when he called Simon's name. What Simon truly wanted to do was go after his wife. But he couldn't imagine the scandal he would cause if he followed her to the ladies' retiring room. And though worse had been said about him, he didn't want to give the gossipmongers anything else to say about Lily.

"She'll be fine, Blackmoor," Charles chided. "Mary will take care of her."

"I just worry," he said, catching himself mumbling.

"I can tell. You remind me of my faithful old dog. He was always such a jolly fellow until someone threatened my existence. Then he came out with teeth flying."

Simon sank into his chair. Surely she would return soon.

⁓

"I must tell you how terribly brave I think you are," Mary said in hushed tones as they walked down the crowded corridor.

"Brave?" Lily echoed, suddenly ill at ease.

"Why, if I were you, I wouldn't even step foot in public yet. I would have waited until the scandal died down a bit." She smiled at Lily. "But then I would imagine Blackmoor would never have married someone without a strong backbone."

Lily stopped walking and turned toward Mary. "I have no idea what you're referring to. Please enlighten me."

"Oh, my," the woman breathed. "You don't know?"

A giggle sounded near them. Lily looked up when she heard someone whisper loudly, "I can't believe she's walking around in public!"

"Know what?" Lily asked, as she drew Mary to the side of the hallway.

"The society columns," Mary mumbled. "The rumors about you and Blackmoor. About why you had to marry quickly." The woman looked down at the floor.

"There are always rumors about His Grace in those pages. It's nothing new." Lily tried to sound light and dignified.

"Yes, but these were about you, dear," Mary said quietly.

Lily shook her head in disbelief. She'd never done anything to provoke a scandal. "What do they say?"

"I've said too much already."

"Please, Mary."

"You should ask His Grace," the woman hedged.

"I'll do just that," Lily said as she turned quickly and stomped back down the corridor.

She heard laughter to her right and looked over to find a group of well-dressed ladies staring at her, tittering behind their fans. *Honestly, didn't they have anything better to do? Obviously not.*

Then the crowd parted, and Lily saw the source of the laughter. Mrs. Teresa Hamilton, stunning as ever, stood amongst them, wearing a smug smile and a low-cut dress. Lily didn't know which was more offensive.

Lily resisted the urge to rip the perfect blond curls from her head. No matter how satisfying that seemed, it certainly wouldn't help Lily's current predicament. She tipped her nose in the air and continued down the hallway, determined to act the role of duchess even if she didn't feel it.

Simon's box came into view, and Lily increased her gait. How could he not tell her what was being said? How could he parade her in front of the *ton* without any warning? In her haste, Lily stumbled just outside their box but managed to catch herself. She took a deep breath and adjusted her slipper.

Then she heard Simon's hushed voice filter through the curtain. "No, Lily doesn't know about me."

What didn't she know? Lily tilted her head to hear better.

"Certainly, you plan to tell her?" Charles asked.

"Lily doesn't need to know about *that* part of my life," Simon snarled.

"Don't bare your teeth at me," Charles growled back.

Did they always fight like that? What an odd family.

"My wife knows all my secrets." The man chuckled. "And adores every last one of them."

"I don't care to know what goes on in your bedroom," Simon replied, and she could hear the frown in his voice.

"*Never* in a bedroom when the moon is full, dear boy."

Simon growled. "What could possibly be keeping Lily?"

Before she knew what happened, Simon barreled out of the box and straight into her.

Thirty-Eight

"Simon!" Lily cried as she nearly stumbled to the floor.

His reflexes were quick, and he snatched her to him, righting her in no time. "I'm so sorry, love."

She stared at him with a mix of fear and barely contained anger. "Why didn't you tell me?" she demanded.

Oh, dear God! What had she overheard? What had Charles said? Simon's mind went back over the conversation. The lout had announced that Mary knew all of *his* secrets and then mentioned the full moon. Certainly Lily hadn't deduced anything from that.

"Tell you what?" he asked cautiously, glancing briefly at the other patrons walking past. Certainly the busy corridor was not the place to have this conversation. Simon directed her inside the box.

When Charles met his eyes, Simon glowered at his cousin. "Out!" he barked.

Charles returned his frown but did as he was bid. Then Simon looked into Lily's furious hazel eyes. Her lips pursed to angry little buds.

"What exactly is my crime, Lily?"

Tears threatened to escape her eyes, but she sniffed them back. "What is being said about me, Simon?"

The gossip! Thank God! Relief washed over him, but only for a moment. Lily looked so forlorn, his heart ached. "I thought it best not to tell you."

She poked him in the chest. Hard. "You thought it would be better for people to laugh at me instead? For me to be completely in the dark?"

The beast threatened to erupt from within him. Someone had laughed at her? He'd kill them. "What happened, Lily?" he growled.

"Take me home," she hissed.

Simon stepped toward her and brushed his knuckles across her soft cheek. "I didn't tell you, love, because I knew it would hurt you. But we can't go yet. If we turn tail and leave, the rumors will persist and grow even uglier. We need to keep our heads high and finish out the play."

"What are they saying about me, Simon?" she asked, her brow furrowed with concern.

He shrugged. "That you're *enceinte*."

Realization reflected in her eyes, and Simon hated to see her hurt. "But I'm not," she barely whispered.

Simon tugged her against him and nuzzled her neck. "You might be. Nothing would make me happier, Lily. But you certainly weren't before we married. And when no child arrives in seven months, or eight, they'll all realize they were wrong."

She sagged against him. "We have to wait *eight* months?"

He lifted his head. "Or sooner, if it's obvious you're not with child. However, since you have expressly demanded that I ravish you nightly, I don't know how long that will remain."

When a giggle escaped her throat, Simon breathed a sigh of relief. He slid his arms around her waist and kissed her soft lips. Now *he* wished they could return home.

"Simon," she said, pushing at his chest.

"Yes, love?"

He'd hoped she would smile at him, or in the very least have a sultry look, but her brow furrowed and her nose scrunched up.

"What else aren't you telling me?"

Simon's stomach dropped. "Nothing," he lied, feigning innocence.

Lily stepped out of his arms. "I'm not a fool, you know."

"Of course not, I—"

She held up her hand to stop his excuse. "I don't want to hear it, unless it's the truth."

"Lily, there's nothing to tell," he insisted as his palms grew sweaty. How long could he keep her in the dark? Would it be safer if he put some distance between them? Lived separately? The idea made him cringe. He didn't want to go on without her. He didn't know if he could.

The theatre grew dim again as intermission ended.

Charles poked his head back inside the box. "Simon…"

He nodded at his cousin. "Sorry to keep you waiting, Charles."

∽∾

Lily stepped from the Blackmoor coach in front of

Madam Pelletier's shop on Bruton Street. She wasn't sure why she was here. When they had intended to stay in London for a time, it had made sense to visit a modiste. However, both she and Simon were now anxious to return to Westfield Hall.

She didn't have a need for gowns befitting a duchess in Hampshire. Yet, Simon had insisted. He grasped her elbow and directed her into the exclusive shop.

An olive-skinned, dark-haired woman rushed forward at their entrance. "Your Grace," she gushed over Simon, her French accent surprising to Lily's ears. "You do me such an honor."

"Madam," Simon began, "you are a visionary. I would never take my wife anywhere else."

The Frenchwoman stood back, placing her hand over her heart. "*Mon dieu!* You've brought me a Greek goddess."

Lily's cheeks warmed at the statement, especially after she'd discovered where Simon had stashed the vicious columns and read them, each one maligning her character and her appearance. *A Long Meg with unfortunate hair and the fashion sense of a medieval peasant.*

"Isn't she, though?" Simon replied, a note of pride in his voice. "We're only to be in London another day. Do you think you can see Her Grace this morning?"

"Oh, indeed!" the modiste answered. Then she took Lily's hand and towed her toward a set of mirrors. "Let's start with your measurements, Your Grace."

"Oh, and, Madam," Simon called, "I'd like to order—"

"I am well acquainted with Your Grace's tastes."

How many women had Simon clothed?

"Thank you," he replied, before leaving Lily to be

poked, prodded, and measured for the better part of the day.

※

With Lily safely in Madam Pelletier's capable hands, Simon made his way to Canis House, an exclusive club to which he and his brothers belonged. The Georgian manor was a bit off the beaten path. In fact, it was so far off the path that he'd had to ride one of the horses from his stables to get there, as the trail wasn't wide enough for his coach.

It was a far cry from White's or other gentlemen's clubs, but only because the members of Canis House had a tendency to grow bushy tails and howl at the moon. Aside from that, it offered the same plush comfort as London's clubs.

Simon stepped into the dimly lit drawing room and allowed his eyes to adjust to the darkness. Within seconds, he spotted his father's oldest friend and confidante, Major Desmond Forster, who occupied a table at the back of the room.

"To what do I owe the honor, Simon? Should I thank that pretty new wife of yours since you have finally paid a visit to your father's old friend?" The man's smile was infectious, and Simon couldn't resist grinning back.

"I'm actually here about something else, Major," Simon confessed as a footman brought a glass of whisky and set it before him. He paused a moment to take a healthy swallow.

"What do you need, Simon?" Leave it to Major Forster to cut right to the meat of the matter.

"I need to find out how many of our kind are enrolled at Harrow."

"Whatever for?" the retired officer said as he sat forward.

"My ward and young cousin will begin school in a few weeks. When we took a tour of the grounds, there was a faint scent. It was almost as though one of our kind had been there. Recently. Do you know of anyone?"

Major Forester nodded. "Actually, there are at least two that I can think of. But there could be more. Not all of our kind offer their information to The Society, as you know."

"I just wanted to ensure Maberley will be safe," Simon said, grateful there would be at least one other boy in residence. "I wonder how much older the others are?" he mused aloud. Oliver could really use a mentor.

"Maberley? By God, is Daniel's son already old enough for Harrow?" A smile overtook the Major's face.

"It took me by surprise as well," Simon said.

"It was quite a tragedy, what happened to his parents. I'm glad the boy has you."

"I never thought I'd say it, but I'm quite happy to have him as well. He came with my wife." Simon's eyes danced with glee. "A bonus."

"I would say so." Major Forester tilted his head and regarded Simon quietly. "I would also dare to say that you're in love."

"Quite," Simon confessed. He heaved a sigh.

"Don't make it sound so dreadful, will you, chap? They say falling in love is quite an occasion. It has been quite a long time since I've done so. I can barely remember what it's like."

"Have you ever…?" Simon stopped himself. "Never mind," he mumbled.

"Have I ever what?" the major prodded. "Ask the question that's eating at you." He motioned for more drinks to be brought to the table.

Perhaps liquid courage would help, Simon thought as he tossed back another shot.

"I'm just wondering," Simon hedged. "My father and mother must have had a very normal relationship. I don't remember him ever leaving when the moon was full."

"And?" Major Forster prompted.

Simon sighed. "Have you ever claimed a mate?" he finally spit out. He refused to even glance in the major's direction for fear that the man would be rolling on the floor with laughter. But the old officer just clapped his big hand on Simon's shoulder, forcing his attention.

"Indeed I have." He smiled at the memory.

"And it… went… well?" Simon couldn't figure out how to ask the questions he needed to have answered.

"Splendidly," the major said, coughing a little to cover the emotion that coated the word. "What's your fear, Simon? You know your parents had a Lycan relationship. And your mother is no worse for wear."

"I've resolved to never claim Lily."

"Why in the world would you do such an idiotic thing?" Major Forster's voice rose an octave.

"Would you keep your voice down?" Simon growled, looking around the room to see who had heard. Fortunately, no one seemed to be paying them a bit of attention.

"Is your Lily a little mouse? Is she fragile?"

"No, not at all."

"Then share your life with her. Or you do an injustice to both yourself and to her. You'll never fully know her until she shares in every part of your life. Don't you want to be a whole man?"

"More than anything," Simon confessed. "But her sister couldn't handle the claiming. I can't risk losing Lily. Or having her look at me the way Emma did Daniel." He couldn't imagine a worse fate.

Thirty-Nine

EXCITEMENT RUSHED THOUGH LILY WHEN WESTFIELD Hall finally came into view from the coach window. She didn't care if she ever returned to London. The city's allure no longer existed for her. But here, in their quiet corner of Hampshire, she could remain forever with Simon.

However, she wasn't certain *he* could. Simon was just as at home in London as he was at Westfield Hall. What if she lost him to the excitement of Town, to his lifestyle?

She glanced up at his ruggedly handsome face. He seemed deep in thought, as he had most of the trip. Troubled. Quiet. Though whenever she asked what had his mind, he forced a smile to his lips and told her it was nothing.

But it was obviously something.

She just couldn't figure out what.

Lily knew he was lying, though she couldn't understand why. Had she done something to make him distrustful of her? If so, she wasn't sure what it was.

The full moon.

Oliver had mentioned it, as had Charles Alstott. *The full moon?* What did that have to do with anything? Thoroughly confused, she heaved a sigh.

Simon gently touched her cheek. "We're almost home, love."

Did he love her, or was their relationship merely physical to him? *If* he loved her, wouldn't he trust her? Lily smiled in return, though she didn't feel it.

"Will said he'd help me with my Latin," her nephew said.

Ever since his excursion to Harrow, Oliver seemed excited about the prospect of going away to school, which was a welcome about-face. Thank heavens! At least something good had come of their trip.

"You'll have to settle for me, Maberley," Simon informed him. "Unless Will sprouted wings and flew to Scotland, it'll be weeks before he and Ben return."

Oliver nodded. "Do you think Lord Benjamin is in some sort of trouble?"

Simon chuckled, shaking his head. "I believe he's into *something*, but I wouldn't necessarily call it trouble. My guess is Ben won't appreciate it when Will shows up unannounced, though it will all be his own fault. I cannot fathom him writing Mother several times a week."

"Simon!" Lily chastised, then looked across the coach at her nephew. "Oliver York, I'll expect a letter from you at least once a week after you start school."

"Of course!" Simon's voice dripped with mirth. "Once a week, Maberley, or I'll be forced to send Will across the countryside looking for you."

Then the two of them howled with peals of laughter, causing the coach to rock on its springs. Lily didn't find them remotely humorous, and she folded her arms across her chest, glaring at her husband.

Simon brought his levity under control and squeezed her shoulder. "I'm sorry, love. I couldn't resist."

She supposed she should be happy that he didn't seem to be the brooding man he'd been since they'd left London. But as she was the brunt of his joke, Lily had a difficult time feeling charitable.

Simon sighed. "Oliver, promise your aunt you'll write her at least once a week when you attend Harrow."

"I promise," he quickly replied as the coach rambled to a stop.

"Thank God," Simon remarked. "Good to be home."

He opened the door, hopped from the carriage, and extended his hand to her.

Lily accepted his help, stepping into the late-afternoon light. Simon was right. It did feel good to be home. His hand snaked around her waist, and he led her up the steps of the manor house.

The door opened wide, and Billings beamed at them. "Welcome home, Your Graces."

The butler took Simon's beaver hat and informed them that the dowager duchess was enjoying tea and entertaining Miss Hawthorne in the blue parlor.

A rumbled growl escaped Simon at Prisca's name, which Lily didn't understand at all. Why did it seem that none of the Westfield men could be civil to her friend? "If you're incapable of behaving yourself, Simon, you and Oliver can entertain yourselves elsewhere."

"I believe that is best," he clipped out and then directed Oliver toward his study.

Lily shook her head, worried she'd never understand

certain aspects of him. She handed her Spencer jacket to Billings and proceeded down the corridor to the blue parlor. Even before she entered the room, she could hear her mother-in-law's laugh mixed with Prisca's giggle.

She stepped over the threshold to find the two women sitting side by side on the settee. "Good afternoon."

"Oh!" they cried in unison, though it was Prisca who leapt from her spot. "Lily, you're home!"

As the two embraced, Alice slowly rose from her seat. "I trust everything went well, dear?"

Lily nodded. It was a lie, but she didn't know how else to respond. It seemed, however, that Alice had keen senses. Her mother-in-law's eyes narrowed, obviously assessing her. "Come join us for tea," Alice continued.

Lily allowed the dowager to lead her to the settee before assuming the spot beside her. "Your letter mentioned you were to see *Richard III*."

"Oh!" Prisca exclaimed as she settled on a chair across from them. "I hear Kean is excellent in the role. I do prefer the comedies however. *Twelfth Night* is my particular favorite."

"Did you enjoy yourself?" Alice asked.

"Yes." Until she learned all of London thought she was of easy virtue, and before she once again laid eyes on Teresa Hamilton. "I met Mr. and Mrs. Alstott."

Alice's grey eyes widened. "Indeed? It's been an age. Did they seem well?"

Lily nodded again and then discussed the play in great detail. After more questions were asked and answered, Prisca announced that it was late and she really should return home. Good-byes and hugs were exchanged, and in no time Lily found herself alone with Alice.

"All right, Lily," her mother-in-law began quietly, "it's just us. I can tell something is bothering you."

It was just them. Lily squared her shoulders. "Does the full moon mean anything to you?" she blurted out.

She expected the dowager to look surprised or taken aback by her question, but Alice smiled instead. "It comes around once a month."

Not a very satisfying answer. Lily scowled. "I know Simon is keeping something from me, and it has to do with the full moon."

Alice heaved a sigh. "Figured all that out by yourself?"

Was it impossible for the woman to give her a helpful response? "Do *you* know what it is?"

Alice rose from her seat. "Dear Lily, I don't often understand my sons' choices. Take Miss Hawthorne, for example. Why William keeps himself from her I have no idea. They'd both be much happier if he didn't. And with Benjamin, there are so many things I don't understand about him that there's not even a good starting place."

"And Simon?" Lily asked, her patience wearing thin.

"Well, Simon I understand. I just don't happen to agree with him."

"What does that mean?"

"It means I can't tell you what you want to know, Lily." Her expression was pained.

"Why not?"

"Do you love my son?"

More than life, or she wouldn't care about any of this. Lily nodded, which made Alice smile and clasp her hand.

"My dear, you've figured out so much on your own. You're on the right path. Follow your heart."

"Why can't you tell me what is going on?" Lily begged.

"Because it's not allowed. Only Simon can do so."

Lily thought she might scream. Only Simon could tell her? That was the most unhelpful thing Alice could have said. Simon had no intention of telling her anything.

She was on her own.

❧

After dismissing Oliver, Simon returned to his desk to pore over a report from his steward. It wasn't the most interesting reading, but it would serve to keep his mind off Prisca Hawthorne.

Truly he shouldn't be so irritated with the meddlesome chit. If she hadn't interfered in his life, he wouldn't have Lily. He should be thanking the girl. But the manipulative way she went about arranging things to her liking made it hard for him to keep a level head where she was concerned. With that in mind, it was perhaps for the best that Will had decided against throwing his lot in with the chit. He'd rather not have to kill his sister-in-law. Now if he could keep her from visiting Lily and his mother...

A knock at the door interrupted his thoughts, and Simon pushed his report to the middle of his desk. "Come."

His mother poked her head inside. "Do you have a moment, dear?"

He gestured to one of the chairs before him. "Of course."

She slipped inside and shut the door firmly behind her. She did not sit, however, as she chose to pace before his desk instead. "You need to tell her, Simon."

"Tell her to ban Prisca Hawthorne from my home? I was considering it," he replied hopefully.

She stopped walking, heaved an irritated sigh, and folded her arms across her chest. "Don't be obtuse. You know exactly what I'm talking about."

His shoulders slumped forward. He did know what she meant; he'd just *hoped* it had to do with his rudeness toward Prisca. "We've already had this discussion. I won't burden Lily with this aspect of my life."

His mother's lips drew up tight. "She knows you're keeping something from her."

Simon dismissed the idea with a wave of his hand. "She knows nothing. Don't put your hopes for Lily above her best interests."

"*My* hopes for Lily," she scoffed. "You really are more stubborn than even your father, Simon. She told me herself that she knows you're keeping something important from her."

He swallowed. "She did?" Lily had asked him numerous times what secrets he kept from her, but he thought he'd convinced her otherwise.

"Hmm," she answered. "And she asked me if the full moon had anything to do with whatever you're hiding."

His limbs all went weak. How could she possibly know that much? "What did you say?"

"I told her it wasn't allowed for me to say anything."

"God damn it, Mother!" He leapt to his feet while his pulse pounded in his ears and fear gripped his chest. Simon's fist struck his desk with such a force that it split along the middle and his report fell to the floor along with all his unopened correspondence.

Well accustomed to his temper, his mother didn't even flinch. "Honestly, Simon, that desk belonged to your grandfather. You should have a care."

"To hell with the desk," he roared, pushing it over as an afterthought. "Why would you tell her such a thing? Now she *knows* I'm hiding something."

His mother rubbed her temple, looking at him as if he were a simpleton. "She *already* knew that, Simon. How long do you think it will take for her to learn the rest of it? Tell her now, before she discovers it on her own."

"Simon," Lily called from the library door.

"Yes, love?" His voice came from a darkened corner. Strange. After they'd arrived at Westfield Hall, he hadn't sought her out, and it was nearly time for dinner. Then there was the disaster she found in his study. It looked as though a wild animal had been trapped inside, destroying everything in sight. The image made chills race down her spine.

Cautiously, Lily stepped into the room, finding her husband reclined in an overstuffed leather chair with a glass of something that smelled like whisky. "Are you all right?" she asked stopping before him.

"Are you?" Simon countered. His grey eyes landed

on her, reflecting a dangerous glint. The intensity of his gaze nearly shook her to her core, and she wasn't at all certain it was her husband staring at her.

A nervous giggle escaped her, and she pressed her nails into her palm, hoping to steady herself. "It is nearly time for dinner."

"I'm not hungry."

"Oh." She frowned at him. She had the feeling she should leave him to his strange mood, but seeing him like this tore at her heart. "Is something amiss?" she asked, edging a bit closer to him.

"Why would you think so?"

"I went to your study first…" her voice trailed off when he winced.

"I received some troubling news, is all. Nothing for you to worry about, Lily."

Troubling news? Though her rational mind screamed for her to leave, she couldn't do so. Lily dropped to her knees before him, clasping one strong hand with both of hers. "You are my husband, Simon. If something is troubling you, I can't help but worry."

Something flashed in his eyes, something she couldn't read. Then he smiled at her, a sad smile that made her heart constrict. "Are you happy with me? With all of this?"

She kissed his hand that she had trapped. "Never doubt it."

Simon brushed her cheek with his free hand. "Lily, you should eat. I won't have you withering away to nothing simply because I'm not hungry."

She tugged at his hand. "If you'd rather not eat, Simon, I'm sure I can think of something more enjoyable."

Forty

SIMON WATCHED LILY CLOSELY OVER THE NEXT SEVERAL days. If he hadn't had that disturbing conversation with his mother, he would never have known anything was amiss. She fussed over Oliver, sweetly insisting he work on his studies. Doting on the lad as if he were two instead of twelve. She worked on frilly sewing with his mother, chatting gaily all the while. And Lily continued to look at Simon with the same adoring, passion-hued eyes. He made love to her every night, and she responded just as she always had.

He would have begun to think his imagination had invented the entire conversation with his mother, if not for the way she continued to pressure him when they were alone, insisting that he tell his wife the truth.

"She'll understand," his mother hissed in the corridor outside the breakfast room.

But he couldn't be sure of that, and he brushed past her on his way to the library. His mother had accepted his father, and Mary Alstott accepted Charles, but there were even more examples where that didn't turn out. Daniel and Emma were only one. And he kept coming back to the fact that Lily was Emma's sister. There was no reason to believe she would feel differently than Emma.

Giving only part of himself to Lily was better than not having her at all. It was a risk he couldn't take.

She couldn't find out. He couldn't lose her.

He watched her across the room, turning the pages of an old book. Her nose crinkled up just a bit when she concentrated, and he loved the look on her.

His attention was diverted from his wife when Billings cleared his throat in the library doorway. "Your Grace, a letter has arrived for you."

Simon dismissed him with a wave of his hand. "Put it with the others, Billings."

"This one is from Major Forster. He had it hand delivered with the instructions that you were to open it right away."

Forster? Simon rose from his seat and started toward his butler, a smile on his face. The old major knew him well. The letter would most assuredly become lost amongst the others if he didn't go to such lengths.

Simon retrieved the letter from the silver salver Billings held and broke the seal.

Dear Blackmoor,

I hope you are well. As per our conversation last week, I have compiled a list of other boys enrolled at Harrow. The list is rather short, however. Only Leopold Schofield from Surrey is both registered with The Society and on the school rolls. The other boys have recently graduated and are already at Cambridge.

I do not know if you are acquainted with the Schofields, but I can attest to the bravery of the boy's father who fought under my command.

I have sent a letter to Lieutenant Schofield, on your behalf, explaining the Earl of Maberley's situation. The lieutenant should be contacting you directly. It would be best, dear boy, if you actually paid close attention to your correspondence over the next fortnight. Not everyone knows how to get your attention as well as I.

Please send my love to your mother. I do hope to see you at Canis House soon.

> *Sincerely,*
> *Maj. Desmond Forster*

"Is everything all right?" Lily asked, rising from her seat.

Simon carefully folded the letter and put it in his pocket. He was surprised to see Lily's gaze concentrated on him when he glanced in her direction. Her brows were drawn together, her hazel eyes troubled.

"News, Simon?" she asked.

"Nothing of importance, love," he replied, trying to make his tone sound light. "Just a note from an old friend of my father's."

"Which old friend?"

Why all the questions? "Major Forster." If he was fortunate, she would leave it at that.

"And what did he want?"

Simon closed his eyes and sighed. *Please don't force me to lie to you more than is necessary.* "He knows of a boy who will be attending Harrow along with Oliver.

He suggests that the boys meet before the session begins so they can become acquainted."

Lily crossed the floor, confusion reflected in her eyes. "I'm certain there will be a number of boys at Harrow for the Michaelmas term."

None like Leopold Schofield. "Yes, but I was looking for a mentor for Oliver. Someone to take him under his wing, so to speak. Major Forster thinks one of his lieutenant's sons would be a good fit."

Lily reached out her hand to Simon, and, when he pulled her toward him, she kissed his cheek. "That was a very sweet thing to do."

Simon nuzzled against her neck, inhaling the soft lilac scent that he had come to identify with Lily. So light and feminine, so different from him. "I'm never sweet," he said gruffly.

She giggled at that, wrapping her arms around his middle. "I beg to differ."

"Not sweet," he repeated, nipping at the base of her neck. "I had ulterior motives."

Lily's lithe body molded against his. "I can't imagine what you mean, Your Grace."

He blew his breath low across her bodice and cupped her bottom, pressing his arousal firmly against her softness. "I think it should be obvious."

"My beastly husband," she began with a teasing lilt to her voice. "If you ruin my new gown, I'll thrash you."

New gown? Simon ran his fingers along her silk-covered back. How had he not noticed she wore something new? "Is this one of Madam Pelletier's?"

Lily nodded. "An entire trunk arrived this morning.

I can't even imagine what you spent to have such an extensive order finished and delivered so quickly."

To hell with the dresses. Simon couldn't hide his grin. If the order was complete, Lily should have received several pieces that were for his eyes only.

"You have a strange look on your face," she told him.

Simon lifted one brow. "That, love, is me imagining what you'll look like in one of your new nightrails."

A pretty blush pinkened her cheeks. "I don't know why you bothered to order them at all. They don't hide a thing. I might as well walk about nude."

Simon couldn't resist squeezing her bottom. "Excellent suggestion."

Lily stepped out of his arms with an enchanting giggle. "Behave yourself, Simon Westfield. And you'll have to be patient as well. I am supposed to leave for Langley Downs in a few moments."

Langley Downs. Simon's smile became a scowl. "I'd rather you not spend time with Prisca Hawthorne."

Lily shook her head. "Why?"

"Who do you think told Mrs. Bostic you were living here unchaperoned?" When Lily stared blankly at him, Simon continued, "That meddlesome chit can manage her brothers' lives all she wants, but I take umbrage when she interferes in mine."

"Simon," Lily began, "if you weren't afraid for my reputation, would you have ever married me?"

No. He'd have suffered without her. He wouldn't have wished his life on her. He wouldn't have tied her future to him.

When he didn't respond, Lily frowned at him. "I see. Are you sorry you married me?"

"No," he assured her and closed the distance between them. "Never believe that. I love that you're mine, Lily." Selfish bastard that he was, he could never let her go now.

"Well," Lily said, folding her arms across her chest. "I didn't know Prisca was the cause. I'll have to thank her over tea."

❧

Langely Downs' butler announced, "The Duchess of Blackmoor," before returning to his post.

As she stepped over the threshold of the green parlor, Lily was surprised to see that Prisca was not alone. "Your Grace." Emory Hawthorne stood and bowed stiffly. "Allow me to offer my felicitations on your recent marriage."

Lily smiled at the gentleman, who seemed suddenly uncomfortable now that she'd arrived. Of course, the last time she'd seen him, she'd been in a terrible state of disarray, courtesy of Simon Westfield. "Thank you, Mr. Hawthorne. I shall pass on your well wishes to my husband."

After a tight smile, he excused himself and left Lily and Prisca to their own company. As Prisca linked her arm with Lily's, her violet eyes twinkled mischievously. "All right, since the dowager isn't with you, you can tell me everything, Lily."

"Everything?"

Prisca nodded enthusiastically. "How is it? How do you like being a duchess?"

"I suppose now would be a good time to thank you for ruining my reputation and forcing me into a marriage with Simon."

Prisca didn't even look ashamed. Her smile grew larger, brightening the room. "It was a stroke of luck. I didn't know what I was going to do until the situation presented itself. I am surprised Will told him, however. No wonder Blackmoor scowled at me when I left Westfield Hall last week. That man does not like to be managed."

"Hmm." Lily agreed. "He mentioned as much."

"But are *you* happy?" Prisca asked, as she sat on the settee and gestured for Lily to join her.

Lily couldn't help but smile. "Very. I do want to thank you for everything, especially for braving Simon's temper."

Prisca giggled. "Please. As I said before, I've known Blackmoor my entire life. I'm not the least bit afraid of him."

The room began to spin in Lily's mind. She may not be able to get her mother-in-law to tell her anything, but Prisca might know what she was after. "I have a strange question to ask you."

"Well, that sounds intriguing."

"As you say, you've known Simon forever…" Lily frowned. He would be furious if he knew she was asking these sorts of questions. She shook off the thought. She was the Duchess of Blackmoor, and she had every right to know what her duke was hiding from her. "Does the full moon mean anything to you?"

When her friend said nothing but stared at her blankly, Lily prodded, "In regards to Simon?"

After a moment, Prisca furrowed her brow. It was a ridiculous thing to ask. Lily felt like a fool the moment the words left her mouth.

Finally, Prisca shook her head. "I don't know, Lily. I've often wondered the same thing. Not about His Grace. He is much older than me. But once upon a time I spent quite a lot of time with Will and Benjamin. It was years ago. Their moods became like clockwork. I didn't notice it at first, and it happens so gradually, but the longer you're with them, the more it becomes apparent. Will always got more agitated as the moon waxed, and Ben always got more quiet."

"Do you know what it means?" Lily asked, leaning toward Prisca who shook her head.

"I asked Will once. I've never seen him so furious. He refused to talk to me about it and… Well, things between us haven't ever been the same since."

Lily felt the wind whoosh out of her lungs. What a horrible tale. What if Simon reacted the same way? She didn't want things to change between them, other than she wished he'd trust her with whatever this was. She didn't want them to constantly hurt each other the way Prisca and Will did.

Maybe it was best not knowing. As long as Simon stayed with her, she could be content. Losing him wasn't an option, even if it meant never learning his secret, even if it meant he didn't fully trust her. At least for now.

Forty-One

LILY STOPPED BEFORE ENTERING SIMON'S STUDY. He'd never summoned her before, and she couldn't imagine what he wanted with her. She took a deep breath and smoothed her skirts with her hands. Then she knocked softly.

"Come," he called.

She pushed the door open and stepped inside. Simon sat behind a new oak desk, and he smiled when she entered. "Ah, there you are, love," he said, rising to his feet.

"You wanted to see me?"

Simon nodded and gestured to one of the two leather seats in front of his desk. "I am terrible at correspondence. Perhaps you've noticed."

Lily laughed and then fell into the first seat. "I am painfully aware of that fact, Simon."

One dark eyebrow rose. "Yes, well, you wouldn't have sought me out if I had been more communicative. So I can't really feel remorse for my failing in this regard."

Lily couldn't help but smile. "I suppose that is true."

"Anyway, I thought you could help me become a bit more organized. Help me go through my post, to be more responsible in this area."

"You want me to go through your post?"

He nodded. "I really have no patience for it alone. But I thought if you assisted me, I might manage to get through it."

"Meaning?" Lily asked.

"Most of my correspondence is destined for the rubbish bin. People wanting things of me. To attend a function or sponsor a charity, things of that nature. Anyone who knows me well would never write to me. Except for Will and Ben. They're the exception to the rule. Even still, neither of them write to me very often."

How did one live like that? Lily couldn't imagine. "Have you ever thought about sponsoring a charity?"

He sat back in his chair and folded his arm across his chest. "I am quite philanthropic, Lily. Major Forster runs a charitable organization that I donate liberally to."

Lily had no idea. All the years she'd kept up with his exploits, she'd believed him to be a self-involved rake-hell. "The man who found a boy to mentor Oliver?"

"Yes. He was an old friend of my father's."

"So you mentioned. What does his organization do?"

Simon hesitated, studying her a moment before answering. "The Lycanian Society helps individuals and families who suffer from certain ailments. Food, shelter, clothing, things of that nature. Will devotes much of his time to The Society."

Lily had never heard of it. "Isn't it usually women who spend their time with charities?"

Simon quirked a grin at her. "I'll be sure to mention that to Will."

Flustered, Lily sat forward, her hand on her chest. "Oh, don't you dare!" Will was such a dear man that she'd never want to insult him.

Simon's warm chuckle put her at ease, and she sank against the back of the chair. "So," he continued, "will you help manage me, Lily?"

She would never refuse an opportunity to spend time with him, and it warmed her to her toes that he wanted the same. "Of course."

"Excellent." He rose from his seat and walked around his desk. "We'll start tomorrow." He pulled Lily from her seat and slid his arms around her waist. "I don't know what I'd do without you, love."

Lily smiled at him. "Oh, you'd probably still be making a name for yourself amongst the society rags, breaking hearts as you went."

Simon smiled wolfishly and then dipped his head down to kiss her right above her heart. "Still intact," he murmured before kissing his way back up her collarbone, her neck, and finally her lips.

The flutters that raced through her nearly robbed her of her breath, and she actually swayed. Simon's arms tightened around her as his tongue slowly traced her lips. When he swept inside her mouth, Lily thought he might devour her. All of her hoped he would.

⌘

Simon watched the sunlight reflect off Lily's pretty locks as she intently studied the pile of letters before her. He was supposed to be looking at his ledger and tending to his Blackmoor holdings, but none of the entries were nearly as engaging as his wife. As if she felt his stare, she looked up and he averted his eyes to the open pages before him.

"Simon," she said quietly.

"Hmm?" He raised his head, as if he had not been gazing at her for the last ten minutes.

"I don't know some of these names. Do you want me to call them out to you?"

He leaned back in his chair and folded his arms across his chest. If she wanted to read Cook's grocery bill, he'd readily listen. "Go ahead."

"Phineas Appleton."

"Toss it."

"What if it's important? Shouldn't I look?"

Simon laughed. "I went to school with Appleton. He was a degenerate then, and he still is. He writes once a month wanting me to join some club of his. I'd rather not."

"Have you told him so?"

"One would think my unresponsiveness would be enough of a hint, Lily."

"Apparently not." She waved the letter in the air. "A simple note stating that you are uninterested might stop Mr. Appleton's interest."

No one who wanted Blackmoor money or name would stop hounding him because of a simple note. But it was endearing that his sweet, naïve wife thought it would. "You may pen one, if you'd like. I'm not going to waste my time on Appleton."

She put the letter aside and lifted the next one to

her nose. "This one doesn't have a name, but it's drenched in some perfume."

Damn! He hadn't thought about Lily coming across *those* sorts of letters. Perhaps he should rethink her helping him. Who knew what she might come across? "As I said before, no one who knows me well would send me a letter. Toss it."

"It's from a female admirer."

This was a bit awkward. "Lily, please toss it."

She smiled at him and put it on top of Appleton's letter. "I could write all of your admirers, too, and inform them that you are married now and that your wife goes through your post."

Simon scowled at Lily until her smile vanished.

She cleared her throat. "This is from Lieutenant Schofield. Isn't that the—"

"Let me have it." Simon sat forward with a start. Who knew what Schofield wrote in his letter? He'd really rather Lily not read whatever it was. He'd give her the edited version later.

Lily looked at the letter and then passed it across the desk to him.

Dear Duke of Blackmoor,

I understand from Major Forster that your ward, the Earl of Maberley, will be in attendance at Harrow for the Michaelmas term along with my son, Leo. Forster suggested we bring the lads together before the start of term, so that Maberley will have someone to guide him.

I was in Spain with my regiment when Leo began his first term at school. I wish that I had been here for him to help make his transition into the human world easier. We would be honored to assist Maberley with his adjustment.

Perhaps the earl could pay us a visit during the September moonful and give the lads the opportunity to sniff each other. I will await your reply.

> *Your humble servant,*
> *Lt. Harold Schofield*
> *Reston House,*
> *Guilford, Surrey*

Transition into the human world? How did the Schofields normally go about their lives? It was a stroke of luck that he'd been able to snatch the letter from Lily's fingers.

The September moonful. That was the perfect excuse. He could take Oliver to Surrey to experience the change with Schofield, while he returned to the woods of Westfield Hall without Lily knowing. He could tell her he was going to London after dropping Oliver off along the way.

He frowned, realizing he would have to come up with a different excuse once a month for the rest of his life. He was going to have to become much more creative, or he'd run out of ideas before their first anniversary.

"What did he say, Simon?" Lily's voice interrupted his thoughts.

Simon looked up from the letter to find Lily's eyes focused on him. "He'd like for Oliver to come visit them next week. Let the boys get acquainted before the start of term."

"Oh. Well, perhaps the Schofield boy could come here instead."

And have *three* wolves in close proximity to Lily? Not a chance. "I think it would be rude to turn down Schofield's offer, love. Perhaps we can invite the boy some other time." Like when the moon was in its crescent state.

"But Oliver will be leaving us so soon anyway," she said sadly.

Simon pocketed the note and rose from his seat. He walked around his desk and placed his hands on Lily's shoulders. "It'll just be for a few days. He needs this. It'll give him a bit of confidence to start school with."

She nodded her head. "I know you're right."

"Come on, love. We've been doing this long enough. I asked Cook to prepare a basket for luncheon and thought we could enjoy the grounds."

She smiled at him. "That is a lovely idea."

❦

Simon took Lily's hand in his as they walked down the garden path. Lily still had trouble reconciling *this* Simon with the dangerous Duke of Blackmoor. He had such a bad reputation, and she knew without a doubt that much of it was earned.

Lily worried her bottom lip between her teeth. She couldn't get the thought of all the perfume-scented letters off her mind. Before they'd left his study, he'd scooped up all the letters with feminine scrawl and tossed them into the wastebasket. Why would he do such a thing? He hadn't read them. Did he have something to hide?

She would like to imagine that the letters meant nothing. But how well did she really know him?

Simon squeezed her hand in his. "Is something bothering you?" His eyebrows drew together.

Lily shook her head. "No. Why do you ask?"

"Because, if you chew on that bottom lip any harder, I'll have to take drastic measures." His eyes twinkled at her, the grey depths reflecting happiness and contentment.

"Drastic measures to do what?"

"To protect those lips I love so much. I might have need of them later." He pulled her closer and touched his lips to hers. "Or now," he murmured, then smiled at her.

He spread a blanket on the soft ground and sat, tugging her fingers until she sat with him, then he drew her to sit between his spread knees. She leaned back against him. The body supporting hers was strong and supple. She sighed with contentment. Yet some doubts still nagged at her.

"Out with it, Lily," he said.

Lily took a deep breath and started. "I never thought I would marry, Simon."

"I am very lucky that some other man didn't snatch you from my path years ago."

"No one was ever very interested in me. You are the first."

"Their loss," he murmured.

"I'm sorry you got stuck with me, Simon," she said, turning to look at him. "But I do need to tell you one thing. And it's something you may not like."

Simon tensed behind her, his body at alert. "Continue."

"I watched Emma change after her marriage to Daniel." Simon inhaled behind her. She turned to look at him. "And I don't think I could stand it if you did to me what Daniel did to her."

"Change in what way?" The calm beneath his voice belied the rigid set of his body. "What did he do to her?"

"Emma was always happy and carefree. She laughed readily. She loved with all her heart. And she loved Daniel."

"If I remember correctly, she had his whole heart as well."

"I'm not so sure."

∽

Simon took a breath and tried to remember snippets of conversations he'd had with Daniel about his marriage.

"I'm fairly certain he loved and adored her," Simon could truthfully say.

"Then why did he have relations with other women?" Lily's eyes dodged his, looking everywhere but at his face.

He captured her chin in his hand and waited for her gaze to rise.

"Daniel was faithful. I can attest to that."

"She always thought he had a mistress," Lily whispered.

"She told you that?"

Lily nodded.

"What made her draw that conclusion?"

"The way he left her all the time. He took trips every month." Lily paused, then looked directly into his eyes. "Perhaps you can explain it to me. Maybe you know something I don't."

"Daniel was faithful. He adored Emma."

"A few months after they married, she changed."

"In what way?" Simon had to find out how much she knew.

"She feared him. They were fine for a few months. And then Emma told me Daniel was taking her with him on one of his trips. And she came back changed."

"And what do you think happened?" Simon thought his heart might pound out of his chest.

"I think he hurt her. She told me as much," she blurted out when Simon tried to deny it.

"It wasn't intentional," Simon sighed. How could he possibly ease her pain?

"You know about it?" Lily gasped.

"I don't know details," Simon said, which was true. He had never delved deeper into the relationship than Daniel wanted him to, so he didn't know specifics. "But I have an idea of what happened." The same thing that could happen if Simon took Lily under the light of the full moon.

"What do you know?"

He closed his eyes and tried to arrange his thoughts. "I know he got too rough with her." Simon shrugged.

"In what way?"

Please let it go, Lily.

"In what way, Simon?" she prodded.

"Intimately," he confessed. "He scared her intimately." He didn't know how else to verbalize it.

"You mean like when they were together?"

"More like when he was inside her." When he

placed his teeth upon her shoulder. When he tore her flesh. When he marked her as his own.

"Oh." Lily looked confused.

"There are times…" Simon started. Then he stopped.

"Times?"

Simon closed his eyes tightly. "Times when a man, men like Daniel and me, feel like we could lose control."

"Do you feel that way with me?"

"I'm sure I will."

"Simon, you would never hurt me." Her hand moved to cup his face. Such tenderness, even when he revealed some of his inner battle. He didn't deserve it.

Simon kissed her palm. "I wouldn't intend to. And neither did Daniel. Once he realized he was capable of it, he took himself away from her."

"Where did he go? To other women?"

"Never."

"I could never bear it if you left me."

"You're stronger than Emma. You would adjust."

Lily shook her head and touched her lips to his. "I'll have to coerce you to stay."

She could try. But even she couldn't stop the cycle of the moon.

Forty-Two

SIMON HATED LYING TO HER. HE SIMPLY DETESTED himself for it. She deserved so much more. But he'd decided before their marriage that she would never know about his Lycan side, so certain measures had to be put in place. *For her safety.* He kept reminding himself that this was *for her safety.*

"You're leaving me?" she asked, her hands on her hips.

"I'll only be in London for a few days," he said as he avoided looking into her eyes. If he did, he would confess all his sins. He would tell her every untruth. Then he would watch her turn from him in revulsion. He couldn't bear it. He simply could not.

"Why can't I go with you?" she asked. Her eyes pleaded with him, demanding that he answer.

"You simply cannot. It's not that kind of journey."

"Then what kind of journey is it?" Lily began to pace from one side of the room to the other.

Simon clenched the bridge of his nose between his thumb and forefinger. He'd been feeling more and more out of control as the days passed. And the night before, he'd nearly taken her too hard when he'd made love to her. She'd cried out when he'd gotten too rough. He couldn't allow himself to hurt her. He surely would if he stayed at Westfield Hall.

"It's the kind you can't go on!" he snapped at her.

Lily's indrawn breath made him cringe.

"Lily," he said softly as he walked to her. Perhaps he should grovel at her feet. He could drop to his hands and knees before her and lay his snout over her slipper. Maybe she would take the hint.

He reached for her.

She raised her hands to fend him off. "Don't touch me, Simon."

He stepped back, surprised by her tone of voice. "This is really bothering you?"

"As though you have to ask," she said before she turned on her heel and left the room, slamming the door behind her so hard that the portrait of an old ancestor in front of a lake shook from its hanger and hit the floor with a bang. His Lily certainly knew how to leave a room.

"Billings!" Simon called. The man appeared in the doorway. "Find Maberley, will you?"

The butler nodded. Since this was the last cycle of the moon before Oliver was to be at Harrow, Simon had, indeed, been fortunate to make arrangements with Lieutenant Schofield. The man's generosity with taking Oliver for a few days so he could become acquainted with young Leo Schofield would not be forgotten.

In the morning, he and Oliver would leave for Surrey. Instead of traveling on to London, as he'd told Lily, Simon planned to return to Westfield land and go deep into the woods to a small crofter's cottage that wasn't used any more. And there he would wait until the moon began to wane. Until he was once again free to love her.

He would wait there alone in sheer misery. He already missed her, and he wasn't even gone yet. It would be torturous to be so close to her, yet so far away.

❦

Lily punched her needle through the fabric with much more force than was necessary, she knew. But she had to take out her frustration on *something*. Simon was out on estate business, and Oliver was in his chamber, sequestered with his Latin text, so the poor fabric she was stitching would have to substitute.

Leaving. How could he possibly leave? They had been married less than a month, and he wanted to *leave* her already. And he wouldn't even tell her what he was doing! Just like Daniel.

She should at least be allowed to accompany him. She'd gotten quite used to having him around. She didn't even know if she would be able to sleep without him wrapped around her, their legs tangled.

Why, just the night before, he'd done things to her that she'd never dreamed possible. He'd even made her cry out so loudly that she worried the servants could hear. It had been sublime. But afterward he had turned from her with a guilty look on his face.

Guilt?

What in the world did he have to feel guilty about? He'd brought her supreme pleasure. Yet he acted as though she was a fragile piece of glass that might break at any moment.

Billings caught her attention when he coughed quietly in the doorway.

"Your Grace?"

"Yes?" She looked up from her sewing and fixed him with a stare.

"I'm sorry to disturb you, but there's apparently a problem in the kitchen and Cook insists on speaking with you."

"Do you know what she needs?"

"She said you were the only one she would speak with, Your Grace."

"Oh, bother," Lily groaned as she set her sewing in the basket at her feet and then went to find Cook to see what the matter was. How strange. What sort of problem did Cook need her for? And in the kitchens? Lily had never entered that room before.

Lily stepped into the kitchen and was assaulted with the smell of freshly baked bread. She hadn't realized she was hungry until she heard her stomach rumble. Did all kitchens smell this delightful?

Concentrating on her work, Cook chopped carrots and onions, and only looked up as Lily approached her. "What seems to be the problem?" Lily asked, pasting a smile she didn't feel across her face.

Cook whispered, "His Grace asked me to prepare food for your retreat in the woods. But he told me not to tell anyone that you were leaving."

"Leaving? I'm not leaving," Lily said. She reached to rub her temples, trying to chase away a headache that threatened.

"You *won't* be going into the woods with His Grace? The dowager always did," she mumbled that last part to herself, though Lily heard it.

"Into the woods? I have no idea what you're referring to." It was becoming more and more strange. Like a house of horrors, where nothing was as it seemed.

"Oh, my," the old woman said. "It seems as I have misspoken. I must have misunderstood." Cook attempted a half-hearted laugh. "My ears aren't what they used to be."

"No, I'm sorry," Lily said, quickly changing her tactics. "His Grace and I will be going away. I have a dreadful headache. Please forgive me."

Cook took a sigh of relief. "I figured you would. The late duke always took his duchess with him."

Why? Lily wanted to scream, but she held her tongue. She'd get more out of Cook if she maintained her composure. "Of course. What day did he say we would be leaving?"

"After leaving the earl in Surrey, he thought he'd be back tomorrow night, Your Grace."

"Excellent." Lily turned to leave.

"Your Grace!" the woman called. "The basket?"

"Oh, I trust your judgment implicitly," Lily called back. She took the stairs at a run, anxious to have time to absorb all she'd just learned.

Simon wasn't going to London. He was going into the *woods*. Why in the world would he do that? And why had his father done the same thing? If she thought she'd get a straight answer out of Alice, she'd ask.

Lily returned to the sitting room, where her sewing waited. But now, on the settee sat Oliver, who had his head buried in a book.

"I do hope that's Latin," Lily remarked as she settled beside him.

"O-of course it is, Aunt Lily," he said. But then he moved to tuck the book between the cushions.

Well, that was obviously not a Latin text. Though her mind was on more important matters than why Oliver would try to hide a book from her. She sat down to think.

Simon appeared in the doorway. "Maberley, I'll have a word with you in my study," he said.

"Yes, Your Grace." Oliver seemed to be much more accepting of Simon's authority now, and he followed him from the room like a faithful puppy.

Lily picked up her sewing but realized she'd lost her thimble. She lifted the settee cushion to see if it had fallen in the crack. She heard a thud as Oliver's book hit the floor.

When Lily bent to pick it up, she turned it over in her hand. Her eyes narrowed as she looked at the black leather cover. Embossed in gold, the title, *Lycans: Legend and Lore*, captured her attention. She turned to the first page, where a rendering of a lone wolf, his snout high in the air, called to the moon. A masculine scrawl marred the inner cover. It simply read: *A Lycan cannot be embraced by another until he embraces the wildness within himself.*

Lycan?

Oliver had tried to hide a book about wolves from her? Why in the world would he hide a fairy tale? Because he didn't want her to know it wasn't his Latin text? Lily turned to the first page.

A folded piece of foolscap fell to the floor. Lily bent and picked it up, unfolding it and pressing the seams flat so she could take a closer look.

A Lycan family tree? Lily scanned through the names. Surely that was the product of someone's overactive imagination. Then she saw Westfield and stopped. Her finger hovered over the three names— Simon… Benjamin… William. Her name was listed along with Simon's, with the date they were married. Lily sat down heavily on the settee. Her finger traced over to Daniel and Emma's names, which also listed the date they were married and the date of their death. Below them, Oliver had been added. Was this Simon's handwriting?

Surely Simon wouldn't have created a family tree, supposedly consisting of werewolf males, as the title suggested. Oliver was a bit too old for fairy tales. And Simon had never struck her as a fanciful sort.

"Finally found it, did you?" Alice asked from the doorway.

Lily jumped and quickly folded the family tree, tucking it back between the pages of the book.

"Found what?" she attempted.

Alice laughed. "You are terrible at evasion, dear girl."

"Alice." Lily stopped and shook her head.

Alice crossed the room to stroke the top of Lily's hair. She picked up the book and pressed it into Lily's hands. "Happy reading."

❧

Alice had nearly jumped for joy when she'd seen Lily with one of Jonathan's old books. If it had taken much longer for one of the men to make a mistake and leave one lying about, she would have been forced to plant one in Lily's path. Or to knock her over the head with it, whichever came first.

All the clues were there. Now Lily just needed time to piece them together.

Alice poured a glass of sherry and watched as Lily went out the door that led to the garden. The girl was smart. Give her enough time, and she would figure it out.

Simon interrupted her thoughts. "Have you seen Lily, Mother?"

"Not for quite some time," Alice lied smoothly. "I think she said she was going to the Hawthornes'. I'm not completely sure."

"She didn't mention that she was leaving," Simon said, his eyebrows drawing together in a frown.

"She was in a bit of a foul mood, son. What did you do?"

"Mother, why must you assume that I *did* something?"

"Because I know you. And I know you're thinking way too much with your head."

"Mother, I don't have time for riddles," he sighed.

"Then let me spell it out for you, Simon." He cringed as she stepped near. He should cringe. If she followed her instincts, she would do him bodily harm. Luckily, she had some restraint. "She loves you."

"I don't doubt it."

"And you love her," Alice continued.

"Of course I do."

"Prove it, Simon."

Forty-Three

LILY WALKED SLOWLY DOWN THE GARDEN PATH, THE book tucked securely under her arm. It was a bit intimidating, knowing she might hold the key to the door Simon kept closed to her.

She brushed a lock of hair from her face as she opened the book and began to read the inscription again. She traced her finger over the words, wondering who'd scrawled the note.

A Lycan cannot be embraced by another until he embraces the wildness within himself.

What did it mean? The definition of a Lycan slowed her reading.

Lycans are defined by their ability to walk upright as humans. The shift from human to were is decided by the phase of the moon.

The moon?

What did this have to do with Simon? Simon was obviously human. As was Will. And all the other Westfield men.

In adolescence, were children grow at a rapid pace, often surpassing the size, strength, and appetite of their contemporaries.

Oliver? Certainly it was a coincidence that Oliver had undergone so many changes. Wasn't it?

Humans affected by the mark of the beast cannot avoid the call of the moon. They are unable to refuse the change.

What change? Becoming wolf? That was impossible.

Some Lycans experience great anger and melancholy because they lose the ability to choose for themselves. They are prone to fits of temper, during which their superior strength and speed can damage objects in their path.

The desk?

When a Lycan takes his mate, he's forced to take a human, which goes against the very basis of human nature. Humans mating with animals? It shakes humanity to the very core.

She could understand why. But the book still seemed to be more of a fairy tale than anything that could possibly be real. She assumed that anyone reading it could find some trait of a werewolf in almost any person, if they looked deeply enough.

Lily read until it was too dark to make out the words, devouring the entire book as the sun moved across the sky. And it wasn't until she reached the very end that she saw it. She tipped the book toward the moon so she could read the words.

There is but one thing that identifies a werewolf. It's presented on the body of the affected person. Every Lycan carries the mark of the beast, a simple moon-shaped mark, on his person.

Lily jumped to her feet. The book thudded to the ground. Simon! Simon had a mark like that. Oliver had a mark like that. Simon said it was a family trait, that Will, Benjamin, and Daniel all had one, too.

Simon was a werewolf? It was too difficult to believe. Lily ran down the path toward the house and through the back door. She had to find more books. She had to read more. Surely there would be more Lycanthropic lore if the men of the household were truly werewolves.

Lily ran down the corridor toward the library. And that was where her wolf stalked her.

~✣~

"Where have you been?" a voice asked from the corner of the darkened library.

Lily spun on her heels, searching the darkness. "Simon?" she asked.

"I asked where you have been, Lily." He leaned forward in his chair so his face was illuminated by the light of the nearly full moon that shone through the window.

"I-I was in the garden. Reading." Lily smoothed her hands on her skirts, trying to remove the wetness from her palms.

"I was looking for you," Simon said as he raised a glass of amber liquid to his lips.

"I'm sorry. I didn't know. Did you need something?"

Simon stood and stalked across the room, moving slowly toward her. "Just you," he said quietly.

She suddenly felt like prey.

"It's nice to be needed." She smiled, raising a hand to touch his face once he was close enough. She gasped as Simon growled and touched his teeth to the inside of her wrist. He abraded her skin and then licked lightly across the area. She felt that lick all the way to her toes.

"Cold?" he asked when she shivered, his eyes, black as night, meeting hers.

"Not a bit," she breathed.

Simon stepped toward her, forcing her to walk backward. She stepped back until she hit the wall. His hands came up to press against the wall on both sides of her head. She couldn't help but think she was well and truly trapped.

His lips pressed against hers, nearly painful with the intensity of his caress. She whimpered against him, but he paid her no heed.

"Is this new?" he asked as he tugged at her bodice when he finally lifted his head.

"Yes," she whispered. "You bought it."

"I'll buy you another." Then the fabric tore as he ripped it from top to bottom and shoved it from her shoulders.

Lily could do no more than gasp. She was terrified. But she was more terrified of her own reaction to Simon than she was of his actions toward her. She grew wet, her center pulsing as he cupped her breasts in his hands and lifted them to his face, pushing the centers together so he could draw both peaks into his mouth at once.

Lily reached for his shoulders when her legs weakened. She glanced toward the door.

"The door's open, Simon," she had the sense to whisper.

"I don't care," he said as he slid his leg between her thighs and rocked her body against it.

She immediately cried out. And then repeated the motion on her own.

His eyes narrowed. "Do it again," he said. She rocked against him once more, wetness flooding his pants leg as she did so.

"I want you," he said quietly. "Here. Now."

"Yes," was all she could say.

Simon pulled his thigh from between her legs and adjusted to free himself from his trousers. Effortlessly, he lifted her, pushing her against the wall as he slid into her in one hard, fast thrust.

Lily cried out. Simon pushed her face into his shoulder. "Someone will hear you," he said. "They'll know that I'm taking you like an animal in the library."

She watched his face shift as he realized what he'd said and began to withdraw from her. Lily leaned forward and nibbled his neck, lightly abrading his skin with her teeth.

He growled and filled her again. She pressed her face into his shoulder as she lifted her legs to wrap around his waist. She took him deeper. He slammed into her again. And again. And again. And finally, when she could take no more, he allowed her to splinter into a million pieces and then followed.

❧

Simon held her there against the wall while he caught his breath. What had he done? He'd lost control. He'd hurt her. He'd used her. He'd taken her in a *library* with the door open like she was a common whore.

"Oh, God, I'm sorry," he mumbled.

"Why?" she asked, her legs still wrapped around his waist.

"I was out of control," he said.

"No…" she began, but he refused to let her speak.

"I was. I was out of control." Simon dropped her legs to the floor and let her stand. "And I ruined your dress." He tried to pull the edges together. But the damage was too severe. He took off his jacket and slid it around her shoulders. He righted his trousers and picked her up in his arms to carry her up the steps. Simon wondered absently where the rest of the household was. But he paid little attention to their absence. He had to get Lily upstairs before someone saw what he'd done to her.

He took the stairs two at a time. He laid her gently on the bed and took her face in his hands. "You deserve better than me," he ground out.

He shushed her protest and lay with her for a moment, until her breaths became regular and quiet.

Once she slept, he got up, dressed, and left the room.

"Billings!" he called once he reached the bottom step.

"Yes, Your Grace?" The man appeared as though magically summoned.

"Have two horses readied and find Maberley. We'll be leaving tonight, instead of tomorrow."

"Yes, Your Grace."

Simon needed to get far away from Lily before he hurt her. Before he went too far and she ended up hating him.

Forty-Four

"YOU WANTED TO SEE ME, BLACKMOOR?" OLIVER asked, rubbing his eyes as he stepped into the study.

Simon stared up at the lad, his vision clear, his memory of losing control still fresh in his mind. "We're starting for Surrey tonight. Grab your satchel and meet me in the stables."

"Tonight?" Oliver covered a yawn with his hand. "I thought we were going to leave in the morning. I didn't get to say good-bye to Aunt Lily, and Cook said—"

"Tonight!" Simon snapped. Then he closed his eyes and tried to maintain his temper. After all, it wasn't Oliver's fault that he had lost control with Lily. He took some calming breaths before slowly opening his eyes.

Oliver looked frightened, standing with his back against the wall, his brown eyes focused like beacons on Simon.

"We're close to the full moon, Oliver. We have to go. I'm afraid I may hurt Lily if we stay another night."

Before he could finish his statement, the lad rushed from the room. At least he now understood the urgency.

Simon awaited Oliver in the stables. Abbadon was saddled and ready, as was Erebus. Simon never would have thought the boy could handle the Anglo-Arabian, but he apparently had Daniel's skill with horseflesh. The gelding adored Oliver, which was nothing short of a miracle.

After only a few moments, Oliver entered the stables, his eyes red-rimmed and with a leather satchel slung over one shoulder. His furious glare brought Simon up short. "If you ever hurt her, I will kill you."

Simon nodded. If he ever hurt Lily, he'd kill himself. There was no need for Maberley to bloody his hands. "Well, that's why we're leaving."

In one fluid move, Oliver mounted the Anglo-Arabian with the grace of an expert horseman. "What are you waiting for, Blackmoor?"

The lad's protective qualities were admirable, especially in a boy so young. Simon mounted Abbadon, all the while keeping his eyes locked with his cousin's. "Follow close, and don't get lost."

Oliver nodded. Then a look of doubt entered his eyes. "Are you not afraid of highwaymen?"

Simon threw back his head and laughed. He needed that release immensely. "God help the highwayman who thinks he can stop two Lycans."

With that, they rode into the night under the bright light of a nearly full moon.

≈

Lily sat at the breakfast table, slowly sipping her tea. A plate of baked eggs and sausages sat in front of her, but she couldn't find her appetite.

It was quite a shock to wake up and discover that her husband and nephew were already gone. No note. No good-bye. Nothing.

Into the woods. That's what Cook had said. Had they even gone to Surrey? Or were they hiding in the woods? Waiting for the moon to wane?

She shook her head. Did she *truly* believe her husband was a werewolf? That Oliver was a werewolf? It sounded insane. Yet everything she'd read seemed to indicate that the impossible *was* possible. It would have been nice to discuss the Lycan book with Simon before he disappeared.

But he hadn't given her that chance. Blast him!

"You should eat something," Alice said as she entered the room and sat across from Lily.

"Apparently I'm not hungry."

Alice frowned, raking her gaze across Lily. "Are you feeling ill?"

Ill tempered. "That depends. Are you not allowed to discuss Lycans with me today?"

A ghost of a smile lit Alice's lips. "Sweet Lily. I told you, only Simon is able to reveal such secrets."

She wasn't denying it though, was she? "I see." Lily drummed her fingers on the breakfast table. "But is that just in regards to Simon? Can you tell me about Will? Or your husband? Oliver perhaps? Is my nephew a… a Lycan?"

Alice took a deep breath. "Dear, after Simon reveals everything to you, we can have as many conversations as you'd like on the subject. For the time being, you are on the correct path. I can't say more than that."

Lily leapt to her feet. This was among the most bizarre conversations she'd ever had. "Why not? Are there werewolf spies that would know if you told me? Will they suddenly appear in the middle of the room in a poof of smoke and drag you off to some wolfy prison for revealing their secrets?"

"I know it's difficult, Lily," Alice began softly.

Lily punched her hands to her hips. "Difficult, Alice, is reading fantastical books about werewolves and starting to believe that the man I married and the boy I raised are such creatures. I should be locked away in Bedlam for even entertaining the idea. Then I woke up to find the two of them gone. And the only person who can give me answers refuses to do so."

"I would if I was able."

Lily started from the room, but Alice's words halted her. "Do you remember when I asked you if there was anything Oliver could do to make you stop loving him?"

"Yes," she answered, looking back over her shoulder.

Alice nodded. "What if he is a Lycan, Lily? What if everything you're entertaining is true? Simon, Will, Oliver... Would you love them less? Or stop loving them all together?"

What if it was all true? What if Simon transformed under the light of a full moon and became a wolf? A memory flashed in her mind of the wolf on the hill she saw the night she spent at Langley Downs. It had seemed as if the creature had called out to her.

Was it Simon?

❧

The sun was barely in the sky when Simon spotted Reston House from atop a hill outside of Guilford. The Elizabethan home was of modest size and settled nicely in the woods, just as Lieutenant Schofield had described. Oliver would be safe here, which was a relief.

He urged Abbadon forward and galloped down the hill. They rode around the back of the house toward the stables, where they dismounted. Almost at once they were surrounded by a pack of russet-haired, freckle-faced children.

"Are you the duke?" asked one bold little girl, about six years old.

Before Simon could answer, a hulking man with auburn hair stepped from the home's back door. "Blackmoor?" the man called.

"Lieutenant Schofield?" Simon asked.

"Who else?" the officer asked, stepping forward and clapping Simon's back as though they were old friends. "We weren't expecting you 'til this afternoon." Then he looked at the swarm of children, who all looked just like him. "Mary, take your brothers and sisters, and run along to your mother."

The oldest girl herded her brothers and sisters and directed them back toward the house.

"Sorry," the lieutenant began. "It's not all that often we have such important guests." Then he looked over Simon's shoulder. "And you must be the Earl of Maberley."

"Oliver," he replied, nodding.

"Well, Oliver," the lieutenant said, "Leo is up in his room making space for you. Come along, and we'll introduce you."

In no time, Oliver and Leo Schofield seemed to be the best of friends and had gone to explore the woods behind Reston House together. Lily would be relieved the two boys had connected so quickly.

Lily.

Simon's thoughts returned to her, and his heart ached, but he could see her again in a few days when the worst of his affliction had passed. When he was certain she'd be safe from him. He accepted a cup of tea from the army officer after sinking into an overstuffed chair, which was heaven after the long ride.

"Would you like to rest, Your Grace?" the lieutenant asked him. "You look exhausted, if you don't mind my saying so."

Simon only hoped he looked better than he felt. "That is very kind, but I should be getting back to Westfield Hall."

The lieutenant winked at him. "Ah, your wife is wanting you home safe for moonful?"

He tried to keep the scowl from his face. "My wife is unaware that I am Lycan."

The officer nodded in understanding as he dropped into a seat across from Simon. "Ah, my first wife was the same way. She was a sweet thing but didn't have the fortitude for a claiming."

Finally, Simon heaved a sigh. Everyone else made it sound as if he'd made the wrong decision, but Lieutenant Schofield seemed to understand.

"In that case, would you like to stay here with us? We have plenty of room."

That Simon doubted, but the offer was generous.

He shook his head. "I don't want to be too far from my wife."

"I understand."

"You say your first wife didn't have the fortitude?"

The lieutenant rubbed his chin. "Leo's mother. When she discovered what I was, she threw herself from the attic. She died on impact. He was just an infant. I'm fortunate my second wife's will was a bit stronger."

The matter-of-fact way Lieutenant Schofield could discuss such a thing made chills race up Simon's spine. An image of Lily's lifeless body flashed in his mind. Surely she wouldn't throw herself from the top floor of Westfield Hall upon learning the truth.

His resolve to keep her distant from this aspect of his life seemed the correct decision. In their vows, he'd promised to protect her, and he appeared to be on the right course.

After finishing his tea, Simon thanked the lieutenant for his generosity and then started back for Hampshire.

Forty-Five

Lily bolted upright in bed, the plaintive call of a wild animal rousing her from her sleep. She ran to the window and searched the darkness. There, limned by the light of the full moon, sat the wild beast that called to her. High on a hill, the lone wolf raised his head and howled.

The sound tore through her like the slice of a sharp blade. She doubled over, seeking relief from the blinding pain. Black danced around the edges of her vision, but she fought it back.

"Simon," she whispered, when she could finally stand again. She pressed her fingertips against the cold, wet glass, using her index finger to trace the wolf's form. The beast raised his head and called again. This call reached past the pain it caused in her body and touched her heart.

"I'm coming," Lily whispered. She turned, ran on her bare feet across the floor, and flung open her door with so much force that it hit the wall and bounced back closed. The sound reverberated through the room. But the call of the one she loved was the only noise she heard. She opened the door again and slipped through.

Lily dashed down the hallway, her frantic pace disguised by the soft carpet beneath her feet. When she reached the lower level of the manor, she turned toward the doorway that led to the garden. As she rounded the corner, her hip collided with the edge of a hallway table. A heavy vase crashed against the hardwood floor.

Lily stopped only briefly to press the heel of her hand to the pain in her hip. She had to reach Simon. She had to get to him. Nothing would stand in her way.

"Lily," a voice called. She barely heard it, her heartbeats loud in her ear, almost as loud as the breaths that rushed in and out of her lungs.

"Lily!" The word finally caught her attention.

Lily turned slowly to find Alice in her nightrail and wrapper, leaning against the doorjamb of the library. She had a glass of amber liquid in her hand, which she raised casually to her lips. A smile played at the corners of her mouth. Lily had no time for the woman. She had to reach Simon. Lily turned back toward the door.

"Are you fully aware of what you're doing?" Alice asked. Her question drew Lily's gaze.

Lily shook her head. She had no idea what she was doing. She simply knew she had to heed the call of the wolf.

Her wolf.

Simon.

"Do not let him hide from you," Alice surprised her by saying. "Do not let him shut you out. Don't accept anything less than *everything*."

Lily nodded.

Alice walked toward her. She cupped Lily's face in her hands and forced Lily to look at her.

"If he hurts you, know that it's not intentional."

"He wouldn't hurt me."

"He won't intend to."

Lily nodded.

"If you weren't his intended mate, you wouldn't *feel* the call."

"I understand. I must go."

Alice stepped back and nodded. "Go. Be well. Love him."

"As though I have a choice." Lily was unable to repress the small smile that erupted before she turned on her heel and ran for the garden door.

Simon sat atop the hill, his need for Lily painful in its intensity. He wanted nothing more than to shift back to human form and go to her. He needed to be with her. He needed to be inside her. He needed her.

Simon arched his neck and called to her. He knew she would not hear, but he needed to make the sound. He needed to scream to the heavens. He needed to cry.

Dear God, he needed.

A rabbit skittered by in the bushes. Simon didn't take his eyes from Westfield Hall. She was in there. She was asleep in his bed. She was snug and safe under the counterpane. She was safe from him.

That thought brought unending pain. She shouldn't need to be safe from him. If he wasn't such a beast, he could be with her. He could be with her and love her always. Love her in every way.

Simon's ears perked up when he heard a door slam at Westfield Hall. He stood up on all four feet. His limbs quivered with the desire to run to her. Instead, he turned away, ready to head back into the dense forest. *Ready to run from her.*

Then his keen hearing picked up the sound of running feet as they crunched against the pea-gravel path in the garden. Someone was outside. He sniffed the air. Damn! The wind blew in the wrong direction to pick up a scent.

Simon closed his eyes and willed the wind to change direction. Despite his close proximity to nature, he had no ability to force the wind to do his bidding. Had he been human, he would have laughed.

But he wasn't. And never would be. Not truly. Sure, he could pretend to be human most of the time. But he was all beast.

Simon heard footfalls pounding against the soft forest floor. Faster and faster they ran. An animal? He sniffed again. Still no scent. He growled at the injustice of it all.

The wind shifted.

He smelled it.

He smelled her.

Lily.

No.

The footsteps grew louder and louder as she ran. He would evade her. He would go farther into the forest. He would run from her. He turned to do just that.

But then she winced. Simon stood and looked down. He could see her there, stopped at the bottom of the hill. She halted and pulled a thorn from her foot. Maybe that would slow her down.

Not his Lily. She ran even faster than before. She was nearly upon him when he turned to run away.

He heard her voice.

❧

A soft rain began to fall. Lily paid it no heed and simply brushed the wet locks of hair from in front of her eyes. She had to find her wolf.

Lily knew it was him the moment she saw him. His black hair shone under the light of the moon. The streak of white that usually graced his temple now shot across one ear and down his back.

"Simon!" she called. He was facing away from her. He was moving in the wrong direction. But she would run forever to catch him. She barely felt the pain in her feet, which were bruised and battered after her barefoot run through the forest.

He didn't turn when she called to him. He ran in the other direction. He moved into the dark until she was unable to tell wolf from shadow.

No!

"Simon," she cried, bending over, the pain of his absence nearly more than she could bear. Lily fell to her hands and knees as tears clouded her vision.

"Don't leave me!" she screamed, the strength of which burned her throat.

A man stepped out of the shadows.

Simon stood completely naked and completely unashamed under the light of the full moon.

"Why are you here, Lily?" he snarled.

She drew in a deep breath, the relief of seeing him nearly palpable.

"Because I need you," she said.

He turned to walk back into the forest. "Go home," he ordered.

"Because I want you!" she cried, louder than before.

He turned and looked at her.

"Because I love you!" she finished.

Lily sat back on her heels and freed her nightrail from around her legs, where she knelt on the ground. Quickly, she tugged it over her head and tossed it to the ground beside her. She sat naked in front of him. She held up her hands, palms facing the sky. "Take me," she cried.

Forty-Six

SIMON FOUGHT THE BEAST. HE FOUGHT IT WITH EVERY bit of his body, mind, and soul.

He came to her and kneeled in front of her, his hands sliding into the hair at her temples.

"Why don't you want me?" she sobbed. But gone was the time that he could have gently wiped the tear from her cheek. Instead, he brutally pulled at her hair, tipping her head so that she was forced to look him in the eye.

"You think I don't want you?" he snarled. How could she possibly think that? He wanted her in the worst way. He wanted to pin her beneath him. He wanted to thrust into her until he could spill himself inside her. He wanted to take her. He wanted it more than he wanted his next breath.

Despite the brutal pressure he applied to her scalp with his hands tangled in her hair, she turned her head and pressed her face into his palm.

He couldn't allow her to show gentleness to him. The beast didn't deserve it. The beast wanted nothing more than to hurt her. Why would she turn to him and seek comfort?

Lily reached up to touch Simon's face, and he flinched. "Don't touch me," he growled.

Yet she persisted. Her hand cupped his cheek. Her thumb brushed across his bottom lip. And Simon gave up control. He allowed the beast to take over.

The pain of the transformation was miniscule compared to the pain in his heart. For he knew that when he showed her his true self, when he came to her in Lycan form, she would turn from him in disgust.

Simon lifted his face to the moon and basked in the light of the night. He dropped to his hands and knees before her and let her watch as his hands became paws with long, black claws, so sharp they dug into the soft, wet earth. Simon watched her face as she watched his. He knew his nose would elongate and his ears would move to the top of his head and become pointy. He'd seen his brothers and others of their kind change. It was a quick process. Yet tonight, it seemed to happen so slowly.

When he was fully Lycan, he stood before her, his face level with hers. He wanted to shout, "Go home! Go to safety!" But now all he could do was whimper. So, he did.

Then the little fool reached a hand toward him. She reached those tiny little fingers out as though she wanted to touch him. Hadn't her mother ever taught her not to touch wild animals?

Simon bared his teeth and growled.

Lily's hand stilled, hanging in the air in mid-reach. He growled again. There, he thought. That is what I am. I am fur and snout and teeth and bite. I am Lycan. I am not human.

Simon closed his eyes and sat very still. He hoped that,

when he opened them, she would be long gone. She would come to her senses and leave him. But even more than that, he closed his eyes because he didn't want to see the revulsion on her face he knew would be there. He knew she wouldn't be able to accept him as he was.

Then she touched him. His eyes flew open, and he bared his teeth. He snarled. He would bite her if she wasn't careful.

"There, now," she whispered as a tear slipped from her eye and rode a path down her cheek. "Growl all you want." Then a laugh broke from her throat. She said very softly, "When Emma and I were young, we had these cats in the stables. No one could touch them. They were feral. They hissed and scratched and bit. But I never gave up."

Her hands threaded into the hair at his neck. She stroked him. She touched him. "I'll never give up on you, either, Simon," she said quietly. "Because I love you."

Simon realized that he'd never told her he loved her. All the times he'd pleasured her. All the times he'd held her. He'd never told her. He suddenly felt a burning desire to do so.

Simon gritted his teeth and forced the physical characteristics of the beast to recede. He fought until he kneeled before her again in his human form.

Simon took her face in his human hands, his palms dirty from the mud under his claws, hands that were unable to be gentle. Hands that wanted to bite cruelly into her flesh. She cried out. He instinctively gentled his touch.

Before tonight, he'd never been able to do that. He'd never been able to control the beast.

"Did you hear me? I said I love you." She repeated the words, her eyes searching his.

"I love you *too much*," he snarled, well aware that his lips lifted from his teeth. But unable to force the beast away completely.

"Love me *enough*," she simply said and held out her arms to him.

Simon kneeled before her on shaky legs. His body wanted to be in Lycan form. His mind wanted to stay in human form. His heart wanted to love Lily.

His heart won.

Simon took her face in his hands. "I cannot be gentle," he growled.

"I know," she said. She took his hand in hers and brought it to the curls at the juncture of her thighs. He slid his fingers into her hot, wet body. "I give myself to you, my wolf, because I know you will keep me safe," she said.

He needed no more urging. She cried out when he picked her up and spun her in his arms. He faced her away from him, her bottom cradled in the saddle of his hips. He pressed against her, ready to take her.

Simon wrapped one arm around Lily's waist and used the other to press her shoulders toward the ground. She extended her arms to hold herself up and looked over her shoulder at him.

Her auburn hair clung to her back like wet ropes. He brushed it to the side, exposing the arch of her spine. The soft rain that fell left droplets of water on her skin.

Control. He needed control.

Simon allowed himself the pleasure of licking a path

up her spine, his tongue lapping at the drops of water until he reached her neck.

"I am yours," she whispered. "Know that it's me who takes you, Simon." She repeated the words he'd said to her their first time together.

"No one else, Lily," he growled before thrusting inside her. Her heat enveloped him as he pushed further. She gasped with undisguised pleasure.

The beast hovered just below the surface. The beast wanted to dominate her. Simon raked her back with his fingernails, hard enough to leave shallow red scratches down her tender white skin. He looked down in horror. What had he done?

"Again," she panted. "Do it again," she begged as she backed up against him and rocked forward. The heat of her slid down his length. She took him farther than ever before.

Simon's nails raked a new path down her back as he slammed into her.

"More," she said. The beast reared and fought. Simon bent low, pressing his chest to her back. One of his hands slipped into her hair and wound a knot around his fist. He tugged until her head was forced to turn. He breathed against her ear.

"It's *me* who takes *you*," he said, just before his teeth punctured the tender skin of her shoulder.

She erupted around him. He stopped to cry out at the sensation of her clamping around his length.

He wailed.

He howled.

He followed her.

❧

Lily sank to the ground under Simon's weight. He pressed her into the cold, soft earth. He slipped from her body within seconds, and she immediately felt the loss.

His hands brushed the hair away from her face. "Are you all right?"

Too weak to do more than nod, she slowly inclined her head. "Better," she murmured. And she was. She was better than ever before. She was Simon's wife. She was his partner. She was his Lycan mate.

"Did I hurt you?" he asked, his voice quavering slightly.

"Not a bit," she assured him.

"I'm sorry I marked you." He reached to touch the small wound on her shoulder.

"I'm not." She smiled.

Simon rolled her over and looked into her eyes. "You're sure you're all right?"

"I'm not fragile, Simon." She cupped his face in her hand.

Simon slid an arm beneath her knees and one under her shoulders and hoisted her against him. She wrapped her arms around his neck, holding tightly to him. Would he disappear if she let him go? Would he walk into the shadows and leave her?

"I'll not leave you again," he said, as though he read her mind. "If you'll have me, all of me, I'll share my Lycan life with you."

"Do I have to wait a whole month to be able to do that again?" she asked, unable to withhold the laughter that erupted at the look on his face.

Simon carried her through the garden, into the house, up the stairs, and into their bedroom, both of them completely naked. He placed her gently on the bed.

"What's this?" she asked, as she saw a note on her pillow, with a tin of salve and a small towel. "For the shoulder," she read aloud. "Love, Alice."

"That's my mother for you," Simon sighed. "I love her, but she really should mind her own matters."

"Why did you fight it, Simon?" She had to know.

"I was afraid."

"That I wouldn't love you?"

"That I would never love myself." He shrugged then joined her on the bed.

"I love you enough for both of us." She kissed his jaw.

"A Lycan cannot be embraced by another until he embraces the wildness within himself." He repeated the words at the front of his father's book.

"Who wrote that?"

"Daniel." He twirled a lock of her hair absently around his finger.

"Daniel?"

Simon just nodded and swallowed hard. "He wrote it when he realized what he'd done, how he'd ruined his chance for a happy life with Emma."

"What do you mean?"

"He never embraced it. He never fully accepted that he was a Lycan. He dabbled at it, much like I did. He ran to hide every time the moon was full.

"By the time he took Emma, there was too much anger, too much despair. Then he hated himself. Every time she looked at him, she cringed. I didn't want that. I didn't want you to be disgusted by me."

"I'm not."

"And that, my dear, is the only thing that saved you." He chuckled.

"Oh, so the big, bad wolf would have hurt me, would he?" She laughed as she sat up and pushed him onto his back. Then straddled his hips.

"This big, bad wolf has officially been tamed," Simon said as he raised his hands above his head and relaxed.

"I actually liked my beastly husband." She pretended to pout. "He has a certain wolfish charm." He sat up quickly, captured her in a tight embrace, and reversed their positions, so that he was over her.

He growled, "Then you, love, may have all of this beast you can stand."

Lily adjusted for him as he settled between her thighs. "I would accept nothing less."

Epilogue

Thoroughly amused, Simon watched Lily rush around her bedchamber in a frenzy. She was looking behind tables and under the mattress, completely unaware of his presence in the doorway.

She blew a stray auburn curl from her face and then took a deep sigh as she planted her hands on her hips.

"You do know we have servants to clean the house," he said, making her jump at least a foot in the air.

"Oh!" Lily spun around to face him. "Don't do that. You nearly scared me to death."

Simon couldn't help but chuckle. "Love, you've married a wolf. You don't scare all that easily." A light blush stained her cheeks, and Simon was certain he'd never tire of the sight. "What are you looking for?"

Lily flopped down on her bed and frowned. "My father's pocket watch. I know it arrived with the rest of my things from Maberley Hall, but I can't find it anywhere."

Simon crossed the floor and stood before her. "Your father's pocket watch?"

She nodded and wiped a tear from her cheek.

Simon took her hands in his and pulled her up from the bed. "This doesn't have anything to do with Oliver leaving, does it?"

The coach was waiting to take the three of them to Harrow, and Oliver was below stairs pacing the parlor, as he was anxious to leave.

Lily frowned at him. "I'd wanted to give it to him before we left. It's the only thing my father had of value, and I thought it would make a good going-away gift. Something for him to remember me by."

Simon touched her cheek. "Ah, love, there's no boy more devoted to his mother than Oliver is to you. He doesn't need a pocket watch to remember you."

She sniffed back another tear. "Do you think he's ready for this? We could wait another year," she added hopefully.

Simon kissed her forehead. "You can't stop him from growing up any easier than I can stop the moon's cycles. It's all part of life. And he'll be fine. He's anxious to see Leo Schofield again."

At this Lily brightened. "He'll keep an eye on Oliver?"

"He promised to do so," Simon told her.

Someone coughed in the doorway, and Simon could have kicked himself for not shutting the door. He looked over his shoulder to find Billings holding a letter. "Your Grace."

"What is it?" Simon asked, stepping toward his butler to take the letter.

Will's seal. It had nearly been a month. Simon tore it open.

Dear Simon,

   I trust you are well at Westfield Hall. You may be interested to know that I have located Benjamin. Please tell Prisca he sends his love. I will return when I am able. Give Lily a kiss for me.

Your devoted brother,
William

"What is it, Simon?" Lily asked, stepping forward.

Simon handed her the letter and watched confusion cross her face.

"He didn't say much," she said softly, giving the note back to him.

Not that Simon was surprised. Will kept quite a bit to himself. He always had. "He said enough."

"He didn't say if they were in trouble, or why Benjamin hadn't written. He... Why did he send Prisca Benjamin's love and not his own?"

Simon pocketed his brother's note. "Don't worry about it, Lily. You have more important things to concern yourself with."

"Oliver," she said wistfully.

"Indeed. Now do you really want your father's pocket watch?"

Lily nodded. "I've looked everywhere, Simon."

"Shh." He touched his fingers to her lips. Then he closed his eyes and focused on the sounds in the room. In the far corner, he heard a faint, muffled ticking. Simon opened his eyes and looked in the direction of the sound. Lily's armoire stood in the corner, and he edged toward it.

The ticking got a bit louder.

When Simon opened a drawer inside the armoire, he could hear it better. His fingers explored through frilly lace and satin until he came across something cold and metallic.

When he withdrew a gold pocket watch, Lily gasped. "How did you find it?"

He winked at her. "My hearing is excellent."

"Will our children inherit all these wonderful traits?" she asked as she reached up to brush her fingers tenderly through the hair that hung over his forehead.

"Only the boys, love. Only the boys."

"Wait." Lily's brow furrowed. "Only the boys inherit Lycan traits? That doesn't seem quite fair."

Simon couldn't help but chuckle. She not only accepted him, but she wanted a house full of others just like him? How had he gotten so lucky?

Simon patted her bottom and shooed her out the door. "With the two of us combined, anything is possible, Lily love."

About the Author

Lydia Dare is an active member of the Heart of Carolina Romance Writers and sits on the organization's board of directors. She lives in a house filled with boys and an animal or two (or ten) near Raleigh, North Carolina.

TALL, DARK, AND WOLFISH

Major Desmond Forster's dark eyes twinkled as he looked up from his drink. "Ah, Benjamin. It's been an age. Please, please." He gestured toward an empty chair at his table. "To what do I owe this honor?"

Ben swallowed. It wasn't something he could just blurt out. In fact, now that he was here, he didn't know what to say to Forster at all. "I, uh, could use your counsel, sir."

"*My* counsel?" The old man leaned back in his seat and grinned. "I am flattered. I thought you generally sought out Blackmoor."

Usually he did want his brother Simon's advice. But this wasn't something he could discuss with either of his brothers. In fact, keeping Simon and Will from learning his secret was of the utmost importance. Ben took a deep breath and leaned in close over the table. "I'm in trouble, Major."

The man's smile vanished instantly. "What sort of trouble, Benjamin?"

He held tightly to the table and willed the words out of his mouth. "I didn't change."

"You didn't change?" the officer echoed.

LYDIA DARE

"With the full moon last night," he explained. "I. Didn't. Change."

For the first time in his life as a Lycan man, Benjamin Westfield hadn't sprouted a tail, long snout, or paws with the coming of the full moon. He'd sought the moon the same way he always did, this time in a clearing in the woods, for his transformation. But last night nothing had happened. A moonbeam touched him, but the change that was so much a part of him didn't come, and he'd stood there for an eternity waiting and wondering why he was broken.

Major Forster's face drained of its color and his mouth fell open. "You didn't *change*?" he repeated, this time in soto voce, with a world of meaning in his words.

Ben shook his head. "Do you know why?"

"Benjamin, we always change."

"Well, not me. Not last night."

The major motioned for two more glasses. "What happened?"

"Nothing happened. The moon hit me like it always does. But I didn't feel the pain, nor the joy, of changing. Nothing happened at all."

Major Forster scratched his head. "Prior to last night, did you feel the same call of the moon in the days leading up to the moonful?" He pushed a glass of whisky toward Ben with the tips of his fingers.

Ben sighed. Now that he mentioned it, he hadn't felt the same call. He hadn't been lusty or angry or felt the need to withdraw. But he hadn't really paid it much attention. Changing was as natural to him as breathing. It had been a part of him for fourteen of his twenty-six years, since adolescence.

Ben could only shake his head in dismay as he slumped in his chair. "No. I don't believe I did."

"Do you believe this has anything to do with that little incident in Brighton last month?" Major Forster raised one eyebrow.

Ben's eyes shot up quickly to meet the major's. "How did you know about that?"

"News travels quickly in our circle, Benjamin."

"I didn't mean to hurt her," Ben mumbled.

"We never do," the major said as he clapped a hand to Ben's shoulder. "What did Blackmoor have to say about it?"

Ben exhaled loudly and shook his head. "What *didn't* he have to say about it?" he breathed.

"That bad, huh?"

"Worse," Ben admitted.

"Those of our kind have to be aware of our strength—and our lust—as the moon grows fuller." His eyes narrowed as he regarded Ben.

"I know. Believe me, I have heard it all from Simon. '*You can't be with a woman that close to the phase of the moon. You could get out of control. How many times do I have to tell you? Now look what happened!*'" He mocked his oldest brother's tone.

Major Forster chuckled.

"The woman was just scared. Really scared. Who would have thought that a whore would have been so squeamish?"

"Blackmoor, obviously."

Ben finally took a sip of his whisky and appreciated the way it made his eyes water. At least he felt something then. "I went to see the woman after the full moon. She's doing just fine. *She* actually apologized to *me* for screaming loud enough to call the watch."

"What did you learn from that experience?" the major asked.

"That I can't control the beast when it's that close to the full moon. I thought I could." He waved a hand in the air. "Other Lycans control themselves with women. They get along beautifully together."

"You will learn more about the type of relationship they have when you meet your own mate, my boy."

"But what do I do about not changing? I think I'm broken. I need to go back."

"There's only one way to go back," Major Forster mumbled as he scrubbed a hand across his mouth.

"Pardon?"

The major coughed into his hand. "There's only one person who can help you." He stopped talking and fixed his stare on his glass of whisky. Ben watched him for a moment.

"Major?" he finally prompted him.

The man finally tore his gaze from the glass. "Yes?" he asked, obviously distracted by his own thoughts.

"You were going to tell me how to fix it."

"Oh, yes." The man sat forward. "You must find a healer."

"A what?"

"A healer," the major repeated.

"You mean a witch?" Ben fought back a hysterical laugh. He'd come to his father's old friend for guidance, and he was going to send him to find a fabled creature that didn't exist. Oh, life was not working in his favor.

"A witch. A healer. Call it what you will. But you must find one."

"Everyone knows that witches are the things of legends and myths."

"As are we, my boy. As are we. But you can take my word for it, Benjamin. They do exist."